A SELECTED EDITION OF W. D. HOWELLS

Volume 17

The Shadow of a Dream

and

An Imperative Duty

W. D. HOWELLS

The Shadow of a Dream

and

An Imperative Duty

Introduction and Notes to the Text
by Martha Banta

Text Established by
Martha Banta, Ronald Gottesman
and David J. Nordloh

INDIANA UNIVERSITY PRESS

Bloomington and London

1 9 7 0

*Copyright © 1969 by Indiana University Press
and the Howells Edition Editorial Board*

*Library of Congress catalog card number: 71–79475
Standard Book Number: 253–35190–1*

Manufactured in the United States of America

Acknowledgments

For indispensable support in money and morale the editors of this volume and the Howells Edition Center gladly express their gratitude to Barnaby C. Keeney and the National Endowment for the Humanities; to William M. Gibson and the Center for Editions of American Authors, Modern Language Association of America; to Joseph L. Sutton, President, and Lynne L. Merritt, Jr., Vice-President and Dean, Research and Advanced Studies, Indiana University; to Herman B Wells and the Indiana University Foundation; and to William White Howells and the heirs of W. D. Howells.

We are pleased to acknowledge the assistance of Robert D. Schildgen, Ann Hofstra and Nancy S. Leonard of the Howells Edition staff, who contributed substantially to the completion of the volume. Our thanks are also extended, for special help, to:

Eugene Bianco
William H. Bond and the staff of the Houghton Library, Harvard
    University
Cecil K. Byrd, Indiana University Library
William Cagle, Lilly Library, Indiana University
Dennis M. Dalrymple, Harper & Row, Publishers
Doris Gardiner, University of California at Santa Barbara Library
Frieda Hagmann, University of California at Santa Barbara Li-
    brary
C. W. Kilpatrick, T. & A. Constable, Limited, London
Ellen McKaskle, University of California at Santa Barbara Library
James B. Meriwether, University of South Carolina
Anthony Shipps, Indiana University Library

Contents

THE SHADOW OF A DREAM

AN IMPERATIVE DUTY

Illustration: Photograph of W. D. Howells, c. 1890. *following page xxi*

Introduction

The Shadow of a Dream

SOME TIME in the spring of 1887 Hamlin Garland paid his first visit to William Dean Howells to talk about his own literary hopes. As Howells accompanied him back to the railroad station, he suddenly asked his young visitor,

> "What would you think of my doing a story dealing with the effect of a dream on the life of a man? I have in mind a tale to be called *The Shadow of a Dream,* or something like that, wherein the principal character is to be influenced to some action—I don't quite know what—through the memory of a vision which is to pursue him and have some share in the final catastrophe, whatever it may turn out to be."

When Garland expressed surprise, Howells spoke for him. " 'You think it is not quite like me? You are right. It *is* rather romantic, and I may never write it.' " But he did, Garland later remarked, in his "own way."[1]

During the 1860's and 1870's Howells as reviewer paid special heed to the presence of occult elements in other men's literary efforts. Howells as novelist delayed a major assessment of whether men of reason might come together on common ground with men of psyche until the appearance of *The Undiscovered Country* in 1880. In his review of Howells' novel, Thomas W. Higginson concluded that, however much it seemed to deviate from Howells' avowed social realism, it showed real promise in its study of character

---

1. "Meetings with Howells," *The Bookman,* XLV (March 1917), 5. Garland's reminiscences are more hindrance than help in the attempt to verify the exact year and month of Howells' reference to *The Shadow of a Dream.* In each of three accounts Garland names different dates (month and year) and hotel locations. An examination of the evidence suggests, however, that the visit may have taken place between 28 April and 1 May 1887.

under stress of invisible forces.[2] Higginson's insight is a true one, but it took another decade before Howells fulfilled the possibilities for fiction (hinted at by his prophetically titled novel) which Howells the private man had long since explored.

As a child living in a Boy's Town, nurtured by superstitious boy-talk and his father's Swedenborgianism and affected by the burgeoning consciousness of his own existence, Howells had early moved between the worlds of the wakened mind and of sleep. The night-side of consciousness had tightened its hold as he entered adolescence; by nineteen the young Howells had suffered the fear of fear that led to nervous collapse. His father's sympathy and his own strong will to return to mental equilibrium were able to offset his psychic fears, but the mark went "deeper than I could say," Howells later wrote. "In self-defense I learnt to practise a psychological juggle . . . ."[3]

One strategy for balancing fears is to assimilate them into art. Howells tried this strategy, and failed, in "Geoffrey Winter" and "The Ghost-Maker"—fragments of interest as his earliest sustained fictional forays into the occult aspects of the "inner life."[4] Another strategy he found useful for controlling the inexplicable was to bring it to the surface in conversation. During his first visit to Boston in 1860 he spoke to Oliver Wendell Holmes "of the intimations of immortality, of the experiences of morbid youth, and of all those messages from the tremulous nerves

---

2. "Howells's 'Undiscovered Country,' " *Scribner's Monthly*, XX (September 1880), 793–795.

3. *Years of My Youth* (New York and London, 1916), p. 94. See also Edwin H. Cady's two studies of the causes and consequences of Howells' fears which examine the "unknown" fiction produced by Howells the "psychological novelist" in the years after 1890: "The Neuroticism of William Dean Howells," *PMLA*, LXI (March 1946), 229–238, and "The Howells Nobody Knows," *The Mad River Review*, I (Winter, 1964–65), 3–25. Indeed, for much of the biographical information, I am indebted to them, as well as to Cady's two-volume biography of Howells—*The Road to Realism* and *The Realist at War* (Syracuse, N.Y., 1956 and 1958)—and to his work on the Twayne Edition (1962) of *The Shadow of a Dream* and *An Imperative Duty*.

4. The manuscripts of the unfinished novels are in the Houghton Library at Harvard University. A story culled from an early version of the first chapter of "Geoffrey Winter" appeared as "A Dream" in *Knickerbocker Magazine*, LVIII (August 1861), 146–150.

which we take for prophecies." Holmes' tactful recognition that "forebodings and presentiments" are part of "the companionship of the whole race in their experience" helped relieve Howells of the dread that he stood alone in his fears.[5] From this background of anxieties, common to most men, and this history, peculiar to Howells, of attempts to surmount anxiety by forcing it into the open through written and spoken words, Howells arrived at the years immediately preceding *The Shadow of a Dream* receptive to the matter of the mind's powers and vulnerabilities.[6]

The old schemes for maintaining mental equilibrium were severely strained in the 1880's, the decade after *The Undiscovered Country*. Howells' younger brother Henry, suffering from a crippled mind, became increasingly violent; his eldest daughter Winifred showed marked signs of mental disorder; as he later observed in an interview in 1896, Howells' own balance "suddenly, and without apparent cause," gave way, and the "'bottom dropped out!'"[7] In the face of these mounting pressures Howells pulled himself together to begin work on *A Hazard of New Fortunes*. On 3 March 1889, the day after the first installment of his new novel appeared serially, Winifred died suddenly. It was on the *other* side of this event that *The Shadow of a Dream* began to evolve into an accomplished fact.

After completing the final chapters of *A Hazard of New Fortunes* in the late summer of 1889, Howells went to work on *The Shadow of a Dream* and then moved on in December to *A Boy's Town*, a reminiscence of his earliest years in Hamilton, Ohio. This fic-

---

5. *Literary Friends and Acquaintance* (New York and London, 1900), pp. 44 and 45.

6. A notebook entry of 1883 lists "The Shadow of a Dream" among other jotted titles, while in another notebook Howells urged himself to write "'A Realistic Ghost Story' to surpass 'A Romance of Old Clothes' and 'A Phantom Lover'—Oct 1886." The 1883 notebook is in the Houghton Library at Harvard University.

Permission to quote unpublished passages from the notebooks and letters written by Howells has been granted by William White Howells for the heirs of the Howells Estate. Permission to quote from other unpublished letters owned by Harvard has been granted by the Harvard College Library. Republication of this material requires these same permissions. The manuscripts of all letters are at Harvard unless otherwise noted.

7. Review by Marrion Wilcox, "Works of W. D. Howells, 1860–96," *Harper's Weekly*, 4 July 1896, pp. 655–656.

tionalized autobiography reveals the source for several details used in the novel; it indicates too the origin of that general atmosphere of guilt-dreams and death-fears common to the two books written during a period of concentrated artistic effort between the autumn of 1889 and the spring of 1890.[8] Also, his recollection of Bret Harte's visit to Boston in 1871 furnished the incident Howells needed to bring the Rev. James Nevil's dilemma to its close.[9] Indeed, the novel offers yet one more solid, if unstartling, example of the ways in which Howells drew experiences from every corner of his life for use in his fiction. It illustrates as well how rapidly he could work under self-imposed pressure.

By 29 October 1889 H. M. Alden of *Harper's Monthly* replied that he liked the first part of the proposed three-part serial "very much," especially the presence of "more dramatic intention in it than you usually have." By the middle of December Howells wrote to his father of the near completion of the novelette he believed the older man would "fancy." The Samuel Clemenses had also enjoyed the early chapters which Howells probably

---

8. *A Boy's Town* (New York, 1890, p. 14) notes that Howells had lived in "the Falconer house," also spelled "Faulkner." After moving away he returned for a visit and was overwhelmed by a sense of loss of home (p. 244), somewhat like the restirrings of memory Basil March feels on revisiting the house of Douglas Faulkner. The havoc caused by an exaggerated sense of guilt, important to an understanding of the Howells-Basil March view of Nevil's dilemma, is depicted in *A Boy's Town*, p. 44. Other autobiographical accounts published in later years give clues to still further sources for Howells' inspiration for this novelette: *Years of My Youth*, pp. 25 and 174–175; *My Literary Passions, Criticism and Fiction* (New York and London, 1891), p. 51; and *My Year in a Log Cabin* (New York, 1893), pp. 37–39.

9. In stepping backward from the railroad car bearing Harte away, Howells barely escaped being crushed against the station walls. He was able "long after, to adapt the incident to the exigencies of fiction, and to have a character, not otherwise to be conveniently disposed of, actually crushed to death between a moving train and such an archway" ("Editor's Easy Chair," *Harper's Monthly*, CVIII [December 1903], 159). The self-mocking tone apparent in Howells' easy eradication of a character from a novel and a man from his mental torment ought to be noted. He had first planned to let Nevil live and have fulfillment of passionate desire (see page xviii of this introduction, Howells' letter to Howard Pyle). When he could no longer allow love to Nevil, Howells seems to have found relief in denying Nevil life. Howells' own fears probably underlie both decisions which give the novel's ending its markedly evasive quality.

read to them during a visit to Hartford on 2 and 3 November; on 23 December Mark Twain wrote to urge Howells to let them hear the rest of his "dream-story."[10] By 29 December Howells could grant their wish; the novel was finished.

When *The Shadow of a Dream* began to appear in serial form in March 1890, Howells was busy planning its May appearance in book form. No manuscript is known to exist, but the changes made between the *Harper's Monthly* serial and the Harper book edition provide good illustrations of the way Howells worked toward increased precision of meaning while protecting himself from implications too strong to be allowed permanency.

Between the serial and book versions, shifts from "duskiness" to "smokiness" (13.4 in the present edition) and from "calm goodness" to "clear goodness" (15.5) seem to indicate verbal fastidiousness rather than significant changes in Howells' attitude toward the material. There are, however, six passages (only three of more than a word or so in length) which perhaps demonstrate more than attention to craft; emotional as well as artistic reasons may lie behind certain of the alterations between the *Harper's Monthly* text and the Harper book edition. Each of these instances concerns the physical appearance of Hermia Faulkner, the woman over whom her husband and James Nevil find their pain and death, and the effect her appearance has upon the observer-narrator Basil March.

Shortly after meeting Hermia, March makes a slightly mocking comparison between Douglas Faulkner's sickly state and his wife's obvious physical allure. The *Harper's Monthly* version reads, " 'And he hasn't got an undulating walk, and he doesn't tilt his head a little on one side as if it were a heavy rose; and he hasn't got a complexion of russet crimsoned; and his hair isn't thick and dull black and fluffy over the forehead; and he isn't round and strong and firm.' " The New York version of the same passage works to undercut Hermia's latent sensuality by turning her

10. *Mark Twain-Howells Letters*, ed. Henry Nash Smith and William M. Gibson (Cambridge, Mass., 1960), II, 625 and 626, footnote 5.

powers into playfully noted abstractions: " 'And he hasn't got a regular two-horse carriage of a walk, nor immortal eyes with starlike sorrows in them . . .' " (22.12–16).

Throughout most of his literary life Howells sought to demolish the follies he found pervading the Romantic stance. Romanticism was untrue in its sentimentality, thus sometimes immoral and often silly. More than that, it was also dangerous; the romantic urge roiled the dark waters of those passions Howells had early discovered he must evade if he were to survive as a man.[11] In *The Shadow of a Dream* more was at stake in his tempering of Hermia's fleshly presence than a canny economic expediency that knew that many readers resisted coming to terms with the implications of flesh they might find on the pages of the novels they bought. Howells had to ward off foolish idealizations of womankind, and much more. In reappraising the original description of Hermia Faulkner's appearance Howells judged that he had made her too vital and desirable. Revisions were made that avoid or neutralize the sensuality of her nature and body, while attention is called to attributes less physical: her tall stature, her "usual American type" of beauty, her aristocratic walk, her "immortal eyes"—all reduced to mortal scope by an irony that defeats any attempt to romanticize or sensualize.

When Basil March later sees the widowed but recently engaged Hermia in the palatial setting of her home, he is aware of the excitement she generates as a woman which he had never before felt. In the revised New York edition Howells replaces a womanly love-object with a neo-Platonic goddess. But by altering the words describing Hermia from "grossness" to "import" (83.34), from "ripeness" to "splendor" (84.1), and from "sumptuous womanhood" to "most regal womanhood" (84.1), Howells commits an error perhaps only a little less distasteful than

---

11. Everett Carter's "The Palpitating Divan," *College English*, XI (1950), 423–428, gives a reasoned assessment of Howells' stand on the place of sex in literature. This article, together with Edwin H. Cady's articles concerning Howells' fears, offers a wider view of Howells' problems as an artist and an insight into why irony was his most characteristic mode of self-defense.

the one he tried to avoid. He removes Hermia from the realm of human fleshliness only to move her nearer the region inhabited by an almost Petrarchan, semi-divine lady of angelic eyes, no flesh, and little solidity of character.

Much of the point of the novelette's psychological meaning is lost when Howells subverts Hermia's reality as a desirable woman who incites maddened jealousy on the part of her husband and who causes Nevil to torment himself over the thought that he may have coveted her, however unconsciously. As seasoned portrayer of the "usual American type" and as experimenter in the depiction of the "inner life," Howells either had to face fully or evade partially the significance of a woman who could foster subconscious desires and bring nightmare madness, remorse, and death into two men's lives. Howells was determined to solve at least one of these problems. His revisions show that, even if he could not surmount all the complexities involved, he chose ironic reductiveness as his best, if ultimately inadequate, weapon.

Even before book publication of *The Shadow of a Dream*, letters from friends indicated what reactions might be expected toward that novelette Howells had characterized as being "not quite like me." Howard Pyle's congratulatory letter judged "that the most tragic element of your story is the pathetic commonness of it all; so much agony, so much torture, and all for the sake of the dryest of dry husks." Pyle speculated on "that paradoxical truth that those who strive so hard to do the right thing insist upon making their own lives and the lives of those dearest to them so uncomfortable."[12] Howells mistook Pyle's remarks as an attack against self-denial, virtue, and goodness upheld for their own sakes and replied:

> Sometimes I feel that I must live entirely on the earthly plane unless I wish to be an arrogant ass, and meddle with things above me; and yet I *must* meddle with them, both in my own defective conduct and in the imagined lives of others. I felt that

---

12. Charles D. Abbott, *Howard Pyle, A Chronicle* (New York and London, 1925), pp. 178–179; letter of 13 April 1890.

Nevil was the helpless prisoner of his traditions, and yet in his place I do not know how I could have acted differently. At first I meant to have him marry Hermia, but he convinced me, as he wormed it out, that this was not possible. Happy for all if they could die out of their difficulties![13]

Letters from James Russell Lowell, Wolcott Balestier, Madison Cawein, William James, and Charles Eliot Norton followed during the summer months of 1890. The power of *A Hazard of New Fortunes* was too strong and immediate to be offset by the "daintily subtle" effects of *The Shadow of a Dream* with its "happy flights of poetry," its "pastel paintings in delicate prose," and its touch, "felicitous & pregnant with exquisite pathos."[14] Still, his friends took note of the pleasure this "slighter" novelette brought them and waited for more and greater achievements.

The Shadow of a Dream received relatively little critical attention; to many it was but one of Howells' "annual" efforts, wedged in between more important novels. The reader for *Critic*, who laid down the book "with a sigh . . . to muse awhile over the exceeding sadness of its theme," felt a sense of wonder "as to the solution of the mystery in ethics it propounds" and the quality of treatment that seemed so unlike Howells'. Since little in the book suggested to him the Howells of *The Rise of Silas Lapham* or the dramatic farces, the reviewer found relief in the solid presences of the Marches, "caught by a mental 'Kodak'. . . ." In Great Britain the *Literary World* and the *Athenæum* passed over it without much to say, while the *Pall Mall Budget* found it "rather tiresome" even if ultimately interesting, and the *Saturday Review* thought the language "not only affected but slipshod" and the story "all about three very unpleasant souls."[15]

---

13. Letter of 17 April 1890; *Life in Letters of William Dean Howells*, ed. Mildred Howells (Garden City, N.Y., 1928), II, 11.

14. Letter of 19 June, *New Letters of James Russell Lowell*, ed. M. A. De Wolfe Howe (New York and London, 1932), p. 341; letter of 20 August, *The Letters of William James*, ed. by his son Henry James (Boston, 1920), I, 298–299; letters of 12 and 25 July and 24 August 1890 at Harvard.

15. *Critic*, 26 July 1890, p. 44; *Literary World*, 27 June 1890, pp. 600–601; *Athenæum*, 3270 (28 June 1890), p. 828; *Pall Mall Budget*, 18 June 1890, p. 798; *Saturday Review*, LXX (5 July 1890), 19.

Two English reviewers took the time and had the acuity to examine the new possibilities for literature the novelette opened up. William Sharp in *Academy* (12 July 1890, pp. 27-28) called it Howells' best novel, welcomed the exposure of "our human helplessness under the dominion of natural laws and occult psychological forces," and saw its author "to be on the verge of a new departure in his art." The reviewer for the *Spectator* (16 August 1890, pp. 213-215) desired to dissociate the novelette from Howells' other works since it newly studied "that borderland of mental impressions and influences" and "the multitudinous chimæras that haunt the half-sick brain . . . ."

Eighteen months after its appearance the book also found an American reader more certain of what it represented in Howells' developing writing life; in contrasting the earlier novelette to *An Imperative Duty*, the reviewer proclaimed *The Shadow of a Dream* "a distinct success as a psychologic study" and called Howells "an acquisition in this special field of modern fiction . . . ."[16] However, an even longer view back toward *The Shadow of a Dream* taken by Marrion Wilcox in *Harper's Weekly* (4 July 1896, p. 655) indicates this judgment did not hold. The book is commended in passing merely for its "literary quality and witty dialogue." In the late 1890's such fiction—especially when sired by that eminent patriarch of the everyday and the external—was still considered a strange animal by those insensitive to clear signs to the contrary.

After *The Shadow of a Dream* was presented to the American world, Howells moved to get it into the hands of readers abroad. In March 1891 Wolcott Balestier corresponded with him from London concerning a newly planned Continental Series that would begin with *Tuscan Cities* and *The Shadow of a Dream*. David Douglas of Edinburgh acted to get the novelette out as part of his "American Authors" series in both cloth and cheap paper editions. Meanwhile, in America, release of the book in wrapper

---

16. *Critic*, 16 January 1892, p. 34. One assumes that this reviewer is not the one who, in the earlier *Critic* article, failed to recognize the kind of fiction *The Shadow of a Dream* represents.

and cloth formats, followed by a remainder binding, ended the first year's history of the novelette. More important than the printings that did take place is the fact that it was nine years before a re-impression was brought out in 1899 and then sixty-three more years until Twayne Press published *The Shadow of a Dream* in conjunction with *An Imperative Duty*. A meager exposure, indeed.

From the first Howells had viewed his novelette as experimental and "not quite like me." Yet among the hundreds of jottings and titles which never emerged from his notebooks into fruition, the idea for *The Shadow of a Dream* was one of those selected to receive finished expression; somehow the novelette was important to him. It is surely of importance to an understanding of the strong new current toward psychological fiction which Howells assessed as a critic and furthered as a novelist.

"The motive is rather romantic," Howells had written his father in December 1889, "but the treatment very realistic." At this point he was still held to "realism" as that scientific notation of outward actions that tends to take the everyday and external as its criteria for reality; he still felt uneasy when he saw the "motive" of this fiction existing separately from its "treatment," each attempting to have its own validity as "romantic" and "realistic." Nine years later (13 March 1898) he wrote Aurelia Howells that for some time he had sensed he ought to "deal more with things of spiritual significance." "Outer life no longer interests me as it once did," he admitted, "and I believe I can find a new audience for my studies of the inner life."[17]

---

17. *The Shadow of a Dream* was followed by a flow of "occult" fiction. Two collections of short stories, *Questionable Shapes* and *Between the Dark and the Daylight*, appeared in 1903 and 1907, and *The Seen and Unseen at Stratford-on-Avon, A Fantasy* was published in 1914. The article "True, I Talk of Dreams" (*Harper's Monthly*, May 1895), an introduction to *Shapes that Haunt the Dusk* (1907), the essay included in *In After Days, Thoughts on the Future Life* (1910), and "Easy Chair" discussions in November 1917 and August 1919 concerning Sir Oliver Lodge's mediumistic meetings with his dead son and the growth of spiritualism offer continuing evidence of Howells' interest in the more obscure corners of the self. Significant portions of *The Landlord at Lion's Head* (1897), *The Son of Royal Langbrith* (1904), and *The Leatherwood God* (1916) are further demonstration of his interest in the powers of the human

It was not until 1903, however, that Howells could fully record the "swing of the pendulum" which took responsible fiction toward a mode that was "unscientific" and yet not romantic in the pejorative sense; only then could he praise "a whole order of literature" that was "calling itself psychological, as realism called itself scientific, and dealing with life on its mystical side." Naming over such practitioners as Tolstoy, Gorky, Ibsen, Björnsen, Hauptmann, Maeterlinck, and Henry James, he concluded, "We have indeed, in our best fiction, gone back to mysticism, if indeed we were not always there in our best fiction, and the riddle of the painful earth is again engaging us with the old fascination."[18]

Modesty may have kept Howells from including his name on this list, but he was certainly aware that from childhood his own concerns, private and literary, had been swinging him toward that same pendulum position where *The Shadow of a Dream* rests.

M. B.

---

mind. His correspondence is filled with letters, too numerous to cite, concerning Swedenborg's views on the immortality of consciousness and his own opinions on psychic research, dreams of the dead, and the "new psychology" of William James.

18. Review of John Bigelow's *The Mystery of Sleep*, "Editor's Easy Chair," *Harper's Monthly*, CVII (June 1903), 149.

W. D. Howells.

The Shadow of a Dream

Part First

————

FAULKNER

DOUGLAS FAULKNER was of a type once commoner in the West than now, I fancy. In fact, many of the circumstances that tended to shape such a character, with the conditions that repressed and the conditions that evolved it, have changed so vastly that they may almost be said not to exist any longer.

He was a lawyer, with a high ideal of professional honor, and in his personal relations he was known to be almost fantastically delicate, generous, and faithful. At the same time he was a "practical" politician; he adhered to his party in all its measures; he rose rapidly to be a leader in it, and was an unscrupulous manager of caucuses and conventions. For a while he was editor of the party organ in his city, and he wrote caustic articles for it which were rather in the line of his political than his personal morality. This employment was supposed to be more congenial than his profession to the literary taste for which he had a large repute among his more unliterary acquaintance. They said that Faulkner could have been an author if he had chosen, and they implied that this was not worth while with a man who could be something in law and politics. Their belief had followed him from Muskingum University, where he was graduated with distinction in letters and forensics. The school was not then on so grand a scale as its name, and a little of the humanities might have gone a long way in it; but Faulkner was really a lover of books, and a reader of them, whether he could ever have been a writer of them or not; and he kept up his habit of reading after he entered active life.

It was during his editorial phase that I came from the country to be a writer on the opposition newspaper in his city, and something I did caught his fancy: some sketch of the sort I was always trying at, or some pert criticism, or some flippant satire of his party friends. He came to see me, and asked me to his house, for a talk, he said, about literature; and when I went I chose to find him not very modern in his preferences. He wanted to talk to me about Byron and Shelley, Scott and Cooper, Lamartine and Schiller, Irving and Goldsmith, when I was full of Tennyson and Heine, Emerson and Lowell, George Eliot and Hawthorne and Thackeray; and he rather bored me, showing me fine editions of his favorites. I was surprised to learn that he was only a few years older than myself: he had filled my mind so long as a politician that I had supposed him a veteran of thirty, at least, and he proved to be not more than twenty-six. Still, as I was only twenty-two I paid him the homage of a younger man, but I remember deciding that he was something of a sentimentalist. He seemed anxious to account for himself in his public character, so out of keeping with the other lives he led; he said he was sorry that his mother (with whom he lived in her widowhood) was out of town; she was the inspiration of all his love of literature, he said; and would have been so glad to see me. I was flattered, for the Faulkners were of the first social importance; they were of Virginian extraction. From his library he took me into what he called his den, and introduced me to a friend of his who sat smoking in a corner, and whom I saw to be a tall young Episcopal clergyman when he stood up. The night was very hot; Faulkner had in some claret punch, and the Rev. Mr. Nevil drank with us. He did not talk much, and I perceived that he was the matter-of-fact partner in a friendship which was very romantic on Faulkner's side, and which appeared to date back to their college days. That was now a good while ago, but they seemed to be in the habit of meeting often, and to have kept up their friendship in all its first fervor. Mr. Nevil was very handsome, with a regular face, and a bloom on it quite girlishly peachy, and very pure, still, earnest blue eyes. He looked physically and spiritually wholesome; but Faulkner certainly did not look wholesome in the matter of his complexion at least. It was pale, with a sort of smokiness, and his black, straight hair strung down in points over his forehead; his beautiful dark eyes were restlessly brilliant; he stooped a little, and he was, as they say in the West, loosehung. I noticed his hands, long, nervous, with fingers that trembled, as he rested their tips, a little yellowed from his cigar, on a book.

It was a volume of De Quincey, on whom we all came together in literature, and we happened to talk especially of his essay on Kant, and of the dreams which afflicted the philosopher's old age, and which no doubt De Quincey picturesquely makes the most of. Then we began to tell our own dreams, the ghastlier ones; and Faulkner said he sometimes had dreams, humiliating, disgraceful, loathsome, that followed him far into the next day with a sense of actual occurrence. He was very vivid about them, and in spite of the want of modernity in his literary preferences, I began to think he might really have been a writer. He said that sometimes he did not see why we should not attribute such dreams to the Evil One, who might have easier access to a man in the helplessness of sleep; but Nevil agreed with me that they were more likely to come from a late supper. Faulkner submitted, but he said they were a real affliction, and their persistence in a man's waking thoughts might almost influence his life.

When I took my leave he followed me to his gate, in his bare head and slippers; it was moonlight, and he walked a long way homeward with me. We led a very simple life in our little city then, and a man might go bareheaded and slipper-footed about its streets at night as much as he liked. Now and then we met a policeman, and Faulkner nodded, with the facile "Ah, Tommy!" or "Hello, Mike!" of a man inside politics. I told him I envied him his ability to mingle with the people in that way, and he said it was not worth while.

"You are on the right track, and I hope you'll stick to it. We ought to have some Western authors; the West's ripe for it. I used to have the conceit to think I could have done something myself in literature, if I'd kept on after I left college."

I murmured some civilities to the effect that this was what all his friends thought.

"Well, it's too late, now," he said, "if ever it was early enough. I was foredoomed to the law; my father wouldn't hear of anything else, and I don't know that I blame him. I might have made a spoon, but I should certainly have spoiled a horn. A man generally does what he's fit for. Now there's Nevil— Don't you like Nevil?"

I said, "Very much," though really I had not thought it very seemly for a clergyman to smoke, and drink claret punch: I was very severe in those days.

Faulkner went on: "Nevil's an instance, a perfect case in point. If ever there was a human creature born into the world to do just the work he *is* doing, it's Nevil. I can't tell you how much that fellow has been to me, March!" This was the second time we had met; but Faulkner was already on terms of comradery with me; he was the kind of man who could hold no middle course; he must stand haughtily aloof, or he must take you to his heart. As he spoke, he put his long arm across my shoulders, and kept it there while we walked. "I was inclined to be pretty wild in college, and I had got to running very free when I first stumbled against Jim Nevil. He was standing up as tall and straight morally as he does physically, but he managed to meet me on my own level without seeming to stoop to it. He was ordained of God, then, and his life had a message for every one; for me it seemed to have a special message, and what he did for me was what he lived more than what he said. He talked to me, of course, but it was his example that saved me. You must know Nevil. Yes, he's a noble fellow, and you can't have any true conception of friendship till you *have* known him. Just *see* that moon!" Faulkner stopped abruptly, and threw up his head.

The perfect orb seemed to swim in the perfect blue. The words began to breathe themselves from my lips:

" 'The moon doth with delight
Look round her when the heavens are bare;' "

and he responded as if it were the strain of a litany:

" 'Waters on a starry night
Are beautiful and fair;' "

and I spoke:

" 'The sunshine is a glorious birth;' "

and he responded again:

" 'But yet I know, where'er I go,
That there hath passed a glory from the earth.' "

His voice broke in the last line and faded into a tremulous whisper. It was the youth in both of us, smitten to ecstasy by the beauty of the scene, and pouring itself out in the modulations of that divine stop, as if it had been the rapture of one soul.

He took his arm from my shoulder, and turned about without any ceremony of adieu, and walked away, head down, with shuffling, slippered feet.

We met several times, very pleasantly, and with increased liking. Then he took offence, as capricious as his former fancy, at something I wrote, and sent me an angry note, which I answered in kind. Not long afterward I went abroad on a little money I had saved up, and when I came home, I married, and by an ironical chance, found myself, with my æsthetic tastes, my literary ambition, and my journalistic experience, settled in the insurance business at Boston. I did not revisit the West, but I learned by letters that our dear little city out there had become a formidable railroad centre; everybody had made or lost money, and Faulkner had become very rich through the real estate which had long kept him land-poor. One day I got a newspaper addressed in his handwriting, which brought me the news of his marriage. The name of the lady struck me as almost factitiously pretty, and I could well imagine Faulkner provisionally falling in love with her because she was called Hermia Winter. The half-column account of the wedding described the Rev. James Nevil as "officiating"; and something in the noisy and bragging tone of the reporter in dealing with this important society event disadvantaged the people concerned in my mind. I chose to regard it all as cruder and louder than anything I remembered of the place in old days; but my wife said that it was characteristically Western, and that probably it had always been like that out there; only I had not felt it while I was in it, though, as she said, I was not of it.

She was a Bostonian herself, and it was useless to appeal to the society journalism of her own city in proof of the prevalence of that sort of vulgarity everywhere. She laughed at the name Hermia, and said it sounded made-up, and that she had no doubt the girl's name was Hannah. I thought I had my revenge afterward when a friend wrote me about the marriage, which was a surprise to everybody; for it had always been supposed that Faulkner was going to marry the beautiful and brilliant Miss Ludlow, long, perhaps too long, the belle of the place. The lady whom he had chosen was the daughter of a New England family, who had lived just out of town in my time and had never been in society. She was a teacher in Bell's Institute, and Faulkner met her there on one of his business visits as trustee. She was a very cultivated girl, though; and they were going abroad for their wedding journey. My correspondent had a special message from Faulkner for me, delivered on his wedding night. He remembered me among the people he would have liked to have there; he was sorry for our little quarrel and was to blame for it; he was coming home by way of Boston, and was going to look me up.

My wife said, Well, he seemed a nice fellow; but it only showed how any sort of New England girl could go out there and pick up the best. For the rest, she hoped they would not hurry home on my account; and if all my Western friends, with their free ideas of hospitality, were going to call on me, there would be no end to it. It was the jealousy of her husband's past every good wife feels that spoke; but long before I met Faulkner again we had both forgotten all about him.

II

ONE DAY seven or eight years later, when I was coming up from Lynn, where we had board for a few weeks' outing in August, I fell in with Dr. Wingate, the nervous specialist. We were members of the same dining club, and were supposed to meet every month; we really met once or twice during the winter, but then it was a great pleasure to me, and I tried always to get a place next him at table. I found in him, as I think one finds in most intelligent physicians, a sympathy for human suffering unclouded by sentiment, and a knowledge of human nature at once vast and accurate, which fascinated me far more than any forays of the imagination in that difficult region. Like physicians everywhere, he was less local in his feelings and interests than men of other professions; and I was able better to overcome with him that sense of being a foreigner, and in some sort on sufferance, which embarrassed me (quite needlessly, I dare say) with some of my commensals: lawyers, ministers, brokers, and politicians. I had a sort of affection for him; I never saw him, with the sunny, simple-hearted, boyish smile he had, without feeling glad; and it seemed to me that he liked me, too. His kindly presence must have gone a long way with his patients, whose fluttering sensibilities would hang upon his cheery strength as upon one of the main chances of life.

We rather rushed together to shake hands, and each asked how the other happened to be there at that hour in the morning. I explained my presence, and he said, as if it were some sort of coincidence: "You don't say so! Why, I've got a patient over at Swampscott, who says he knows you. A man named Faulkner."

I repeated, "Faulkner?" In the course of travel and business I had met so many people that I forgave myself for not distinguishing them very sharply by name, at once.

"He says he used to know you in your demi-semi-literary days, and he rather seemed to think you must be concealing a reputation for a poet, when I told him you were in the insurance business, and I only knew of your literary tastes. He's a Western man, and he met you out there."

"Oh!" said I. "*Douglas* Faulkner!" And now it was my turn to say, "*You* don't say so! Why of course! Is it possible!" and I lost myself in a cloud of silent reminiscences and associations, to come out presently with the question, "What in the world is he doing at Swampscott?"

The doctor looked serious; and then he looked keenly at me. "Were you and he great friends?"

"Well, we were not sworn brothers exactly. We were writers on rival newspapers; but I rather liked him. Yes, there was something charming to me about him; something good and sweet. I haven't met him, though, for ten years."

"He seemed to be rather fond of you. He said he wished I would tell you to come and see him, the next time I met you. Odd you should turn up there in the station!" By this time we were in the train, on our way to Boston.

"I will," I said, and I hesitated to add, "I hope there's nothing serious the matter?"

The doctor hesitated too. "Well, he's a pretty sick man. There's no reason I shouldn't tell you. He's badly run down; and—I don't like the way his heart behaves."

"Oh, I'm sorry—"

"He had just got home from Europe, and was on his way to the mountains when he came to see me in Boston, and I sent him to the sea-side. I came down last night—it's the beginning of my vacation—to see him, and spent the night there. He's got the Mallows place—nice old place. Do you know his wife?"

"No; he married after I came East. What sort of person is she?" I asked.

I remembered my talk with my wife about her and her name, and I felt that it was really a triumph for me when the doctor said: "Well, she's an exquisite creature. One of the most beautiful women I ever saw, and one of the most interesting. Of course, there's where the ache comes in. In a case like that, it isn't so much that one dies as that the other lives. It's none of my business; but she seemed rather lonely. They have no acquaintance among the other cottagers, and—did you think of taking your wife over? Excuse me!"

"Why of course! I'm so glad you suggested it. Mrs. March will be most happy to go with me."

III

MRS. MARCH dissembled her joy at the prospect when I opened it to her. She said she did not see how she entered into the affair. Faulkner was an old friend of mine; but she had nothing to do with him, and certainly nothing to do with his wife. They would not like each other; it would look patronizing; it would complicate matters; she did not see what good it would do for her to go. I constantly fell back upon the doctor's suggestion. In the end, she went. She professed to be governed entirely by Dr. Wingate's opinion of our duty in the case; I acknowledged a good deal of curiosity as well as some humanity, and I boldly proposed to gratify both. But in fact I felt rather ashamed of my motives when I met Faulkner, and I righted myself in my own regard by instantly shifting my visit to the ground of friendly civility. He seemed surprised and touched to see me, and he welcomed my wife with that rather decorative politeness which men of Southern extraction use toward women. He was not going to have any of my compassion as an invalid, that was clear; and he put himself on a level with me in the matter of health at once. He said it was very good of Dr. Wingate to send me so soon, and I was very good to come; he was rather expecting the doctor himself in the afternoon; he had been out of kilter for two or three years; but he was getting all right now. I knew he did not believe this, but I made believe not to know it, and I even said, when he asked me how I was, that I was so-so; and I left him to infer that everybody was out of kilter, and perhaps just in his own way.

"Well, let us go up to the house," he said, as if this gave him a pleasure, "and find Mrs. Faulkner. You never met my wife,

March? Her people used to live just outside the city line, on Pawpaw Creek. They were of New England origin," he added to my wife; "but I don't know whether you'll find her very much of a Yankee. She has passed most of her life in the West. She will be very glad to see you; we have no acquaintances about here. Your Eastern people don't catch on to the homeless stranger quite so quickly as we do in the West. I dare say they don't let go so easily, either."

We had found Faulkner at the gate of his avenue, and we began to walk with him at once toward his cottage, under the arches of the sea-beaten, somewhat wizened elms, which all slanted landward, with a writhing fling of their gray and yellow lichened boughs. It was a delicious morning, and the cool sunshine dripped in through the thin leaves, here and there blighted at the edge and faded, and seemed to lie in pools in the road. The fine air was fresh, and brought from a distance apparently greater than it really came the plunge of the surf against the rocks, and the crash of the rollers along the beach. The ground fell away in a wide stretch of neglected lawn toward the water; and the autumnal dandelions lifted their stars on their tall slender stems from the long grass, which was full of late summer glint and sheen, and blowing with a delicate sway and tilt of its blades in the breeze that tossed the elms.

"What a lovely place!" sighed my wife.

"You haven't begun to see it," said Faulkner. "We've got twenty acres of land here, and all the sea and sky there are. Mrs. Faulkner will want to show you the whole affair. Did you walk up from the station? I'll send for your baggage from the house."

"That won't be necessary; I have it on my arm," said my wife, and she put her little shopping bag in evidence with a gay twirl.

"Why, but you're going to stay all night?"

"Oh, no, indeed! What would become of our children?"

"We'll send to Lynn for them."

"Thank you; it couldn't be managed. I won't try to convince you, Mr. Faulkner, but I'm sure your wife will be reasonable," she said, to forestall the protests which she saw hovering in his eyes.

I noticed that his eyes, once so beautiful, had a dull and suffering look, and the smokiness of his complexion had a kind of livid stain in it. His hair straggled from under his soft felt hat with the unkempt effect I remembered, and his dress had a sort of characteristic slovenliness. He carried a stick, and his expressive hands seemed longer and languider, as if relaxed from a nervous tension borne beyond the strength.

"Well, I'm sorry," said Faulkner. "But you're booked for the day, anyway."

My wife apparently did not think it worth while to dispute this; or perhaps she was waiting to have it out with Mrs. Faulkner. He put up his arm across my shoulder, and gave me a little pull toward him. "It's mighty pleasant to see you again, old fellow! I can't tell you *how* pleasant."

I was not to be outdone in civilities, and my cordiality in reply retrospectively established our former acquaintance on a ground of intimacy which it had never really occupied. My wife knew this and gave me a look of surprise, which I could see hardening into the resolution not to betray herself at least into insincerities.

"You'll find another old acquaintance of yours here," Faulkner went on. "You remember Nevil?"

"Your clerical friend? Yes, indeed! Is he here?" I put as much factitious rapture into my tone as it would hold.

"Yes; we were in Europe together, and he's spending a month with us here." Faulkner spoke gloomily, almost sullenly; he added, brightly, "You know I can't get along without Jim. He was in Europe with us, too, a good deal of the time. Yes, we've always been great friends."

"You remember I told you about Mr. Nevil, my dear," I explained to my wife.

"Oh, yes," she said, non-committally.

Faulkner slipped his hand from my shoulder into my arm, and gently stayed my pace a little. I perceived that he was leaning on me; but I made a feint of our being merely affectionate, and slowed my step as unconsciously as I could. He looked up under the downward slanted brim of his hat. "I expected them before this. Nevil went up to the house for my wife, and then we were going down on the rocks."

He stopped short, and rested heavily against me. I glanced round at his face: it was a lurid red, and, as it were, suffused with pain; his eyes seemed to stand full of tears; his lips were purple, and they quivered.

It was an odious moment: we could not speak or stir; we suffered too, and were cruelly embarrassed, for we felt that we must not explicitly recognize his seizure. In front of us I saw a gentleman and lady who seemed to be under something of our constraint. They were coming as swiftly as possible, without seeming to hurry, and they must have understood the situation, though they could not see his features. Before they reached us, Faulkner's face relaxed, and began to recover its natural color. He stirred, and I felt him urging me softly forward. By the time we encountered the others, he was able to say, in very much his usual tone, "My dear, this is Mrs. March, and my old friend March, that I've told you about. Nevil, you remember March? Let me present you to Mrs. March."

My astonishment that he could accomplish these introductions was lost in the interest that Mrs. Faulkner at once inspired in my wife, as I could see, equally with myself. She must then have been about thirty, and she had lost her girlish slenderness without having lost her girlish grace. Her figure, tall much above the wont of women, had a mature stateliness, while fitful gleams of her first youth brightened her face, her voice, her manner. There could be no doubt about her refinement, and none about her beauty; the one was as evident as the other. The beauty was of a usual American type; the refinement was from her eyes, which were angelic; deep and faithful and touching. I am sure this was the first impression of my wife as well as myself.

I shook hands with Nevil, whom I found looking not so much older as the past ten years should have made him. His dark golden hair had retreated a little on his forehead, and there were some faint, faint lines down his cheeks and his shaven lips. I saw the look of anxiety he cast furtively at Faulkner; but for that he seemed as young and high-hearted as when we first met. I searched his eyes for the clear goodness which once dwelt in them, and found it, a little saddened, a little sobered, a little more saintly, but all there, still. I cannot tell how my heart went out to him with a tenderness which nothing in his behavior toward me had ever invited. On the few occasions when we met, he had always loyally left me to Faulkner, who made all the advances and offered all the caresses, without winning any such return of affection from me as I now involuntarily felt for Nevil. Of course I looked at my wife to see what she thought of him. I saw that something in her being a woman, which drew her to Mrs. Faulkner, left her indifferent to Nevil.

IV

"HERMIA," said Faulkner, sounding the canine letter in her name with a Western strength that was full of the charm of old associations for me, "these people have got some children at Lynn, and they can't stay here overnight because they didn't bring them. I'm going to send over for them."

"Oh, I should like to see your children," she answered to my wife, cordially, yet submissively, as the way of one wise woman is with another concerning her children.

Mrs. March explained how it was in no wise possible to have the children sent for; and how we had only come for a short call. I perceived that all Mrs. Faulkner's politeness could not keep her mind on what my wife was saying: that she was scanning her husband's face with devoted intensity. The same absence showed itself in Nevil's manner. Of course they were both terribly anxious; I could understand that from what I had already seen of Faulkner's case; and in his interest they were both trying to hide their anxiety. Of course, too, he knew it on his part, and he tried to ignore their efforts at concealment. We were all playing at the futile and heart-breaking comedy which humanity obliges us to keep up with a dying man, and in which he must bear his part with the rest. We began to be even gay. Faulkner insisted again that we were good for the whole day; his wife joined him; he appealed to Nevil to put it to Mrs. March as a duty (that would fetch any New England woman, he said), and we consented to stay over lunch, in a burlesque of being kept prisoners. While this went on, I could not help noticing the quality of the look which Faulkner turned upon his wife and Nevil when he spoke to either: a sort of deadliness passing into a piteous appeal. It was very curious.

He asked if we should go down on the rocks, or up to the house, and we decided that we had better go to the house, and do the rocks after lunch: the tide was coming in, and the surf would be better and better.

"All right," he said, and we let Mr. Nevil lead the way with the ladies, while we came at a little distance behind. Faulkner began at once to praise Nevil, for his goodness in staying on with him so long after he had given up to him the whole past year in Europe. I said the proper things in appreciation, and Faulkner went on to say that Nevil had the richest and the poorest parish in our old home now, the most millionaires and the most paupers; and he had made St. Luke's a refuge and a sanctuary for them all. He said he did not suppose a man had ever been so fortunate as he was in his friendship with Nevil. At first his wife had been jealous of it, but now she had got used to it; and though he did not suppose she would ever quite forgive Nevil for having been his friend before her time, she tolerated him. I said I understood how that sort of thing was; and he added that there was also the religious difference: Mrs. Faulkner's people were Unitarians, and she was strenuous in their faith, where he never allowed her to be molested. We got to talking about the old times in the West, and the people whom we had known in common, and how the city had grown, and how I would hardly know where I was if I were dropped down in it. But he kept returning to Nevil and to his wife, and I became rather tired of them.

The cottage, when we reached it, afforded a relief by its extremely remarkable prettiness. Though it was so near the sea, it was almost hidden in trees, and as Faulkner said, if you did not purposely look out to the water, you could easily imagine yourself in the depths of the country. As we sat on the veranda that shaded three sides of the house, he named the different points on the coast, with the curious accuracy which some people like to achieve in particulars wholly unimportant to other people. I suppose he had amused the sad leisure of his sickness in verifying the geography, and I tried to be interested in it, though I was so much more interested in him. He sat deeply sunken in a low Japanese arm-chair of rushes, with his long lean legs one crossed on the other, and fondling the crook of his stick with his thin right hand, while he looked out to seaward under the brim of his hat pulled down to his eyes. Nevil went directly to his room when we reached the cottage, and after a little while Mrs. Faulkner took my wife away to show her the house, which was vast and extravagantly furnished for a summer cottage. "It had gone unlet until very late in the season," Faulkner said, "and you've no idea how cheap we got it. I suppose it's a little out of society, off here on this point; you see it's quite alone; but as we're out of society too, it just suits us."

He looked after his wife as she left the veranda with Mrs. March, and I fancied in his glance at her buoyant, strenuous grace and her beauty of perfect health, something of the despair with which a sick man must feel the whole world slipping from his hold, too weak to close upon the most precious possession and keep it for his helplessness even while he stays.

The ladies were gone a good while, and he rambled on incessantly as if to keep me from thinking about his condition; or at least I fancied this, because I could not help thinking of it. Just as they returned, he was asking me, "Do you remember our talking that night about Kant's dreams, and—" He stopped, and called out to my wife, "Well, don't you think we are in luck?"

"Luck doesn't express it, Mr. Faulkner. You're in clover,

knee-deep. I didn't imagine there was such a place, anywhere."

"After lunch we must show you our old garden, as well as the rocks," said Faulkner. "At present I don't see how we could do better than stay where we are."

I thought he was going to recur to the subject he had dropped at sight of the returning ladies, but he did not. He asked my wife if Mrs. Faulkner had shown her the copy they had made of Murillo's Madonna, and he talked about its qualities with an authoritative ignorance of art which I should have found amusing in different circumstances. He had made a complete collection of all the engravings of this Madonna, and of all the sentimental Madonnas of the Parmesan school. He considered them very spiritual, and said he would show them to us, some time; he always carried them about with him; but he wanted to keep something to tempt us back another day. He asked her if she cared for rare editions, and said he wished he had his large paper copies with him. He told her I would remember them, and I pretended that I did. I do not think Faulkner had read much since I saw him. He talked about Bulwer and Dickens and Cherbuliez and Octave Feuillet as if they were modern. But nobody came up to Victor Hugo. Of course we had both read *Les Misérables?* Mrs. Faulkner, he said, was crazy about a Russian fellow: Tourguénief. Had we read him, and could we make anything out of him? Faulkner could not, for his part. Were we ever going to have any great poets again? Byron was the last that you could really call great.

His wife listened in a watchful abeyance to see if he needed anything, or felt worse, or was getting tired. From time to time he sent her for some book, or print, or curio that he mentioned, and whenever she came back, he gave her first that deadly look. Afterward, I fancied that he despatched her on these errands to make experiment of how the sight of her would affect him at each return.

The sea stretched a vast shimmer of thin grayish blue under the perfect sky; and the ships moved half sunk on its rim, or seemed buoyantly lifting from it for flight in the nearer distance.

The colors were those of an aquarelle, washes of this tint and that, bodyless and impalpable, and they were attenuated to the last thinness in the long yellow curve of beach, and the break of the shallow rollers upon it. Faulkner said they never got tired of looking; there was one effect on the wide wet beach, which he wished we could see, when people were riding toward you, and seemed to be walking on some kind of extraordinary stilts.

Mr. Nevil came down, and then Mrs. Faulkner said it must be near lunch-time, and asked my wife and me if we would not like to go to our room first.

v

As SOON AS the door closed upon us, my wife broke out: "*Well*, my dear! it's just as I imagined. What a tiresome creature! And how ignorant and arrogant! Is *that* what you called a cultivated person in the West?"

"Well, I don't think I shall quite hold myself responsible for Faulkner; I'll own he hasn't improved since I saw him last. But I always told you he was a sentimentalist."

"Sentimentalist! He's one *sop* of sentiment; and as conventional! Second-rate and second-hand! Why my *dear !* Could you ever have thought there was anything to that man?"

"Well, certainly more than I do at present. But I don't recollect that I ever boasted him Apollo and the nine Muses all boiled down into one."

She did not relent. "Why, compared with him, that Mr. Nevil is a burning and a shining light."

"Nevil has certainly gathered brilliancy somehow," I admitted.

"It's quite like such a man as Faulkner to want a three-cornered household. I think the man who can't give up his intimate friends after he's married, is always a kind of weakling. He has no right to them; it's a tacit reflection on his wife's heart and mind."

"Yes, I think you're quite right, there," I said, waiting for her to put the restorative touches to the bang which the sea-breeze had made a little too limp for social purposes; and we went over together the list of households we knew in which the husband supplemented himself with a familiar friend. We agreed that it was the innocence of our life that made it so common, but we said all the same that it was undignified and silly and mischievous. It kept the husband and wife apart, and kept them from the absolutely free exchange of tendernesses at any and every moment, and forbade them the equally wholesome immediate expressions of resentments, or else gave their quarrels a witness whom they could not look at without remembering that they had quarrelled in his presence. We made allowance for the difference in the case of Nevil and the Faulkners; there was now at least a real reason for his being with them; they would have been singularly lonely and helpless without him.

"They have no children!" said my wife. "That says it all. They are really not a family. Oh, dear! I hope it isn't wicked for us to be so happy in our children, Basil."

"It's a sin that I think I can brazen out at the Day of Judgment," I answered. "What does she say when you have her alone with another woman?"

"Well, there you've hit upon the true test, my dear. If a person's genuine, and not a *poseuse*, she's more interesting when you have her alone with another woman, than when you have her with a lot of men. And Mrs. Faulkner stands the test. Yes, she's a great creature."

"Why, what did she say?"

"Say? Nothing! You don't have to *say* anything. You merely have to *be*."

"Oh! That seems rather simple."

"Stuff! You know what I mean. You're the true blue, if you don't begin to fade or change your tone, in the least. If you remain just what you were, and are not anxious to get away. If you have repose, and are unselfish enough to be truly polite. If you make the other woman that you're alone with feel that she's just as well worth while as a man. And that can't be done by *saying*. Now do you understand?"

"Yes; and it appears difficult."

"Difficult? It's next to impossible!"

"And it can all be conveyed by manner?"

"Of course we talked—"

"She must have flattered you enormously."

"She praised *you!*"

"Oh!" I said, in admiration of the way my point was turned against me. But I was not satisfied with my wife's judgment of Faulkner. I could not say it was unjust to the facts before her; but I felt that something was left out of the account: something that she as a woman and an Easterner could not take into the account. We men and we Westerners have a civilization of our own.

She went on to say, "Of course, I couldn't be with her for a quarter of an hour, and especially after I had seen what *he* was, without understanding her marriage. She's a great deal younger than he is; and she was earning her own living, poor thing, and perhaps supporting her family—"

"Oh, oh! What jumps!"

"At any rate, she was poor, and they were poor; and she was dazzled by his offer, and might easily have supposed herself in love with him. Her people would be flattered too, if they were not quite up to her, and he was a great swell among you, out there, and rich, and all that. Of course, she simply *had* to marry him. And then—she outgrew him. With her taste and her sense, it could only be a question of time. I know she was writhing inwardly through all his pretentious, ignorant talk about art and literature; but with her ideal of duty, she would rather *die* than let anybody see that she *didn't* think him the greatest and wisest of human creatures. They have no children; and that might be fatal to any woman that was less noble and heroic than she is. But she's simply made *him* her child, since his sickness, and devoted herself to him, and that's been their salvation. She won't let herself see any fault in him, or anything offensive or conceited or petty."

"Did she tell you all this?"

"What an idea! I *knew* it from the way she kept lugging him in, and relating everything to him. You could see she was simply determined to do it."

"Oh, then you've romanced all this about her! Suppose I begin, now, and romance poor old Faulkner?"

"You're welcome—if you can make anything out of him."

"Well, of course, I'm at a disadvantage. In the first place, he isn't quite so pretty as his wife—"

"No, he *isn't!*"

"And his name isn't Hermia, or Hannah."

"Oh, it *is* Hermia!" my wife interrupted. "I'm satisfied of that. But what geese her parents must have been to call her so!"

I ignored the interpolation. "And he hasn't got a regular two-horse carriage of a walk, nor immortal eyes with starlike sorrows in them; he seems plainer and limper than ever, poor old fellow. Ah, my dear, our miseries don't embellish our persons very much, whatever they do for our souls; and Faulkner's good looks—"

My wife had quite finished repairing her disordered bang, and we had abandoned ourselves entirely to controversy. A knock at the door startled us, and it was Mrs. Faulkner's voice which said outside, "Lunch is ready."

My wife seized my wrist melodramatically, and almost at the moment of answering, in a sweet, high society tone, "Yes, yes, thank you! We're *quite* ready too!" she hissed in my ear, "Basil! Do you suppose she *heard* you?"

"If she did," I said, "she must have thought I was praising Faulkner's beauty."

VI

THE LUNCH was a proof of Mrs. Faulkner's native skill as a house-keeper, in all its appointments, and of her experience and observation of certain details of touch and flavor, acclimated and naturalized to the American kitchen from the cuisines of southern Europe. It meant money, but not money alone; it meant sympathy and appreciation and the artistic sense. I could see that my wife ate every morsel with triumph over me: I could feel that without looking at her: and she rendered merit to Mrs. Faulkner for it all, as much as if she had cooked it, created it. In fact I knew that my wife had fallen in love with her: and when you have fallen in love with a married woman you must of course hate her husband, especially if you are another woman.

I thought this reflection rather neat, and I wished that I could have a chance to put it to my wife; but none offered till it was forever too late; none offered at all in effect. After lunch we went that walk they had planned, and this time Faulkner took the two ladies in charge, or rather he fell to them, that he might tacitly be under his wife's care. I heard him, as I lagged behind with Nevil, devoting himself to Mrs. March with his decorative politeness, and I longed in vain to beg the poor man to spare himself.

Nevil and I spoke irrelevancies till we had dropped back out of ear-shot. Then he asked, "How do you find Faulkner?" and looked at me.

There was no reason why I should not be honest. "Well, I confess he gave me a great shock."

"When he had that seizure?"

"Yes."

"But generally speaking?"

"Generally speaking he seems to me a very sick man."

"You see him at his best," said Nevil; and he fetched a deep sigh. "This is an exceptionally good day with him."

"Does he suffer often in that way?"

"Yes, rather often."

"And is he in danger at such times?"

"The greatest. The chance is that he will not live through such a seizure; he may die at any moment without the seizure. Any little excitement may bring on the paroxysm. I suppose it was seeing you unexpectedly."

"Of course, I didn't know we should meet him."

"Oh, no one was to blame," said Nevil. "The inevitable can't be avoided. Somehow it must come."

We were silent. Then I said, "He seemed to be in great agony."

"I suppose we can't imagine such agony."

"And is there no hope for him?"

"I understand, none at all."

"And he must go on suffering that way till— It's horrible! He'd better be dead!" I said, remembering the atrocity of the anguish which Faulkner's face had betrayed: the livid lips, the suffused eyes, the dumb ache visible in every fibre of his dull, copper-tinted visage.

"Ah!" said Nevil, with another long, quivering sigh. "We mustn't allow ourselves to say such things, or even to think them. The appeal to death from the most intolerable pain, it's going from the known to the unknown. Death is in the hands of God, as life is; he giveth and he taketh away. Blessed be the name of the Lord! Blessed, blessed!" He dropped his head, and lifted it suddenly. "We must say that all the more when we see such hopeless, senseless torment as Faulkner's. I've often tried to think what Christ meant by that cry of his on the cross, 'My God, why hast thou forsaken me?' It couldn't have been that he doubted his Father; that's monstrous. But perhaps in the exquisite torture that he suffered, his weak, bewildered human nature forgot, lost for the dire moment, the reason of pain."

"And is there any reason for pain?" I asked, sceptically. "Or any except that it frays away the tissues whose tatters are to let the spirit through?"

"I used not to think so, and I used to groan in despair when I could see no other reason for it. What can we say about the pain that does not end in death? Is it wasted, suffered to no end? Shall mortal man be more just than God? Shall man work wisely, usefully, definitely, and God work stupidly, idly, purposelessly? It's impossible! Our whole being denies it; whatever we see or hear, of waste or aimlessness in the universe, which seems to affirm it, we know to be an illusion: our very nature protests it so. But I could not reason to the reason, and I owe my release to the suggestion of a friend whose experience of suffering had schooled him to clearer and deeper insight than mine. He had perceived, or it had been given him to feel, that no pang we suffer in soul or sense is lost or wasted, but is suffered to the good of some one, or of all. How, we shall some time know; and why. For the present the assurance that it is so is enough for me, and it enables me to be patient with the suffering of a man who is more to me than any brother could be. Sometimes it seems to me the clew to the whole labyrinthine mystery of life and death, of Being and Not-being."

"It's a great thought," I said. "It's immensely comforting. What does Faulkner think of it? Have you ever suggested it to him?"

I could not tell whether he fancied an edge of irony in my question; but it seemed as if he spiritually withdrew from me a little way, and then disciplined himself and returned. "No," he said, gently. "Faulkner rejects everything. As he says, he is going it blind. He says it will soon be over with him, and then if he sleeps, it will be well with him, and if he wakes, it can't be worse with him than it is now; and so he won't worry about the why or wherefore of anything, since he can't help it."

"That doesn't seem a bad kind of philosophy," I mused aloud.

"No. Whatever we call such a frame of mind, it's practically trust in God. And I don't judge Faulkner, if his resignation is sometimes rather contemptuous in its expression. I wish it were otherwise; but I doubt if he's always quite master of himself."

We walked slowly on. Faulkner, I knew, was aware of his condition, and I thought his courage splendid, in view of it. I wondered if his wife knew it as fully as he; probably she did; and when I considered this, I appeared to myself the most trivial of human beings, though I am not so sure now that I was. We are all what the absence, not the presence, of death has made us.

I found myself at a stand-still, and I perceived that Nevil had halted me. "Did it strike you—have you seen anything strange—peculiar—in Faulkner's manner?"

"No," I returned. "That is, how do you mean?"

"I've sometimes fancied, lately—I've been afraid—that his mind was giving way under the stress of his suffering. It's something that often happens—it's something that Dr. Wingate has apprehended."

"Good heavens! That would be too much. I saw no sign of it.

He recurred once, just before lunch, to that night when we first met at his house, and had that talk about Kant's dreams, and De Quincey. I thought he was going to say something; but just then the ladies came back to us, and he began to talk to them."

Nevil looked at me fixedly. "Very likely I'm mistaken. Perhaps my own mind isn't standing it very well! But the fear of that additional horror—I assure you that it makes my heart stop when I think of it. I ought to go away. I ought to be at home; I've spent the past year in Europe with the Faulkners, as—as their guest—and I have no right to a vacation this summer. There are duties, interests, claims upon me, that I'm neglecting in my proper work; and yet I can't tear myself away from him—from them."

We stood facing each other, and Nevil was speaking with the perturbation of an anxiety still suppressed, but now finding vent for the first time, and carrying us deep into an intimacy unwarranted by the casual character of our acquaintance.

I heard my wife's voice calling, "Come, come!" and I looked up to see both of the ladies waving their handkerchiefs from an open gate where they stood, and beckoning us on.

"Oh, yes," said Nevil. "That's the old garden."

VII

SOME former proprietor had built a paling of slender strips of wood ten or twelve feet high, and set so close together as almost to touch one another; and in this shelter from the salt gales had planted a garden on the southward, seaward slope, which must once have flourished in delicious luxuriance. The paling, weather-beaten a silvery gray, and blotched with lichens, sagged and swayed all out of plumb, with here and there a belvedere trembling upon rotting posts, and reached by broken steps, for the outlook over a tumult of vast rocks to the illimitable welter of the sea. Within the garden close there were old greenhouses and graperies, their roofs sunken in and their glass shattered, where every spring the tall weeds sprang up to the light, and withered in midsummer for want of moisture, and the Black

Hamburgs and Sweetwaters set in large clusters whose berries mildewed and burst, and mouldered away in never-riping decay. Broken flower-pots strewed the ground about them, and filled the tangles of the grass; but nature took up the work from art, and continued the old garden in her wilding fashion to an effect of disordered loveliness that was full of poetry sad to heart-break. Neglected rose-bushes straggled and fell in the high grass, their leaves tattered and skeletoned by slugs and blight; but here and there they still lifted a belated flower. The terraced garden beds were dense with witch-grass, through which the blackberry vines trailed their leaves, already on fire with autumn; young sumach-trees and Balm of Gilead scrub had sprung up in the paths, and about among the abandon and oblivion of former symmetry, stiff borders of box gave out their pungent odor in the sun that shone through clumps of tiger-lilies. The pear-trees in their places had been untouched by the pruning-knife for many a year, but they bore on their knotty and distorted scions, swollen to black lumps, crops of gnarled and misshapen fruit that bowed their branches to the ground; some peach-trees held a few leprous peaches, pale, and spotted with the gum that exuded from their limbs and trunks; over staggering trellises the grape-vines clung, and dangled imperfect bunches of Isabellas and Concords.

"Well, how do you like it?" asked Faulkner, with a sort of pride in our sensation, as if he had invented the place.

"Perfect! Perfect!" cried my wife, absorbing all its sentiment in a long, in-drawn sigh. "Nothing could possibly be better. You can't believe you're in America, here!"

He smiled in sympathy, and said, "No; for all practical purposes this is as old as Cæsar. That's what I used to feel, over there. You can hold only just so much antiquity. The ruin of twenty years, if it's complete in its way, can fill you as full as the ruin of a thousand."

"Yes, that's true," my wife answered, and I saw her eyes begin to light up with liking for a man who could express her feeling so well.

"But to enjoy perfectly a melancholy, a desolation, a crazy charm, a dead and dying beauty like this," he went on, "one ought to be very young, and prosperous and happy. Then it would exhale all the sweetness of its melancholy, and distil into one's cup the drop of pathos that gives pleasure its keenest thrill." His voice broke with a feeling that forbade me to censure his words for magniloquence.

It seemed to make his wife uneasy; perhaps from long, close observation of him she knew how often the spiritual throe runs into the physical pang, and feared for the effect of his mood upon him.

"Shall we go on and show them the rocks from the Point, or from one of the belvederes here?" she asked.

"I don't care," he said, wearily; and again I saw that deadliness in the look he gave her. Then he seemed to recollect himself, and added, politely, "I'm afraid of those belvederes; you can't tell what moment they're going to give way. Better go out to the Point."

"Do you think," she entreated, "you had better walk so far?"

"Well, perhaps March will stay here with me awhile, and we can follow you later. I'm all right; only a little tired."

I acquiesced, of course, and the ladies, after the usual flutter of civilities, started on. Nevil lingered to ask, "Doug, don't you think I'd better go back and leave word for the doctor where he'll find you, if he happens to come before we return to the house?"

"Oh, I've arranged all that," said Faulkner, with a kind of dryness, as it seemed, though it might have been merely a sick man's impatience; and he did not look up after Nevil as he turned away.

We stood silent a moment, after he left us, and I said, to break the constraint, "How much all this seems like those been-there-before seizures which we used to make so much of when we were young! This garden, this sky, the sea out there, the very *feel* of the air, are as familiar to me as any most intimate experience of my life, and yet I know it's all as unreal, as unsubstantial historically, as the shadow of a dream."

"How horribly," said Faulkner, as if he had not heard me, "those old flower beds look like graves! I was going to sit down on one of them, but I can't do it."

"It would have been pretty damp, anyway; wouldn't it?" I suggested.

"Perhaps. We can sit in that idiotic arbor, I suppose."

He nodded at the frail structure on the terrace below where we stood: two sides of trellis meeting in an arch, and canted over like the belvederes; a dead grape-vine hung upon it. I stepped down, and made sure of the benches which faced each other under the arch. "Yes; they're all right. Nothing could be better;" and Faulkner followed me, and took one of them. After some experiment of its strength, he leaned back in the corner of the arbor, and put his legs up along the seat.

The hoarse plunge and wash of the surf on the rocks below the garden filled the air like the texture of a denser silence; around us the crickets and grasshoppers blent their monotonies with it.

"Why do you call the shadow of a dream unsubstantial?" he demanded.

"Well, I don't know," I said. "I don't suppose I meant to say that it was more unsubstantial than other shadows."

"No. Of course." He dropped his eyelids, and went on talking with them closed: the effect was curious; perhaps he found he could keep himself calmer in that way. "I began to speak to you a little while ago of the talk we had that night at my house about old Kant's nightmares."

"Oh, yes; poor old fellow! It was awful, his being afraid to go to sleep because he was sure to have them. I don't know but that's a touch worse than not being able to go to sleep at all. Just imagine: as soon as you drop off to refreshing slumber, as you would otherwise expect, you find you've dropped as it were into hell."

"Yes; that's it," said Faulkner. "I wonder if it was the same thing over and over?"

"I don't remember what De Quincey says about that; and I don't know whether that would be worse or not. Perhaps, torment for torment, infernal monotony would be more infernal than infernal variety. But there couldn't be much choice."

Faulkner did not speak at once. Then he asked, "Did you ever have a recurrent dream?"

"A dream that repeated itself several times the same night? Yes; I've waked from a dream—or seemed to wake—and then fallen asleep and dreamed it again; and then waked and slept and dreamed it a third time. I suppose nearly every one has had that experience."

"I don't mean that kind of dream," said Faulkner. "I mean a dream that recurs regularly, once a week or so, with little or no change in its incidents."

"No, I never had that kind of dream; I don't know that I ever heard of such a dream. I remember your speaking that night about shameful dreams, that projected a sense of dishonor over half the next day. I've had that kind. They're a great nuisance. And then, if I've made free, as one's appallingly apt to do in such dreams, with persons of my acquaintance, it's extremely embarrassing to meet them." Faulkner smiled, and I asked, "Do you find that your dream habit has changed since you were younger?"

"Yes; the dreams are more vivid; but usually I don't remember them so distinctly. I suppose it's like life: we experience things with a sharper and fuller consciousness than we once did, but they leave less impression."

"Yes, yes!" I assented. "I wonder why?"

"Oh, I suppose because the fact is inscribed upon a surface that's already occupied. We're all old palimpsests by the time we reach forty. In youth we present a *tabula rasa* to experience."

"Then I should think we wouldn't receive impressions with that sharper and fuller consciousness," I suggested. "And yet I know we do."

"I don't understand it either," said Faulkner.

"There's one thing I've noticed of late years in my own dream habit, which I don't remember in the past. I go to sleep some-times—almost always in my afternoon naps—with a perfectly wide-awake knowledge that I'm doing so; and I'm able to pass the bounds with my eyes open, as it were. I can say to myself as I drowse off, 'This is a dream thought,' if I find something grotesque floating through my mind, and then, 'This is a waking thought,' when there is something logical and matter-of-fact. I come and go, that way, half a dozen times before I lose myself."

"That is very curious, very interesting," said Faulkner; and he raised his heavy eyelids for a smiling glance at me, and then let them drop. His face sobered almost to frowning sternness as he went on. "There's a whole region of experience—half the map of our life—that they tell us must always remain a wilderness, with all its extraordinary phenomena irredeemably savage and senseless. For my part, I don't believe it. I will put the wisdom of the ancients before the science of the moderns, and I will say with Elihu, 'In a dream, in a vision of the night, when deep sleep falleth upon men, in slumberings upon the bed; then He openeth the ears of men, and sealeth their instruction.'"

"It's noble poetry," I said.

"It's more than that," said Faulkner. "It's truth."

"Perhaps it was in the beginning, when men lived nearer to the origin of life, but I doubt if it's more than noble poetry now; though that of course is truth in its way."

Faulkner opened his eyes and let his legs drop to the ground. I saw that my dissent had excited him, and I was sorry; I resolved to agree with him at the first possible moment.

"Why should God be farther from men in our days than He was in Job's?" he demanded.

"It isn't that," I said. "It's men who are farther from God."

"Oh! *That's* a pretty quibble. But it gives you away, all the same. Do you mean to say that if you had a graphic and circumstantial dream, about something of importance to you—something you intended to do, a journey you intended to take, or an enterprise you were thinking of—and your dream contained a forecast or warning, do you mean to say you wouldn't be influenced by it?"

"Certainly I should," I answered; and I couldn't help adding, "or rather, the ancestral tent-dweller within me would be influenced."

"Oh!" Faulkner sneered. "God's neighbor, or the neighbor of God?"

I had made a bad business of trying to agree with him. I braced myself for another effort. "Why, Faulkner, *I* don't deny anything. All that I contend for is that we should not throw away 'the long result of time,' and return to the bondage of the superstitions that cursed the childhood of the race, that blackened every joy of its youth, and spread a veil of innocent blood between it and the skies. There may be something in dreams; if there is, our thoughts, not our fears, will find it out. I am a coward, like everybody else; perhaps rather more of a coward; but if I had a dream that contained a forecast or a warning of evil, I should feel it my duty in the interest of civilization to defy it; though I don't say I should be able to do it. On the contrary, I think very likely I should lie down under it, and shudder out some propitiatory aspiration to the offended fetich that was threatening me."

Faulkner seemed a little placated. "I understand what you mean; and I know the danger of giving way to the nervous tremors that vibrate in us from the horrible old times when, on this very coast, a wretched woman would have been caught up and flung in jail, and hung on the gallows, because some distempered child had dreamed that it saw her with the Black Man in the forest. But I'm not ready to say that a dream, recurring and recurring with the clearest circumstance, and without variation in its details, is idle and meaningless. Who is that Frenchman who wrote about the diseases of personality? Ribot! Well, he tells how people about to be attacked by disease are 'warned in a dream' of what is to happen. A man dreams of a mad dog, and wakes up with a malignant ulcer in the spot where he was bitten; dreams of an epileptic, and wakes to have his first fit; dreams of a deaf-mute, and wakes with palsied tongue. He says that these are intimations of calamity from the recesses of the organism to the nerve centres, which we don't notice in the hurly-burly of conscious life."

"Yes, I remember that passage. And I have had one such experience myself," I said.

"Very well, then," said Faulkner. "If in the physical, why not in the moral world? If you dream persistently of evil, of perfidy, of treachery, so distinctly and perfectly bodied forth that when you wake the dream seems the reality, and your consciousness the delusion, why should you treat your vision with contempt? Why should not the psychologist respect it as something quite as gravely significant in its way as those dream hints of impending malady which no pathologist would ignore?"

I now perceived that I was in the presence of what was on Faulkner's mind. I did not know what it was, and I did not expect that he would tell me. I did not wish him to tell me; I fancied that I might help him better, if I did not know just the make and manner of his trouble; and I longed to help him, for I saw that he longed for help. I felt that his logic was false, and I believed that he had entangled himself in it only after many attempts to escape it; but I did not know just which point of it to touch first. I felt him looking at me with imploring challenge, but I did not lift my head till I heard a step in the long, tangled grass, and heard the voice of Dr. Wingate in a cheerful, "Hello! hello! You here, March? Well, that's good!"

Another step, another voice would have been startling; but these were with us, in a manner, before we heard them, and they brought support and repose with them.

"I'm glad to see you, doctor," I said, without making ceremony of the greetings which I saw he was disposed to ignore.

He shook hands impartially with Faulkner and with me as if he were no more interested in one than the other; his large, honest, friendly stomach bowed out as he stood a moment wiping the sweat from his forehead, and looking round him. "*Isn't* this a nice old place? I never see this garden without a kind of satisfaction in it as one of the things that money can't buy. There are mighty few of them. But here's one that only the loss of money can buy. Heigh?"

Wingate sat down, tentatively at first, on the other end of my seat, and faced Faulkner, still without seeming to take any special interest in him.

I repeated, "I'm glad to see you, doctor; and I'm particularly glad to see you in a metaphysical mood, for Faulkner, here, has got me in a corner, and I want you to get me out."

"Ah? Am I in a metaphysical mood? What's your corner?" The doctor worked his elbow into the trellis behind him, and then swayed back on it.

"We were talking about dreams," I said, "and we had got as far as Ribot, and his instances of dreams that prophesy maladies. You know them."

"Oh, yes. Well?"

"Well, Faulkner says if a man dreams of physical evil, and the dream is prophetic, or worthy of scientific regard, why shouldn't the dream that forebodes moral evil be considered seriously too; why shouldn't it be held to be truly prophetic?"

The doctor smiled. "It seems to me you're pretty easily cornered. I should say that the dream of moral evil should certainly be seriously considered: not as prophetic in the least of what it foreboded, but as prophetic of very grave mental disturbance,— if it persisted. I should be afraid that it was the rehearsal of a mania that was soon to burst out in waking madness. If it persisted," said the doctor, looking still at me, "and he yielded to it, I should feel anxious for the dreamer's sanity."

Faulkner sat with his face twisted away from us, as if the doctor had been looking at him, and he wished to avoid his eye. "I don't see," I said, "but what that settles it, Faulkner?"

"Oh, it's a very good answer in its way," said Faulkner, still without looking at us. "But it takes no account of the spiritual element in such experiences."

"No," said the doctor; "and I should be ashamed of it if it did. As long as we have on this muddy vesture of decay, the less medicine meddles and makes with our immortal part, the better. Of course, I'm not speaking for the Christian Scientists."

"Then you don't consider the mind immortal?" demanded Faulkner.

"I don't consider the brain immortal. And I think I've seen the mind in decay."

We were all silent. I found a comfort in this robust and clear refusal of Wingate's to dally with any sort of ifs and ands, and to deal only with the facts of experience, which I felt must impart itself in some measure to Faulkner, even through his refusal. At the same time I was a little ashamed of not having myself been able to come to his rescue. The silence prolonged itself, and I began to see that the doctor wished to be alone with his patient, who perhaps was willing to part with me too.

Wingate asked, "Where's Mrs. Faulkner?" and this gave me my chance to get away with dignity.

"She and my wife are off at the Point, looking at the rocks. I'll go and tell her you've come."

"Oh, there's nothing especial. I merely wanted to ask her a few little things. You needn't hurry her back."

He left his place beside me, and went over to Faulkner, whose wrist he took between his fingers. He had dropped it, when I looked back, after I left them, and then, with the distinctness that one sense lends another, I partly heard, partly saw him say: "If you don't, it will not only drive you mad; it will kill you."

The doctor's voice came to me in the same key of strenuous, almost angry remonstrance, after I hurried into the lane from the garden, but I could not make out the words any longer.

VIII

I REACHED the cliff that overlooked the rocks, and stood a moment staring out on that image of eternity: the infinite waters, seasonless, changeless, boundless. The tide was still coming in, with that slow, resistless invasion of the land which is like the closing in of death upon the borders of life. In successive plunges, it pounded on the outer reef, and brawled foaming in over the broken granite shore, lifting and tossing the sea-weed of the bowlders, which spread and swayed before it like the hair of drowned Titans, and lunged into the hollow murmuring caverns, to suck back again, and pull down a stretch of gravelly beach, with a long snarl of the pebbles torn from their beds. A mist was coming up from the farther ocean; and the sails on the horizon were melting into it.

I saw my wife down on the rocks near the water, with Nevil; on a height nearer me stood Mrs. Faulkner, fronting seaward, a solitary figure that looked wistful on the peak that lifted and defined her against the curtain of the waters. She was quite motionless, like a statue there. She stirred, and exchanged with those below gesticulations of the gay, meaningless sort which people make one another for no reason in the presence of scenes of natural grandeur. She faced about, and at sight of me began instantly to run toward me. I waved to her not to come, and hurried down the rocks to meet her. But I could not stop her, and she was quite breathless when we reached each other.

"What—what is it?" she gasped.

"Nothing whatever!" I returned. "Doctor Wingate is with Mr. Faulkner, and I've profited by the opportunity to come off and admire your rocks. Will you tell me how my wife ever got down there alive, or expects to get back?"

"Does he want me? Did the doctor send for me?"

"Not just at present," I answered her first question. "He asked for you, but he said there was no occasion for hurry."

"Oh, then, I'll go at once," she said, quite as if I had begged her not to lose a moment.

My wife and Nevil had now caught sight of us together, and started excitedly up the rocks. I waved and beckoned to them in vain; it was a panic. I laughed to see Nevil clamber upward forgetful of my wife, and then, recollecting her, go back, and pull her after him. At one point of his progress he lost his balance, and rolled down to her feet. Mrs. Faulkner laughed hysterically with me, and then began to cry.

"He's up again—he isn't hurt!" I shouted. "Good heavens! What an unnecessary excitement! Didn't you all expect me to come? Did you suppose I could come invisibly?"

"No—no! But we expected Mr. Faulkner with you!"

"Yes, that's all right. But he preferred to remain with the doctor. I should have staid myself, if I could have imagined the trouble I was going to make."

"I will run on," she said. "You can wait for them."

"Why, there's no occasion for running." But she had already started, and was flying down the long slope that rose to the cliff, and I had no choice but to wait, and try to keep the others from following her at the same breakneck speed. I was getting angry, and my temper was not improved when my wife called out as soon as she was within ear-shot, "What is it? What is it? Has anything happened?"

"No! Nothing whatever!"

"Then what made you wave to us? You have almost killed us!"

"I waved, to stop you."

She did not regard the words. "What is Mrs. Faulkner running so, for?"

"You'd better ask her, if you ever overtake her. *I* don't know. I told her the doctor said she needn't hurry, and she started off like the wind."

"Oh my goodness! Is the *doctor* there?"

"Really, my dear—" I began; but Nevil interposed in time.

"We rather expected him to-day," he said to my wife.

"Oh, yes! Mr. Faulkner said so," she recollected. "But of course Mrs. Faulkner is so anxious about her husband that she can't bear to lose a word of what the doctor says to him."

"Well, that's something intelligible," I said, as we moved slowly after her: she was just vanishing into the wilding growth of trees that skirted the old garden. "But you can imagine my astonishment in coming up with a reassuring message, to have it act upon her like a fire-alarm. However, my calming presence seems to have had that effect upon everybody."

Nevil did not concern himself with my personal grievance. In that tumble of his he must have fallen upon some scene of extinct revelry, for he carried on his back a collection of broken egg-shells, clam-shells, bits of charred drift-wood, burnt sea-weed, and other vestiges of a former clam-bake. "Allow me!" I said, and I brushed some of them off, as he walked and talked along unheeding.

"No one can imagine," he said, "the perpetual tension of her anxiety, her incessant devotion."

"Oh, *I* can!" said my wife, with a meritorious effect of being one of the true faith as regarded Mrs. Faulkner, and of excluding me tacitly from the communion, which I found much harder to bear than Nevil's indifference.

"Oh," I said, coolly, "isn't it such as any woman would feel in her circumstances?"

My wife gave me a look that I should have deserved, perhaps, if I had blasphemed.

"No one," said Nevil, "was ever in quite such painful circumstances. If you had seen the strain she is under, as I have, for a whole year, you would understand this."

"Yes, yes. Of course. It's as painful as it can be; but it isn't more painful than the case of many another woman who has seen her husband suffering, and dying by moments under her eyes." I obeyed a perverse impulse to go on and say, though I felt my wife's eyes dwelling in horrified reproach upon me, "I don't mean to depreciate Mrs. Faulkner in any sense, or to question the exquisite poignancy of her trials and her self-sacrifice."

"But you *do!*" said my wife. "You do *both!* You are talking of something you don't know about. If you did, you couldn't— or, I hope at least you wouldn't—talk so."

Nevil said, with the humane wish to mitigate the effect of her severity, "Mrs. March has divined the peculiarly painful feature in the case. It isn't a thing we should have ventured to speak of, if we hadn't somehow seemed to approach it simultaneously."

"You mean," I said, "his aversion to her?"

"Yes!" answered Nevil, in astonishment. "Have you—have *you* noticed it, too?"

"From the first moment I saw them together. But it wasn't a

thing I could make sure of until now. I suppose I was waiting to approach it simultaneously, too."

Nevil did not heed the little jibe, and my wife noticed it only to contemn it with a look. "And how do you account for it?" he implored. "How can you explain such a terrible thing? That he should have conceived this unkindness, this repulsion for that hapless creature, whose whole existence is centred in her love of him? Ah, you haven't seen— There have been times— I suppose I am speaking to friends of his who feel exactly as I do about him?"

"Oh, yes, indeed!" cried my wife, as one in authority for both of us.

"There have been times, within the past six months, and especially during the past month, when, if I hadn't known it was the same man, I could hardly have believed it was Faulkner, in his treatment of her."

"Perhaps it wasn't Faulkner," I suggested.

"You mean that—"

"He isn't himself. You mentioned it."

"Yes. I should be glad to believe that, sometimes, dreadful as it is. It's so much less dreadful than the idea that he could change toward her in this hour of their dire need and mutual helplessness; and should leave her widowed of his love before she is widowed of his life." Nevil went on: "You couldn't at all appreciate the situation unless you had known them together from the beginning of their acquaintance, as I have. In fact, I was the means of bringing them together; at least I introduced them to each other. With him it was a case of love at first sight. He was much older than she—ten or twelve years; but I don't believe anybody had ever struck Faulkner's fancy before, in spite of all that talk about Miss Ludlow."

"Oh," I said, with a smile of reminiscence, "everybody was expected to be in love with Miss Ludlow, and to be rejected by her."

"I'm sure Faulkner was neither," said Nevil. "You know his romantic nature. He kept it hidden in his public life, but in all his personal relations he gave it full play. He's a man who has lived the poetry that another man would have written; and he's such a *great* soul that I think it rather pleased him to be that one of the two who must always love the most, in every marriage. To give more love than she gave him, I think he was glad to do that, and that he looked forward to all the future as the field for winning her to a love as perfect as the trust which she had in him. He used to talk with me about it before they were married— you know how boyishly simple-hearted he always was; of course since that, not a syllable. But his victory came sooner than he could have expected. Shortly after their marriage—in fact on their wedding journey to Europe—she fell very sick, and hovered between life and death for a long time. He made himself her nurse; he wouldn't allow any one else to come near her; he brought her back to health and the full strength of her youth. I don't know whether I ought to repeat a conjecture of Dr. Wingate's—it's merely a conjecture, and Mrs. Faulkner of course has never heard the slightest hint of it. But you know Faulkner was always a delicate fellow, with a force that was entirely nervous; and the doctor once said to me that he might have developed the tendency he was born with, by overtasking himself in care of her. The bending over, so much, was bad; the lifting, in that posture; and then, when she left her bed, he used to carry her about in his arms, up and down stairs, and everywhere."

"Ah!" sighed my wife, "how cruel life is! But how beautiful, how grand!"

"A nature," I said, without looking at her, "that might impress the casual observer as a mere sop of sentiment, is often capable of that sort of devotion. In fact I suppose that the people we call sentimentalists are merely poets who lack the artistic faculty of expression, and have to live their poetry, as you say, instead of writing it."

I spoke to Nevil, but he replied to my wife, who cried out, "Oh, I hope she'll never know it! I hope she'll die without knowing it!"

"She's a woman who could bear to know it," he said, "if any woman ever could. But if she had known it she could not possibly have lived more singly for him than she has done ever since. I don't know," he went on in a kind of muse, "whether her devotion was love in the usual way. It has always seemed to me to ignore that, to leave that out of the question; perhaps to take that for granted, as a trivial thing that need hardly be reckoned in the large account. Their not having children, that, too, has kept them, in a way, like a young couple; they have had only each other to dedicate themselves to. I don't mean that they have not had higher interests, spiritual interests. Faulkner, you know, has always been a faithful churchman, and Mrs. Faulkner, in her way—it may be your way, too—"

"We are Unitarians," said my wife, firmly.

Nevil bowed tolerantly. "Mrs. Faulkner is a very religious person. But one could not live with them, as I have done, for months at a time, and now for a whole year past, without seeing that he was first of all things with her. She was what St. Paul describes the wife to be. She took thought of the things of this world, how she might please her husband. And she did please him. Even after his physical trouble began to show itself—or to be distressing—she made him exquisitely happy, so happy that I trembled for him, knowing that change must come to every state, and since nothing could bring him more happiness, something must bring him less. And then, this—blight came."

As he spoke Nevil knit his fingers together, and rent them apart in an anguish of pity, of sympathy.

"And you can't imagine—you have no clew—no hint—" my wife began.

"No. No. No. He keeps the horror, whatever it is, wholly to himself. I think if he could tell somebody he could escape it. But he can't! The one thing evident is, that it somehow refers to *her;* and so—he *can't* speak!" We walked on in silence a moment, and then Nevil began again, falteringly, "If—if Faulkner, if he had ever shown the slightest question of her—the least anxiety—the smallest wavering, with or without reason, you might suppose it was jealousy, in some suppressed form. But there never was anything of that! He is too noble, too magnanimous for that; he honors her too devoutly. Ah-h-h!"

He went along with his head fallen, and his hands clinging together behind him. We were very near the gate of the old garden. When he reached it he turned and said to us, "I almost dread to see them together; I always dread to see them: his aversion, and her bewilderment—"

I did not accuse the man of anything wrong in his intense feeling; in my heart I pitied him as the victim of a situation which he ought never to have witnessed, which should have been known only to the two doomed necessarily to suffer in it. I wanted to say to my wife that here was another instance, and perhaps the most odious we could ever know, of the evil of that disgusting three-cornered domestic arrangement which we had both always so cordially reprobated. But I had no chance for that. In fact we found ourselves in the presence of a scene from which we should all have retired, no doubt, if we had known just how.

Dr. Wingate was standing in the arbor, looking down at Faulkner, who sat in the place where I had left him. But now his wife sat beside him, and held his hand in her left, while she had drawn his head over on her shoulder with her right. I fancied, from the weak and fallen look of his face, with its closed eyes, that he had just recovered from one of those agonies.

The stir of our feet, or rather the cessation of it as we came involuntarily to a stop in the grass, roused the group in the arbor. Dr. Wingate and Mrs. Faulkner turned their heads toward us; Faulkner opened his eyes. He remained looking a moment, as if he did not see us. Then his gaze seemed to grow and centre upon Nevil. He flung his wife's hand away, and started suddenly to his feet, and made a pace toward us.

She rose too, and "Ah, Douglas!" she cried out.

He put his hand on her breast and pushed her away with a look of fierce rejection. Then he caught at his own heart; a change, the change that shall come upon every living face, came upon his face. He fell back upon the seat, and his head sank forward.

———

Part Second

HERMIA

I

THE DEATH of Faulkner precipitated in the same compassion all the doubts and reserves of its witnesses. Perhaps one of the reasons why sickness and death are in the world is that they humanize through the sympathies the nature that health and life imbrute. They link in the chain which must one day gall every mortal, the strong and happy with the weak and sorrowing, and unite us in the consciousness of a common doom, if not the hope of a common redemption. "Some day," each of us tries to realize to himself in their presence, "I shall suffer so; some day I shall lie dumb and cold like that;" and at least we perceive that it is the mystery of our origin speaking to us in those groans, in that silence, of the mystery of our destiny. We have no refuge then but to forget ourselves in pity; and it is sorrow and shame forever if we fail of it. The pity of those who saw Faulkner die was not for him. He was swiftly past all that. In a moment, in the twinkling of an eye, he had been changed. The fire that burned so fiercely, the flame that was the sum of his passions, his hates, his loves, had been quenched in a breath; but his end had been such as each of us might desire for himself if he were at peace with himself.

A little wind, cold, keen, stirring the leaves overhead and the long grass underfoot, was coming in from the sea; the sun was growing pale before the rising fog; the roar of the ocean seemed solidly to fill the air. I do not know how long we stood still. All

43

of us knew that Faulkner was dead; no one made the ghastly
pretence that he had fallen in a faint; but none of us recognized
the fact till my wife, with a burst of tears, took his widow in her
arms. Then it was as if we had each wept, and found freedom to
move, to speak, to act, by giving way to our grief.

Mrs. March had never before had occasion in our happy life
to deal with such an event, and now her instinct of usefulness
surprised me; or rather it afterward surprised me, when I
thought of it. From moment to moment she knew what to do,
and she knew what to make me do. The doctor, whose office was
with life, went away; and the priest, whose calling concerned
after-life, was so stunned by what had happened, that he remained helpless in the presence of death. If it had not been for
my wife and myself, I hardly know who would have grappled
with all those details which present themselves in such a situation
with the same imperative claim upon us as eating, drinking and
sleeping, and the other commonplace needs of existence. I was
struck by their equality with these; in their order, they came like
anything else.

Just before dark my wife sent me back to our children at
Lynn. "Poor little things! They will be frightened to death at
our staying so long; and you must explain to them as well as you
can why I didn't come with you. Mrs. Wakely will get them to
bed for you; and be sure that you see they have a light burning
in the hall, if they're nervous without it. You won't be needed
here. Of course I can't leave her now. You must do the best you
can without me."

"Yes, yes," I said. "But how strange, Isabel, that we should
be mixed up with these unhappy people in this way! Do you
remember the critical mood in which we came here to-day?"

"Yes; perhaps we've always been too critical, and held ourselves too much aloof—tried to escape ties."

"Death won't let us escape them, even if life will," I answered,
and for the first time I had a perception of the necessary solidarity of human affairs from the beginning to the end, in which no
one can do or be anything to himself alone. "It makes very little

difference now what that poor man's taste in literature and art was. It seems a great while ago since we smiled at him for it. Was it only this morning?"

"This morning? It seems a thousand years—in some pre-existence."

"Why, it *was* in a pre-existence for *him !*"

"Yes; how strange that is!"

II

I DID NOT SEE Wingate again till I met him at our first dinner in the fall. Then, as we sat at our corner together, with our comfortable little cups of black coffee before us, at a sufficient distance from the others, who had broken up the order of the table, and grouped themselves in twos and threes for the good talk that comes last at such a time, we began to speak of the Faulkners. They had probably been in both our minds, vaguely and vividly, the whole evening. He asked me if I had heard anything from Mrs. Faulkner lately; and I said, Oh, yes; my wife heard from her pretty often, though irregularly; and I told him how, with every intention and prepossession to the contrary, my wife had grown into what I might call an intimate friendship with her. The widow had gone back to the city where Faulkner and I had lived together, and had taken up her life again in the old place, with the old surroundings and the old associations.

"Then you were not especially intimate with him when you lived there?"

"No," I said; "it was a friendly acquaintance for a while, and then it was an unfriendly non-acquaintance;" and I explained how. "To tell you the truth, I never cared a great deal for him; and I was surprised to find that he seemed to care a good deal for me; though perhaps what seemed affection for me was only the appeal for sympathy that a dying man addresses to the whole earth."

"Perhaps," said the doctor.

"I hope I don't appear very cold-hearted. I liked his friend the parson a great deal better, and for no more reason than I liked Faulkner less. Faulkner was a sentimental idealist; he tried to live the rather high-strung literature that he might have written, if his lot had been cast in a literary community. You understand?"

"Yes."

"I have known several such men in the West; they're rather characteristic of a new country."

"Yes; I can understand how. I didn't know but you had been intimate," said Wingate, in a half tone of disappointment.

I recognized it with a laugh. "Well, Faulkner was intimate, doctor, if I wasn't. Will that serve the purpose?"

"I'm not sure." The doctor broke off the ash of his cigar on the edge of his saucer. "I should like to ask one thing!" he said.

"Ask away!"

He hitched his chair nearer me, setting it sidewise of the table, on which he rested his left arm, and then dropped his face on his lifted hand. "That day, just before I came, had he been telling you his dream?"

"No."

The doctor now used a whole tone of disappointment. "Well, I'm sorry. I should have liked to talk it over with you."

"You can't be half so sorry as I am. I should like immensely to talk it over. I always had a fancy that his dream killed him."

"Oh, no! oh, no!" said the doctor, with a smile at my unscientific leap to the conclusion.

"Hastened it, then."

"We can't say, very decidedly, whether a death is hastened or not—that kind. The man was destined to die soon, and to die what is called suddenly. He might have died at that very moment and in that precise way if he had never had any such dream. Undoubtedly it wore upon him. But I should say it was an effect rather than a cause of his condition. There's where you outsiders are apt to make your mistakes in these recondite cases. You want something dramatic—like what you've read of—and you're fond of supposing that a man's trouble of mind caused his disease, when it was his disease caused his trouble of mind: the physical affected the moral, and not the moral the physical."

"You mean that his mind was clouded?"

The doctor laughed. "No, I didn't mean that. But it's true, all the same. His mind was clouded, by the pain he had suffered, perhaps, and his dream came out of the cloud in his mind. If he had lived, it would have resulted in mania, as I told him substantially that day. But it was very curious, its recurrence and its unvarying circumstantiality. I don't know that I ever knew anything *just* like it; though there's a kind of similarity in all these cases."

I saw that Wingate would like to tell me what Faulkner's dream was; but I knew that he would not do so unless he could fully justify the confidence to his professional conscience. I said to myself that I should not tempt him, but I tried to tempt him. "He told you how long he had been having his dream?"

The doctor appeared not to have heard my question. "And you say she has gone back to their old place?"

"Yes, and to every circumstance of their life as nearly as possible." I did not like his running away with my bait in that fashion very well, but I thought it best to give him all the line he wanted, and then play him back as I could. "You know—but of course you don't know—that his mother always lived with them when they were at home—or they lived with her: it was the old lady's house, I believe: and the widow has even repeated that feature of their former ménage, and has her mother-in-law with her."

"And what's become of the parson?"

"The parson? Oh—Nevil! Nevil's given up his parish there, and gone further west—to Kansas, where he has charge of a sort of mission church—I don't understand the mechanism of those things very well—and is doing some good work. I believe he has ritualized somewhat. That seems to be the way with them when they take to practical Christianity. Curious; but it's so."

"And she lives with her mother-in-law," the doctor mused aloud. "Property tied up so she had to?"

"No. I think not. It seems to be quite her own choice. I dare say they get on very well. The old lady is romantic, I believe, like Faulkner; and probably she's in love with her daughter-in-law."

"Well," said the doctor, "it isn't a situation that every woman could reconcile herself to, under the best conditions. But if she thought she ought to do it, she would do it. She has pluck enough. I should like to tell you one thing," and the doctor hitched his chair a little closer as he said this, and again he broke the ash of his cigar off on his saucer.

He did not go on at once, and lest it might be for want of prompting I said, "Well?"

"I don't know whether this is something your wife ever knew about or not?" he began, askingly.

"Really, I can't say," I answered, impatiently, "till I know myself."

He did not mind my impatience, but pulled comfortably at his cigar for a moment before he went on. "She came to my office with her."

"When they went to see you just before she started West? I understood she called on business."

"To pay my bill? Yes; and then she asked to see me alone. I suppose your wife thought she wished to consult me; and so did I. But it wasn't the usual kind of consultation; in fact she wasn't the usual kind of woman! She didn't lose an instant; she went right at me. 'Doctor,' said she, 'do you know what was on my husband's mind?' I like to deal with any one I can be honest with, and I saw I could be honest with her. 'Yes,' I said; 'he told me.' She caught her breath a little, and then said she, 'Can you tell me the form, the kind, of trouble it was?' 'Yes,' I said; 'it was a dream. A dream that kept coming, again and again, and finally had begun to color his waking thoughts and impressions.' She gave another gasp—I can see her now, just how she looked with the black crape round her face, all pale and washed out with weeping—and then she asked, 'Did it relate to—me?' 'Yes,' I said, 'it related to you, Mrs. Faulkner.' She came right back at me. 'Doctor Wingate,' said she, 'is it something that he could

ever have told me, if he had lived?' I had to think awhile before
I said, 'No, as I understood his character, I don't think he ever
could.' She came right back again—I could see that she had
made up her mind to go through it all in a certain way, and that
she was ready for anything—and said she, 'I know that whatever it was, he was always struggling against it; and that when
it forced itself upon him, he did not believe it at the bottom of
his heart. I have seen that; and now I will ask you only one thing
more. Is it something that for his sake—not for mine, remember!
—you wouldn't wish me to know?' 'I would rather you wouldn't
know it, for his sake,' said I. 'Then,' said she, 'that is all;' and
she got up, and put out her hand to me, and gave mine a grip as
strong as a man's, and went out."

"Splendid!" I said, overmastering my own disappointment,
and wishing that in my interest Mrs. Faulkner had been a little
less heroic.

"Splendid?" said Wingate. "It was superhuman! Or superwoman. Just think of the burden she shouldered for life! I don't
know how much or how little she had divined, but all the worse
if she had divined anything. She denied herself the satisfaction
of her curiosity, and left me to make whatever I chose of her
motives. She didn't explain; she simply asked and acted. I might
suspect this, or I might suppose that; she left me free. I never
saw such nerve. It was superb."

"Perhaps a little topping," I suggested.

"Yes, perhaps a little topping," the doctor consented. "But
still, it was a toppingness that could have consisted only with the
most perfect conscience, the most absolute freedom from self-
reproach in every particular."

"C'était magnifique, mais ce n'était pas la guerre. I think I
should have preferred a little more human nature in mine. I
should have liked her better if she had gone down on her knees
to you, and begged you to tell her what it was; and when you
had told her, if it inculpated her at all, would never have left
you till you had exculpated her. That would have been more
like a woman."

"Yes, much more like most women," said the doctor. "But the type is not the nation, or the race, or the sex. The type is cheap, dirt cheap. It's the variation from the type that is the character, the individual, the valuable and venerable personality."

"Since when did you set up hero-worship, doctor? Really, you're worse than my wife. But I expect her to be worse than you when I tell her this story of Mrs. Faulkner. You will let me tell her?"

"Oh, yes. I suppose you would tell her whether I let you or not."

"There's always a danger of that kind," I admitted.

"I wonder," said Wingate, "whether the eagerness of women to hear things isn't a natural result from the eagerness of men to tell them?"

"Possibly they may have spoiled us in that way. Do you think you were as eager not to tell, as Mrs. Faulkner was not to hear?"

The doctor laughed tolerantly.

III

I WAS SURPRISED at the way my wife took the doctor's story when I repeated it to her the next morning at breakfast.

"Well," she said, "that is the first thing I've ever heard of Mrs. Faulkner that I don't like."

"It was certainly a base treason to her sex to go back on its reputation for curiosity in that manner."

"Oh, it was enough like a woman to do that—a certain kind of woman."

"The *poseuse ?*"

"The worse than *poseuse*. The kind of woman that overtasks her strength, and breaks down with what she's undertaken, and makes us all ridiculous, and discourages us from trying to bear what we really could bear."

"Doctor Wingate admires her immensely for her courage in trying it."

"And I suppose you admire her too."

"No. When it comes to that, I'm all woman—the kind of woman that wouldn't attempt more than she could perform, unless she could get some man to carry out her enterprise for her. But perhaps she might do that."

"What do you mean?"

"I don't mean *what*, at all. I mean *whom*. Nevil."

"Basil," said my wife, "when you talk that way you make me lose all respect for you. No. She may be too exalted, but at least she isn't degraded."

"She couldn't very well be both," I admitted.

"And it shows what a really low idea you have of women, my dear. I'm sorry for you."

"Bless my soul! Why do you object to her being superwoman, as Wingate says, in one way, and not superwoman in another?"

"We both agreed, from the very beginning, that that ridiculous friendship was entirely between him and Faulkner. I think it was as silly as it could be, and weak, and sentimental in all of them. She ought to have put a stop to it; but with him so sick as he was, of course she had to yield, and then be subjected to— to anything that people were mean enough to think."

"Why not say base enough, vile enough, grovelling enough, crawling-in-the-mire enough?"

"Very well, then, I *will* say that. And I will say that any one who will insinuate such a thing is as bad—as bad as Faulkner himself."

"But not so much to blame, I hope. At least I didn't bring Nevil into his family."

"You admired him!"

"Yes, if I may say it without further offence, I liked him. I pitied him; it seemed to me that he was the chief victim of Faulkner's fondness. He couldn't get away without inhumanity; but I believe he was thoroughly bored by the situation. He felt it to be ridiculous."

"And she, what did she think of it?"

"I don't believe she thought of it at all. She was preoccupied with her husband. He had to stay and simply look on, and see her suffer, because he couldn't get away. It was an odious predicament."

"Yes. I think it was too," said my wife. "And I felt sorry for him, though I didn't admire him. And I must say that he escaped from his false position as quickly and as completely as possible."

"Ah, I don't know that I've altogether liked his leaving the town. That looked, if anything, a little conscious. I should have preferred his staying and living it all down."

"There was nothing to live down!"

"No; nothing."

"You are talking so detestably," said my wife, "that I've got a great mind not to tell you something."

I folded my hands in supplication. "Oh, I will behave! I will behave! Don't keep anything more from me, my dear. Think what I've endured already from the fortitude of Mrs. Faulkner!"

"The letter came last night, by the last distribution, after you'd gone to your dinner," said Mrs. March, feeling in her pocket for it, which was always a work of time: a woman has to rediscover her pocket whenever she uses it. "He's engaged."

"Who?"

"Who? Mr. Nevil. Now, what do you have to say?"

I threw myself forward in astonishment. "What! Already! Why it isn't six months since—"

"Basil!" cried my wife, in a voice of such terrible warning that I was silent. I had to humble myself very elaborately, after that. Even then it was with great hauteur and distance that she said, "He's engaged to a young lady of his parish out there. The letter's from Mrs. Faulkner." She tossed it across the table to me with a disdain for my low condition that would have wounded a less fallen spirit. But I was glad of the letter on any terms, and I eagerly pulled it open and flattened it out.

"Just read it aloud, please," commanded my wife, from her remote height, and I meekly obeyed.

" 'DEAR MRS. MARCH,—You will be surprised to get a letter from me so soon after the last I wrote; but I have a piece of news which has excited us all here a good deal, and which I think will interest you and Mr. March. Mr. Nevil has just written my mother, Mrs. Faulkner, of his engagement.'

"What an astonishing woman!" I broke off. "Why in the world didn't she keep it for the postscript, after she had palavered over forty or fifty pages about nothing?"

"Because," said my wife, "she isn't an ordinary woman in any way. Go on."

I went on.

" 'His letter is rather incoherent, of course. But he tells us she is very young, and he encloses a photograph to show us that she is pretty. She is more than that, however; she is a beautiful girl; but the photograph does not paint character, and so we have to take Mr. Nevil's word for the fact that she is very good, and cultivated and affectionate.'

"Affectionate, of course!" I broke off again; and my wife came down from her high horse long enough to laugh; and then instantly got back again.

" 'He seems very much in love, and we feel as happy as we can about him without knowing his *fiancée*. He has been so long like a son to Mrs. Faulkner, that of course it is a little pang to her, but she reconciles herself to losing him by thinking of his good. I am thoroughly glad, for I think his life was very lonely, and that he longed for companionship. He is of a very simple nature—you cannot always see it under the ecclesiasticism— and I think he has missed Douglas almost as much as we have. He hints in his letter that if Douglas were living, and the old place here could welcome him as of old, he could wish for no other home.'

"Look here, Isabel!" I broke off again. "These seem to me rather wild and whirling words. If Mrs. Faulkner *mère* is so very happy, why does she have a little pang and have to brace up by thinking of his good? And if Mr. Nevil is so very ecstatic about his betrothed, why does he intimate that if the old home of his friends could still be his, he would not want a new home of his own?"

"That is very weak in him," my wife admitted.

"Yes; let's hope the future Mrs. Nevil may never get hold of that letter of his. She probably hates the very name of Faulkner already."

"If you will go on," said my wife, "you will see what Hermia says of all that."

"Hannah," I corrected her; but I went on.

" 'I suppose,' " the letter ran, " 'that this is the last of Mr. Nevil, as far as we are concerned. I could not adopt his old friends, if I were in her place, and I am persuading Mrs. Faulkner to disappear out of his life as promptly and as voluntarily as possible, after his marriage. I know that this is one of the things that men laugh at us for; but I cannot help it, and I grieve to think now that I could not help showing poor Douglas that his friends were less welcome to me than they were to him. Mrs. Faulkner sees the matter as I do; but she will have to play the part of mother-in-law at least so far as the infare is concerned. Mr. Nevil has no relations of his own (he is the most bereft and orphaned person I ever knew), and she has asked him to bring his bride here as he would to his mother's house. Of course it will all be very quiet; but we must go through some social form of welcome. The marriage is to be very soon—in a month. I will write you about it.' "

I folded up the letter and gave it back to Mrs. March.

"Now, what have you got to say?" she demanded.

"I? Oh! May I ask why you didn't tell me about this letter in the beginning, instead of allowing me to go on with my defamatory conjectures?"

"I wanted to see you cover yourself with confusion; I wished to give you a lesson."

"Pshaw, Isabel! You know that you were so curious about what Wingate told me that it put the letter all out of your head."

"And do you say now," she retorted, quite as if she had got the better of me, and were making one triumph follow upon another, "do you still mean to say that she expected to get him to help her bear the—the shadow of Faulkner's dream?"

"Isn't that rather attenuating it?" I asked. But upon reflection I found that the phrase accurately expressed the case. "Why yes, that's just what it is. It's the burden of a shadow! In spite of Wingate's scientific reluctances, I believe that it crushed poor Faulkner; and I'm glad the weight of it isn't to fall upon her or upon Nevil. Weight! Why, Isabel, that letter has simply removed mountains from my mind! And the affair was really none of my business, either."

"Yes, I'm glad it's all over," said my wife, with a sigh of relief. "Now I *can* respect her without the slightest reservation."

"And isn't it strange," I suggested, "that this kind of burden she can bear alone, but if she had divided it with him she could not bear it?"

"Yes, it's strange," she answered. "And, as you say, this letter is a great relief. Dr. Wingate may account for it all on scientific grounds if he chooses, and say that Faulkner's disease caused the dream, and not the dream his disease. But if this had not happened, if this engagement did not give the lie so distinctly to the worst that we ever thought when we thought our worst about it, I never could have felt exactly easy. There would always have been, don't you know, the misgiving that there was a consciousness of something drawing them together during his life that frightened them apart after his death. But now I feel *perfectly* sure!"

There had never been any doubt with us as to the nature of Faulkner's dream, though we could only conjecture its form and facts. Sometimes these appeared to us very gross and palpable, and again merely a vaguely accusing horror, a ghastly adumbration, a mere sensation, a swiftly vanishing impression. We had talked it over a great deal at first, and then it had faded more and more out of our minds. We had our own cares, our own concerns, which were naturally first with us; and I feel that in giving the idea of our preoccupation with those of others, however interesting, however fascinating, I am contributing to one of those false effects of perspective which have always annoyed me in history. The events of the past are pressed together in that retrospect, as if the past were entirely composed of events, and not, like the present, of long intermediate stretches and spaces of eventlessness, which the rapidly approaching lines and the vanishing point can give no hint of. In spite of everything, since the story only secondarily concerns ourselves, we must appear concerned in it alone, though for that very reason we ought to be able to seem what we really were: spectators giving it a sympathetic and appreciative glance now and then, while we kept about our own business.

IV

For a while we expected with vivid interest Mrs. Faulkner's account of the infare, and her description of the bride, and of the bridegroom in his new relations. Then we ceased to talk of it, and I, at least, forgot all about it. The time for her letter had passed when it came, and then we reckoned up the weeks since the last one came, and found that this was almost a month overdue. When we had ascertained this fact, my wife opened the letter, and began to snatch a phrase from this page and another from that, turning to the last and returning to the first, in that provoking way women have with a letter, instead of reading it solidly through from beginning to end. As she did this I saw her eyes dilate, and she grew more and more excited.

"Well, well?" I called out to her, when this spectacle became intolerable.

"Oh, my *dear*, my dear!" she answered, and went on snatching significant fragments from the letter.

"What is it? Doesn't the bride suit? Was Nevil too silly about her? Were the dresses from Worth's? Or what's the matter?"

"The engagement—the engagement is *off!* Nevil is perfectly killed by it; and he's back on their hands, down sick, and they're taking care of him. Oh, horrors *upon* horrors! I never heard of anything so dreadful! And the details—well, the whole thing is simply inexpressible!"

"Suppose you give Mrs. Faulkner a chance at the inexpressible. I'd rather hear of the calamity at first hands and in a mass, than have it doled out to me piecemeal by a third person, and snatched back at every mouthful." I put out my hand for the letter, and after a certain hesitation my wife gave it me.

"Well, see what *you* can make of it."

"I shall make nothing of it; I shall leave that to the facts."

These appeared to be that the engagement had gone on like other engagements up to a certain point. The preparations were made; the dresses were bought; the presents were provided, presumably with the usual fatuity and reluctance; the cards were out; the day was fixed. All this had gone forward with no hint of misgiving from the young lady. She seemed excited, Nevil could remember; but to seem excited in such circumstances was to seem natural. Suddenly, a week before the day fixed for the wedding, she discovered that she had made a mistake: she could never have truly loved him, and now she was sure that she did not love him at all. She was not fit to be a clergyman's wife; she never could make him happy. He must release her; that was the substance of it; but there were decorative prayers to be forgiven and forgotten and accepted in the relation of a friend. She was the only daughter of rich and vulgar parents, and her father added a secret anguish to Nevil's open shame by offering to make it right with him in any sum he would name; the millionaire wished to act handsomely. Nevil could perhaps have borne both the secret anguish and the open shame; but the Sunday edition of the leading newspaper of the place found the affair a legitimate field of journalistic enterprise. It gave column after column of imagined and half-imagined detail; it gave biographical sketches of what it called the high retracting parties; it gave Nevil's portrait, the young lady's portrait, the portraits of the young lady's parents. It was immensely successful, and it drove Nevil out of town. He came back crushed and broken to his old home, and sought refuge with his old friends from the disgrace of his wrong. He would not see any one but the doctor, outside of their house; he was completely prostrated. The worst of it was that he seemed really to have been in love with the girl, whom he believed to have been persuaded by her parents to break off the match; though he could not understand why they should have allowed her to go so far. Mrs. Faulkner had her own opinions on this point, which she expressed in her letter, and they were to the effect that the girl was weak and fickle, but that she was right in thinking she never had loved him, however wrong she had been in once thinking differently. This could not be suggested for Nevil's comfort, and they were obliged tacitly to accept his theory of the matter; he could not bear to think slightingly of her. In fact, it had been a perfect infatuation, and it had been all the more complete because Nevil, though past thirty-five, had never been in love before, and gave himself to his passion with the ardor of an untouched heart, and the strength of a manhood matured in the loftiest worship, and the most childlike ignorance of women, and especially girls. This was what Mrs. Faulkner gathered at second-hand from his talk with her mother-in-law; and she found herself embarrassed in deciding just how to treat the bruised and broken man, so strangely cast upon their compassion. He wanted to talk with her about his misery, but it seemed to her that she ought not to let him; and yet she could not well avoid it, when he turned to her with such a confident expectation of her sympathy. It was very awkward having him in the house; but they could not turn him out of doors; and he clung to Douglas's mother with all the trusting helplessness of a sick son. It was pathetic to see a man who had once been to her the very embodiment of strong common-sense and spiritual manliness, so weak and helpless. The doctor said he must get away as soon as he could; and he had better go to Europe and travel about. But Nevil was poor; they could send him, of course, and would be glad to do so; but he was sensitive about money, and had none of that innocent clerical willingness to take it.

The letter closed rather abruptly with civil remembrances to me.

"Isn't it cruel, dear?" my wife said, pleadingly, as if to forestall any ironical view I might be inclined to take of the case.

"Yes, it is cruel," I answered, quite in earnest, and we went on to talk it over in all the lights. We said, what a strange thing it was, in the distribution of sorrow and trouble, that this one should receive blow after blow, all through life, and that one go untouched from the beginning to the end. Any man would have thought that Mrs. Faulkner had certainly had her share of suffering in her husband's sickness and death, without having this calamity of his friend laid upon her; for in the mystery of our human solidarity it was clear that she must help him support it. But apparently God did not think so; or was existence all a miserable chance, a series of stupid, blundering accidents? We could not believe that, for our very souls' sake; and for our own sanity we must not. We who were nowhere when the foundations of the earth were laid, and knew not who had laid the measures of it, or stretched the line upon it, could only feel that our little corner of cognition afforded no perspective of the infinite plan; and we left those others to their place in it, not without commiseration, but certainly without trying to account for what had happened to them, or with any hope of ever offering a justification of it.

V

THE SITUATION, which seemed to our despondent philosophy tragically permanent, was of course only a transitory phase; and we quickly had news of a change. Nevil had grown better; he had been invited to resume his former charge, with a year's leave of absence for travel and the complete recovery of his health. The sort of indignant tenderness with which all his old friends had taken up his cause against his cruel fate had gone far to console and restore him. Mrs. Faulkner spoke of his joy in their affection as something very beautiful, and she dwelt upon the pleasure it gave them to see the old Nevil coming back day by day, in the old unselfish manliness. He had been troubled, in his depression, by the consciousness that it was ignoble to give way to it, and his courage was rising with his strength to resist. But still it was thought best for him to go abroad and complete his recovery by an entire change; and he was going very soon. He had accepted the means from his people as an advance of salary for services which he expected to render, and so the obstacle of his poverty and pride was got over.

I cannot say that it pleased us greatly to learn that Nevil thought of sailing from Boston, and hoped to see us; but we had our curiosity to satisfy, as well as our intangible obligation of hospitality to fulfil, and my wife wrote asking him to our house for such time as he should have between arriving and departing. He was delayed in one way or other so that he came in the morning, and sailed at noon; she did not meet him at all, but I went over to the ship in East Boston, and saw him off, and then gave her such report of him as I could. I am afraid it was rather vague. I said he seemed shy, as if he were embarrassed by his knowledge that I knew his story; he seemed a little cold; he seemed a little more clerical. I suppose I had really expected him to speak with intense feeling of the Faulkners, and that it disappointed me when he only mentioned them in giving me the messages they had sent. I do not know why I should have felt repelled, almost hurt by his manner; but I dare say it was because I had met him so full of a sympathy which I could not express and which he could not recognize. I was aware afterward of having derived my mood rather from Mrs. Faulkner's representations of him than from my own recollections. Perhaps I had a romantic wish to behold a man whom the waters had passed over, and who gave evidence of what he had undergone. But Nevil appeared as he had always appeared to me: pure, gentle, serene; not broken, not bruised, and by no means prepared for the compassion which I was prepared to lavish upon him. I did not reflect that the intimacy had proceeded much more rapidly on my part than on his.

He was in company with a wealthy parishioner, and he presented me as a fellow-Westerner. His friend ordered some champagne in celebration of this fact and of the parting hour, and we had it in their large state-room, the captain's room, which the parishioner was very proud of having secured. He filled Nevil's glass slowly, so that he should lose nothing in mere effervescence, and said, "Doctor's orders, you know." He explained to me that for his own part he did not care about Europe; he had seen too much of it; but he was going along to watch out that Nevil took care of himself.

My wife was even less satisfied with this interview at second-hand than I was at first-hand. She insisted that I should search my conscience and say whether I had not met Nevil with too great effusion, which he might justly resent as patronizing. I brought myself in not guilty of this crime, and then she said she had always thought he was tepid and limited, and she was disposed to console herself by finding in my rebuff, as she called it, a just punishment for my having liked Nevil so much. "You can see by that champagne business," she said, "that, after all, he's just as much a Westerner at heart as Faulkner. I doubt if he was so much hurt by that newspaper notoriety of his broken engagement as he pretended to be."

I admitted that he was a fraud in every respect, and that he had been guilty of something very like larceny in depriving her of a hero. "But," I said, "you have your heroine left."

"Yes, thank goodness! *She's* a *woman!*"

"A heroine usually is—unless she's an angel."

Nevil was gone a year, and during this time the correspondence between Mrs. Faulkner and Mrs. March, fevered to an abnormal activity by recent events, fell back into the state of correspondence in health, which tends to an exchange of apologies for not having written. Mrs. Faulkner's letters contained some report of Nevil's movements; and we had got so used to his being abroad that it seemed very sudden, when one came saying that he had got home, perfectly well, and had gone at once to work in his parish, with all his old energy. She sent some newspapers with marked notices of him; and then it seemed to me that we heard nothing more from her till the next spring, when a most joyful letter burst upon us, as it were, with the announcement of her engagement to Nevil.

I cannot say exactly what it was about this fact that shocked us both. The affair, superficially, was in every way right and proper. We were sure that, as Hermia reported, Faulkner's mother was as happy in it as herself, and that it was the just and lawful recompense of suffering that Hermia and Nevil had jointly and severally undergone for no wrong or fault of theirs; we ought to have been glad for them; and yet, somehow, we could not; somehow we were not reconciled to that comfortable close for the most painful passage of life we had ever witnessed. Instead of being the end of trouble, it seemed like the beginning. It brought up again with dreadful vividness all the experiences of that day when Faulkner died. It was as if he rose from the dead, and walked the earth again in the agony of body we had seen, and the anguish of mind we had imagined. Once more I saw him, with a face full of hate, push her from him, and fall back and gasp and die.

Hermia's letter came in the morning; and during the forenoon I received a telegram at my office from her asking if Dr. Wingate were in Boston. I sent out and found that the doctor was at home, and answered accordingly. Then I sent the telegram to my wife, and I hurried away from the office rather early in the afternoon, to learn what she made of it.

She had just got a telegram herself from Mrs. Faulkner, saying that she should start for Boston by the eleven o'clock train that night, and asking if she might come to our house.

VI

THE GENERAL CHANGE in Hermia, no less than a phase of her character which had never before shown itself to us, struck me at the station where I went to meet her on the arrival of her train; and when I brought her home, I saw that she affected my wife in the same way. Personally we had known her only as the submissive and patient subject of an invalid's sick will, anxious to devote herself to the gratification of his whims. We remembered her as all gentleness, abeyance, self-effacement, and then as a despair so quiet that the wildest grief would have been less pathetic to witness. From Wingate's report of her interview with him we had inferred a strength which was rather hysterical; and though her letters of the last two years had given us the impression of a clear and just mind, able to decide impartially from uncommon insight, we had still kept our old idea of her, and thought only of the self-abnegation we had seen, and the somewhat abnormal self-assertion of which we had heard.

She now appeared younger than before, which I suppose was an effect of her having really grown thinner; and with her return to her youthful figure she had acquired an elastic vigor which we did not perceive at once to be moral rather than physical. It was when we fairly saw her face in the light of the half-hour which we had with her before dinner, that we knew this was the spirit's school of the body; and that underneath her power over herself was a weakness that had to be constantly watched and disciplined. She was like an athlete who knows the point in which lies the danger of his failure, and who guards and fortifies it. I am aware that this gives a false and theatrical complexion to the simple truth that touched and fascinated us; but I do not know how otherwise to express it; and I am not able to describe as I would like the appearance of a great happiness suddenly arrested and held in check, which we both believed we saw in her. It was this, I fancy, that kept us silent with those congratulations upon her engagement which we should both have felt it fit to offer. To tell the whole truth, we were a little quelled and overawed by the resolute strength of which she gave the effect, and we left it for her, if she would, to enlarge the circle of our talk from the commonplaces of her journey East, and her ability to sleep on the cars, and of her health, and Mrs. Faulkner's health, and ours; and include an emotional region where Nevil should at least be named. But she did not mention him, and she only departed from these safe generalities in asking if we could probably see Dr. Wingate that evening.

I said that he had no office hours in the evening, but I knew he was to be found at home between half past seven and nine, and we might chance it.

"I must see him to-night," she answered, quietly, "and I wish you and Mrs. March would come with me. It's a matter that I may want you to know about. I may need—need"—she faltered a breath—"your help."

"Why, of course," said my wife; and then I had one of my inspirations, as she called them.

I said, "Why not send a messenger round for Dr. Wingate to come here? It will catch him at dinner, and then we can make sure of him," and I modestly evaded the merit I might have acquired through this suggestion, by going off to ring for a messenger, who arrived, of course, just when we had forgotten him, and made my wife believe it was the doctor.

We had a moment together before dinner for the exchange of impressions and conjectures, and I made my little objections to the hardship of being involved again in Mrs. Faulkner's affairs. "What do you suppose she meant by needing our help? Really I think I must be excused from being present at her consultation of Dr. Wingate! If she's going to break down on our hands—"

My wife saw the parody of her customary anxieties in the presence of any aspect of the unexpected. "Nonsense! It's nothing of that kind, poor thing! If it only were! But it's something that's on her mind—that Dr. Wingate knows about and she doesn't. And now the time's come when she must."

"Do you mean—the dream?"

"Yes. Or something connected with it. I saw it in an instant. Well, she's got her punishment!"

"Her punishment? What in the world is she punished for?"

"For trying to bear more than she could. For trying not to know what she must know before she could really ever take another step in life. I suppose at that time she expected to die. But she lived."

"Ah, that's a mistake we often make!"

"Yes, she could have borne it if nothing else had happened after that."

"But something else happened."

"And now she has to provide for this world instead of the next."

"Poor mortality!" I sighed. "Between the two worlds, how its difficulties are multiplied!"

VII

DR. WINGATE arrived with his professional face, in which I fancied a queer interrogation of mine. Then I said, "It's Mrs. Faulkner who wishes to see you. You remember? She's here with us."

But he only asked, "How long has she been in town?" and he gave a poke or two at his hair after taking his hat off in the hall, where I went out to meet him when I heard his ring.

"Since four o'clock."

"Oh!"

"She was anxious to see you at once, and I made bold to send for you, instead of taking the chance of not finding you in."

"Oh, that's all right," he said, and he rubbed his hands with an air of impatience which decided me not to tell him, as I had imagined myself doing, of her engagement to Nevil by way of preparation. I saw that it was not my affair; and I decided not to put my fingers between the bark and the tree.

He preceded me into the library, where Mrs. Faulkner sat waiting with my wife, and I saw him make a special effort to temper his bluff directness with a kindly deference. It was she who was brusque, and who put aside the preliminaries which he would have interposed.

"Doctor Wingate, I have come to Boston to see you in the hope that you can help me. But now I almost think that no one can help me. You can't change the truth!"

"Rather an undertaking, Mrs. Faulkner, I admit," he said with a smile for her exaltation. "But it depends somewhat upon the nature of the truth. I have known cases in which I could change the truth *back*. They're not so very uncommon." He looked at her with smiling insinuation, and she smiled pathetically in response.

"This isn't one of that kind," she said, and she had to make the effort of beginning afresh. "Do you remember when I came to you just—just after my husband's death, and spoke to you about the dream that killed him?"

"The dream didn't kill him," said Wingate. "But I remember the interview you refer to." He looked round at my wife and me, and then at Hermia, as if to question whether it was really her intention that we should be present, and we both made an instinctive motion to rise.

"Don't go," she said. "I wish you to stay. I was afraid, then, to face it alone, and now I wish to know what it was. Oh, yes! I made a feint of refusing to know it for his sake. I believed that I was sincere, but I was a miserable hypocrite. I was sparing myself, not him. Now, all that must come to an end. I ask you to tell me what his dream was, and to tell it in the presence of those who saw him suffer from it, *die* of it." Wingate opened his mouth to protest again, but she hurried on. "You said then that his dream concerned me, and I want them to judge me by it, and I will judge myself by their judgment."

"Really, Mrs. Faulkner," said Wingate, with the laugh of a man whose perplexity passes any other expression, "you are almost as bad as *he* was! Where shall I begin? How much can you bear? The whole thing's very painful! Why must you know it now, when you've held out against it so bravely, so wisely, for two years?"

"Because," she answered, as if she had prepared herself for some such question, "I was going to take a great step, and I wished to look at every thought and fact of my life, to be sure that I was worthy to take such a step. I got to thinking of that dream, which you said concerned me; and I found that I could have no peace, no certainty of the kind I wanted till I knew what it was. I must have been—there must have been something in me—terribly wrong, terribly bad, to have inspired such a dream, and—"

"Ah-h-h!" the doctor broke out, "you're as wild as he was in that reasoning," and to both of us men her logic was pitiably childlike; but I could see that for my wife it had a force inappreciable to us, because she was a woman too; no doubt she would judge Hermia as severely as she judged herself. "What you say," the doctor went on, "is perfectly monstrous, and I should not feel justified in telling you anything about it, unless I could bring you to see the matter in a reasonable light. And in the first place, I want you to realize that whatever you were, or whatever you were not, it had absolutely no more to do with his dream, than the character of an inhabitant of Saturn, if there is one. Why, just consider! You wish to judge yourself, and if possible condemn yourself—I can see that!—for something he dreamed about you; and yet I suppose you dream things about others—we all do!—that dishonor and defame them, without thinking evil of them for it?"

I laughed. "Why, of course!" but the two women were silent.

My wife said, finally, "Why, of course, we don't blame them for it; but we can't *feel* exactly the same toward them afterward; and if I knew that a person had such a dream about me, I should not be comfortable till—till—"

"Till you knew just why they had it," I suggested; and I tried to lighten the situation with another laugh.

Hermia gave my wife a grateful look for her sympathy, quite as if it had eased her of her self-accusal, instead of darkening her case against herself, and asked the doctor, "Did his dream dishonor me—defame me—to you?"

"No!" the doctor cried out. "I did not say that. His dream concerned you, and it distressed him; but I couldn't say that it was one to make me or any one think wrong of you. Now, won't that do! Isn't that enough?"

"No," said Hermia, "it isn't enough. I must be judge of whether I was guilty of anything wrong, and I must know what his dream accused me of. Why did it keep coming and coming?"

"How do you know it kept coming and coming?"

"Because I know. Because—because— His mother and I were looking over some things he had left—I wished to do it—letters and papers; and we found a scrap that said—that said—that spoke of his having a dream, and how he had been dreaming the same thing for months, sometimes every night, sometimes once a week. And I can remember how he would be very good to me for days, and then some morning he would not speak to me or hardly look at me; so that—so that I was afraid his mind—"

"Did you keep that scrap?" Wingate interrupted.

Hermia took it out of her pocket, where she must have been keeping her hand upon it, and gave it him. He read it over, glanced again at the characters, and handed it back to her.

"If you needed any proof of what I must say to you now, Mrs. Faulkner," he began, very gravely and tenderly, "you could get it of the first alienist whom you showed that paper. I suppose, if you've been brooding over this matter, it will be a relief, a help to know that your fears were right. When your husband wrote that paper, he was not in his right mind. The signs are simply unmistakable; they couldn't be counterfeited; there's insanity in every line, in every word of that handwriting. It would be interesting to know whether his hand was the same when he wrote of other things. But that's irrelevant. What's certain is that on one point he had a delusion, and that this delusion had begun to show itself in the form of a dream. Isn't it enough, now, if I assure you that his dream had no more real significance, no more rightful implication, than any other form of mania?"

She shook her head. "No. Why should it persist?"

"Ha-a-a!" he breathed in desperation. "Why should any mania persist in a disordered mind?"

"It isn't the same thing at all."

"But it is exactly and perfectly the same thing! It was the presence in his sleep of a maniacal delusion that was gradually overshadowing his waking consciousness, and that must have ended in his open insanity if death had not come to his relief."

She simply asked, "What was it?"

"What was it?" he echoed. "Well, you have a sort of right to know; perhaps you had better know. But I wish—I wish you had the strength to forego it—to accept my assurance, the most solemn, the most sincere I could give any one on a matter of life and death, that although his dream involved you, it no more rightfully inculpated you than it inculpated me, and that it ought to have no more consideration, no more influence, in your life than the ravings of any lunatic that came to you from an asylum window as you passed in the street. Now, won't that do? Can't you accept my assurance, and go home satisfied?"

"When I know what his dream was," she answered. "I can never rest again, now, till I know it."

"But there is this to be considered, Mrs. Faulkner," he urged. "There is the regard you have for him, his memory. He was no more responsible for dreaming his dream than you are for having been the subject of it. But you know how involuntary, how helpless, we often are in our judgments of others; and I warn you—it's my duty to warn you—that the danger is not that you may not be able to forgive yourself, but that you may not be able to forgive *him*."

"I must take the risk of that. I must know everything, now, at any cost. I am not afraid of being unjust to him. I saw him suffer, and I can make every allowance." Wingate was silent, with his head down, and she began with a kind of gasp: "Did he—was he afraid of me? I know how suspicious people are who are affected as you say he was beginning to be—though I can't believe it, I can't imagine it!—and I can understand, if he *was!* Did he think I would hurt him, somehow? Was that what he dreamed? Did he dream that I was going to do him some harm —kill him—?"

"Oh, no! no! no!" cried Wingate, getting to his feet. "Nothing of that kind, I assure you!" He spoke with the relief, as I fancied, of having found out the worst she had feared, and of being able to console her with something indefinitely less terrible. I had often known my wife push out a skirmish line of apprehension far beyond the main body of her anxiety, so as to have the comfort of finding herself within the utmost she had imagined of evil; and I understood the feminine principle on which Wingate counted, and shared his relief.

"Then what was it?" Hermia asked.

"What was it? Nothing. Nothing at all, in a manner! Nothing

of the kind you feared. But if you must know"—Wingate glanced at us where we sat spellbound by our sympathy and interest— "though it's ridiculously unimportant in comparison with what you've suggested, I think perhaps you'd better hear it alone, Mrs. Faulkner."

"By all manner of means!" I said, and my wife said, "Yes, indeed!" as we rose together.

I felt from the first an odious quality in the part we had been obliged to bear; and I confess that I was beginning to bear it with some measure of resentment, in spite of my curiosity, and with some misgiving as to the delicacy of the woman who had required our presence at this interview. But perhaps I judged her too severely. In some of the most intimate affairs and sentiments, in which women are conventionally supposed to play a veiled and hidden part, they really have an overt, almost a public rôle, which nature no doubt fits them to sustain, without violence to their modesty, without touching susceptibilities that in men would be intolerably wounded.

I was impatient of the mechanical effort Hermia made to detain my wife, to whose hand she clung, and whom I had to draw from her with me out of the room. My wife agreed with me that we must have gone, but I doubt if she perfectly thought so; and they both had an effect of yielding out of regard to the sensibilities of us men.

VIII

I WAS IN no humor to tempt any confidence from Wingate when I hurried out to the street door to see him off after I heard him come out of the library. My curiosity, such as I had, was damped by a sense of the indecency of knowing in brutal vocables what I already conjectured, and I was still resentful of having been obliged to enter into the affair to the extent I had.

Wingate let me help him on with his overcoat, and he put his hand on the door-knob before he spoke. "The next time you have a case of this kind, old fellow, I hope I shall be in Europe."

He looked hot and dry, and he breathed harder than even a stout man need after being helped on with his overcoat. "I made a mistake in sending your wife and you out of the room. It was no easier for me, and Mrs. Faulkner says she shall tell her at once, anyway, and you might as well have had it at first-hand. She takes it worse than I expected. Good-night!" he added abruptly, after a pause, and an evident intention to say something else; and he flung himself down my steps and seemed to rebound into his coupé, which was standing before them.

I waited the next turn of events with an increasing sense of injury at the hands of our guest, for I knew that ultimately I must be drawn upon for the nervous force which my wife would spend in sympathizing with her; and I had not yet recognized the claim that she seemed to think our purely accidental relations had established for her upon us.

But the next turn of events was apparently to wait our motion. I mechanically expected Hermia to come out of the library, where I was mechanically impatient to take my book and pity her at my ease; but she did not come out, and I had to go and sit down in the parlor, which was less commodious for my compassion, and unusual for my book. I sat there, disconsolately trying to read, for what I thought a long time, till my wife came down stairs.

"Where is Mrs. Faulkner?" she asked, under her breath. I nodded toward the library. "But I thought the doctor had gone?"

"So he has. He went some time ago; but he didn't take her with him."

"I've been expecting her to ask for me," said my wife, vaguely. "I hated to go to her. It would have seemed like prying."

"To a lady who was willing to have the whole matter, whatever it was, talked out before us both?"

"That is true," said my wife. "Would you knock?"

"Perhaps I would listen at the key-hole first," said I, and I felt myself growing more and more sardonic, for no reason, except that I had such a good chance.

My wife meekly went and listened, and then, after a look at me, opened the library door and went in. It was nearly an hour before she rejoined me in our own room, having first gone with our guest to hers, and staid with her there a little while.

Then she said, "Well, Basil, I never knew anything so sad in my life. I don't know what we are going to do. She must go home at once, and I don't see how she is ever to get there. That is what we have got to talk over now."

"I supposed you had talked it over already," I suggested, still perversely affecting that cheap cynicism.

My wife took it for what it was, and ignored it.

"Poor, stricken creature!" she sighed. "I don't believe she had moved after the doctor left her till I came in, and then she hardly moved. She had that awful stony quiet that people— strong people—have, when you bring them bad news. I could hardly get her to speak. She said she wanted me to know everything, but she did not know how to tell me, unless I asked her; and so, little by little, we got it out together. But I think I'd better not tell you, dear, just in so many words, till she's out of the house; do you?"

"No; I guess I know pretty well what you have to tell," I answered, honestly enough, and without any ironical slant, even in my tone.

My wife went on: "I'm afraid Dr. Wingate didn't manage very well: he had something finer than nerves to deal with. But I don't blame *him*, poor man, either. He was thrown off his guard by her asking if her husband had dreamed that she was going to hurt him, and he thought that what he really did dream was so much less dreadful that it would relieve her; and I'm afraid he went at it too lightly. But it seems that she had never imagined that he could have dreamed *that*, and it perfectly crushed her. Basil! Don't you believe there are some natures so innocent that they have no suspicion of suspicion, that they can't conceive of it? Well, that is Hermia Faulkner! She is on such a grand scale, she's so noble and faithful and loyal, that she can't even understand the kind of nature that could attribute wrong to her: its baseness, its cruelty. She's crushed under the ruin of her own ideal of that wretched man!"

"Oh, oh, oh!" I cried. "Isn't that rather a high horse you're on? I don't think poor old Faulkner was to blame for his crazy dream. I wouldn't like to shoulder the responsibility for my dreams!"

"*You* are very different. *You* are *good*," said my wife, "and you couldn't have such a dream, if you tried; but if you go, now, and think it was worse than it really was, I shall hate you. I should like to tell you *just* what it was; but you are such a fool, dear," she added, tenderly, "that you'd be conscious the whole way, and couldn't help showing it every minute."

"The whole way? Every minute? What do you mean?"

"I've decided that you must take Hermia home."

"Oh, I see! That was why you were so willing we should inquire how she could get there. But supposing I can't leave my business?"

"But I know you can. You were going to New York with me next week, and we can give that up. There's nothing else for it. We must! It will give you a chance to see your old friends out there, and you've simply got to do it; that's all." She added, in terms expressive of the only phase of her anxiety that could be put concretely, and by no means representative of her entire motive: "I can't have her getting sick here on my hands; and there's no other way. Her mother-in-law is too old to come for her, and—"

"We might telegraph the Reverend James Nevil to come," I suggested.

"Basil!" cried my wife.

"Oh, it's no use, my dear! I'd better know just what I'm to be conscious of."

"You know it already; we've both known it from the beginning; but I can't tell you. It isn't her fault, though it covers her with such cruel shame that she can't look herself in the face. It's *his* fault for having him there to dream about; and it's HIS fault for being there to be dreamt about." I knew that my wife meant

Faulkner by her less, and Nevil by her greater, vehemence of accent. "I suppose she felt, all the time—such a woman would— that he had no right to bring his friendship into their married life that way. She must have felt hampered and molested by it; but she yielded to him because she didn't want to seem petty or jealous. There's where I blame *her*. Basil! A woman's jealousy is God-given! It's inspired, for her safety and for her husband's. She *ought* to show it."

"How about a man's?"

"Oh, that's different! Men *have* no inspirations. Jealousy's a low, brutal instinct with them. Just see the difference between her feeling that his friend had no business in their family, and his making that very friend the object of his suspicions!"

"If you conjecture one fact," I said, "and hold Faulkner responsible for the other, the difference is certainly very much against him. But, as I understand from Dr. Wingate, Faulkner's dream foreshadowed his alienation."

"Oh, don't talk to me of Dr. Wingate!" she cried. "He doesn't know anything about it. No! It was his miserable jealousy that turned his brain; it wasn't his insanity that caused his jealousy; and if you keep saying that, Basil, I shall think you are trying to justify him."

"Bless my soul! What question of justification is there?"

"If he was not responsible for his dream," she went on, "he was certainly responsible for the occasion of his dream, and so it comes to the same thing at last. It was his folly, his silly, romantic clinging to a sentiment that he ought to have flung away the instant he was married, which did all the harm. A husband shouldn't have any friend but his wife."

"You will never get me to deny that, my dear, at least as long as you're in this dangerous humor."

"I know I'm ridiculous," she said, nervously. "But I do feel so sorry for that poor creature! She seems to me like some innocent thing caught in a trap; and she can't escape, and no one can set her free. I shall begin to believe that there is such a thing as Fate, in that old Greek sense: something that punishes you for your sorrows and for the errors of others."

"There is certainly something that does that," I said, "whether we call it Fate or not. We suffer every day for our sorrows, and for the sins of men we never saw, or even heard of. There's solidarity in *that* direction, anyway."

"Yes, and why can't we feel it in the other direction? Why can't we feel that we're helped, as well as hurt, by those unknown people? Why aren't we rewarded for our happiness?"

"It's all a mystery; and I don't know but we *are* rewarded for our happiness, quite as much as we're punished for our misery. Some utterly forgotten ancestral dyspeptic rises from the dust now and then, and smites me with his prehistoric indigestion. Well, perhaps it's some other forgotten ancestor, whose motions were all hale and joyous, that makes me get up now and then impersonally gay and happy, and go through the day as if I had just come into a blessed immortality."

"Ah, those awful dead! Basil," she entreated, "from this time on, let's live so that whichever dies first, the other won't have anything to be remorseful for!"

"We can't do that, and I don't believe we were meant to do it. We have to live together as if we were going to live together forever."

"Why, we *are*, dearest! Don't you think we are?"

"I can't imagine anything else; but I don't understand that this is the prospect that now looks so disheartening for Mrs. Faulkner. If it were a question of her going on forever with Faulkner, it would be very simple, or comparatively simple. In that case the wrong he had helplessly done her in his crazy dream would only endear him to her the more, for it would be something for her perpetually to exercise her love of forgiving upon. But the difficulty is that she now wishes to go on living with somebody else forever. I don't blame her for that; on the contrary I think it's altogether well and wholly right, something to be desired and praised. But if the one she now wishes to go on living with forever happens to be the very person whom her dead husband's dream foreboded—"

"Basil!"

"Why, you see, it complicates the affair." We had touched

the quick, and we were silent a moment, quivering with sympathy. "It's all a mystery, and one part no more a mystery than another; but I suppose that when we come really to know, it will all be so very, very simple that we shall be astonished. Mrs. Faulkner's trouble isn't about the future, though; that has to be left to take care of itself; her trouble is about the present and about the past. I haven't the least idea that she ever gave a thought to Nevil as long as her husband lived, or for long after he died."

"Oh, Basil! I *like* to hear you say that!"

"I dare say you'd like to say it yourself: it's very magnanimous. But I can understand how such a woman would now begin to question whether she had not thought of him, and would end by bringing herself in guilty, no matter what the facts were. I didn't like her attempting to ignore the tenor of Faulkner's dream when she went to talk with Wingate about it immediately after his death. That was romantic."

"I didn't like that either," said my wife. "Yes, it was romantic."

"If she had made Wingate tell her then, it would have been all over with by this time. Either she would have resented it, and set about forgetting Faulkner, and living a denial of all fealty to the memory of a man who could wrong her so—"

"Basil! You said he was not responsible for it!"

"Or else she would have succumbed to it, and refused ever to see Nevil, and this frightful quandary that she's got us all into never would have been brought about."

My wife could not laugh with me at our personal entanglement in Mrs. Faulkner's affair, which my words reminded her of. She began to enlarge upon the hardship of it; and she was not reconciled to it by my arguments going to show how nothing any one did or suffered could be done or suffered to one's self alone, and that probably at that very moment some nameless savage in Central Africa was shaping our destiny in some degree, and was making favor with his fetich for our disaster, when he supposed himself to be merely invoking protection against a raid of

Arab slavers. Those were the days of frequent railroad accidents, and she recurred to her fixed principle that I must never go a railroad journey alone, because it was necessary that when I was killed on the train she and the children must be there to be killed with me. Nothing less than the infatuation she had for Mrs. Faulkner would have supported her in the sacrifice of such a principle, and I am not sure that even that would have been enough without the lively fear of having Mrs. Faulkner break down with a nervous fever, or something, before we could get her out of the house. I recurred to this consideration, which Isabel had already touched upon, and treated it in a philosophic spirit, as an instance of the grotesque and squalid element which is so apt to mar a heroic situation, in order apparently to keep human nature modest; but she could not follow me. She said, yes, that decided it; and she drew a sigh of relief, which she cut short to express her wonder that Dr. Wingate should have told Hermia what Faulkner's dream was when he knew it would perfectly kill her. She said she had long had her doubts of his wisdom, and she now proceeded to disable it, with that confidence in her ability to judge him which all women feel in regard to physicians. At least, she said, if he had any sort of intuition, or even the smallest grain of common-sense, or the slightest delicacy, he would not have told her that the man whom the dream involved was the very man she was going to marry. I said that perhaps Wingate did not know she was going to marry Nevil; and she acknowledged that this was true, and began to rehabilitate him. I was in hopes that she would not ask me why I had not told him; for I now saw, or thought I saw, that I had been mistaken in the delicacy which had kept me from doing it. But I was not to escape: the question came, in due course, and all my struggles to free myself only served to fix the blame for the whole trouble more firmly upon me. She said that now she saw it all; and that I need not go to Central Africa for the cause of our predicament.

I spent a troubled night, tormented, whether sleeping or waking, by a fantastic exaggeration of the whole business, and exasperated by a keen sense of its preposterousness. It seemed to me intolerable that I should be made the victim of it: that this gossamer nothing, which might perhaps accountably involve the lives of those concerned through a morbid conscience, should have power upon me, to drag me a thousand miles away from my family, and subject me to all the chances of danger and death which I must incur, seemed to me atrocious. I spent myself in long imaginary dialogues with my wife, with Hermia, with Nevil, in which I convinced them to no effect that I had nothing whatever to do with the matter, and would not have. Faulkner appeared to me a demoniac presence, at the end of the lurid perspective, running back to that scene in the garden—implacable, immovable, ridiculous like all the rest, monstrous, illogical, and no more to be reasoned away than to be entreated.

I woke in the morning with the clear sense that there was only one thing for it, and that was simply to refuse to go with Mrs. Faulkner. I spent the forenoon in arranging my business for a week's absence, and I started West with her on the three o'clock train.

Part Third

―――――――

NEVIL

I

IN SPITE OF my wife's care that I should not be made conscious in Mrs. Faulkner's presence by knowing just the terms of her husband's dream, I must have been rather embarrassed in setting off upon her homeward journey with her if she had seemed aware of any strangeness in it. But she seemed aware of nothing. I could not help seeing that my company, or the supervision of some one, was essential to her. She was like a person mentally benumbed; all the currents of her thought were turned so deeply inward, toward the one trouble which engrossed them, that she appeared incapable of motion from herself. She did what I bade her with a mute passivity, as if she were my mesmeric subject, and with a sort of unseeing stare, like a sleep-walker's. My wife came with us to the station to take leave of her, but Hermia had parted with her at the moment of being left alone with Dr. Wingate the night before, and I think could not have been fully sensible of any of us since. I had a fantastic notion of being like something in a dream to her, and I am afraid I must have been like something very harassing, with the attentions I was obliged to offer her.

I tried to make them as few as possible, and to confine them to the elemental questions of eating and sleeping. These were very simply settled: she neither ate nor slept throughout the journey. I spent all the time I could in the smoking car. When I came to her with the announcement that at this or that next

79

station we were to have five, or ten, or twenty minutes for re-
freshment, after the barbarous custom of the days before dining
cars, she said she wanted nothing, so definitively that I could not
urge her; and in the morning, after my nightmares in my berth,
I found her sitting in one corner of the section I had secured for
her, with every appearance of not having moved from her place
since she first took it on coming aboard the car. Her cheek was
propped on the palm of one hand, and she had that blind,
straightforward stare.

It was a strange journey; and if our fellow-passengers made
their conjectures about us, it must have been to the effect that
I was in charge of a mild case of melancholia, and was rather
negligent of my charge. I left her as much to herself as I could,
for I understood with what a painful strain she would have to
detach herself from the trouble on which her thoughts were bent,
if I interrupted them, and that I could in no manner relieve her,
or help her to puzzle it out. Toward the end of the second afternoon we came to one of the last stations between us and our
destination, and then she started up with a long sigh, and after a
moment began to put together the little bags and wraps which
women travel with.

"Here we are at Blue Clay," I said, coming up to her.

"Yes," she answered; "this is the last stop the express makes
before we get home."

Probably she had taken note of every point and incident in
the journey with that superficial consciousness which is so active
in times of trouble. She now showed an alertness like that of one
awakened from a refreshing sleep, and I had an increasing sense
of her having cast off the burden that had oppressed her. There
was nothing of levity in her apparent relief; her exaltation was
noble and dignified as her dejection had been. Perhaps she had
not reached any solution of her trouble; perhaps she had simply
cast it from her by a natural reaction as we do when we have
suffered enough, for one time, and was destined to take it up
again. But I felt that I could not be mistaken in the fact of her
relief. If I was mistaken, then it was because she had a strength

to conceal her suffering which I could not imagine because she had so frankly shown her suffering before. Her present behavior might have been a woman's ideal of the way she would wish to behave in the circumstances; but I still think Hermia Faulkner had found freedom, at that moment, from the stress of her preoccupation, and began to assume a certain hospitality of manner toward me, because she was able without pain to do so. She thanked me with ingenuous sweetness for coming home with her, and expressed a sense of the sacrifice which would have satisfied even the exacting woman who had made me make it. She asked if I had slept well, as if I had just got up; and she hoped I would not suffer by the great kindness which Mrs. March and I had both shown her, and which she would never forget. I protested, of course, that it was all nothing, and said that I had long wished to revisit the scenes of my youth, and had eagerly seized the excuse that the hope of being useful to her gave me for coming now. She answered, "Yes; that is what Mrs. March told me." As we drew near our destination she sympathized with the interest I felt in approaching the place where I had spent the happiest years of my young manhood, and helped me to make out some of the landmarks by which I hoped to identify the city I remembered. But the new city was built all out over and beyond them, and our approach was hurried by finding them within it, so that before I realized it the train was slowing up in the grandiose depot of vaulted brick and glass which replaced the shabby wooden shed of former days. I had intended to renew there the emotions with which I parted from a friend long since dead, the night I started for Europe; but I was distracted by the change, as well as by the hurly-burly of arrival, and I willingly abandoned myself to the friendly care of the black serving-man of Mrs. Faulkner who was there to meet us, and who at once brevetted me one of the family. He took my bag, and led the way out to Mrs. Faulkner's carriage, and put it in with her things before I thought to stop him.

"Oh, I can't let you take the trouble of driving me to a hotel," I said. "I will get a hack here."

"Why, surely," she answered in a tone of wounded expectation, "you are coming to *us*?"

"No; I shall be here such a little while, and—"

"But that's all the more reason why you should be our guest. My mother would be hurt if you went anywhere else; we will leave you free to come and go as you like; only you *must stay* with us."

It was useless to protest, and I got into the carriage with her.

II

BOTH THEN and afterward, when we reached the Faulkner mansion, I was aware of not having done the Faulkners justice as personages, in our meeting at Swampscott. I had understood, in a careless way, that their occupation of that villa and the style of their living in it meant money; but Faulkner himself was such an informal sloven, and Hermia was so little attributable in character to anything about her, and the doom hanging over them was so exclusive of all other interest in them, that I had not conjectured the degree of state from which they were detached. The quiet richness of the equipage that had met us now was the forerunner of a sumptuous comfort, far beyond any expectation of mine, in all Mrs. Faulkner's belongings and surroundings. She was not a person you could imagine caring for the evidences or uses of wealth; she affected you at once as exterior to all such sordid accidents; as capable of being a goddess in any gown. As a matter of fact, however, the costliness in which her whole life was clad was certainly very great.

I had forgotten the spacious grounds in which Faulkner's house stood, or perhaps I now noticed them more because all the neighborhood had been closely built up in the process of the city's growth. In the heart of the town the mansion rose from the midst of ample lawns and gardens, enclosed by a high brick wall, such as I had always said was my ideal of stately bounds; and it all looked much older than anything at the East, from the soft-coal smoke with which wall and mansion and garden trees were blackened. I suppose it was the smell of this in the air, and the mat of ivy on the house front, that confused my memories of the farther past with more recent recollections of England, and imparted to my present sensations the vagueness of both, as we rolled up under the *porte cochère*. I saw that the house must have been vastly enlarged since I had been there last, and the bulk of the elms that overtopped it, and the height of the slim white birches on the lawn before it, warned me how long ago that had been. Within, I was met by the fresh, brisk warmth of a fire of hickory limbs, that burnt on the wide hall hearth, and I at once delivered myself up to the caresses of the velvety ease in which all life moved there. These influences are so subtly corrupting that a vulgar question formed itself in my mind, as I followed the servant up the broad staircase to my room, and I wondered how much the invitation of such luxury might tempt a man fagged in heart and mind. I said to myself that if I were Nevil, for example, and I were in love with the heart of this material bliss, I should certainly let no fantastic scruple bar me from possession. I cannot exactly say how the formulation of this low thought affected me with a perception of Hermia's charm in a way it was not apt to make its appeal. But when I went down to dinner, and met her again, mellowed to harmony with all that softness and richness by a dress that lent itself in color and texture to her peculiar beauty, I was abashed by her youth and loveliness. I had till then thought of her so much as a mysteriously stricken soul, that I had never done justice to her as a woman that some favored man might be in love with, as men are with women, and might marry. When I now realized this I was ashamed of realizing it, and was afraid of betraying it somehow, by some levity, some want of conformity in mood or manner to what I knew of her. I suffered myself to wonder if Nevil ever had this unruly sense of her, against which something sadly reproachful in her beauty itself seemed to protest, and which I feel that I have given undue import and fixity in putting it into words. I suppose it was all from seeing her for the first time in colors, and from perceiving with a distinctness unfelt before that she was in the perfect splendor of a most regal womanhood. Something perversely comic mixed with my remorse, when I met her eye with these thoughts in my mind, and fancied a swift query there as to the impression I had of her. I wished to tease, to mystify her, to keep her between laughing and crying, as a naughty boy will with some little girl whom he pretends to have found something wrong about. I have since thought she may have been questioning whether I read in her costume any conclusion as to the matter pending in her mind; and that she meant to express by this assertion of her right to be beautiful the decision which she had reached. If this was so, she had chosen a means too finely, too purely feminine; my wife might have understood her, but I certainly did not.

The dowager Mrs. Faulkner was there with her in the drawing-room, a plain old lady, whom I could see her son had looked like, in a rich old lady's silk. She welcomed me with a motherly cordiality, and put me on that footing of intimacy with Faulkner in the past which I was always wishing in vain to refuse. I perceived that I had for her only the personality that he had given me; she could not detach me from the period of my first acquaintance with him. She began at once to talk literature with me, as if that were the practical interest of my life; and I found her far better read, and of a far more modern taste, than her son had been. She was one of those old ladies who perhaps reach their perfection a little away from the centres of thought, or rather of talk, and in some such subordinate city as that where her life had been passed. She had kept the keen relish for books which seems to dull where books are written and printed, and she had vivid opinions about them which were not faded by constant wear. I found also that she knew personally a great many of the authors we discussed: it was still in the palmy days of lecturing, and the Faulkners had made their house the hospitable sojourn of every writer who had come to the place to read his essay or poem. She told me that I had the authors' seat at her table, and that the very chair I then sat in had been occupied by Emerson, Curtis, Wendell Phillips, Saxe, Dr. Holland, Bayard Taylor, Mark Twain, and I do not know who else.

I confess that she fatigued me a little with all that enthusiasm, but except for her passion for authorship in books and out of them, I found that I must revise my impression that she was a romantic person. Her relations with her daughter-in-law had nothing, certainly, of romantic insubstantiality; they were of the solidest and simplest affection, founded apparently upon a confidence as perfect as could have existed between them if Hermia had been her own child. She gave her the head of the table, and she let herself be ruled by her in many little things in which old ladies are apt to be rebellious to younger women. She seemed to wish only to lead the talk, but she deferred to Hermia in several questions of fact as well as taste, and though she always spoke to her as "child," it was evidently with no wish to depose or minify her. On her part Hermia, without seeming to do so, showed herself watchful of Mrs. Faulkner's comfort and pleasure at every moment, and evidently returned her liking in all its cordiality. There was no manner of jealousy between them, perhaps because Mrs. Faulkner could never have been a beauty, and could not even be retrospectively envious of Hermia's magnificence, and partly also because they were temperaments that in being wholly opposite did not in the least wear upon each other.

This at least was my rapid formulation of the case. The dinner was exquisite, and Mrs. Faulkner praised it with impartial jollity, assuring me that I should have had no such dinner if she had been in authority, but that Hermia's genius for house-keeping was such that its inspirations ruled even in her absence. As for herself, she did not know what she was eating.

"Nor, I hope, how much I am," I said.

In fact I felt quite torpid, after dinner. As we sat before the fire I began to have long dreams between the syllables of the words I heard spoken, and I had a passage of conversation with my wife and Faulkner, in which it was all pleasantly arranged in regard to Nevil, while I was dimly aware of Mrs. Faulkner's asking me whether I thought George Eliot would live as a poet.

I do not know whether I perceptibly disgraced myself or not. But we made a short evening, and a little after nine o'clock I acquiesced with an alacrity for which I am sure my wife would never have forgiven me, in Hermia's suggestion that I must be very tired, and would like to go to bed.

III

IT WAS CERTAINLY a most anomalous situation, and I woke with the brilliant idea that for my own part in it the whole thing was to take it as naturally as possible; which was probably reflected into my waking thought from some otherwise wholly vanished dream.

I found it early, as to the daylight, but in that smoke-dimmed November air it might very well be still rather dark at seven o'clock. I went out for a breath of the pensive confusion which I found still persisted in it, and inhaled my glad youth and my first joy of travel in the odor of those bituminous fumes. The grass was still brightly green on the lawn;

"And parting summer lingering blooms delayed"

in the garden, which stretched with box-bordered walks and grape-vined trellises to the wall at one side of the house. The leaves had dropped from the trees, and I picked up from the fallen foliage, soft and dank under my feet, a black walnut, pungently aromatic, and redolent of my boyhood. At the same time a faint scent rose from the box, and transported me to that old neglected garden by the sea, where I saw Faulkner die. A thrill of immense pity for him pierced my heart. I thought with what a passion of tenderness for that woman he must have planned this house, from which he was now in eternal exile, and her willingness to forget him in her love for another seemed monstrous. It was hard to be a philosophical spectator; I found myself taking the unfriended side of the dead.

In the house, when I returned to it, I was met by Faulkner's mother, before that cheerful hall fire. She put aside the damp morning paper which she had just opened to dry in the heat, and gave me her old, soft hand.

"Do you find many familiar points about the place?" she asked.

"No; I'm afraid I hadn't kept any distinct remembrance of it. At least, it's all very strange."

"You would recognize my son's room, I suppose," she said, turning and leading the way down a corridor that branched away from the hall. "The old house is all here; the new one was built round it; and we've kept poor Douglas's den, as he used to call it, just as it was."

I thought it an odd fancy she should wish me to visit the place with her, but I concluded that perhaps she wished to tell her daughter I had already seen it, if she should ask. At any rate, I had no comment to make even in my own mind: we all deal as we best can with our bereavements, and it is but lamely, helplessly at the best.

We had to pass through the library, and I recognized some of the rare editions and large-paper copies with which poor Faulkner had so quickly surfeited me; and there were two or three of his ridiculous Madonnas hung about, cold engravings with wide mats in frigid frames of black, after a belated taste for the quiet in art. They made me shiver; and in the room which we entered from the library that night, and found Nevil smoking there, we were now met by a ghostly scent of tobacco, as if from the cigars that Faulkner kept on nervously consuming, one after another, as we had talked. It brought back my youth, which seemed haunting the city everywhere: not my youth bright and warm as we find it imagined in the lying books, but cold and dead: the spectre that really revisits after years, and makes us glad it is dead.

The stout-hearted old lady pushed back a blind that had swung to across an open casement, and let in the morning sun. "We keep it aired every day; I can't bear to let it seem to be getting out of use. Hermia feels as I do about it, and she would have asked you to come here and smoke and write your letters; but I thought perhaps I had better bring you first. She was very tired, and we sat up late, talking. Will you sit down? Breakfast will not be ready till half past eight."

I obeyed, and she sat down too. I wondered what could be her motive in wishing to keep me there, and what her theory was in bringing up the last matter that I should have supposed she would like to talk of in that place. Perhaps she spoke from that absence of sensation in regard to certain interests of life which we imagine callousness in the old: those interests are simply extinct in them, and they are no harder than the young who still feel them so keenly. Perhaps she still felt them, and meant to make a supreme renunciation of the past on the spot hallowed to her by the strongest associations. I do not know; I only know that she began to speak, and to speak with a plainness that I have no right to call obtuseness.

IV

"Mr. March, Hermia has been telling me of what she learnt in Boston from Dr. Wingate."

"Yes?" I said feebly.

"It was my wish that she should go there, and see him, and find out to the last word all that he remembered of Douglas. She would not have gone without my wish; but it was her wish, too; or rather it was the necessity of both of us. After we found that paper of Douglas's, which she took with her, we could neither of us rest till we knew everything."

I nodded, for want of wit to say anything relevant, and she went on.

"I wish to say at once that I thoroughly approve of Hermia's engagement to Mr. Nevil, and that nothing she heard from Dr. Wingate has changed me in the least about it. At first, the engagement was rather a shock to me; but not more so than his offer was to Hermia; perhaps not so much." There was no faltering in Mrs. Faulkner's voice, but a tear ran down her cheek. "We are very strangely made, Mr. March. It is twenty years since my husband died, and I have never once thought of marrying again; but I cannot honestly say that I would not have married if I had met any one I loved. I know that such a thing was possible, though I did not know it then. At first, after we have lost some one who is very dear to us, it seems as if henceforward we must live only for the dead: to atone to them for the default of our lives with them, and to make reparation for unkindness. That is the way I felt when my husband died. I wanted to keep myself in communion with him. But that was not possible. Nature soon teaches us better than that; she shows us that as long as we live upon the earth, we cannot live at all for the dead: we can live only for the living."

"Yes," I said. "I never thought of it before, though."

"Have you ever known any deep bereavement?"

"No; I have been very fortunate."

"If you ever have such a sorrow, you will understand what I say as you never can without it. I had learned the truth when my son died, and I tried to make my daughter accept it from me. But she could not; she could only accept it from experience. He had been her whole life so long that she did not wish to live any other. No woman ever devoted herself more utterly than she did to him. She could not realize that as long as she remained in the world she could not devote herself to him any more; that all that had come absolutely to an end. The truth was the harder for her to learn 'by reason of great strength.' She thought that for his sake she could bear not to know what was the trouble of mind in which he died. That was a mistake."

"My wife and I thought so, when we heard of it. Dr. Wingate told me about it. But it was very heroic."

"It was heroic, yes; but it was impossible. I knew it at the time. If she had made Dr. Wingate tell her then, she could have thought it out and lived it down; or, if she couldn't have done that, then at least what makes it so cruel now would never have happened."

"Yes, I see," I said, in the pause which Mrs. Faulkner made.

"I have always been willing," she resumed, "and sometimes I have been anxious that Hermia should marry again. Marriage is for this world. We are told that by Christ himself, and we know it instinctively. Death does dissolve it inexorably; and although

I believe, as Swedenborg says in one of his strange books, that one man and one woman shall live together to all eternity in a union that will make them one personality, still I believe that, as he says, that union may or may not begin on earth, and that it will be formed hereafter without regard to earthly ties. I was not a fool, and I saw that Hermia was young and attractive, and I expected her to have the feelings of other young and attractive women."

There was a mixture of mysticism and matter-of-fact in this dear old lady's formulation of the case which was bringing me near the verge of a smile, but I said, gravely, "Of course."

"But she never showed the least sign of it; and when, after Mr. Nevil came back from Europe, their engagement took place, I was entirely unprepared for such a thing. He had been with us a great deal. We nursed him through a long sickness after that broken engagement of his in Nebraska, and he was quite like one of ourselves. In fact, his friendship with Douglas dates back so far—to the very beginning of their college days—that I can hardly remember when James did not seem like a son to me. You mustn't suppose, though, that I ever objected to the engagement, or do now. I highly approve of it. But I had always fancied that the very intimacy that Hermia was thrown into with him, was unfavorable to her forming any fancy for him. In fact, she has always been rather critical of him; and I know that she rather dislikes clergymen—as men, I mean. She is a religious person in her own way: I've nothing to say against her way. So, as I say, I was sufficiently astonished; but that is neither here nor there. I gave my cordial consent at once. James has not had a very joyous life; he has made it rather hard for himself, and I suppose that the idea of putting some brightness into it may have first made Hermia— But at any rate they were very happy together; and though Hermia had her morbid feelings occasionally about Douglas, and seemed to think it was wicked to turn from him to anybody else, and a kind of treason, still, she always listened to me about it, and would be reasonable when I showed her how foolish she was. I wanted her to put his things away, and there I suppose I made a little mistake, especially the things connected with his last days—writings and letters, and odd scraps, that she was always intending to look over, and never quite had the strength for. She consented to burn them; but she could not bring herself to do that without reading them; and so we found that paper which she carried to Dr. Wingate. Do you know what was in it?"

"No, certainly. She showed it to him in our presence, and I think she was willing we should know, but he decided very wisely that he would rather speak with her alone about it."

My feeling did not seem to make much impression upon Mrs. Faulkner.

"I suppose you do know, Mr. March, that my son was not quite in his right mind when he died?"

I admitted that I had some misgivings to that effect.

"I don't understand," she went on, "why we should be so ashamed to acknowledge that any one connected with us is not perfectly sane. As if the world were not full of crazy people! As if we were not all a little crazy on some point or other! The pain he suffered had affected his mind; it's very common, I believe; and he had a delusion that showed itself in the form of a dream, but that would have been sure, if he lived, to have broken out in a mania."

She stopped, as if she expected me to prompt her or agree with her, and I said, "Yes, Dr. Wingate told me something of the kind."

"But he gave you no hint of what the dream—the delusion—was?"

"None."

"We used often to try to think what it could be. It seemed to give him a dislike or distrust for Hermia; and we thought—we hardly ever spoke of it openly; now we must handle it without shrinking, no matter what pain it gives! We thought—that it involved some fear of violence from her. People whose minds are beginning to be affected, often have such dreadful fancies about those who are dearest to them."

"Yes, yes, I know," I said, and I hope I did not let my tone express the slight impatience I felt at being obliged to traverse ground I had been over with Hermia already in this quest.

"But it was nothing of that kind whatever. It was"—Mrs. Faulkner hesitated, as if to prepare me for a great surprise—"jealousy."

"Jealousy?" I repeated, and I could not help throwing into the word a touch of the surprise which she evidently expected of me. I had not followed her so far without perceiving that an old lady so devoted to literature valued the literary quality of the situation; that with all her good sense and true and just feeling she had the foible of being rather proud of a passage in her family life which was so like a passage of romance.

"Yes," she went on. "And of all things, jealousy of her with— with James." I could say nothing to a fact which I had conjectured long before, and she continued: "Dr. Wingate seemed to think that now she had better know exactly what the dream was, since the paper we had found distressed her so much, and take it in the right way. It was a scribble in one of his note-books, on a leaf that he had torn out and probably meant to tear up. It had the date, and it spoke of his having that dream again; that he had begun to have it every night, and if he fell asleep by day. The leaf was torn out at the side in places, and you could only read scraps of sentences, but it all accused her of wishing his death. It would have driven any other woman wild, but Hermia had been through too much already. She told me something of it, to explain the paper as well as she could; and she said that she knew you and Mrs. March had noticed something strange in Douglas's manner toward her the day you were there; and I urged her to go right on and consult you both, and see Dr. Wingate, and find out exactly what the trouble was."

I was silent, for want of anything fitting to say, though she seemed to expect me to speak.

"The doctor told her that Douglas had been having the dream almost a year before he died: at first every month or two, and then every week. So far as he could remember it was always exactly the same thing from the very beginning. He dreamed that she and James were—attached, and were waiting for him to die, so that they could get married. Then he would see them getting married in church, and at the same time it would be his own funeral, and he would try to scream out that he was not dead; but Hermia would smile, and say to the people that she had known James before she knew Douglas; and then *both* ceremonies would go on, and he would wake. That was all."

"It seems to me quite enough. Horrible! Horrible! I'm surprised that Wingate should have told her."

"He had to do so. There was nothing else. She got it from him by questioning; though I suppose he thought it best she should know just what the trouble was, so that she could see how perfectly fantastic it was, and be able to deal with it accordingly."

"Poor man! How he must have suffered from that unrelenting nightmare! And it seems too ghastly to drag from his grave the secret he kept while he lived." These thoughts were so vivid in my mind that I should not have been surprised if Mrs. Faulkner had replied to them like spoken words.

But she only said: "There were some strange details of the dream, which it seems Dr. Wingate recalled; he may have written it down after hearing Douglas tell it; and from the description of the church which he gave, Hermia recognized it as one here in the city: James's own church. Of course," said the old lady, ignoring the shudder with which I received this final touch, "Dr. Wingate might not have been so explicit if he had known of Hermia's engagement to James. I suppose you hadn't told him?"

"No," I said, and I set that omission down as the chief enormity in a life which has not been free from some blunders worse than crimes.

"Well, that is the whole affair, and we must act at once," said Mrs. Faulkner.

"Break off the engagement, of course," was at my tongue's end; but I found out I had said nothing when she added:

"James must know it all without delay. He has been out of town, but he will be home to-night, and he must know it before he meets Hermia again."

"Of course," I said.

"We talked it over late into the night, and we both came to that conclusion. In fact, Hermia had thought it out on the way home; and she said that just as the train came in sight of home yesterday, it all flashed upon her what she must do. She must leave the future wholly to James, to do whatever he thought right after he knew everything. She says it came to her like a sudden relief from pain. You must have thought it strange we could keep up, as we did in the evening, but it was the revulsion of feeling with her, and I knew nothing till you left us. She merely said, when we met, 'It is all right, mother,' and I should have thought so, if she had told me every word. The decision she reached is the only one. We must leave it to James. She rests in that, and I can't say whether the thought of my poor son's illusion troubles her or not, in itself. I know that it ought not to trouble her; but at the same time I know that it is something which we ought not to keep from James. Men often look at things very differently from women, the best of women."

V

IT WENT THROUGH my mind that the affections being the main interest of women's lives, perhaps they dealt with them more practically if not more wholesomely than men. Certainly their treatment of them seems much more business-like.

Heaven knows what was really in that old woman's heart, as she talked so bravely of a future from which even her son's memory was to be obliterated. Whether it was a sacrifice of herself she was completing, or whether she was accomplishing an end which she freely intended, I shall never be certain; but I thought afterward that she had perhaps schooled herself to look only at Hermia's side of the affair, and had come to feel that she could do no wrong to the dead, whom she could no longer help, by seeking the happiness of the living, whom she could help so much. I myself have always reasoned to this effect, and in what I had to do with it I did my best to bring others to the same mind; and yet at that moment, in that place, it seemed a hellish thing. I saw Faulkner with the inner vision, by which alone, doubtless, we

see the dead, standing there where I first met him, by that table
where we were sitting, with his long nervous fingers, yellowed at
their tips by his cigar, trembling on an open page; and then I
saw him fall back on the seat of the arbor in the old sea-side
garden and die. What a long tragedy it was that had passed between those two meetings! Had not his suffering won him the
right to remembrance? None of us would have denied this; but
what was proposed was to forget him; to blot his memory and
his sorrow, as he had himself been blotted, out of the world
forever. The living must do this for their lives' sake; the dead
must not master us through an immortal grief. All the same I
pitied Faulkner, pitied him for his baleful dream, whose shadow
had clouded his own life, and seemed destined to follow that of
others as relentlessly; and I pitied him all the more because
there seemed no one to do it but me who had cared for him so
little while he lived. He had suffered greatly, and by no fault of
his own, unless you could blame his folly in having his friend so
familiarly a part of his home that his crazy jealousy must make
him its object almost necessarily. But even this weakness, cul-
pable as it was, was a weakness and not a wrong; and no cas-
uistry could prove it malevolent. Something impersonally sinister
was in it all, and the group involved was severally as blameless as
the victims of fate in a Greek trilogy. Neither I nor any other
witness of the fact considered for a moment that Faulkner had
cause for the dark suspicion which was the beginning and the
end of his dream.

I do not know whether Mrs. Faulkner had been saying anything else before I woke from these thoughts and heard her say,
"I have spoken very fully and freely to you, Mr. March, both
because you knew much of this matter already, and because I
need—Hermia needs—your help. We depend upon your kindness; we are quite helpless without you; and you were one of my
son's early friends, and can enter into our feelings."

"I assure you, Mrs. Faulkner—" I began; and I was going to
say that the matter of my early friendship with her son had somehow always been strangely exaggerated; but I found that I could
not decently do this, under the circumstances, and I said—

"There is nothing in my power that I wouldn't gladly do for you."

"I was certain of that," she answered. "James must know of this—of the whole fact—as soon as he gets back. But Hermia can't write to him about it, and I can't speak to him." I began to feel a cold apprehension steal over me; at the same time a light of intelligence concerning Hermia's hospitable eagerness to make me her guest dawned upon me. Could that exquisite creature, in that electrical moment of relief from her trouble, have foreseen my usefulness by the same flash that showed her the simple duty she had in the matter? I do not think I should have blamed her, if that were the case; and I was prepared for Mrs. Faulkner's conclusion: "We must ask *you* to speak to James."

I was prepared, but I was certainly dismayed, too; and I promptly protested: "My dear Mrs. Faulkner, I don't see how I could possibly do that. I am very sorry, very sorry indeed; but I cannot. I should not feel warranted in assuming such a confidential mission to Mr. Nevil, by my really slight acquaintance, or by anything in my past relations with your son. I have been most reluctant to know anything about this painful business," and if this was not quite true, it was certainly true that I had not sought to know anything. "At every point my wife and I have respected the secrecy in which we felt it ought to remain, even against the impulse of sympathetic curiosity."

"Then Mrs. March did not tell you what it was when you started home with Hermia?"

"Surely not! She would have thought it a betrayal of Mrs. Faulkner that would have been embarrassing to me; and how could you suppose I would let you go on and tell me the whole story if I knew it already?"

"I didn't think of that," said Mrs. Faulkner. "Hermia and I both took it for granted that Mrs. March had told you." I did not say anything, and she added ruefully, "Then I don't know what we shall do. Is it asking too much to ask if you can suggest anything?"

I knew from her tone that she was hurt as well as disappointed by this refusal of mine to act for them; strange as it appears, she must have counted unquestioningly upon my consent. I said, to gain time as much as possible, for I had no doubt on that point, "Excuse me, Mrs. Faulkner: do I understand this request to come from you both?"

"No; my daughter knows nothing about it. The idea of asking you was entirely my own; and I made a point of seeing you as soon as possible, this morning. If you must refuse, I beg you will not let her know."

"You may depend upon my silence, Mrs. Faulkner. But," and I rose and began to walk about the room, "why should you tell Mr. Nevil what the dream was; or at least that it concerned him? We must consider that, in the light of reason, the thing is non-existent. It has no manner of substance, or claim upon any one's conscience or even interest. Dr. Wingate did not wish Mrs. Faulkner to know it; and I really think that when she insisted, he would have done wisely and righteously to lie to her about it. I'm sure he would have done so if he had known that she was engaged to Mr. Nevil. But it's too late now; the mischief's done, as far as she's concerned. The question is now how to stop the evil from going farther; and I say there is no necessity for Mr. Nevil's knowing anything about it. Treat it from this moment as the unreality which it is; ignore it."

I went on to the same effect; but as I talked, I knew more and more that I was wasting my breath, and in a bad cause, and I saw that Mrs. Faulkner even ceased to follow me. One of the maids came to my rescue with the announcement that breakfast was served. We followed her, and I ate with the appetite to which I have noticed that the exercise of the sympathies always gives an edge of peculiar keenness.

VI

HERMIA did not join us at breakfast, but I had no need to account for her absence upon that theory of extreme fatigue from her journey, which Mrs. Faulkner urged with so much superfluous apology. I began to have my reluctances about that old lady, to wish to escape from her, because I had refused to oblige her in that little matter of interviewing Nevil, and I was afraid she would recur to it. I made an excuse of wanting to look about the town, and I went out as soon as I could get away after breakfast.

Now that I was there, and had come so far, I was willing to see all I could of the place, and of several people in it whom I remembered as very charming; and I felt exasperated by the terms of my presence. I reviled myself for going to the Faulkners', though I knew I could not help it; but being their guest I could not leave them except to leave town. I strolled about harassed with the notion that I would go on the night express, and denying myself in the interest of this early departure all those little lapses into sentiment concerning the past which I had always expected to indulge when I returned to its scenes. I found myself unwilling to meet my old friends, with the burden on me of having to say that I was there only for the day, and to explain that I had come on with Mrs. Faulkner, and was her guest. I hated the air of mystery the affair would have; but there was one person whom I could not really think of going away without seeing. As a young man I used to come and go in her house as freely as in my own home, at any time between nine in the morning and twelve at night; she had been kind to me, and helpful and inspiring, as only a brilliant woman of the world, who is also good, can be to an ambitious, shy, awkward young fellow of twenty-two; and I decided to make hers stand for all the friendships of the past.

She made me so sweetly welcome that in a moment we had broken through the little web of alienation that the spider years had been spinning between us; and found ourselves exactly in the old relations again. I had been a little curious, after seeing so much of the world, to see whether she would appear as clever and accomplished as she used to seem; and I was glad to find she bore the test of my mature experience perfectly. After all, it is such women who make the polite world, wherever we find it;

not the world them. Her tact divined, without any motion of mine, all the external points of the case, and made it seem even to me the most natural thing possible that I should have seized the occasion of Mrs. Faulkner's being in Boston to run out with her to my old home, if only for a day, and give my old friends a glimpse of me. She supposed that I must be devoted to the Faulkners for the short time I staid, and she would merely insist upon my lunching with her; she would make my peace with Mrs. Faulkner. Was not she exquisite? Had I ever met any one just like her? And what a life of self-devotion, and then of sorrow! No, no one could understand what she had been through, unless they had seen something of it day by day. But I had seen something; the most tragical thing of all, perhaps; and my wife had been so good! Mrs. Faulkner had told her about Mrs. March.

The talk naturally confined itself to Mrs. Faulkner for a time, and it naturally returned to her from whatever excursions it made in other directions. After a while, it began, somehow, to include Nevil, whom I found to be another of my friend's enthusiasms; she celebrated him with the fervor that is rather characteristic of hero and heroine worship in small places, where people almost have their noses against the altar. I trembled inwardly for the secret I was guarding, for I felt that my friend would have it out of me in an instant if she suspected me of its custody, but apparently she knew nothing of the engagement. She asked me if I had heard of that horrid affair out West which had given poor Mr. Nevil back to them again; and she said she supposed he would never think of marrying, now. She wished that he would marry Hermia Faulkner; it would be more than appropriate, it would be ideal; they were exactly suited to each other; and she could help him in his work as no other woman could. She deserved some happiness; but it would be like her to go on dedicating her whole existence to the memory of a man who was really her inferior, and who had nothing to commend him to her constancy except his love for her. Of his love for her you could not say enough; but my friend reminded me that she had never considered him the wonderful person that some people thought him; and she scouted the notion of his having married beneath him in marrying Hermia Winter. Her people were very nice people, though they were so poor; they were idealists; and her father had come West and settled on Pawpaw Creek after the failure of one of those communities in New England, which he had been connected with. As for Hermia herself, whom my friend remembered in her Bell's Institute days, she was a girl of the rarest intelligence and character; a being quite supernally above a ward politician and a pretentious dilettante like Douglas Faulkner, whose "three times skimmed sky-blue" Virginia blood was full of the barbaric pride of a race of slave-holders. As my friend went on she characterized poor Faulkner with a violent excess which would have satisfied even Mrs. March the day when she first met him at Swampscott, and he betrayed his defective tastes in literature and art. Of course, I said that this was exactly the way in which he had impressed my wife; and I defended him. But she told me I might spare my breath; that she knew I really thought just as my wife and she did about him; and that if James Nevil had not been a saint upon earth he never could have endured the man.

"We are both saints," I suggested. "I endured him."

"Oh, no, you're not. Nevil really loved him, and I believe he loves his memory to this day."

"Well, at any rate Faulkner's out of the story," I urged.

"I'm not so sure of that!" cried my friend. "I'm afraid it's their foolish constancy to him that keeps those two from thinking of each other."

"Are you, really?" I asked, and I found a perverse amusement in playing with her shrewd ignorance so near my knowledge, which it could so easily have penetrated. "It seems to me that if they were inclined to each other, their allegiance to the dead would have very little effect. I suspect that conscience, or the moral sentiments, or whatever we call the supersensuous equipment, has nothing to do with people's falling in love, except to find reasons and justifications for it, and to add a zest to it."

"I will write that to Mrs. March," said my friend, "and ask her if those are her ideas, too."

"Oh, I know!" I answered airily. "You ladies like to pretend that it's an affair of the soul, or if possible, of the intellect; and as your favor is the breath of the novelists' nostrils, they all flatter you up in your pretension, till you get to believing in it yourselves. But at the bottom of your hearts, you know, as *we* do, that it's a plain, earthly affair, for this life, for this trip and train only."

"Shocking! shocking!" said my friend, shaking her head, which had grown charmingly gray, in a marquise manner, and evincing her delight in the boldness with which I handled the matter.

"You may be sure," I concluded, "that if these two people have not fallen in love, it's because they don't fancy each other. If they did, there would be no consideration of sentiment, no air-woven tie of fealty to a love or a friendship of the past, which would hold them in the leash. If Faulkner's ghost rose between them, they would plunge through it into each other's arms."

"Ah, now you *are* talking atrociously!" said my friend.

I had indeed been hurried a little beyond myself by a sudden realization of the fact that so far as Hermia was concerned, the past was obliterated by her determination to leave everything to Nevil; and that as soon as Nevil knew everything, he would decide, as I should have decided, that every consideration of honor and delicacy and duty, as well as of love, bound him to her. An added impulse had been given to my words by the consciousness that I was the only means of making her determination known to him, that whether she had inspired her mother to ask this service of me or not, she tacitly hoped it, and that in the end I should probably somehow render it.

But I instinctively fought off from it as long as I could, and I resolved to leave town without rendering it if possible. I spent most of the afternoon with my friend; and she sent a late embassy to the Faulkners to know if she might keep me to dinner. They consented, as they must; Hermia herself wrote that she consented only because she was so completely prostrated that she could not hope to see me at dinner, and her mother was not well; they counted upon having me several days with them, and they would not be selfish.

VII

THE FAULKNERS of course knew nothing of my intention of going that night, and I staid rather late after dinner, so that I should not have much more time than I needed to pack my bag and catch my train. I thought that if I could not altogether escape an embarrassing urgence from them to stay longer, I could at least cut it short. But I found that it was a needless precaution when I went back to them. Mrs. Faulkner, the mother, received my reasons for hurrying home with all the acquiescence I could have wished. She said she knew I must be anxious to get back to my family whom I had left at such short notice; that Hermia and herself appreciated my kindness and my wife's goodness more than they could ever express; and they hoped and prayed that if our need should ever be like theirs we might find such friends in it as we had been to them. I felt an unintentional irony in these thanks so far as they concerned the perfection of my own friendship, but I still had no disposition to repair its lack by offering to see Nevil for her. That, I felt, more and more, I could not do; but I stood a moment, questioning whether I ought not to renew my expressions of regret that I could not do it. I ended by saying that I hoped all would turn out for the best with them; and I added some platitudes and inanities which she seemed not to hear, for she broke in upon them with excuses for Hermia, who would not be able to see me, she was afraid. I said, I knew what a wretched day she had been having, and I left my adieux with Mrs. Faulkner for her. Perhaps if I had not myself been so distraught I might have noticed more the incoherent attention Mrs. Faulkner was able to give me throughout this interview. But I did not realize it till afterward. I went to my room, glad to have it over so easily, and resolved to get out of the house with all possible despatch. I had a carriage at the gate, and I looked forward to waiting an hour and a half in the depot before my train started with more pleasure than such a prospect ever inspired in me before.

In the confusion which afterward explained and justified itself, Mrs. Faulkner had failed to offer me the superfluous help of a servant to fetch down my bag, and I was descending the stairs with it in my hand when I heard a door close in the corridor which led to Faulkner's den. Steps uneven and irregular advanced toward the square hall at the foot of the stairs, and in a moment I saw a man stagger into the light, and stay himself by a clutch at the newel-post. He looked around as if dazed, and then vaguely up at me, where I stood as motionless and helpless as he. I have no belief he saw me; but at any rate, Nevil turned at the cry of "James! James!" which came in Hermia's voice from the corridor, and caught her in his arms as she flew upon him. She locked her arms around his neck, and wildly kissed him again and again, with sobs such as break from the ruin of life and love; with gasps like dying, and with a fond, passionate moaning broken by the sound of those fierce, swift kisses.

I pitied her far too much to feel ashamed of my involuntary witness of the scene; though as for that I do not believe she would have foregone one caress if she had known that all the world was looking. I perceived that this was the end; and I understood as clearly as if I had been told that she had confided her secret to him, had left their fate in his hands, and that he had decided against their love. It maddened me against him, to think he had done that. I did not know, I did not care, what motive, what reason, what scruple had governed him; I felt that there could be only one good in the world, and that was the happiness of that woman. For the moment, this happiness seemed centred and existent solely in her possession of him. But I was sensible, through my compassion and my indignation, that whatever he had done, she was admiring, adoring him for it. I saw that, in a flash of her upturned face, as I stood, with my heart in my mouth, before the tragedy of their renunciation. The play suddenly ended. With one last long kiss, she pushed him from her, and fled back into the corridor.

VIII

I FOUND MYSELF outside in the night, and at the gate I found Nevil in parley with my coachman, who was explaining to him that he was engaged to take a gentleman inside the house, there, to the depot, and could not carry Nevil home.

"Get in, Mr. Nevil," I said. "I've plenty of time, and can drop you wherever you say."

It was as if we had both just come out of the theatre, and actor and spectator had met on the same footing of the commonplace world of reality.

"Oh, Mr. March!" he said. "Is that you? I *will* drive with you as far as my study, if you'll let me. I don't feel quite able to walk."

"Yes, certainly. Get in."

He gave the direction, "St. Luke's Church," and I followed him into the hack, and he shrank into the corner, and scarcely spoke till we reached the church. By the gleams that the street lamps threw into the windows as we passed them I had glimpses of his face, haggard and estranged. He tried to fit his latch-key to the door in the church edifice, and then gave it to me, saying with pathetic feebleness, "You do it. I can't. And don't go— don't leave me," he added, as we entered. "Come in, a moment."

I told the driver to wait, and I suppose he had his conjectures as to the condition in which I was getting the Rev. James Nevil into his study. He was like one drunk, and he went reeling and stumbling before me. Once within he seemed almost unconscious of me, where he sat sunken in an arm-chair, staring at the fire in the grate, and I waited for him to speak. At last I made a movement, and he took it as a sign of departure, and put out his hand entreatingly. "No, no! You mustn't go. I want to tell you—" And then he lapsed again into his silence. At last he broke from it with a long sigh: that "Ah-h-h!" which I remembered from the time when he spoke, on the cliffs by the sea, of Faulkner's unkindness to Hermia. "Well, it is ended!"

I had not the heart to pretend that I did not know what he meant. I said nothing, and he lifted his face toward me where I stood, leaning on his chimney-piece.

"Hermia has told me that you know about this unhappiness of ours," he said, hoarsely. "Your knowledge makes you the one human being whom I can speak to of it; perhaps it gives you the right to know all—all there is."

"No, no," I protested. "I have no claim, and I haven't the wish." I mechanically referred to my watch, and seeing that I had abundant time before my train went, I dropped into the chair beside the hearth, and ended by saying, "But I should be glad if I could in any way serve you or help you. I do know the painful situation in which you are placed, and though I can truly say that neither my wife nor I have ever tried to know of it, I confess that we have been most deeply interested, and you have both had our sympathy in a measure which I needn't try to express." I instinctively calmed my tone to an effect of quiet upon his agitation.

"You have been very good—far kinder friends than we could have hoped to find, and there is nothing that such friends as you may not know, so far as we are concerned. But there is very little more to tell. It is all over."

I thought he wished me to ask how, and I said, "Mrs. Faulkner's mother told me this morning that they were waiting to see you—or rather to let you know on your return—"

"Yes. I expected to return to-night, but I came back late this afternoon, and I went directly to them, of course. It was not what Hermia wished—it was what she dreaded most—but it was doubtless for the best; at any rate it happened. In a moment we were confronted with our question. She told me, fully and fearlessly, as she deals with everything, just what it was, and we set ourselves to solve it—to solve it, if possible, in favor of ourselves, our weakness, perhaps our sin!" His head dropped on his breast, and I saw his eyes fixed with a dreary stare on the smouldering fire. I was sensible, without looking about it much, of the character of the room. It was one of those studies which clergymen for their convenience sometimes have in their church buildings, and where I suppose they go to read and write and think, and transact church business with the officers of their church, and receive people who come to them for counsel or comfort in such straits as those which bring us in piteous entreaty before the ministers of conscience. It is a kind of Protestant confessional; and while I waited for Nevil to speak again, I recalled stories I had heard of guilty souls seeking such an asylum for that relief which we shall all know at the judgment-day, when we shall be stripped bare before the divine compassion down to our inmost thoughts and purposes. Women who have betrayed their husbands go there to own their shame; men that have cheated and stolen and lied, go there to lay the burden of their wrong-doing upon the priest of God; and with these a mass of minor sinners, with their peccadilloes of temper and breeding and deceit; as well as the self-accusers who wish to purge their spirits even of the dread of sin, and to receive the acquittal which they cannot give themselves. More and more as Nevil went on it seemed to me that the place was not favorable to a judicial examination of his own case; that the color of things he had heard there must stain and blacken the facts of his own experience, and prevent him from seeing them aright.

"The question was," he said, lifting his head, and bending that hopeless stare on me, "not what we should do, with that shadow of Faulkner's dream hanging over us, but what we *had* done—what *I* had done—to cause him the torment of such a dream."

"For Heaven's sake, Mr. Nevil," I broke in, "don't take that way of looking at it. You had no more to do with causing that dream than I had. The pain he suffered—the physical pain— caused the craze which his dream came from. It was a somnambulic mania—nothing more and nothing less. Dr. Wingate assured Mrs. Faulkner in the most solemn manner—"

"Ah, the sincerity of a doctor with his patient! He is a skilful

man, very able, very learned; he knows all about the body, but
the soul and its secrets are beyond science. There are facts in
the case that he has never had before him. I knew Hermia first,
in the loveliness of her young girlhood, and I brought her and
Faulkner together."

I murmured, "Yes, I remember you told me."

"I saw the impression she instantly made upon him: it was
love at first sight. But though the love of her had possessed his
whole soul, he was first faithful to his friendship with me. In that
childlike, simple, cordial truthfulness of his, which no one ever
knew so fully as I, and which I shall never see in any other man,
he pressed me to tell him whether I had any feeling for her myself, for then he would go away, and live his passion down, as
best he could, and leave her to me. I assured him that I had no
such feeling, no feeling but that pleasure in her beauty and goodness which every one must have in her presence; and they were
married."

The silence following upon the gasp in which these words
ended was not such as I could break. After a moment Nevil went
on.

"I believed what I said; I have never doubted it till this day.
But—how do I know—how do I know—that I was not in love
with her then, that I have not always been in love with her
through all his life and death? It is such a subtle, such a fatal
thing in its perversion! I have seen it in others; why shouldn't it
be in me? Why shouldn't we have been playing a part unknowingly to ourselves, hypocrites before our own souls? Why should
I ever have consented to be with them, to qualify their home by
an alien presence, through the daily, hourly lie of friendship for
him, except that I loved her, and longed to be near her? Why
could not I have kept the love of that poor foolish young girl,
innocent and harmless, for all her levity, which she gave me out
there in the West, except that in the guilty inmost of my heart
there was no room for anything but love for my friend's wife,
whom it had made his widow? Why—"

"Hold on! Wait! This is monstrous!" I broke in upon him.

"It's atrocious. You're the victim of your own morbid introspection, of a kind of self-analysis that never ends in anything but self-conviction. I know what it is, every one knows; and it's your right, it's your duty as a man to stand out against it, and not let the honest and lawful feeling you now have damn the past to shame!"

I spoke vehemently, far beyond any explicit right I had to adjure him, but I could see that my words had not the slightest weight with him.

"And Hermia," he went on, "why should she have cared nothing for Faulkner at first? Why, when she believed she had schooled herself to love him, should she have suffered the ever-repeated intrusion of my presence in her home? Why should she have refused so long to know what his dream was? Why should we have made such haste to separate after Faulkner's death; and then why should my thoughts have turned so instantly to her, with such longing for her pity, in that shame I underwent; and why should she have honored and not despised me for a misfortune that my own folly had provoked? There is one answer to it all!"

"And the answer is that your view of the case is as purely an aberration as Faulkner's dream."

"Ah, you can't account for everything on the ground of madness! Somewhere, some time, there *must* be responsibility for wrong."

"Even if we have to find it in innocence! I tell you that your view of the situation is as false as that which the lowest scandal-mongering mind of an enemy could take of it. You are bound to let your own character—or if not your character, then her character, her nature—count for something in making up such a judgment. I will leave you out of the question, if you like, but I would stake my life upon the singleness of her devotion, in thought, feeling, and deed, to that wretched man whose misery seems such an inextinguishable poison. It's preposterous that I should be defending her to you; but if you have suffered her to share these misgivings of yours, I say you've done a cruel thing.

I know—her mother told me—that after what she underwent from learning just what Faulkner's dream was—and my wife and I saw something of her suffering, both in Boston and on the way out here—"

"Ah—h—h!" he breathed.

"She had found peace in her reliance, her perfect faith in your conscience, in your sense of justice, and your instinct of right; and, if you will allow me to say so, you were most sacredly bound not to let any perverse scruple, any self-indulgent misgiving, betray her trust in you. You are a man, with a man's larger outlook, and you should have been the perspective in which she could see the whole matter truly. If you have failed her in this, you have been guilty of something worse than anything you accuse yourself of. Take the thing at its worst! I refuse to consider that she ever allowed her fancy to stray from her duty, but suppose that you *were* in love with her, in that unconscious way you imagine: who was hurt, who was deceived by it? What harm was done? I will go farther, and ask what harm was there, even if you knew you were in love with her? You let no one else know it—her, least of any." The words, when I had got them out, shocked me; they certainly did not represent my own feeling about such a situation; I was glad my wife had not heard them; and I saw the horror of me that came into Nevil's face. I felt myself getting hot and red, and I hastened to add, "You will forgive me, if I try to put before you the mere legal, practical, matter-of-fact view of the affair"; and I could not help remembering that it was also the romantic view, which I had found celebrated in many novels, as something peculiarly fine and noble and high, something heroic in the silently suffering lover. "I admit that I have no right to speak to you at all—"

"Go on; I invite you to speak," he said gently.

"Then I will say that my only desire is to—to—how shall I say it?—urge that this is altogether an affair of the future, and that if you allow the unhappy past, which is dead, and ought to be buried with Faulkner, to dominate you, or to shape your relations, you seem to me to be—"

I found myself talking sophistries, and I had nothing to say when he took up the word where I broke off.

"Recognizing the fact that the future is the creature, the mere consequence of the past! Without what has been, nothing can be. Oh, we have looked at it in every light! At first, when she told me, I was as bold, as defiant, as a man can be who finds himself unjustly defamed. I said that if ever we had felt reluctance or doubt in our allegiance to the dead, now it was our right, our duty to feel none. We should accuse ourselves if we admitted that any accusal could lie against us. The very innocence of our lives demanded vindication; we should be recreant to our good consciences if we did not treat that wretched figment of a dreaming craze as it deserved. For a moment—for an hour—we were happy in the escape which my defiance won for us, and we built that future without a past, which you think can stand. It fell to ruin. We had deceived each other, but the deceit could not last. Our very indignation at the treason imputed to us by Faulkner's dream made us examine our hearts, and question each other. We could not tell when our love began, and that mystery of origin which love partakes of with eternity, and which makes it seem so divine a thing, became a witness against us. We said that if we could not make sure that no thought we had ever had of each other in his lifetime was false to him, then we were guilty of all, and we must part."

"Oh," I groaned out, "what mere madness of the moon!"

"It was not I who pronounced our sentence; she saw herself that it must be so; it was she who sent me from her."

"Yes; only a woman could be capable of it, could be such a moral hypochondriac! But if she sent you away, and you know, as you must know, that in her heart she wished you to stay, why not in Heaven's name go back to her?"

"Ah, you think I didn't go back! You think we parted once only! We parted a hundred times!"

"But," I said, "you will see it all differently to-morrow, and you must go back to her, and whether she bids you go or not, you must never leave her."

"And what sort of life would that be? A life of defiance, of recklessness, a mere futureless present! I am a priest of the Church, and I teach submission, renunciation, abnegation, here below, where there can be no true happiness, for the sake of a blessed eternity. Shall I cleave to this love which we feel cannot innocently be ours, and preach those things with my lying tongue, while my life preaches rebellion, indulgence, self-will? Every breath I drew would be hypocrisy. What heart should I have to counsel or admonish others in temptation, when I was all rotten within myself? What—"

"Ah, but only listen a moment! This would be all well enough if you were guilty of what you accuse yourself! But don't you see that in this reasoning, or this raving, of yours, you have violated the very first principle, the very highest principle of law? You have held yourself guilty till you were proven innocent, and you offer no proof that you are guilty, not the least proof in the world. You are only *afraid* that you are guilty; it amounts to that, and it amounts to nothing more; for I hold that Faulkner's crazy jealousy forms no manner of case against you. I confess that though I may have seemed to imply the contrary, I should not feel it lawful for you to marry his widow if you had ever allowed yourself to covet his wife. But you never did; the very notion of such a thing fills you with such shame and horror that you accuse yourself of it. I know that kind of infernal juggle of the morbid conscience; but I thank Heaven I have my own conscience in such good training now that it accuses me of nothing I haven't done; it finds it has quite enough to do in dealing with the facts; I don't supply it with any fancies! It ought to be on your conscience not to leave that noble and beautiful creature to be the prey of doubts and fears, of ifs and ands, that will blast her whole life with the shame of a thief who has given up his booty to escape punishment! Suppose you look at that side of it! You say you left her because she bade you, but she bade you only because she knew you believed you ought to go; and now you must go back to her not only for her sake and for your sake, but in the interest of human enlightenment, from the duty every educated man has to resist the powers of darkness that work upon our nerves through the superstitions of the childhood of the world. You not only ought not to let Faulkner's dream have any deterrent influence with you, but, as you saw yourself, exactly and entirely because of his dream you ought to act in defiance of it, if you have the good conscience which you've said nothing yet to prove you haven't."

I saw that I had touched some points that had escaped him; we talked a long time, and at last I pulled out my watch in a scare, lest I had overstaid my time. I jumped to my feet. "Good heavens! I've lost my train!"

Nevil looked at his watch. "You have Eastern time; there's nearly a whole hour yet. I'll go to the station with you."

I would not sit down again. "Suppose, then, we let the driver take my bag, and we walk? We can talk better."

"You are very good," he said; "I should like that."

The night was dark, and we had the seclusion of a room for our talk, as we walked along together; and in the vast depot, starred with its gas jets far overhead, there was an unbroken sense of communion. Long before we parted, Nevil had consented to revise his own conclusions, and so far to take my view of the situation as at least to see Hermia again, and lay it before her.

My spirits rose with my success, and I set myself to cheer the melancholy in which he assented to my urgence. I understood afterward that he was yielding to reason against that perverse and curious apparatus which we call the conscience; and I perceived that he was loath to have me leave him, as if he were afraid to be left alone, or wished to be still farther convinced. He followed me into the sleeping car, and there he fell into the hands of that rich and cordial parishioner of his whom I remembered meeting when I went down to the steamer at East Boston to see Nevil off for Europe. The gentleman recalled himself to my recollection, and rejoiced that we were to be fellow-travellers as far as Albany.

Nevil could not hide his disappointment and vexation from me, though his parishioner did not see it. He made us both light cigars with him in the smoking-room, and he talked us silent.

The car began to move, and I said, "Well, good-by," and followed Nevil out upon the platform for a last word. "Remember your promise! Better get off!"

"Oh, I sha'n't forget that. If I live, I will see her again, and tell her all you have said. And I thank you—thank you—" Clinging to my hand, he pressed it hard, and stepped backward from the car to the ground. I saw him look up at me, and then he gave a wild cry, and I could feel the car grinding him up against the stone jamb of the archway through which the train was passing. There was a hideous crashing sound from his body, and I jumped at the bell-rope. The train stopped; Nevil stood upright, with his face turned toward the light, and a strange effect of patience in his attitude. When the train slowly backed and set him free, he dropped forward a crushed and lifeless lump.

IX

HERMIA DIED a year later, and was buried by Faulkner's side; his mother lived on for several years.

It was inevitable, of course, that Hermia should accept Nevil's death as a judgment; we become so bewildered before the mere meaninglessness of events, at times, that it is a relief to believe in a cruel and unjust providence rather than in none at all. What is probably true is that she sank under the strain of experiences that wrung the finest and most sensitive principles of her being, or, as we say, died of a broken heart.

My wife and I have often talked of her and Nevil, and have tried to see some way for them out of the shadow of Faulkner's dream into a sunny and happy life. As they are both dead, we have dealt with them as arbitrarily as with the personages in a fiction, and have placed and replaced them at our pleasure in the game, which they played so disastrously, so that we could bring it to a fortunate close for them. We have always denied, in the interest of common-sense and common justice, any controlling effect to the dream itself, except through their own morbid conscientiousness, their exaggerated sensibility. We know people, plenty of them, who would have been no more restrained from each other by it than by a cobweb across their path: Hermias who would never have told their Nevils of it; Nevils who, if they had known it, would have charged their Hermias on their love to spurn and trample upon it. That evil dream had power upon the hapless pair who succumbed to it only because they were so wholly guiltless of the evil imputed to them.

Our Nevil's death, violent and purely accidental as it was, seemed to us a most vague and inconclusive catastrophe, and no true solution of the problem. Yet our Hermia being what she was, and Nevil being Nevil, we saw that it was impossible Faulkner's dream should not have always had power upon them; and the time came when we could regard their death without regret. I myself think that if Nevil had seen Hermia again, as he promised me, it would have been only to renew in her and in himself their strength for renunciation; and I have sometimes imagined a sort of dramatic friendship taking the place of their love, and uniting their lives in good works, or something of that kind. But I have not been satisfied with this conception; it is too like what I have found carried out in some very romantic novels; and my wife has always insisted that if they had met again, they would have married, and been unhappy. She insists that they could not have kept their self-respect and their perfect honor for each other, if they had married. But this again seems abominably unfair: that they should suffer so for no wrong; unless, indeed, all suffering is to some end unknown to the sufferer and the witnesses, and no anguish is wasted, as that friend of Nevil's believed. We must come to some such conclusion; or else we must go back to a cruder theory, and say that they were all three destined to undergo what they underwent, and that what happened to them was not retribution, not penalty in any wise, since no wrong had been done, but simply fate.

Of course there is always the human possibility that the dream was a divination of facts; that Hermia and Nevil were really in love while Faulkner lived, and were untrue to him in their hearts, which are the fountains of potential good and evil; but knowing them to be what they were, we have never admitted this hypothesis for a moment. For any one to do so, my wife says, would be to confess himself worse than Faulkner dreamed them to be. She does not permit it to be said, or even suggested, that our feelings are not at our bidding, and that there is no sin where there has been no sinning.

THE END

Notes to the Text

7.1 ff.   From Wordsworth, "Ode: Intimations of Immortality," stanza 2.

31.16–18   'In a dream . . .': Job, XXXIII, 15.

43.15–16   in the twinkling of an eye: I Corinthians, XV, 52.

49.30   C'était magnifique: a paraphrase of the famous remark attributed to Marshal Bosquet at the time of the Charge of the Light Brigade at the Battle of Balaclava in the Crimean War, 25 October 1854.

59.13–14   laid the measures of it, or stretched the line upon it: Job, XXXVIII, 5.

86.16   From Goldsmith, "The Deserted Village," l. 4.

TEXTUAL APPARATUS

Textual Commentary

No manuscript or proof stage of *The Shadow of a Dream* is known to exist. The text was first printed in *Harper's Monthly* in three installments between March and May 1890. Howells' British publisher, David Douglas of Edinburgh, prepared the first book edition (BAL 9650) in a single impression which was listed in the *Athenæum* on 24 May 1890 and noted as "now ready" on 31 May. The first American impression of this edition (BAL 9651) appeared under the imprint of Harper and Brothers in New York, also in 1890. Three different formats have been identified: the Franklin Square Library paperbound series, deposited for copyright on 31 May 1890; the standard Harper hardbound format, in red cloth stamped in gilt; and a remainder binding of red cloth stamped in black ink.[1] The Harper records indicate that the first printing consisted of 1,500 copies, but do not specify format.[2] At least one later impression was made of this edition, in 1899, without any textual changes. Finally, David Douglas prepared a Pocket Edition, in his shilling series of "American Authors," with a first printing of 3,000 copies on 13 November 1890,

---

1. The editors of *BAL* theorize that the three formats may represent distinct impressions. Machine collation has disclosed two states of one page, which may possibly distinguish impressions: all copies in the remainder format which we have examined have one full page (196) which is a resetting, without textual changes, of the plate used in the Douglas first edition and the other two Harper formats.

2. Harper Memorandum Books, 1887–1891, p. 75. The records are in the "Treasure Chest" at Harper & Row, Publishers; for a discussion of these materials, see Edwin and Virginia Price Barber, "A Description of Old Harper and Brothers Publishing Records Recently Come to Light," *Bulletin of Bibliography*, XXV (1967), 1–6, 29–34, 39–40. In a letter to Thomas Sergeant Perry on 9 September 1890 Howells reported that so far sales of the book were nearly eight thousand copies (MS at Duke University).

though the book carries a title-page date of 1891.[3] The only later impression was made in 1901, without any textual changes, some copies containing sheets from the first impression. No other editions were called for during Howells' lifetime.[4]

The text of the first book edition was probably set in type by Douglas from proof of the *Harper's Monthly* text, in accordance with Howells' normal practice of the time of having plates made by Douglas both to secure British copyright (which required setting and deposit of text in Great Britain before publication anywhere else) and to obtain plates at a lower cost to himself. After Douglas had plated the type and used these plates to print his first book edition, he sent them to the United States, where Harper in turn used them for the American impressions.[5] The Pocket Edition, however, was a completely new setting prepared by Douglas from his first-edition printing.

Examination of the texts and information about Howells' working methods make it clear that the magazine version of *The Shadow of a Dream* should be copy-text for the present edition: it is the extant text closest to Howells' hand, and the closest therefore to his most clearly

---

3. These figures are drawn from the records of T. & A. Constable, London, and are cited with the permission of P. J. W. Kilpatrick.

4. The "Bibliographical" introduction containing details about *The Shadow of a Dream*, which Howells wrote about 1909 for the proposed Library Edition of his works to be published by Harper, has not been considered part of the present text because it was intended for a collection of stories dealing with Basil and Isabel March, and not for *The Shadow of a Dream* only; see George Arms, "Howells's Unpublished Prefaces," *NEQ*, XVII (1944), 585–587.

The following printed items, including at least first and last known impressions, were collated in the preparation of the present text: copies of *Harper's Monthly* in the Indiana University and University of California at Santa Barbara libraries; copies of the first Douglas edition, BAL 9650, in the British Museum (012632.m.30), the Library of Congress (PS3.H84sh) and the Bodleian Library (2712.e.387); copies of the 1890 Harper printing, BAL 9651, in the Indiana University (PS2025.S5), University of Illinois (813.H83s, copy 3), University of California at Los Angeles (PS2025.S52), Newberry (Case Y, 255.H8745) and Lilly (PS2025.S5 1890) libraries, and of the 1899 re-impression in the University of Chicago (PS2025.S54 1899) and University of California at Berkeley (955.H859sh) libraries; copies of the Douglas Pocket Edition, 1891, in the British Museum (12703.de.32) and in the University of Michigan (828.H86.sh2) and Bodleian (2712.f.197) libraries, and of the 1901 re-impression in the Northwestern (813.4 H85sh) and McGill (YF H833sh) libraries.

5. According to his general contract with Harper and Brothers, Howells supplied the plates for his own books, in return for a higher royalty on sales; for *The Shadow of a Dream* he received a 20% royalty on sales of the hardbound copies and 12½% on the paperback.

realized intentions in accidentals—spelling, punctuation, and other stylistic refinements. We have reproduced this text, in all but its visual appurtenances (type-style, styling of section and paragraph openings, spacing of indentations, the use of capitals and lower-case letters in running titles and section titles), in the present edition, incorporating into it the substantive changes in the book editions which appear to have Howells' authority.[6]

Howells made several such changes—typically in single words or short phrases—when he prepared the first Douglas text, which also introduced some corruptions in substantives and a good many in accidentals. Before the Harper edition was printed from these same plates, he made further revisions in substantives and one revision in accidentals (at 67.24). These revisions constitute all the differences between the first Douglas printing and the Harper text, and all appear to have Howells' authority; so far as we can tell, the Harper editors made no independent changes in the text.[7] The Pocket Edition, which derives from the first Douglas edition, does not contain the readings which Howells introduced into the Harper plates, and evidences further corruption in both substantives and accidentals.

All variants from the magazine copy-text in the book texts which have been accepted as authorial in the present text are recorded in the Emendations list. In addition, this list records emendations of accidentals which seemed necessary to clarify meaning. The first text which reflects changes of the latter sort is cited as their source, but only for documentary reasons, not because Howells is thought to have made them. The non-authorial substantive variants of the book editions are listed in Rejected Substantives.

D.J.N.

---

6. This text therefore accords with both the intention and the practices outlined in the Center for Editions of American Authors, *Statement of Editorial Principles: A Working Manual for Editing Nineteenth Century American Texts*, July 1967.

7. In addition to preparing new title, copyright and colophon pages for their printings, Harper and Brothers did make a minor styling change in the format of the text by removing from the chapter opening pages of the plates the page numbers which had appeared in the Douglas first edition.

Emendations

The following list records all substantive and accidental changes introduced into the copy-text. The reading of the present edition appears to the left of the bracket; the authority for that reading, followed by a semicolon, copy-text reading, copy-text symbol, and variant substantive readings in intermediate texts and their symbols appear to the right of the bracket. The curved dash ~ represents the same word that appears before the bracket and is used in recording punctuation variants. Occasionally changes in accidentals have been made on the authority of the Howells Edition, with the first book edition which records them cited as their source, though these editions of course have no general authority for accidentals; that is, an edition is cited because it is the first to incorporate a change and not because the change is thought to have resulted from Howells' intervention. *Om.* means that the reading to the left of the bracket does not appear in the text cited to the right of the semicolon. The reading of any text which falls between the copy-text and the authority cited for the present edition may be assumed to agree substantively with the copy-text reading if not listed; accidental variants in these uncited texts have not been recorded here. The abbreviation HE indicates emendation made on the authority of the Howells Edition.

The following texts are referred to:

S   *Harper's Monthly,* LXXX (March–May 1890)
A   David Douglas, 1890: First Edition
B   Harper and Brothers, 1890
C   David Douglas, 1891: Pocket Edition

5.5	smokiness] A; duskiness S
8.33	hospitality,] A; ~ S
12.17	came] A; ~, S
13.4	smokiness] A; duskiness S

14.27–28   Her figure . . . while] B; This was still almost pathetically present in the *embonpoint* to which she tended, and S

14.31–33   The beauty . . . which] B; Her hair was a dull black; her tint a rose under brown; her eyes S

15.5   clear] A; calm S

22.12–16   a regular . . . . looks—"] B; an undulating walk, and he doesn't tilt his head a little on one side as if it were a heavy rose; and he hasn't got a complexion of russet crimsoned; and his hair isn't thick and dull black and fluffy over the forehead; and he isn't round and strong and firm." S

23.7   put] A; say S

32.2   me] A; ~, S

34.26   me, "and he yielded to it,] A; me—"if it persisted, S

35.6   ands] HE; ans S

59.27   fate] A; ~, S

62.12   agony] B; anguish S

62.13   anguish] B; agony S

67.24   me—] B; ~ S

82.20   sumptuous] A; luxurious S

83.34   import] B; grossness S

84.1   splendor] B; ripeness S

84.1   a most regal] B; her sumptuous S

84.11–12   finely, too purely] B; purely, too finely S

87.23   kept on nervously consuming] B; himself nervously had consumed S

87.24   had] B; *om.* S

87.24   talked.] A; ~ S

88.12   obtuseness] B; bluntness S

100.15   art.] A; ~ ; S

111.30   of ifs] B; ifs S

114.7–8   so wholly] B; *om.* S; themselves A

114.8   evil] A; evil it S

114.10   vague] B; squalid S

114.28   Nevil's] A; Nevil S

114.29   else] A; else we feel that S

Rejected Substantives

The following list records all substantive variants in editions published after copy-text and rejected as non-authorial in the present text. The reading of the present edition appears to the left of the bracket; the authority for that reading, followed by a semicolon, the variant reading and its source appear to the right of the bracket. *Om.* means that the reading to the left of the bracket does not appear in the text cited to the right of the semicolon. The reading of any unlisted text, other than copy-text, may be presumed to agree with the reading to the left of the bracket, unless recorded in Emendations. If the authority cited for the reading of the present text is other than copy-text, the reading of the copy-text and any text which falls between it and the authority for the present reading are recorded in Emendations.

The following texts are referred to:

S   *Harper's Monthly*, LXXX (March–May 1890)
A   David Douglas, 1890: First Edition
B   Harper and Brothers, 1890
C   David Douglas, 1891: Pocket Edition

7.15	shoulder] S; shoulders A–C
13.14	shoulder] S; shoulders A–C
14.27–28	Her figure . . . while] B; This was still almost pathetically present in the *embonpoint* to which she tended, and C
14.31–33	The beauty . . . which] B; Her hair was a dull black; her tint a rose under brown; her eyes C
19.14	called] S; call A–C
20.9	expressions] S; expression A–C
21.13	a] S; *om.* A–C
22.12–16	a regular . . . . looks—"] B; an undulating walk, and he doesn't tilt his head a little on one side as if it were a heavy rose; and he hasn't got a complexion of russet crimsoned; and his hair isn't thick and dull black and

fluffy over the forehead; and he isn't round and strong and firm." C

27.4	work] S; word A–C
32.35	with] S; with a A–C
42.16–17	how. ¶ Dr. Wingate] S; how. Dr. Wingate A–C
49.8	ask you only] S; only ask you A–C
49.33	you to] S; you A–C
50.8	You] S; I suppose you A–C
57.1	hands] S; hand C
62.12	agony] B; anguish C
62.13	anguish] B; agony C
62.20	I] S; *om.* A–C
63.8	suppose] S; supposed C
75.31	with somebody else forever] S; for ever with somebody else A–C
77.1	railroad] S; railway A–C
83.34	import] B; grossness C
84.1	splendor] B; ripeness C
84.1	a most regal] B; her sumptuous C
84.11–12	finely, too purely] B; purely, too finely C
85.26	inspirations] S; inspiration A–C
87.23	kept on nervously consuming] B; himself nervously had consumed C
87.24	had] B; *om.* C
87.27	after years] S; after-years A–C
88.12	obtuseness] B; bluntness C
91.12–13	Faulkner. ¶ "I] S; Faulkner. "I A–C
95.12	him] S; him even A–C
98.10	Faulkners'] S; Faulkners A–C
102.17	and they] S; but they A–C
111.12	yourself] S; yourself of A–C
111.30	of ifs] B; ifs C
111.30	ands] S; ans B
114.7–8	so wholly] B; themselves C
114.10	vague] B; squalid C
114.27	and] S; or A–C

Word-Division

List A records compounds or possible compounds hyphenated at the end of the line in copy-text and resolved as hyphenated or one word as listed below. If Howells' manuscripts of this period fairly consistently followed one practice respecting the particular compound or possible compound, the resolution was made on that basis. Otherwise his *Harper's* or other periodical texts of this period were used as guides. List B is a guide to transcription of compounds or possible compounds hyphenated at the end of the line in the present text: compounds recorded here should be transcribed as given; words divided at the end of the line and not listed should be transcribed as one word.

LIST A

6.7	foredoomed
10.11	newspapers
19.34–20.1	sea-breeze
27.6–7	heart-break
27.27	in-drawn
29.9	grape-vine
29.27	nightmares
36.7	seaward
37.19	overtake
38.1	clam-shells
40.9	simple-hearted
45.34	cold-hearted
47.35	-in-law
48.3	daughter-in-
56.12	infare
57.2	piecemeal
58.13–14	manhood
61.31–32	newspapers
68.16	handwriting
68.25	disordered
70.2	spellbound
70.33	door-knob
74.17	foreshadowed

84.1	womanhood
86.17	box-bordered
100.33	supersensuous
104.11–12	commonplace
106.18	self-accusers
109.26	matter-of-
110.23	lifetime
112.19	overhead

LIST B

4.31	matter-of-
5.7	loose-hung
19.34	sea-breeze
22.12	two-horse
27.6	heart-break
27.16	pruning-knife
28.32	-there-before
38.1	sea-weed
38.24	self-sacrifice
49.28	self-reproach
58.16	mother-in-
61.6	second-hand
108.12	ever-repeated
108.27	scandal-mongering

An Imperative Duty

Introduction

An Imperative Duty

IN a notebook entry of 1883 William Dean Howells set down the title "The Letters of Olney." In another, undated notebook filled with incidents, some of which were eventually worked into *Indian Summer*, he wrote, "In Town out of Season—Might be a thing in autobiographic form of young man rich, cultivated, well-born who notices all these handsome negroes we saw last summer, and falls in love with an octoroon."[1] From these notebook entries emerged *An Imperative Duty*.

Long before these jottings of the early 1880's, the novel—which was not to appear as a serial until 1891—had been prepared for. Like most of his literary works, *An Imperative Duty* expressed the social conscience Howells had known from childhood. It also gave him the occasion to express ideas less overtly social and more complexly psychological that had been coming in growing force to the surface of his consciousness in the 1880's.

The strong Abolitionist leanings of both sides of Howells' family gave his reason standards of conduct toward the oppressed

1. The 1883 notebook (which also includes the title "The Shadow of a Dream") is at the Houghton Library at Harvard University. Just which summer Howells refers to in the undated notebook (also at the Houghton) is uncertain, but a letter of 27 October 1885 (microfilm at Duke University) suggests the preceding months when the Howellses stayed at a fashionable hotel kept by a family of octoroons in Woodland Park, Auburndale, Massachusetts.

Permission to quote unpublished passages from the notebooks and letters written by Howells has been granted by William White Howells for the heirs of the Howells Estate. Permission to quote from other unpublished letters owned by Harvard has been granted by the Harvard College Library. Republication of this material also requires these permissions. The manuscripts of all letters cited are at Harvard unless otherwise noted.

Negro;[2] but a small boy growing up in the Hamilton, Ohio, of the pre-war years was stirred more by emotions than reason. Howells the boy understood only that there was "an impassable gulf" between the races; Howells the adult admitted "it would not be easy to give a notion" of how the white boys felt toward the town's Negroes.[3] The same boy who paid proud allegiance to the radical Whig cause which his family upheld to the point of martyrdom became part of a night mob set against a Negro rumored to have struck a white boy, and then—alone in that same dark night, afraid of ghosts—was ready to welcome "the company of the lowest-down black boy in town."[4] Even after Howells the adult walked the straight, well-lighted path of rational good-will in regard to the Negro, he did not lose sight of the fact that boys and men respond with their pulses to the matter of race. Of more psychological interest to us than the condemnations of the slave system uttered by the enthusiastic young man[5] is the awareness by the self-probing older man of the ambivalent responses to the kinds of blackness the bewildered boy encountered that night in Hamilton, Ohio.

Howells' first careful literary look at the Negro came after the Civil War when the black race was legally free but not assimilated into white culture. "Mrs. Johnson," which appeared in the *Atlantic Monthly* of January 1868, seems a pleasant "suburban sketch" about the quaint ways and easy-going nature of a Negro cook hired in Cambridge by the Howellses. More importantly it is an examination, however brief, of what it is about the Negroes that white America did not—and feared to—assimilate. The

---

2. *Years of My Youth* (New York and London, 1916), pp. 12 and 15, and *A Boy's Town* (New York, 1890), pp. 11, 126, and 131.

3. *A Boy's Town*, pp. 229–230.

4. *A Boy's Town*, pp. 129–130.

5. Howells' youthful Abolitionist fervor found partial outlet in letters written to his father during the John Brown episode, in his poem "Old Brown" which appeared in the Ashtabula *Sentinel* of January 1860, and in "The Pilot's Story," a melodramatic poem about an abused octoroon, which appeared in the *Atlantic Monthly* in September of the same turbulent year. In these instances, as in *A Chance Acquaintance* of 1873 where he sketched in a personal history of Abolitionist martyrdom, Howells stressed the effect of the Negroes' plight upon white men who suffer directly or vicariously out of a sense of sympathetic brotherhood.

Negro possessed passion, and it was passion which the nine-
teenth-century white had been tutored to repress. In Mrs. Johnson Howells detected those primitive, wild traits he suspected
lay within himself and all men. It was the concern over the hidden
connection between the savage inner self and the civilized outer
man which attracted Howells increasingly as the years passed,
rather than the social inequalities that clearly showed themselves
upon the surface of life.

For all his lasting, deep-rooted interest, it was not until the
1880's that Howells turned toward making the implications for
psyche and society represented by the Negro part of a full-scale
literary work. In 1886 he signed an important contract with
Harper and Brothers which committed him to the writing of a
yearly novel which was first to appear serially in *Harper's Monthly*.
In writing Howells on 10 February 1886 to acknowledge the fif-
teenth of the month as the start of this new relationship, H. M.
Alden indicated that the firm wished to have "The Letters of
Olney" before "A Little Swiss Journey." After that the Olney
story is not mentioned for over four years. The appearance of
The Minister's Charge and *Indian Summer*, the writing of *April Hopes*
and *Annie Kilburn*, Winifred Howells' illness and death, the Hay-
market Riots, and Howells' work on *A Hazard of New Fortunes*,
The Shadow of a Dream, and *A Boy's Town* intervened.

Suddenly, out of the silence covering the long-delayed proj-
ect, Howells wrote Hamlin Garland on 27 August 1890 that he
was at work on the novelette, now entitled *An Imperative Duty;* he
judged (erroneously) that it would be longer than *The Shadow of
a Dream*.[6] Alden wrote Howells on 8 September to tell him that
Harper's could not say definitely when the novelette would appear
in serial form. The magazine had to plan for two other new
serials, but Alden hoped Howells would concur with a July 1891
starting date for *An Imperative Duty*. On the next day Howells
wrote T. S. Perry that he was nearing completion of his fiction;[7]

6. MS at University of Southern California Library.
7. MS at Duke University Library.

within two weeks he had finished, and announced to Henry James on 25 September that he was through with his contracted writing for the year, with three months of leisure ahead as his reward.[8] Alden had not received the manuscript by 13 November, however, and pressed Howells to send it along for possible illustration.[9] By 14 April 1891 Alden was planning within the week to send Howells the first part of the serial for revision; by 7 May David Douglas in Edinburgh acknowledged Howells' letter of 25 April and receipt of the first part of the novelette due for British publication. A further letter from Alden on 14 May called Howells' attention to the need to adjust the number of parts and length of each so that *Harper's* might not be overweighted by the simultaneous appearance of his novelette and a longer story by George Du Maurier. But on the whole *An Imperative Duty* was prepared for its serial appearance in America with a fortunate minimum of fuss and an unfortunate paucity of commentary on the part of its author.

The book publication of *An Imperative Duty*, both in England and America, had a chequered history. In his letter of 7 May 1891 David Douglas wrote to Howells,

> I have sent it to avoid an hours delay to the printer reserving that pleasure [of reading it] until it comes back in proof— which will also be sent to you as fast as it can be set up. Now comes the question can we have it printed & electrotyped in time to ship from this country by June 15th so as to secure entry in the States before July 1st the date at which this one sided "International" Copyright Bill becomes law?

The answer proved no. Douglas wrote on 2 October that he could not meet the deadline imposed by the new law that penalized

---

8. *Life in Letters of William Dean Howells*, ed. Mildred Howells (Garden City, N.Y., 1928), II, 7.

9. *Harper's* finally chose not to illustrate Howells' novelette but provided lavish drawings for the George Du Maurier and Mary Murfree serials which were running simultaneously in the magazine. Perhaps it was a matter of economy that kept Howells' characters from receiving representational form; perhaps it was delicacy over the question of how to show Rhoda Aldgate's strange, dusky beauty.

American books whose type was set abroad. Only thirty-two pages intended for Howells' use in an American edition had been completed, so Douglas gave up the attempt, even though he proceeded with plans to include *An Imperative Duty* in his "American Authors" series for British distribution.

Meanwhile, Howells was keeping his eye upon the plans for the American publication of *An Imperative Duty*. On 26 July 1891 he wrote Harper and Brothers to clarify in advance certain matters concerning royalties and publication dates for both *An Imperative Duty* and *The Quality of Mercy*, then running in serial form. "I had thought of suggesting that you should publish both books together; but *An I.D.* is making so much more impression than I expected that it seems a pity to risk losing any interest it has aroused, by such a delay."[10] No sales records remain for *An Imperative Duty* to substantiate the results of Howells' pleased claim. Even the novelette's subsequent printing history is uncertain. Several new printings of the American and the English editions were called for soon after its publication, but whatever success *An Imperative Duty* enjoyed was fleeting. No new edition was feasible between 1903 and the Twayne Edition of 1962 (in conjunction with *The Shadow of a Dream*).

No manuscript exists of *An Imperative Duty*, but an examination of the revisions made between the magazine serialization and the Harper first edition of 14 November 1891 gives no evidence that Howells' attitude changed toward his main characters.[11] However, the notebook entries of 1883 and 1886 indicate that before writing the original version he changed his mind about how to present the materials. References to "The Letters of Olney" and the story's "autobiographic form" show that Howells initially considered using first-person narrative so that love for a girl with part Negro blood might be seen as it directly affected her white lover. When or why Howells decided to use the third-person

---

10. The letter is part of the "Treasure Chest" collection retained by Harper & Row, Publishers.

11. The publishing date is that given by *A Bibliography of William Dean Howells* compiled by William M. Gibson and George Arms (New York Public Library, 1948).

narrative form is unknown, but one can conjecture that he recognized that to fix the subject within Olney's consciousness alone would greatly limit its possibilities. Olney's reactions to Rhoda Aldgate before and after he learns of her racial antecedents are kept simply to those of a white man with certain quick mental adjustments to make. Far more interesting than Olney's conventionally manly responses are the observations the authorial voice makes in depicting Rhoda. Even when her innocent image of herself is shattered, Rhoda's reactions are still those of a white woman, cruelly at odds with that other dark part of herself cast suddenly into psychological exile.

Once Howells got into his narrative and completed the magazine serial, it appears he knew how he would present his characters, as well as the kind of testing incidents he would pass them through. However, he made a number of changes in wording between the two versions of the opening chapters; although falling to the side of the central issue, these changes deserve notice by the way they point up a general attitude toward alien races and cultures.

In the serial version sharply worded phrases degrade the Irish who fill Boston's summer streets, while paternalistically elevating the Negroes in the opinions delightedly shared by Olney and Rhoda Aldgate. The many references made and the vehemence of tone used to describe this influx that mark the *Harper's Monthly* version are underscored by their absence in the first edition. In a letter of 17 July 1891 to his sister Aurelia, Howells referred to his annoyance over the "noise" being made concerning the slurs against the Irish in the first part of the *Harper's* serial. "They can't see that it is not I who felt and said what Olney did." This confusion of Howells with Olney, however, may have been sufficient reason for Howells to make the revisions that either drop references to the Irish altogether or suggest that "hard work and hard circumstances" are extenuating causes for their unpleasing appearance and manner. But as Olney's antipathy toward the Irish is removed, a way of indicating by contrast his high regard for Negroes is also removed.

The problems attendant upon how a decent White Anglo-Saxon Protestant ought to feel toward the two alien races of Irish and Negro were somehow merged in Howells' mind. (The Irish beat the Chinese in California as others beat Negroes, he noted editorially.[12] The Howells family replaced shiftless Irish servants with the Negress, Mrs. Johnson.) Howells had long been free of overt prejudices against the Negro, but he was aware of how closely his anti-Irish attitudes matched those of his generation. He was ashamed of his essentially illogical reactions, and he never forgot the rebuke James Russell Lowell gave him concerning the "grudge (a mean and cruel grudge, I now think it)" that Howells held against the Irish.[13] It is revealing, therefore, that these passions appear strongly in the magazine serial—even though under Olney's name—and are just as decisively cut out in the New York book edition. The novelette gains its main power from its recognition of how akin all men are psychologically, whether white or Negro. It also adds as a kind of fleeting footnote: akin, whether Yankee or Irish.

The handful of reviewers who made note of *An Imperative Duty* thought they knew clearly what the novelette was about and, in general, sharply objected to what they saw. The *Critic* (16 January 1892, p. 34) stated that the story was a failure, probably due to Howells' "ignorance of the subject." "He likes the race . . . as the Princess Napraxine likes the wolves in Russia—in theory and at a distance. Brought into actual contact with these people, the inference is that he would dislike them cordially without the excuse of 'having injured them.' " The *Nation* (25 February 1892, p. 154) was more moderate, and intelligent, in its objections; but even while praising "that lucidity, force, and grace which give to all Mr. Howells's stories a rare distinction," it had doubts whether the solutions offered (moral duty or love) would work in the very peculiar circumstances depicted. The Boston *Literary World* (5 December 1891, p. 470) also hedged its praise.

---

12. Review of *The New West: or California in 1867* by Charles Loring Brace in the *Atlantic Monthly*, XXIV (August 1869), 259.

13. *Literary Friends and Acquaintance* (New York and London, 1901), p. 219.

Recognition of the importance of the problem the novelette faced, of the maturity of approach, and of the presence of Howells' characteristic "acuteness and cleverness" is tempered by an involved belaboring of Howells' intense self-consciousness and hypercritical view. The last line writes off this, and all Howells' novels, with: "Mr. Howells is no more an artist of the first order than Henry James. He lacks the eye for color and the heart sympathies. He works by rule, and the result is the product of high talent, but not of genius."

In Great Britain, the *Dublin Review* was not impressed; the London *Literary World*, the *Athenæum* and the *Westminster Review* gave passing faint praise; and the *National Observer* missed the point badly as it dwelt upon the ways Howells treated "the feeling about Negroes as a different and inferior race which is ineradicable in the minds of white people who have any considerable experience of them."[14]

Perhaps the most interesting of the immediate responses came from David Douglas in Edinburgh. Douglas did more than glance at the proof-sheets that crossed his desk during the autumn of 1891 in preparation for the British publication of *An Imperative Duty*. "This powerfully touches and deals with a social difficulty of vast importance and one requiring careful handling," Douglas wrote Howells on 2 October. "A few years ago a painful story dealing with the same subject was sent to me, the joint production of a white & a coloured man. The authors could not find a publisher in America and asked me to take charge of it here . . . ." That story's sadness and the exaggeration of its telling led him to fear "it would stir up the bad passions" of both races. In contrast to the novel he rejected, Howells' version was "eminently impartial." Douglas planned to include it in his shilling series even though "ashamed to say I share in the Race antipathy . . . ." Others in Great Britain shared his antipathy without his honesty. Both the British reviews and the letter from Douglas' office that

---

14. The *Dublin Review*, 1 April 1892, p. 464; London *Literary World*, 25 December 1891, p. 554; *Athenæum*, 3355 (13 February 1892), 210–211; *Westminster Review*, CXXXVII (February 1892), 224; *National Observer*, 2 January 1892, pp. 176–177.

reported on 21 January 1892 that the novelette "has not as yet taken with our public" make the book's critical and public failure amply clear.

The relationship between a white man of "pure blood" and his beloved tainted by the lack of such purity which *An Imperative Duty* offered as its narrative line threatened those of Howells' readers with prejudices to burn. It irritated others because of the uniqueness of the case or the perverse emotional attitude that the author, via Olney, seemed to take toward it; that is, the literary values of the story were too often tested on grounds of supposed emotional or social realism and judged a failure of taste at worst and a passing aberration at best. A comparison of Howells' novelette with "Was it an Exceptional Case?" by Miss Matt Crims (which appeared in *In Beaver Cove and Elsewhere* in 1892) demonstrates the greatly different ways that materials of an extraordinarily similar nature can be handled—with psychological realism in Howells' case and a most ludicrous sentimentality and evasion on Miss Crims' part.

Howells' public role in assuming part of the white man's burden in the historical struggle of the Negro for his social rights is a significant one; it continually found expression, whether he was giving editorial praise for the lives of Booker T. Washington and Frederick Douglass, championing Paul L. Dunbar's poetic career, or adding his signature to the petition which led to the founding of the NAACP.[15] Howells' social efforts are rightly studied for the extra-literary light they shed on earlier cultural relationships between Negroes and white men that were con-

---

15. See *Harper's Weekly*, 27 June 1896, for Howells' review of Dunbar's *Majors and Minors* in the "Life and Letters" department; letter to Ripley Hitchcock of 29 July 1896 (MS at Columbia University); Howells' introduction of "Lyrics of Lowly Life," *The Complete Poems of P. L. Dunbar* (New York, 1921); letter from Alphonso Stafford of 10 August 1896; reviews of life studies of Booker T. Washington and Frederick Douglass, "An Exemplary Citizen," *North American Review*, CLXXIII (1901), 280–288; the final sentence of *Familiar Spanish Travels* (New York and London, 1913). Also see W. E. B. Du Bois' tribute to Howells, Boston *Transcript*, 24 February 1912 (Part III, p. 2); Calvin Kytle, "The Story of the NAACP," *Coronet*, XL (August 1956), 140–146; and James B. Stronks, "Paul Laurence Dunbar and William Dean Howells," *The Ohio Historical Quarterly*, LXVII (1958), 95–108.

sidered enlightened at the turn of the century. Of far greater importance, however, to the understanding of Howells' ever-advancing movements as a novelist is our awareness of the ways he increasingly sought out social situations which would initiate exploration of his characters' psychological lives; the situations were perhaps *outré*, but the explorations revealed the common-ness of the passions depicted. In doing so Howells sometimes placed himself in a vulnerable position among those of his reading public who were more deserving than he of the pejorative label "genteel." *An Imperative Duty* is one of the first of the fictions that made Howells' public queasy over the insistence that it stop evading the facts of its humanity. It is in this respect that *An Imperative Duty* takes its prophetic place in Howells' writing career.

M. B.

An Imperative Duty

I

OLNEY got back to Boston about the middle of July, and found himself in the social solitude which the summer makes more noticeable in that city than in any other. The business, the hard work of life, was going on, galloping on, as it always does in America, but the pleasure of life, which he used to be part of as a younger man, was taking a rest, or if not a rest, then certainly an outing at the sea-shore. He met no one he knew, and he continued his foreign travels in his native place, after an absence so long that it made everything once so familiar bewilderingly strange.

He had sailed ten days before from Liverpool, but he felt as as if he had been voyaging in a vicious circle when he landed, and had arrived in Liverpool again. In several humiliating little ways, Boston recalled the most commonplace of English cities. It was not like Liverpool in a certain civic grandiosity, a sort of lion-and-unicorn spectacularity which he had observed there. The resemblance appeared to him in the meanness and dulness of many of the streets in the older part of the town where he was lodged, and in the littleness of the houses. Then there was a curious similarity in the figures and faces of the crowd. He had been struck by the almost American look of the poorer class in Liverpool, and in Boston he was struck by its English look. He could half account for this by the fact that the average face and figure one meets in Boston in midsummer is hardly American; but the other half of the puzzle remained. He could only conjecture an approach from all directions to a common type among those who work with their hands for a living; what he had seen in Liverpool and now saw in Boston was not the English type or the American type, but the proletarian type. He noticed it especially in the women, and more especially in the young girls, as he met them in the street after their day's work was done, and on the first Sunday afternoon following his arrival, as he saw them in the Common. By far the greater part of those listening to the brass band which was then beginning to vex the ghost of our poor old Puritan Sabbath there, were given away by their accent for those primary and secondary Irish who abound with us. The old women were strong, sturdy, old-world peasants, but the young girls were thin and crooked, with pale, pasty complexions, and an effect of physical delicacy from their hard work and hard conditions, which might later be physical refinement. They were conjecturably out of box factories and clothier's shops; they went about in threes or fours, with their lank arms round one another's waists, or lounged upon the dry grass; and they seemed fond of wearing red jerseys, which accented every fact of their anatomy. Looking at them scientifically, Olney thought that if they survived to be mothers they might give us, with better conditions, a race as hale and handsome as the elder American race; but the transition from the Old World to the New, as represented in them, was painful. Their voices were at once coarse and weak; their walk was uncertain, now awkward and now graceful, an undeveloped gait; he found their bearing apt to be aggressive, as if from a wish to ascertain the full limits of their social freedom, rather than from ill-nature, or that bad-heartedness which most rudeness comes from.

But, in fact, Olney met nowhere the deference from beneath that his long sojourn in Europe had accustomed him to consider politeness. He was used in all public places with a kindness mixed with roughness, which is probably the real republican manner: the manner of Florence before the Medici; the manner of Venice when the Florentines were wounded by it after the Medici corrupted them; the manner of the French when the

Terror had done its work. Nobody proved unamiable, though everybody seemed so at first; not even the waiters at his hotel, where he was served by adoptive citizens who looked so much like brigands that he could not help expecting to be carried off and held somewhere for ransom when he first came into the dining-room. They wore immense black mustaches or huge whiskers, or else the American beard cut slanting from the corners of the mouth. They had a kind of short sack of alpaca, which did not support one's love of gentility like the conventional dress-coat of the world-wide waiter, or cheer one's heart like the white linen jacket and apron of the negro waiter. But Olney found them, upon what might be called personal acquaintance, neither uncivil nor unkind, though they were awkward and rather stupid. They could not hide their eagerness for fees, and they took an interest in his well-being so openly mercenary that he could scarcely enjoy his meals. With two of those four-winged whirligigs revolving on the table before him to scare away the flies, and working him up to such a vertigo that he thought he must swoon into his soup, Olney was uncomfortably aware of the Irish waiter standing so close behind his chair that his stomach bulged against it, and he felt his breath coming and going on the bald spot on his crown. He could not put out his hand to take up a bit of bread without having a hairy paw thrust forward to anticipate his want; and he knew that his waiter considered each service of the kind worth a good deal extra, and expected to be remembered for it in our silver coinage, whose unique ugliness struck Olney afresh.

He would not have been ready to say that one of the negro waiters, whom he wished they had at his hotel, would not have been just as greedy of money; but he would have clothed his greed in such a smiling courtesy and such a childish simple-heartedness that it would have been graceful and winning. He would have used tact in his ministrations; he would not have cumbered him with service, as from a wheelbarrow, but would have given him a touch of help here, and a little morsel of attention there; he would have kept aloof as well as alert. That is, he would have had all these charms if he were at his best, and he would have had some of them if he were at his worst.

In fact, the one aspect of our mixed humanity here which struck Olney as altogether agreeable in getting home was that of the race which vexes our social question with its servile past, and promises to keep it uncomfortable with its civic future. He had not forgotten that, so far as society in the society sense is concerned, we have always frankly simplified the matter, and no more consort with the negroes than we do with the lower animals, so that one would be quite as likely to meet a cow or a horse in an American drawing-room as a person of color. But he had forgotten how entirely the colored people keep to themselves in all public places, and how, with the same civil rights as ourselves, they have their own neighborhoods, their own churches, their own amusements, their own resorts. They were just as free to come to the music on the Common that Sunday afternoon as any of the white people he saw there. They could have walked up and down, they could have lounged upon the grass, and no one would have molested them, though the whites would have kept apart from them. But he found very few of them there. It was not till he followed a group away from the Common through Charles Street, where they have their principal church, into Cambridge Street, which is their chief promenade, that he began to see many of them. In the humbler side-hill streets, and in the alleys branching upward from either thoroughfare, they have their homes, and here he encountered them of all ages and sexes. It seemed to him that they had increased since he was last in Boston beyond the ratio of nature; and the hotel clerk afterward told him there had been that summer an unusual influx of negroes from the South.

He would not have known the new arrivals by anything in their looks or bearing. Their environment had made as little impression on the older inhabitants, or the natives, as Time himself makes upon persons of their race, and Olney fancied that Boston did not characterize their manner, as it does that of almost every other sort of aliens. They all alike seemed shining with good-nature and good-will, and the desire of peace on earth. Their barbaric taste in color, when it flamed out in a crimson necktie or a scarlet jersey, or when it subdued itself to a sable that left no gleam of white about them but a point or rim of shirt collar, was invariably delightful to him; but he had to own that their younger people were often dressed with an innate feeling for style. Some of the young fellows were very effective dandies of the type we were then beginning to call dude, and were marked by an ultra correctness, if there is any such thing; they had that air of being clothed through and through, as to the immortal spirit as well as the perishable body, by their cloth gaiters, their light trousers, their neatly buttoned cutaway coats, their harmonious scarfs, and their silk hats. They carried on flirtations of the eye with the young colored girls they met, or when they were walking with them they paid them a court which was far above the behavior of the common young white fellows with the girls of their class in refinement and delicacy. The negroes, if they wished to imitate the manners of our race, wished to imitate the manners of the best among us; they wished to be like ladies and gentlemen. But the young white girls and their fellows whom Olney saw during the evening in possession of most of the benches in the Common and the Public Garden, and between the lawns of Commonwealth Avenue, apparently did not wish to be like ladies and gentlemen in their behavior. The fellow in each case had his arm about the girl's waist, and she had her head at times upon his shoulder; if the branch of a tree overhead cast the smallest rag or tatter of shadow upon them, she had her head on his shoulder most of the time. Olney was rather abashed when he passed close to one of these couples, but they seemed to suffer no embarrassment. They had apparently no concealments to make, nothing to be ashamed of; and they had really nothing to give them a sense of guilt. They were simply vulgar young people, who were publicly abusing the freedom our civilization gives their youth, without knowing any better, or meaning any worse. Olney knew this, but he could not help remarking to the advantage of the negroes, that among all these couples on the benches of the Common and the Garden and the Avenue he never found a colored couple. He thought that some of the young colored girls, as he met them walking with their decorous beaux, were very pretty in their way. They had very thin, high, piping voices that had an effect both of gentleness and gentility. With their brilliant complexions of lustrous black, or rich *café au lait*, or creamy white, they gave a vividness to the public spectacle which it would not otherwise have had, and the sight of these negroes in Boston somehow brought back to Olney's homesick heart a sense of Italy, where he had never seen one of their race.

II

OLNEY was very homesick for Italy that Sunday night. After two days in Boston, mostly spent in exploring the once familiar places in it, and discovering the new and strange ones, he hardly knew which made him feel more hopelessly alien. He had been five years away, and he perceived that the effort to repatriate himself must involve wounds as sore as those of the first days of exile. The tissues then lacerated must bleed again before his life could be reunited with the stock from which it had been torn. He felt himself unable to bear the pain; and he found no attraction of novelty in the future before him. He knew the Boston of his coming years too well to have any illusions about it; and he had known too many other places to have kept the provincial superstitions of his nonage and his earlier manhood concerning its primacy. He believed he should succeed, but that it would be in a minor city, after a struggle with competitors who would be just, and who might be generous, but who would be able, thoroughly equipped, and perfectly disciplined. The fight would be long, even if it were victorious; its prizes would be hard to win, however splendid. Neither the fight nor the prizes seemed so attractive now as they had seemed at a distance. He wished he had been content to stay in Florence, where he could have had the field to himself, if the harvest could never have been so rich. But he understood, even while he called himself a fool for coming home, that he could not have been content to stay without first coming away.

When he went abroad to study, he had a good deal of money, and the income from it was enough for him to live handsomely on anywhere; in Italy it was enough to live superbly on. But the friend with whom he left his affairs had put all of Olney's eggs into one basket. It was the Union Pacific basket which he chose, because nearly every one in Boston was choosing it at the same time, with the fatuous faith of Bostonians in their stocks. Suddenly Olney's income dropped from five or six thousand a year to nothing at all a year; and his pretty scheme of remaining in Italy and growing up with the country in a practice among the nervous Americans who came increasingly abroad every year had to be abandoned, or at least it seemed so at the time. Now he wished he had sold some of his depreciated stock, which everybody said would be worth as much as ever some day, and taken the money to live on till he could begin earning some. This was what Garofalo, his friend and fellow-student in Vienna, and now Professor of the Superior Studies at Florence, urged him to do; and the notion pleased him, but could not persuade him. It was useless for Garofalo to argue that he would have to get the means of living in Boston in some such way, if he went home to establish himself; Olney believed that he should begin earning money in larger sums if not sooner at home. Besides, he recurred to that vague ideal of duty which all virtuous Americans have, and he felt that he ought, as an American, to live in America. He had been quite willing to think of living in Italy while he had the means, but as soon as he had no means, his dormant sense of patriotism roused itself. He said that if he had to make a fight, he would go where other people were making it, and where it would not seem so unnatural as it would in the secular repose of Florence, among those who had all put off their armor at the close of the sixteenth century. Garofalo alleged the intellectual activity everywhere around him in science, literature, philosophy. Olney could not say that it seemed to him a life referred from Germany, France, and England, without root in Italian soil; but he could answer that all this might very well be without affording a lucrative practice for a specialist in nervous diseases, who could be most prosperous where nervous diseases most abounded.

The question was joked away between them, and in the end there never seemed to have been any very serious question of Olney's staying in Florence. Now, if there had not been really, he wished there really had been. Everything discouraged him, somehow; and no doubt his depression was partly a physical mood. He had never expected to find people in town at that time in the summer, or to begin practice at once; he had only promised himself to look about and be suitably settled to receive the nervous sufferers when they began to get back in the fall. Yet the sight of all those handsome houses on the Back Bay, where nervous suffering, if it were to avail him, must mainly abide, struck a chill to his spirit; they seemed to repel his intended ministrations with their barricaded doorways and their close-shuttered windows. His failure to find Dr. Wingate, with whom he had advised about his studies, and with whom he had hoped to talk over his hopes, was peculiarly disheartening, though when he reasoned with himself he saw that there was an imperative logic in Wingate's absence; a nervous specialist of his popularity must, of course, have followed nervous suffering somewhere out of town. Still it was a disappointment, and it made the expense of Olney's sojourn seem yet more ruinous. The hotel where he had gone for cheapness was an old house kept on the American plan; but his outgo of three dollars a day dismayed him when he thought of the *arrangiamento* he could have made in Florence for half the money. He determined to look up a boarding-house in the morning; and the thought of this made him almost sick.

Olney was no longer so young as he had been; we none of us are as young as we once were; but all of us have not reached the great age of thirty, as he had, after seeming sweetly destined to remain forever in the twenties. He belonged to a family that became bald early, and there was already a thin place in the hair on his crown, which he discovered one day when he was looking at the back of his head in the glass. It was shortly after the Union Pacific first passed its dividend, and it made him feel for the time decrepit. Yet he was by no means superannuated in other respects. His color was youthfully fresh; his soft, full beard was of a rich golden red; what there was of his hair—and there was by no means little except in that one spot—was of the same mellow color, which it would keep till forty, without a touch of gray. His figure had not lost its youthful slimness, and it looked even fashionable in its clothes of London cut; so that any fellow-countryman who disliked his air of reserve might easily have passed him by on the other side, and avoided him for a confounded Englishman.

He sat on the high-pillared portico of the hotel, smoking for a half-hour after he returned from his evening stroll, and then he went to his room, and began to go to bed. He was very meditative about it, and after he took off his coat, he sat on the edge of the bed, pensively holding one shoe in his hand, until he could think to unlace the other.

III

THERE CAME a shattering knock at his door, such as rouses you in the night when the porter mistakes your number for that of the gentleman he was to call at four. Olney shouted, "Come in!" and sat waiting the result, with his shoe still in his hand. The door opened, and one of those Irish faces showed itself.

"Are you a doctor, sor?"

"Yes."

"Ahl right."

The face was withdrawn, and the door was closing, when Olney called out: "Why? What of it? Does any one want me?"

"I don't know, sor. There's a lady in Twenty-wan that sah your name in the paper; but she said not to disturb ye if ye wahsn't a doctor."

"A lady?" said Olney. He rapidly reasoned that the lady, whoever she was, had found his name printed in the Sunday papers among the arrivals at that hotel, and that she must have some association with it. "Is she ill? Does she know me?"

"I don't know, sor," said the man, with an air of wishing to conceal nothing. "She don't be in bed, annyway."

Olney reflected a moment, hesitating between a certain vexation at being molested with this ridiculous message and a vague curiosity to find out who the lady could be. As a man, he would have wished to know who any unknown woman could be; as a man of science he divined that this unknown woman was probably one of those difficult invalids who have to be coaxed into anything decisive, even sending for a doctor; this tentative question of hers must represent ever so much self-worry and a high degree of self-conquest.

"Tell her, yes, I'm a doctor," he said to the man. He added, for purposes of identification, "Doctor Edward Olney." He thought for an instant he would send his card; but he decided this would be silly.

"Ahl right, sor. Thank ye, sor," said the man.

He went away, and Olney put on the shoe he had taken off, and got into his coat again. He expected the man back at once, and he wished to be ready, but the messenger did not come for ten or twelve minutes. Then he brought Olney a note, superscribed in a young-lady-like hand, and diffusing when opened a perfume which was instantly but indefinitely memoriferous. Where had he last met the young lady who used that perfume, so full of character, so redolent of personality? The mystery was solved by the note, and all the pleasure of the writer's presence returned to him at the sight of her name.

"DEAR SIR,—My aunt, Mrs. Meredith, is so very far from well, that she asks me to write for her, and beg you to come and see her. She hopes she is not mistaken in thinking it is Dr. Olney whom she met at Professor Garofalo's in Florence, last winter; but if it is not, she trusts you will pardon the intrusion, otherwise unwarrantable at such an hour.

Yours very truly,

RHODA ALDGATE."

"Where is the room?" Olney demanded, putting the note into his breast pocket, and taking up his hat. He smiled to think how much less distinctive the diction was than the perfume; he fancied that Miss Aldgate had written down her aunt's words, which had a formality alien to the nature of the young girl he remembered so agreeably. As he followed along through the apparently aimless corridors, up and down short flights of steps that seemed to ascend at one point only to descend at another, he recalled the particulars of her beauty: her slender height, her rich complexion of olive, with a sort of under-stain of red, and the inky blackness of her eyes and hair. Her face was of almost classic perfection, and the hair, crinkling away to either temple, grew low upon the forehead, as the hair does in the Clytie head. In profile the mouth was firmly accented, with a deep cut outlining the full lower lip, and a fine jut forward of the delicate chin; and the regularity of the mask was farther relieved from insipidity by the sharp wing-like curve in the sides of the sensitive nostrils. Olney recalled it as a mask, and he recalled his sense of her wearing this family face, with its somewhat tragic beauty, over a personality that was at once gentle and gay. The mask, he felt, was inherited, but the character seemed to be of Miss Aldgate's own invention, and expressed itself in the sunny sparkle of her looks, that ran over with a willingness to please and to be pleased, and to consist in effect of a succession of flashing, childlike smiles, showing between her red lips teeth of the milkiest whiteness, small, even, and perfect. These looks, the evening he remembered first meeting her and her aunt, were employed chiefly upon a serious young clergyman sojourning in Florence after a journey to the Holy Land. But they were not employed coquettishly so much as sympathetically, with a readiness for laughter that broke up the inherited mask with a strange contradictory levity. Olney was himself immersed in a long and serious analysis of *Romola* with the aunt, who appeared to have a conscience of prodigious magnifying force, cultivated to the last degree by a constant training upon the ethical problems of fiction. She brought its powerful lenses to bear upon the most intimate particles of Tito's character; his bad qualities seemed to give her almost as much satisfaction as if they had been her own. In knocking at Mrs. Meredith's door, he now remembered how charmingly that pretty little head of Miss Aldgate's, defined by the black hair with its lustrous crinkle, was set upon her shoulders.

IV

THE YOUNG GIRL herself opened the door, and faced him first with the tragic family mask. Then she put out her hand to him with the personal gayety he had recalled. Her laugh, so far as it bore upon the situation, recognized rather the good joke of their finding themselves all in an American hotel together than expressed anxiety for her aunt's condition. It was so glad and free, in fact, that Olney was surprised to find Mrs. Meredith looking quite haggard on the sofa, from which she reached him her hand without attempting to rise.

"Isn't it the most fortunate thing in the world," said Miss Aldgate, "that it should *really* be Dr. Olney? We couldn't believe it when we saw it in the paper!" she added; and now Olney perceived that the laugh which he might have thought indifferent, was a laugh of happy relief, of trust that since it was he, all must go well.

"Yes, it is indeed," said Mrs. Meredith; but she had none of the gayety in putting the burden upon Olney, under Providence, which flashed out in her niece's smile; she appeared to doubt whether Providence and he could manage it, and to relinquish it with misgiving. "There were so many chances against it that it scarcely seemed possible." She examined Olney's face, which had at once begun to hide the professional opinion he was forming, and seemed to find comfort in its unsmiling strength. "And I hated dreadfully to trouble you at such an hour."

"I believe there's no etiquette as to the time of a doctor's visits," said Olney, pulling a chair up to the sofa, and looking down at her. "I hope, if things go well after I'm settled here, to be called up sometimes in the middle of the night, though ten o'clock isn't bad for my second day in Boston." Miss Aldgate laughed with instant appreciation of his pleasantry, and Mrs. Meredith wanly smiled. "You must be even more recent than I am, Mrs. Meredith. I'm afraid that if I had found your names in the register when I signed mine, I should have ventured to call unprofessionally. But then it would very likely have been some other Mrs. Meredith."

Miss Aldgate laughed again, and Olney gave her a look of the kindness a man feels for any one who sees his joke. She dropped upon the chair at the head of the sofa, and invited him with dancing eyes to say some more of those things. But Mrs. Meredith took the word.

"We only got in this morning. That is, the steamer arrived too late last night for us to come ashore, and we drove to the hotel before breakfast. You must be rather surprised to find us in such a place."

"Not at all; I'm here myself," said Olney.

"Oh!" Miss Aldgate laughed.

"I don't assume," he added, "that you came here for cheapness, as I did. At the hotels on the European plan, as they call it, they charge you as much for a room as they do for room and board together here."

"Everything is very expensive," sighed Mrs. Meredith. "We paid three dollars for our carriage from the ship; and I believe it's nothing to what it is in New York. But it's a great while since I've been in Boston, and I told them to bring me here because I'd heard it was an old-fashioned, quiet place. I felt the need of rest, but it seems very noisy. It was very smooth all the way over; but I was excited, and I slept badly. The last two or three nights I've scarcely slept at all."

"Hmm!" said the doctor, feeling himself launched upon the case.

Miss Aldgate rose.

"My dear," said her aunt, "I wish you would look up the prescription the ship's doctor gave me. I was thinking of sending out to have it made up, but I shouldn't wish to try it now unless Dr. Olney approves."

Olney profited by Miss Aldgate's absence to feel Mrs. Meredith's pulse and look at her tongue. He asked her a few formal questions. He was a little surprised to find her so much better than she looked.

"You seem a little upset, Mrs. Meredith," he said. "You may be suffering from suppressed seasickness, but I don't think it's anything worse." He tried to treat the affair lightly, and he added: "I don't see why you shouldn't be on good terms with sleep. You know Tito slept very well, even with a bad conscience."

Mrs. Meredith would not smile with him at the recurrence to their last conversation. She sighed, and gave him a look of tragical appeal. "I sometimes think he had an enviable character."

"Or temperament," Olney suggested. "There doesn't seem to have been much question of character. But he was certainly well constituted for getting on in a world where there was no moral law—if he could have found such a world."

"Then you do believe there *is* such a law in *this* world?" Mrs. Meredith demanded, with an intensity that did not flatter Olney he had been light to good purpose.

He could not help smiling at his failure. "I would rather not say till you had got a night's rest."

"No, no," she persisted. "Do you believe that any one can rightfully live a lie? Do you believe that Tito was ever really at rest when he thought of what he was concealing?"

"He seems to have been pretty comfortable, except when Romola got at him with her moral nature."

"Ah, don't laugh!" said Mrs. Meredith. "It isn't a thing to laugh at."

Miss Aldgate came in, with a scrap of paper fluttering from her slim hand, and showing her pretty teeth in a smile so free of all ethical question that Olney swiftly conjectured an anxiety of Mrs. Meredith concerning a nature so apparently free of all personal responsibility as the young girl looked at that moment. He was aware of innocently rejoicing in this sense of her, which came from the goodness and sweetness which she looked as much as the irresponsibility. It might be that Mrs. Meredith had lost sleep in revolving the problems of Miss Aldgate's character, and the chances of her being equal to the duties that had left so little of Mrs. Meredith. If such an aunt and such a niece were formed to wear upon each other, as the ladies say, it was clear that the niece had worn the most. With this thought evanescently in mind, Olney took the prescription from her.

He read it over, but he did not perceive that the sense of it had failed to reach his mind till Mrs. Meredith said,

"If it is one of those old-fashioned narcotics—he called it a sleeping draught—I would rather not take it."

Though Olney had not been thinking of the prescription, he now pretended that he had. "It would be rather a heroic dose for a first-cabin passenger," he said; "though it might do for the steerage." He took out his pocket-book and wrote a prescription himself. "There! I think that ought to get you a night's rest, Mrs. Meredith."

"I suppose we can get it made up?" she said, irresolutely, lifting herself a little on one elbow.

"I'll take it out and have it done myself," said Olney. "There's an apothecary's just under the hotel."

He rose, but she said: "I can't let you be at that trouble. We can send. Will you—"

"I will ring, Aunt Caroline," said Miss Aldgate, and she ran forward to press the electric button by the door.

The bell was answered by the same man who came to call the doctor to Mrs. Meredith. Miss Aldgate took the prescription, and rapidly explained to him what she wanted. When she had finished, he looked up from the prescription at Olney with a puzzled face.

Olney smiled and Miss Aldgate laughed. The man had not understood at all.

"You know the apothecary's shop under the hotel?" Olney began.

"Yes, I know that forst-rate, sor."

"Well, take that paper down and give it to the apothecary, and wait till he makes up the medicine, and then bring it back to us."

"This paper, sor?"

"No; the medicine."

"And lave the paper wid um?"

"Yes. The apothecary will give you the medicine and keep the prescription. Do you understand?"

"Yes, sor."

"Well?"

"Is the 'pot'ecary after havin' the prescription now, sor?"

Olney took the paper out of his hand and shook it at him. "This paper—this—is the prescription. Do you understand?"

"Yes, sor."

"Take it to the apothecary—"

"The man under the hotel, sor?"

"Yes, the one under the hotel. This prescription—this paper—give it to him; and he will make up a medicine, and give it to you in a bottle; and then you bring it here."

"The bottle, sor?"

"Yes, the bottle with the medicine in it."

"Ahl right, sor! I understand, sor!"

The man hurried away down the corridor, and Miss Aldgate shut the door and broke into a laugh at sight of Olney's face, red and heated with the effort he had been making.

Olney laughed too. "If the matter had been much simpler, I never should have got it into his head at all!"

"They seem to have *no* imagination!" said the girl.

"Or too much," suggested Olney. "There is something very puzzling to us Teutons in the Celtic temperament. We don't know where to have an Irishman. We can predicate of a brother Teuton that this will please him, and that will vex him, but we can't of an Irishman. You treat him with the greatest rudeness and he doesn't mind it; then you propose to be particularly kind and nice, and he takes fire with the most bewildering offence."

"I *know* it," said Miss Aldgate. "That was the way with all our cooks in New York. Don't you remember, aunty?"

Mrs. Meredith made no answer, and

"We can't call them stupid," Olney went on. "I think that as a general thing the Irish are quicker-witted than we are. They're sympathetic and poetic far beyond us. But they can't understand the simplest thing from us. Perhaps they set the high constructive faculties of the imagination at work, when they ought to use a little attention, and mere common-sense. At any rate they seem more foreign to our intelligence, our way of thinking, than the Jews—or the negroes even."

"Oh, I'm glad to hear you say that about the negroes," said Miss Aldgate. "We were having a dispute this afternoon," she explained, "about the white waiters here and the colored waiters at the Hotel Vendome. I was calling on some friends we have there," and Miss Aldgate flushed a little as she said this; "or rather, they came here to see us, and then I drove back with them a moment; and it made me quite homesick to come away and leave those black waiters. Don't you think they're charming? With those soft voices and gentle manners? My aunt has no patience with me; she can't bear to have me look at them; but I never see one of them without loving them. I suppose it's because they're about the first thing I can remember. I was born in the South, you know. Perhaps I got to having a sort of fellow-feeling with them from my old black nurse. You know the Italians say you do."

She turned vividly toward Olney, as if to refer the scientific point to him, but he put it by with a laugh.

"I'm afraid I feel about them as Miss Aldgate does, Mrs. Meredith; and I hadn't an old black nurse, either. I've been finding them delightful, wherever I've seen them, since I got back." Miss Aldgate clapped her hands. "To be sure, I haven't been here long enough to get tired of them."

"Oh, I should *never* tire of them!" said the girl.

"But so far, certainly, they seem to me the most agreeable, the most interesting feature of the social spectacle."

"There, Aunt Caroline!"

"I must confess," Olney went on, "that it's given me a distinct pleasure whenever I've met one of them. They seem to be the only people left who have any heart for life here; they all look hopeful and happy, even in the rejection from their fellow-men, which strikes me as one of the most preposterous, the most monstrous things in the world, now I've got back to it here."

Mrs. Meredith lay with her hand shading her eyes and half her face. She asked, without taking her hand away, "Would you like to meet them on terms of social equality—intermarry with them?"

"Oh, now, Aunt Caroline!" Miss Aldgate broke in. "Who's talking of anything like that?"

"I certainly am not," said Olney, "as far as the intermarrying is concerned. But short of that I don't see why one shouldn't associate with them. There are terms a good deal short of the affection we lavish on dogs and horses that I fancy they might be very glad of. We might recognize them as fellow-beings in public, if we don't in private; but we ignore, if we don't repulse them at every point—from our business as well as our bosoms. Yes, it strikes one as very odd on getting home—very funny, very painful. You would think we might meet on common ground before our common God—but we don't. They have their own churches, and I suppose it would be as surprising to find one of them at a white communion table as it would to find one at a white dinner party."

Olney said this without the least feeling about the matter, except a sense of its grotesqueness. He was himself an agnostic, but he could be as censorious of the Christians who denied Christ in the sacrament, as if he had himself been a better sort. He added:

"Possibly the negroes would be welcome in a Catholic church; the Catholics seem to have kept the ideal of Christian equality in their churches. If ever they turn their attention to the negroes—"

"Oh, I can't imagine a colored Catholic," said Miss Aldgate. "There seems something unnatural in the very idea."

"All the same, there are a good many of them."

"In Boston?"

"No, not in Boston, I fancy."

Mrs. Meredith had taken no farther part in the conversation;

she lay rigidly quiet on her sofa, with her hand shading her eyes.

There was a knock at the door, and Miss Aldgate sprang to open it, with the effect of being glad to work off her exuberant activity, in that or any other way: with Mrs. Meredith so passive, and Olney so acquiescent, the discussion of the race problem was not half enough for her.

The man was there, with the bottle from the apothecary's, and he and Miss Aldgate had a beaming little interview. He exulted in getting back with the medicine all right, and she gratefully accepted his high sense of his offices, and repaid him his outlay, running about the room, and opening several trunks and bags to find her purse, and then added something for his trouble.

"Dear me!" she said, when she got rid of him, "I wish they wouldn't make it *quite* so clear that they expected to be 'remembered.' They've kept my memory on the *qui vive* every moment I've been in the hotel."

Olney smiled in sympathy as he took the bottle from her. "I've found it impossible to forget the least thing they've done for me, and I never boasted of my memory."

She stood watching his examination of the label of the bottle, and his test of its contents from a touch of the inner tip of the cork on his tongue. "A spoon? I've got one here in aunty's medicine chest. It would have cost its weight in silver to get one from the dining-room. And there happens to be ice-water, if you have to give it in water. *Don't* say water without ice!"

"Ice-water will do," said Olney. He began to drop the medicine from the bottle into the spoon, which he then poured into the glass of water she brought him. "I believe," he said, stirring it, "that if the negroes ever have their turn—and if the meek are to inherit the earth they must come to it—we shall have a civilization of such sweetness and good-will as the world has never known yet. Perhaps we shall have to wait their turn for any real Christian civilization."

"You remember the black Madonna at Florence that used to be so popular? What Madonna was it? I suppose they will revere *her* when they get to be all Catholics. Were you in any of their churches to-day? You were saying—" Miss Aldgate put out her hand for the glass.

"No; I never was in a colored church in my life," said Olney. "I'm critical, not constructive, in my humanity. It's easier."

He went himself with the glass to Mrs. Meredith. She seemed not to have been paying any attention to his talk with her niece. She lifted herself up at his approach, and took the glass from him.

"Shall I drink it all?"

"Yes—you can take all of it."

She quaffed it at one nervous gulp, and flung her head heavily down again. "I don't believe it will make me sleep," she said.

Olney smiled. "Well, fortunately, this kind doesn't require the co-operation of the patient. It will make you sleep, I think. You may try keeping awake, if you like."

She opened her eyes with a flash. "Is it chloral?"

"No, it isn't chloral."

"Tell me the truth!" She laid a convulsive clutch upon his wrist, as he sat fronting her and curiously watching her. "I will not let you justify yourself by that code of yours which lets the doctor cheat his patient! If you have been giving me some form of chloral—"

"I haven't been giving you any form of chloral," said Olney, beginning to smile.

"Then you are trying to hypnotize me!"

Olney burst into a laugh. "You certainly need sleep, Mrs. Meredith! I'll look in during the forenoon about the time you ought to wake, and de-hypnotize you." He moved toward the door; but before he reached it he stopped and said, seriously: "I don't know of any code that would allow me to cheat you, against your will. I don't believe any doctor is justified in doing that. Unless he has some sign, some petition for deception, from the patient, you can depend upon it that he finds the truth the best thing."

"It's the only thing—at all times—in life and death!" cried Mrs. Meredith, perfervidly. "If I were dying, I should wish to know it!"

"And I *shouldn't* wish to know it!" said Miss Aldgate. "I think there are cases when the truth would be cruel—positively wicked! Don't you, Dr. Olney?"

"Well," said Olney, preparing to escape through the door which he had set open, "I couldn't honestly say that I think either of us is in immediate danger. Good-night!"

V

OLNEY DID NOT go to see Mrs. Meredith until noon, the next day. He thought that if she were worse, or no better, she would send for him, and that if she did not send, he might very well delay seeing her. He found her alone. Miss Aldgate, she said, had gone to drive with their friends at the Vendome, and was to lunch with them. Olney bore her absence as politely as he could, and hoped Mrs. Meredith had slept.

"Yes, I slept," she said, with a kind of suppressed sigh, "but I'm not sure that I'm very much the better for it."

"I'm sure you are," said Olney, with resolute cheerfulness; and he began to go through with the usual touching of the pulse, and looking at the tongue, and the questions that accompany this business.

Mrs. Meredith broke abruptly away from it all. "It's useless for us to go on! I've no doubt you can drug me to sleep whenever you will. But if I'm to wake up, when I wake, to the trouble that's on my mind, the sleep will do me no good."

She looked wistfully at him, as if she longed to have him ask her what the matter was; but Olney did not feel authorized to do this. He had known, almost from the first moment he met Mrs. Meredith, the night before, that she had something on her mind, or believed so, and that if she could tell him of her trouble, she would probably need no medicine; but he had to proceed, as the physician often must, upon the theory that only her body was out of order, and try to quiet her spirit through her nerves, when the true way was from the other direction. It went through his mind that it might be well for the nervous specialist hereafter to combine the functions of the priest and the leech, especially in the case of nervous ladies, and confess his patients before he began to prescribe for them.

But he could not help feeling glad that things had not come to this millennial pass; for he did not at all wish to know what Mrs. Meredith had on her mind. So much impression of her character had been left from their different meetings in Florence that he had already theorized her as one of those women, commoner amongst us than any other people, perhaps, to whom life, in spite of all experience, remains a sealed book, and who are always trying to unlock its mysteries with the keys furnished them by fiction. They judge the world by the novels they have read, and their acquaintance in the flesh by characters in stories, instead of judging these by the real people they have met, and more or less lived with. Such women get a tone of mind that is very tiresome to every one but other women like them, and that is peculiarly repulsive to such men as Olney, or if not repulsive, then very ridiculous. In Mrs. Meredith's case he did not so much accuse her of wishing to pose as a character with a problem to work out; there was nothing histrionic about the poor woman; but he fancied her hopelessly muddled as to her plain, every-day obligations by a morbid sympathy with the duty-ridden creatures of the novelist's brain. He remembered from that first talk of the winter before—it had been a long talk, an exhaustive talk, covering many cases of conscience in fiction besides that of Tito Melema—that she had shown herself incapable of sinking the sense of obligation in the sense of responsibility, and that she apparently conceived of what she called living up to the truth as something that might be done singly; that right affected her as a body of positive color, sharply distinguished from wrong, and not shading into and out of it by gradations of tint, as we find it doing in reality. Such a woman, he had vaguely reflected, when he came to sum up his impressions, would be capable of an atrocious cruelty in speaking or acting the truth, and would consider herself an exemplary person for having done her duty at any cost of suffering to herself and others. But she would exaggerate as well as idealize, and he tried to find comfort now in thinking that what she had on her mind was very likely a thing of bulk out of all proportion to its weight. Very likely it was something with reference to her niece; some waywardness of affection or ambition in the girl. She might be wanting to study medicine, or law, or divinity; perhaps she wanted to go on the stage. More probably, it was a question of whom she should marry, and Mrs. Meredith was wrestling with the problem of how far in this age of intense individualization a girl's inclinations might be forced for her good, and how far let go for her evil. Such a problem would be quite enough to destroy Mrs. Meredith's peace if that was what she had on her mind; and Olney could not help relating his conjecture to those people at the Vendome, whom Miss Aldgate had gone to drive with and lunch with to-day, after having been to drive with them yesterday. Those people in turn he related to the young clergyman she had spent the evening in talking with in Florence, when he was himself only partially engaged in exploring her aunt's conscience. He wondered whether Mrs. Meredith favored or opposed the young clergyman, and what was just the form of the trouble that was on her mind, but still without the intention to inquire it out.

"Well, perhaps," he suggested, half jocosely, "the trouble will disappear when you've had sleep enough."

"You know very well," she answered, "that it won't—that what you say is simply impossible. I remember some things you said that night when we talked so long together, and I know that you are inclined to confound the moral and the physical, as all doctors are."

Olney would have liked to say, "I wish, my dear lady, you wouldn't confound the sane and insane in the way you do." But he silently submitted, and let her go on.

"That made me dislike you; but I can't say it made me distrust you. I think that if you had been an untruthful person you would have concealed your point of view from me."

Olney could not say he might not have thought it worth while to do that. On the contrary, he had a sort of compassion for the lofty superiority of a woman who so obviously felt her dependence upon him, and was arming herself in all her pride for her abasement before him. He knew that she was longing to tell him what was on her mind, and would probably not end till she had done it. He did not feel that he had the right to prevent her doing that, and he smiled passively in saying, "I couldn't advise you to trust me too far."

"I must trust *some* one too far," she said, "and I have literally no one but you." The tears came into her eyes, and Olney, who knew very well how easily the tears come into women's eyes, was broken up by the sight.

"My dear Mrs. Meredith, I should be very glad to be trusted even too far, if I could really be of use to you."

"Oh, I don't know that you can," she said. After a pause she added, abruptly, "Do you believe in heredity?"

Olney felt inclined to laugh. "Well, that's rather a spacious question, Mrs. Meredith. What do you mean by heredity?"

"You know! The persistence of ancestral traits; the transmission of character and tendency; the reappearance of types after several generations; the—"

She stopped, and Olney knew that he had got at the body of her anxiety, though she had not yet revealed its very features. He determined to deal with the matter as reassuringly as he could in the dark. He smiled in answering, "Heredity is a good deal like the germ theory. There's a large amount of truth in it, no doubt; but it's truth in a state of solution, and nobody knows just how much of it there is. Perhaps we shall never know. As for those cases of atavism—for I suppose that's what you mean—"

"Yes, yes! Atavism! That is the word."

"They are not so very common, and they're not so very well ascertained. You find them mentioned in the books, but vaguely, and on a kind of hearsay, without the names of persons and places; it's a notion that some writers rather like to toy with; but when you come to boil it down, as the newspapers say, there isn't a great deal of absolute fact there. Take the reversion to the inferior race type in the child of parents of mixed blood—say a white with a mulatto or quadroon—"

"Yes!" said Mrs. Meredith, with eagerness.

"Why, it's very effective as a bit of drama. But it must be very rare—very rare indeed. You hear of instances in which the parent of mixed race could not be known from a white person, and yet the child reverts to the negro type in color and feature and character. I should doubt it very much."

Mrs. Meredith cried out as if he had questioned holy writ. "You should doubt it! Why should you doubt it, Dr. Olney?" Yet he perceived that for some reason she wished him to reaffirm his doubt.

"Because the chances are so enormously against it. The natural tendency is all the other way, to the permanent efface-ment of the inferior type. The child of a white and an octoroon is a sixteenth blood; and the child of that child and a white is a thirty-second blood. The chances of atavism, or reversion to the black great-great-great-grandfather are so remote that they may be said hardly to exist at all. They are outside of the probabilities, and only on the verge of the possibilities. But it's so thrilling to consider such a possibility that people like to consider it. Fancy is as much committed to it as prejudice is; but it hasn't so much excuse, for prejudice is mostly ignorant, and fancy mostly educated, or half-educated." Olney folded one leg comfortably across the other, and went on, with a musing smile. "I've been thinking about all this a good deal within the past two days— or since I got back to Boston. I've been more and more struck with the fact that sooner or later our race must absorb the colored race; and I believe that it will obliterate not only its color, but its qualities. The tame man, the civilized man, is stronger than the wild man; and I believe that in those cases within any one race where there are very strong ancestral proclivities on one side especially toward evil, they will die out before the good tenden-cies on the other side, for much the same reason, that is, because vice is savage and virtue is civilized."

Mrs. Meredith listened intently, but at last, "I wish I could believe what you say," she sighed, heavily. "But I don't know that that would relieve me of the duty before me," she added, after a moment's thought. "Dr. Olney, there is something that I need very much to speak about—something that must be done —that my health depends upon—I shall never get well unless—"

"If there is anything you wish to say concerning your health, Mrs. Meredith," he answered, seriously, "it's of course my duty to hear it."

He sat prepared to listen, but she apparently did not know how to begin, and after several gasps she was silent. Then, "No, I can't tell you!" she broke out.

He rose. "Are you to be some time in Boston?" he asked, to relieve the embarrassment of the situation.

"I don't know. Yes, I suppose a week or two."

"If I can be of use to you in any way, I shall be glad to have you send for me."

He turned to the door, but as he put his hand on the knob she called out: "No! Don't go! Sit down! I must speak! You remember," she hurried on, before he could resume his chair, "a young gentleman who talked with my niece that night at Professor Garofalo's—a Mr. Bloomingdale?"

"The young minister?"

"Yes."

"I remember him very well, though I don't think I spoke with him."

Olney stared at Mrs. Meredith, wondering what this Rev. Mr. Bloomingdale had to do with the matter, whatever the matter might be.

"It is his mother and sisters that my niece is lunching with," she said, with an air of explaining. "He is expected on the next steamer, and then—then I must speak! It can't go on, so. There must be a clear and perfect understanding. Dr. Olney," she continued, with a glance at his face, which he felt growing more and more bewildered under the influence of her words, "Mr. Bloomingdale is very much attached to my niece. He—he has offered himself; he offered himself in Liverpool; and I insisted that Rhoda should not give him a decisive answer then—that she should take time to think it over. I wished to gain time myself."

"Yes," said Olney, because she seemed to expect him to say something.

"I wished to gain time and I wished to gain strength, but I have lost both; and the affair has grown more difficult and complicated. Mr. Bloomingdale's family are very fond of Rhoda; they are aware of his attachment—they were in Florence at the time you were, and they came home without him a few months ago, because he wished to stay on in the hope of winning her—and they are showing her every attention; and she does not see how her being with them complicates everything. Of course they flatter her, and she's very headstrong, like all young girls, and I'm afraid she's committing herself—"

"Do they live at the Vendome?" Olney asked, with a certain distaste for them, and he was conscious of resenting their attentions to Miss Aldgate as pushing and vulgar under the circumstances, though he had no right to do so.

"No. They are just waiting there for him. They are New York State people—the western part. They are very rich; the mother is a widow, and they are going to live in Ohio, where Mr. Bloomingdale has a call. They are kind, good people—very kind; and I feel that Rhoda is abusing their kindness by being so much with them before she has positively accepted him; and I can't let her do that until everything is known. She refused him when he offered himself first in Florence—I've always thought she had some other fancy—but at Liverpool, where he renewed his offer just before we sailed, she was inclined to accept him; I suppose her fancy had passed. As I say, I insisted that she should take at least a week to consider it, and that he should change his passage from our steamer to the next. I had no idea of finding his family in Boston, but perhaps in the confusion he forgot to tell us. They found our names in the passenger list, and they came to see us directly after lunch, yesterday. If the match is broken off now, after—"

Mrs. Meredith stopped in a sort of despair, which Olney shared with her as far as concerned the blind alley in which he found himself. He had not the least notion of the way out, and he could only wait her motion.

"I don't see," she resumed, "how my niece can help accepting him if she goes on at this rate with his family, and I don't know how to stop her without telling her the worst at once. I'm afraid she has got her heart set on him." Mrs. Meredith paused again, and then went on. "I have shrunk from speaking because I know that the poor young man's happiness, as well as Rhoda's, is involved, and the peace and self-respect of his family. There have been times when I have almost felt that if there were no danger of the facts ever coming to light, I could make up my mind to die, as I have lived, in a lie. But now I know I cannot; it is my duty to speak out; and the marriage must not take place unless everything is known. It will kill her. But it must be done! Those ancestral traits, those tendencies, may die out, but I can't let any one take the risk of their recurrence unknowingly. He must know who and what she is as fully as I do: her origin, her—"

Olney believed that he began to understand. There was some stain upon that poor child's birth. She was probably not related to Mrs. Meredith at all; she was a foundling; or she was the daughter of some man or woman whose vices or crimes might find her out with their shame if not their propensity some day. Whatever sinister tendency she was heiress to, or whatever ancestral infamy, it could only be matter of conjecture, not inquiry, with Olney; but he imagined the worst from hints that Mrs. Meredith had thrown out, and attributed her to a family of criminals, such as has here and there found its way into the figures of the statisticians. He was not shocked; he was interested by the fact; and he did not find Miss Aldgate at all less charming and beautiful in the conclusion he jumped to than he had found her before. He said to himself that if the case were his, as it was that young minister's, there could be no question in it, except the question of her willingness to marry him. He said this from the safe vantage of the disinterested witness, and with the easy decision of one who need not act upon his decision.

VI

In his instantaneous mental processes, Olney kept his attention fixed upon Mrs. Meredith, and he was aware of her gasping out:

"My niece is of negro descent."

Olney recoiled from the words, in a turmoil of emotion for which there is no term but disgust. His disgust was profound and pervasive, and it did not fail, first of all, to involve the poor child herself. He found himself personally disliking the notion of her having negro blood in her veins; before he felt pity he felt repulsion; his own race instinct expressed itself in a merciless rejection of her beauty, her innocence, her helplessness because of her race. The impulse had to have its course; and then he mastered it, with an abiding compassion, and a sort of tender indignation. He felt that it was atrocious for this old woman to have allowed her hypochondriacal anxieties to dabble with the mysteries of the young girl's future in that way, and he resented having been trapped into considering her detestable question. His feeling was unscientific; but he could not at once detach himself from the purely social relation which he had hitherto held toward Miss Aldgate. The professional view which he was invited to take seemed to have lost all dignity, to be impertinent, cruel, squalid, and to involve the abdication of certain sentiments, conventions, which he was unwilling to part with, at least in her case. Sensibilities which ought not to have survived his scientific training and ambition were wounded to rebellion in him; he perceived as never before that there was inherent outrage in the submission of such questions to one of the opposite sex; there should be women to deal with them.

"How—negro descent?" he asked, stupidly, from the whirl of these thoughts.

"I will try to tell you," said Mrs. Meredith. "And some things you said about that—race—those wretched beings, last night— You were sincere in what you said?" she demanded of the kind of change that came into his face.

"Sincere? Yes," said Olney, thinking how far from any concrete significance he had supposed his words to have for his listeners when he spoke them. He added, "I do abhor the cruel stupidity that makes any race treat another as outcast. But I never dreamed—"

Mrs. Meredith broke in upon him, saying:

"It is almost the only consolation I have in thinking she is rightfully and lawfully my niece, to know that in the course I must take now, I shall not be seeming to make her an outcast. I honored my brother for honoring her mother, and giving her his name when there was no need of his doing it. He did not consult me, and I did not know it till afterward; but I should have been the first to urge it, when it came to a question of marriage or— anything else. For one of our family there could *be* no such question; there was none for him.

"He went South shortly after the war, as so many Northern men did, intending to make his home there; his health was delicate, and his only hope of strength and usefulness, if not of life, was in a milder climate. He outlived the distrust that the Southerners had for all Northern men in those days, and was establishing himself in a very good practice at New Orleans—I forgot to say he was a physician—when he met Rhoda's mother. I needn't go over the details: she was an octoroon, the daughter and the granddaughter of women who had never hoped for mar- riage with the white men who fell in love with them; but she had been educated by her father—he was a Creole, and she was edu- cated in a Northern convent—and I have no doubt she was an accomplished and beautiful girl. I never saw her. My brother met her in her father's house, almost beside her father's death- bed; but even if he had met her in her mother's house, on her mother's level, it would not have been possible for him to do otherwise than as he did. He thought at first of keeping the mar- riage secret, and of going on as before, until he could afford to own it and take all the consequences; but he decided against this, and I was always glad that he did. They were married, after her father's death; and then my brother's ruin began. He lost his practice in the families where he had got a footing, among the well-to-do and respectable people whom he had made his friends; and though he would have been willing to go on among a poorer class who could pay less, it was useless. He had to go away; and for five or six years he drifted about from one place to another, trying to gain a hold here and there, and failing everywhere. Sooner or later his story followed him.

"I don't blame the Southern people; I'm not sure it would have been better in the North. If it had been known who his wife was, she would not have been received socially here any more than she was there; and I doubt if it would not have affected my brother's professional standing in much the same way. People don't like to think there is anything strange about their doctor; they must make a confidant, they must make a familiar of him; and if there is anything peculiar, unusual— My husband was a very good man, one of the best men who ever lived, and he approved of my brother's marriage in the abstract as much as I did; but even he never liked to think *whom* he had married. He was always afraid it would come out among our friends, somehow, and it would be known that his sister-in-law was—

"At last the poor young creature died, and my brother came North with his little girl. We hoped that then he might begin again, and make a new start in life. But it was too late. He was a mere wreck physically, and he died too within the year. Then it became a question what we should do with the child. As long as she was so merely a child it was comparatively simple. We had no children of our own, and when my brother died in another part of the State—we were living in New York then, and he had gone up into the Adirondack region in the hope of getting better —it was natural that we should take the little one home. In a place like New York, nothing is known unless you make it known, and Rhoda was brought up in our house, without any conjecture or curiosity from people outside; she was my brother's orphan, and nobody knew or cared who my brother was; she had teachers and she had schools like any other child, and she had the companionships and social advantages which our own station and money could command.

"At first my husband and I thought of letting her think herself our child; but that would have involved a deceit which we were unwilling to practise; besides, it was not necessary, and it would have been great pain for her afterward. We decided to tell her the truth when the time came, and never anything but the truth, at any time. We never deceived her, but we let her deceive herself. When she came to the age when children begin to ask about themselves, we told her that her father had married in the South, and that her mother, whom she did not remember, was of French descent; but we did not know of her family. This was all true; but still it was not the truth; we knew that well enough, but we promised ourselves that when the time came we would tell her the truth.

"She made up little romances about her mother, which she came to believe in as facts, with our sufferance. I should now call it our connivance."

Mrs. Meredith appealed to Olney with a glance, and he said, in the first sympathy he had felt for her, "It was a difficult position."

"She easily satisfied herself—it's astonishing how little curiosity children have about all the mystery of their coming here—and as she had instinctively inferred something strange or unusual about her mother's family, she decided that she had married against her grandfather's wishes. We left her that illusion too: it seemed so easy to leave things then! It was when she ceased to be a child, and we realized more and more how her life might any time involve some other life, that the question became a constant pressure upon us. Neither my husband nor myself ever justified the concealment we lived in concerning her. We often talked of it, and how it must come to an end. But we were very much attached to her, and we put off thinking definitely about the duty before us as long as we could. Sometimes it seemed to us that we ought to tell the child just who and what she was, but we never had the courage; she does not know to this day. What do you think our duty to her really was?"

"Your duty?" Olney echoed, vaguely. A little while ago he would have answered instantly that they had no duty but to keep her in ignorance as long as she lived; but now he could not honestly do this. The only thing that he could honestly do was to say, "I don't know," and this was what he said.

Mrs. Meredith resumed: "My husband had gone out of business, and there was nothing to keep us at home. But we had nothing definitely in view when we went abroad, or at least nothing explicitly in view. We said that we were going abroad for Rhoda's education; but I think that in my husband's heart, as well as in mine, there was the hope that something might happen to solve the difficulty; we had no plan for solving it. I thought, at any rate, if he did not, that in Europe there would be less unhappiness in store for her than here. I knew that in Europe, especially on the Continent, there was little or none of that race prejudice which we have, and I thought—I imagined—I should find it easier to tell Rhoda the truth if I could tell her at the same time that it made no difference to the man she was to marry."

Olney understood; and he was rather restive under Mrs. Meredith's apparent helplessness to leave anything to his imagination.

"I hoped it might be some Italian—from the first I liked the Italians the best. We lived a great deal in Italy, at Rome and Naples, at Florence, at Venice, even at Milan; and everywhere we tried to avoid Americans. We went into Italian society almost entirely.

"But it seemed a perfect fatality. Rhoda was always homesick for America, and always eager to meet Americans. She refused all the offers that were made for her—and they began to come, even before she was fairly in society—and declared that she would never marry any one but an American. She was always proclaiming her patriotism, and asserting the superiority of America over every other country in a way that would have made anybody but a very pretty girl offensive. The perplexities simply grew upon us, and in the midst of them my husband died, and then I had no one to advise with or confide in. When his affairs were settled up, it turned out that we were much poorer than we had believed. For a while I thought that I should return home, and Rhoda was always eager to come back, but we staid on at Florence, living very quietly, and we had scarcely been out at all for a year when you first met us at Professor Garofalo's. It was there that she met Mr. Bloomingdale, and he was so attentive to her. I could see at once that he was greatly taken with her, and he followed up the acquaintance in a way that could not leave me any doubt. It was certainly not her money that attracted him.

"I liked him from the beginning; and his being a minister gave me a kind of hope, I can hardly tell why. But I thought that if it ever came to my having to tell him about Rhoda, he would be more reasonable. He was so very amiable, very gentle, very kind. Did you ever meet him afterward, anywhere?"

"No," said Olney, briefly.

"I am sorry; I hoped you had; I thought you might have come to know him well enough to suggest— I don't like his family, what I've seen of them, so well. If they know at all what is pending between him and Rhoda, it doesn't seem very nice of them to be pursuing her so."

Mrs. Meredith sat so dreary in her silence that Olney pitied her, and found a husky voice to say, "Perhaps they don't know."

"Perhaps not," she assented, sadly. "But my only hope now is in his being able to take it, when I tell him, as I have hardly the hope that any other American would. I must tell him, if she accepts him, or decides to accept him, and the question is whether I shall tell him before I tell her. If I tell him first, fully and frankly, perhaps—perhaps—he may choose to keep it from her and she need never know. What—what do you think?" she entreated.

"Really," said Olney, "that's a matter I have no sort of opinion about. I'm very sorry, but you must excuse me."

"But you feel that I must tell him?"

"That's another question for you, Mrs. Meredith. I can't answer it."

She threw herself back on the sofa. "I wish I were dead! I see no way out of it, and whatever happens, it will kill the child."

Olney sat silent for some time in a muse almost as dreary as her own. After having despised her as a morbid sentimentalist with a hypochondriacal conscience, he had come to respect her, as we respect any fellow-creature on whom a heavy duty is laid, and who is struggling faithfully to stand up under the burden. He said suddenly, "You mustn't tell him first, Mrs. Meredith!"

"Why?"

"Because—because—the secret is *hers*, to keep it or to tell it. No one else has the right to know it without her leave."

"And if—if she should choose to keep it from him—not tell him at all?"

"I couldn't blame her. It is no fault, no wrong of hers. And who is to be harmed by its concealment?"

"But the chances—the future—the—the—"

Olney could not bear the recurrence to this phase of the subject. He made a gesture of impatience.

Mrs. Meredith added, with hysterical haste: "It might come out in a hundred ways. I can hear it in her voice at times—it's a *black* voice! I can see it in her looks! I can feel it in her character— so easy, so irresponsible, so fond of what is soft and pleasant! She could not deny herself the amusement of going with those people to-day, though I said all I could against it. She cannot forecast consequences; she's a creature of the present hour; she's like them *all*! I think that in some occult, dreadful way she feels her affinity with them, and that's the reason why she's so attracted by them, so fond of them. It's her race *calling* her! I don't believe she would ever tell him!"

"I think you ought to leave it to her," said Olney.

"And let her live a lie! Oh, I know too well what that is!"

"It's bad. But there may be worse things. It seems as if there might be circumstances in which it was one's *right* to live a lie, as you say; for the sake—"

"Never!" said Mrs. Meredith vehemently. "It is better to die —to kill—than to lie. I know how people say such things and act them, till life is all one web of falsehood, from the rising to the going down of the sun. But I will never consent to be a party to any such deceit. I will tell Rhoda, and then she shall tell me what she is going to do, and if *she* is not going to tell him, *I* will do it. Yes! I will not be responsible for the future, and I should *be*

responsible if he did not know. In such a case I could not spare
her. She is my own flesh and blood; she is as dear to me as my
own child could be, but if she *were* my own child it would be all
the same. I would rather see her perish before my eyes than married to any man who did not know the secret of her— O-o-o-o-o!"
Mrs. Meredith gave a loud, shuddering cry, as the door was flung
suddenly open, and Miss Aldgate flashed radiantly into the
room.

She kept the door-knob in her hand, while she demanded,
half frightened, half amused, "What in the world is the matter?
Did I startle you? Of course! But I just ran in a moment as we
were driving by—we're going over to do our duty by Bunker Hill
Monument—to see how you were getting on. I'm so glad *you* are
here, Dr. Olney." She released the door-knob, and gave him her
hand. "Now I can leave Aunt Caroline without a qualm of
conscience till after lunch; and I *did* have a qualm or two, poor
aunty!"

She stooped on one knee beside the sofa, and kissed her aunt,
who seemed to Olney no better than a murderess in the embrace
of her intended victim. In this light and joyous presence, all that
he had heard of the girl's anomalous origin became not only
incredible, but atrocious. She was purely and merely a young
lady, like any other; and he felt himself getting red with shame for
having heard what he had been told against his will.

He could not speak, and he marvelled that Mrs. Meredith
could command the words to say, in quite an every-day voice:
"You silly child! You needn't have stopped. I was getting on
perfectly well."

"Of course you were! And I suppose I've interrupted you in
the full flow of symptoms! I can imagine what a perfectly delightful time you were having with Dr. Olney! I think I'll change these
gloves." She ran into the room that opened from Mrs. Meredith's
parlor, and left him unable to lift his eyes from the floor in her
brief absence. She came back pulling on one long mousquetaire
glove, while the other dangled from her fingers, and began to
laugh. "There's one of those colored waiters down there that

even *you* couldn't have anything to say against my falling in love
with, Aunt Caroline. He's about four feet high, and his feet are
about eighteen inches long, so that he looks just like a capital L.
He doesn't lift them, when he walks, but he slips along on them
over the floor like a funny little mouse; I've decided to call him
Creepy-Mousey: it just exactly describes him, he's so small and
cunning. And he's so sweet! I should like to *own* him, and keep
him as long as he lived. Isn't it a shame that we can't *buy* them,
Dr. Olney, as we used to do? There! I'll put on the other one in
the carriage."

She swooped upon her aunt for another kiss, and then flashed
out of the room as she had flashed into it, and left Mrs. Meredith
and Olney staring at each other.

"Well!" she said. "You see! It is the race instinct! It must as-
sert itself sooner or later."

Olney became suddenly sardonic in the sort of desperation he
fell into. "I should say it was the other-race instinct that was
asserting itself sooner," and when he had said this he felt somehow a hope, which he tried to impart to Mrs. Meredith.

At the end of all their talk she said: "But that doesn't relieve
me of the duty I owe to her and to him. I must tell her, at least,
cost what it may. I cannot live this lie any longer. If she chooses
to do so, perhaps—"

VII

Miss Aldgate came in late in the afternoon. She came in softly,
and then, finding her aunt awake, she let herself fall into an easy-
chair with the air of utter exhaustion that girls like to put on,
after getting home from a social pleasure, and sighed out a long
"O-o-o-h, dear!"

Her aunt let her sit silent, and stare awhile at the carpet just
beyond the toe of her pretty boot before she suggested, "Well?"

"Oh, nothing! Only it got to be rather tiresome, toward the
last."

"Why did you stay so long?"

"I couldn't get away; they wouldn't let me go. They kept proposing this and that, and then they wanted to arrange something for to-morrow. But I wouldn't."

"They are rather persistent," said Mrs. Meredith.

"Yes, they are persistent. But they are very kind—they are very good-natured. I wish—I wish I liked them better!"

"Don't you like them?"

"Oh, I like them, yes, in a kind of way. They're a very familyish sort of a family; they're so much bound up in one another. Of course they can do a great many nice things: Miss Bloomingdale is really wonderful with her music; and Josie sketches very nicely, and Roberta sings beautifully; there's no denying it; but they don't talk very much, and they're all so tall and handsome and blond; and they sit round with their hands arranged in their laps, and keep waiting for me to say things; and then their mother starts them up and makes them do something. The worst is that she keeps dragging in Mr. Bloomingdale all the time. There isn't anything that doesn't suggest him—what he thinks, what he says, where he's been and what he did there; just how far he's got on his way home by this time; how he's never seasick, but he doesn't like rough weather. I began to dread the introduction of a new subject: it was so sure to bring round to him. Don't you think they're of rather an old-fashioned taste?"

"I never liked his family very much," said Mrs. Meredith. "They seemed very estimable people, but not—"

"Our kind? No, decidedly. Did Dr. Olney stay long?"

"No. Why do you ask?" Mrs. Meredith returned, with a startled look.

"Oh, nothing. You seemed to be quite chummy with him, and not to want me round a great deal when I came in." Miss Aldgate had discovered the toe of her boot just beyond her skirt, apparently with some surprise, and she leaned forward to touch it with the point of her parasol, as if to make sure of it. "Is he coming again this evening?" she asked, leaning back in her chair, and twisting her parasol by its handle.

"Not unless I send for him. I have his sleeping medicine."

"Yes. And I know how to drop it. Did he think it strange my being away from you so much when you needed a doctor?"

"He knew I didn't need any doctor. Why do you ask such a question as that?"

"I don't know. I thought it might have struck him. But I thought I had better try and see if I could get used to them or not. They're pretty formal people—conventional. I mean in the way of dress and that kind of thing. They're formal in their ideals, don't you know. They would want to do just what they thought other people were doing; they would be dreadfully troubled if there was anything about them that was not just like everybody else. Do you think Mr. Bloomingdale would be so?"

"I never liked his family very much," Mrs. Meredith repeated. "What little I saw of them," she added, as if conscientiously.

"Oh, that doesn't count, Aunt Caroline!" said the girl, with a laugh. "You never liked the families of any of the Americans that you thought fancied me. But the question is not whether we like his family, but whether he's like them."

"You can't separate him from his family, Rhoda. You must remember that. Each of us is bound by a thousand mysterious ties to our kindred, our ancestors; we can't get away from them—"

"Oh, what stuff, aunty!" Miss Aldgate was still greatly amused. "I should like to know how I'm bound to my mother's family, that I never saw one of; or to her father or grandfather?"

"How?" Mrs. Meredith gasped.

"Yes. Or how much they were bound to me, if they never tried to find me out or make themselves known by any sort of sign? I'm bound to you because we've always been together, and I was bound to Uncle Meredith because he was good to me. But there isn't anything mysterious about it. And Mr. Bloomingdale is bound to his family in the same way. He's fond of them because he's been nice to them and they've been nice to him. I wonder," she mused, while Mrs. Meredith felt herself slowly recoil from the point which she had been suddenly caught up to, "whether I really care for him or not? There were very nice things about him; and no, he wasn't tiresome and formal-minded like them. I wish I had been a little in love with some one, and then I could tell. But I've never had anything but decided dislikings, though I didn't dislike *him* decidedly. No, I rather liked him. That is, I thought he was *good*. Yes, I respected his goodness. It's about the only thing in this world you *can* respect. But now, I remember, he seemed very young, and all the younger because he thought it was his duty as a minister to seem old. Did *you* care very much for his sermon?"

Rhoda came to the end of her thinking aloud with a question that she had to repeat before her aunt asked drearily in answer, "What sermon?"

"Why, we only heard him once! The one he preached in Florence. I didn't have a full sense of his youth till I heard that. Isn't it strange that there are ever young ministers? I suppose people think they can make up in inspiration what they lack in experience. But that day when I looked round at those men and women, some of them gray-haired, and most of them middle-aged, and all of them knowing so much more about life, and its trials and temptations, and troubles and sorrows, than poor Mr. Bloomingdale—I oughtn't to call him *poor*—and heard him going on about the birds and the flowers, I wondered how they could bear it. Of course it was all right; I know that. But if the preacher *shouldn't* happen to be inspired, wouldn't it be awful? How old do you suppose Dr. Olney is?"

"I don't know."

"He seems rather bald. Do you think he is forty?"

"Dear me, no, child! He isn't thirty yet, I dare say. Some men are bald much earlier than others. It's a matter of—heredity."

"Heredity! Everything's heredity with you, Aunt Caroline!" the girl laughed. "I'll bet he's worn it off by thinking too much in one particular spot. You know that they say now they can tell just what place in the brain a person thinks this or that; and just where the will power comes from when you wink your eye, or wiggle your little finger. I wonder if Dr. Olney knows all those things? Have you tried him on your favorite heredity yet?"

"What do you mean, Rhoda?"

"I know you have!" the girl exulted. "Well, he is the kind of man I should always want to have for my doctor if I had to have one; though I don't think he's done you a great deal of good yet, Aunt Caroline: you look wretched, and I shall feel like scolding Dr. Olney when he comes again. But what I mean is, he has such noble ideas: don't you think he has?"

"Yes—yes. About what?"

"Why, about the negroes, you know." Mrs. Meredith winced at the word. "I never happened to see it in that light before. I thought when we had set them free, we had done everything. But I can see now we haven't. We do perfectly banish them, as far as we can; and we don't associate with them half as much as we do with the animals. I got to talking with the Bloomingdales this afternoon, and I had to take the negroes' part. Don't you think that was funny for a Southern girl?" Mrs. Meredith looked at her with a ghastly face, and moved her lips in answer, without making any sound. "They said that the negroes were an inferior race, and they never could associate with the whites because they never could be intellectually equal with them. I told them about that black English lawyer from Sierra Leone that talked so well at the *table d'hôte* in Venice—better than anybody else—but they wouldn't give way. They were very narrow-minded; or the mother was; the rest didn't say anything; only made exclamations. Mrs. Bloomingdale said Dr. Olney must be a very strange physician, to have those ideas. I hope Mr. Bloomingdale isn't like her. You would say he was a good deal younger than Dr. Olney, wouldn't you?"

"Yes—not so very. But why—"

Rhoda broke out into a laugh of humorous perplexity. "Why, if he were only a little older, or a good deal older, he could advise me whether to marry him or not!" The laughter faded suddenly from her eyes, and she fell back dejectedly against her chair, and remained looking at her aunt, as if trying to read in her face the silent working of her thought. "Well?" she demanded, finally.

Mrs. Meredith dropped her eyes. "Why need you marry any one?"

"What a funny question!" the girl answered, with the sparkle of a returning smile. "So as to have somebody to take care of me in my old age!" The young like to speak of age so, with a mocking incredulity; they feel that, however it may have fared with all the race hitherto, they never can be old, and they like to make a joke of the mere notion. "You'll be getting old yourself some day, Aunt Caroline, and then what shall I do? Don't you think that a woman *ought* to get married?"

"Yes—yes. Not always—not necessarily. Certainly not to have some one to take care of her."

"Of course not! That would be a very base motive. I suppose I really meant, have somebody for *me* to take care of. I think that is what keeps one from being lonesome more than anything else. I do feel so alone sometimes. It seems to me that there are very few girls so perfectly isolated. Why, just think! With the exception of you, I don't believe I've got a single relation in the world." Rhoda seemed interested rather than distressed by the fact. "Now there are the Bloomingdales," she went on; "it seems as if they had connections everywhere. That is something *like* a family. If I married Mr. Bloomingdale, I could always have somebody to take care of as long as I lived. To be sure, they would be Bloomingdales," she added, dreamily.

"Rhoda!" said her aunt, "I cannot let you speak so. If you are in earnest about Mr. Bloomingdale—"

"I am. But not about his family—or not so much so."

"You cannot take him without taking his family; that is always the first thing to be thought of in marriage, and young people think of it the last. The family on each side counts almost as much as the couple themselves in a marriage."

"Mine wouldn't," the girl interpolated. "There's so very little of it!"

If Mrs. Meredith was trying to bring the talk to this point, she now seemed to find herself too suddenly confronted with it, and she shrank back a little. "I don't mean that family is the *first* thing."

"You just *said* it was, aunty!"

"The first thing," Mrs. Meredith continued, ignoring the teasing little speech, "is to make sure of yourself, to be satisfied that you love *him*."

"It's so much easier," the girl sighed in mock-seriousness, "to be satisfied that I don't love *them*."

"But that won't do, Rhoda," said Mrs. Meredith, "and I can't let you treat the matter in this trivial spirit. It is a most important matter—far more important than you can realize."

"I can't realize anything about it—that's the trouble."

"You can realize whether you wish to accept him or not."

"No; that's just what I can't do."

"You've had time enough."

"I've had nearly a week. But I want all the time there is; it wouldn't be any too much. I must see him again—after seeing so much of his family."

"Rhoda!" her aunt called sternly to her from the sofa.

But Rhoda did not respond with any sort of intimidation. She was looking down into the street from the window where she sat, and she suddenly bowed. "It was Dr. Olney," she explained. "He was just coming into the hotel, and he looked up. I wonder how he knew it was our window? He seems twice as young with his hat on. I wish he'd wear his hat in the room. But of course he can't."

Everything that had happened since Rhoda came in made it more difficult for Mrs. Meredith to discharge the duty that she thought she had nerved herself up to. She had promised herself that if Rhoda had decided to accept Mr. Bloomingdale, she would speak, and tell her everything; but she was not certain yet that the girl had decided, though from the way in which she played with the question, and her freedom from all anxiety about it, she felt pretty sure that she had. She wished, vaguely, perversely, weakly, that she had not, for then the ordeal for them both could be postponed indefinitely again. She sympathized with the girl in her trials through the young minister's family, who were so repugnant to her in their eagerness for her, and she burned with a prophetic indignation in imagining how such people would cast her off when they knew what she really was. The young man himself seemed kind and good, and if it were a question of him alone, she believed she could trust him; but these others! that mother, those sisters! She recoiled from the duty of humiliating the poor girl before them, so helplessly, innocently, ignorantly guilty of her own origin. The child's gayety and lightness, her elfish whimsicality and thoughtless superficiality, as well as those gleams and glimpses of a deeper nature which a word or action gave from time to time, smote the elder woman's heart with a nameless pain and a tender compassion. By all her circumstance Rhoda had a right to be the somewhat spoiled and teasing pretty thing that she was; and all that sovereign young-ladyishness which sat so becomingly upon her was proper to the station a beautiful young girl holds in a world where she has had only to choose and to command. But Mrs. Meredith shuddered to think with what contempt, open or masquerading as pity, all this would be denied to her. Doubtless she exaggerated; the world slowly changes; it condones many things to those who are well placed in it; and it might not have fared so ill with the child as the woman thought; but Mrs. Meredith had brooded so long upon her destiny that she could see it only in the gloomiest colors. She was darkling in its deepest shadow when she heard Rhoda saying, as if at the end of some speech that she had not caught, "But *he* doesn't seem to have any more family than I have."

"Who?" Mrs. Meredith asked.

"Dr. Olney."

"You don't know anything about his family."

"Well, I don't know anything about my own," Rhoda answered, lightly. She added, soberly, after a moment: "Don't you think it's rather strange that my mother's family never cared to look us up in any way? Even if they were opposed to her marrying papa, one would think they might have forgiven it by this time. The family ties are so strong among the French."

Mrs. Meredith dropped her eyes, and murmured, "It may be different with the Creoles."

"No, I don't believe it is. I've heard it's more so. Did papa never see any of mamma's family but her father? It seems so strange that she should have been as much alone as I am. I know I have *you*, Aunt Caroline. Well, I don't know what to think about Mr. Bloomingdale. I'm always summing up his virtues: he's very good, and he's good-looking, and he's good-natured. He's rich, though I don't let that count. He parts his hair too much on one side, but that doesn't matter, I could make him part it in the middle, and it's a very pretty shade of brown. His eyes are good, and his mouth wouldn't be weak if he wore his beard full. I think he has very good ideas, and I'm sure he would be devoted all his days. It isn't so easy to sum a person up, though, is it? I wish I knew whether I cared for him. I don't believe I've ever been in love with anybody yet. Of course I've had my fancies. I do respect Mr. Bloomingdale, and when I think how very anxious he was to have me care for him, I don't know but I could if I really tried. But ought one to have to try? That's the question. Oughtn't the love to go of itself, without being pushed or pulled? I wish I knew! Aunt Caroline, do you believe in 'learning to love' your husband after marriage? That's what happens in some of the stories; but it seems very ridiculous. I wish it was my *duty* to marry him—or not to; then I could decide. I believe I'm turning out quite a slave of duty. I must have 'caught it' from you, Aunt Caroline. Now I can imagine myself sacrificing anything to duty. If Mr. Bloomingdale were to step ashore from the next steamer, and drive to the hotel without stopping to take breath, and get himself shown up here, and say, 'I've just dropped in, Miss Aldgate, to offer you the opportunity of uniting your life with mine in a high and holy purpose—say working among the poor on the east side in New York, or going down to educate the black race in the South'—I believe I should seize the opportunity without a murmur. Perhaps he may. Do you think he will?"

Rhoda ended her monologue with a gay look at her aunt, who was silent at the end, as she had been throughout, turning the trouble before them over and over in her mind. As happens when we are preoccupied with one thing, all other things seem to tend toward it and bear upon it; half a dozen mere accidents of the girl's spoken reverie touched the sore place in Mrs. Meredith's soul and fretted it to an anguish that she asked herself how she could bear. It all accused and judged and condemned her, because she had kept putting by the duty she had to discharge, and making it contingent upon that decision of the girl's which she was still far from ascertaining. In her recoil from this duty she had believed that if it need not be done at this time, it somehow need never be done; or she had tried to believe this. If Rhoda rejected this young man, she might keep her safe forever from the fact which she felt must wreck the life of the light-hearted, high-spirited girl. That was the refuge which Mrs. Meredith had taken from the task which so strongly beset her; but when she had formulated the case to herself, the absurdity, the impossibility of her position appeared to her. If Rhoda cared nothing for Mr. Bloomingdale, the day would come when she would care everything for some one else; and that day could not be postponed, nor the duty of that day. It would be crueler to leave her unarmed against the truth until the moment when her heart was set upon a love, and then strike her down with it. Mrs. Meredith now saw this; she saw that the doubt in which she was resting was the very moment of action for her; and that the occasion was divinely appointed for dealing more mercifully with the child than any other that could have offered. She had often imagined herself telling Rhoda what she had to tell, and with the romantic coloring from the novels she had read, she had painted herself in the heroic discharge of her duty at the instant when the girl was radiant in the possession of an accepted love, and had helped her to renounce, to suffer, and to triumph. She had always been very strong in these dramatized encounters, and had borne herself with a stony power throughout, against which the bruised and bleeding girl had rested her broken spirit; but now she cowered before her. She longed to fall upon her knees at her feet, and first implore her forgiveness for what she was going to do, and not speak till she had been forgiven; but habit is strong, really stronger than emotion of any sort, and so Mrs.

Meredith remained lying on her sofa, and merely put up her fan to shut out the sight of the child, as she said, "And if it were your duty to give up Mr. Bloomingdale, could you do it?"

"Oh, instantly, Aunt Caroline!" answered Rhoda, with a gay burlesque of fortitude. "I would not hesitate a single week. But why do you ask such an awful question?"

"Is it a very awful question?" Mrs. Meredith palpitated.

"Well, rather! One may wish to give a person up, but not as a *duty*."

Mrs. Meredith understood this well enough, but it was her perfect intelligence concerning the whole situation that seemed to disable her. She made out to say: "Then you have decided not to give him up yet?"

"I've decided—I've decided—let me think!—not to decide till I see him again! What do you mean by if it were my duty to give him up?"

"It would be your duty," Mrs. Meredith paltered, "to give him up unless you were sure you loved him."

"Oh, yes; certainly. *That*."

"You wouldn't wish him, after you've seen so much of his family, not to know everything about yours, if you decided to accept him?"

"Why, you're all there is, Aunt Caroline! You're the end of the story. I should hope he understood that. What else is there?"

"Nothing—nothing— There is very little. But we ought to tell Mr. Bloomingdale all we know—of your mother's family."

"Why, certainly. I expected to do that. There was nothing disgraceful about them, I imagine, except their behavior toward mamma."

"No—"

"You speak as if there *were*. What are you keeping back, Aunt Caroline?" Rhoda sat upright, and faced her aunt with a sort of sudden fierceness which she sometimes showed when she was roused to self-assertion. This was seldom, in the succession of her amiable moods, but when it happened, Mrs. Meredith saw in it the outbreak of the ancestral savagery, and shuddered at it as a self-betrayal rather than a self-assertion; but perhaps self-assertion is this with all of us. "What are you hinting at? If there was anything dishonorable—"

Mrs. Meredith found herself launched at last. She could not go back now; she could not stop. She had only the choice, in going on, of telling the truth, or setting sail to shipwreck under some new lie. For this both will and invention failed her; she was too weak mentally, if she was not too strong morally, for this. She went on in with a kind of mechanical force.

"If there were something dishonorable that was not their fault, that was their wrong, their sorrow, their burden—what should you think of your father's marrying your mother, with a full knowledge of it?"

"I should think he did nobly and bravely to marry her. But that's nothing. What was the disgrace? What had they done, that they had to suffer innocently? You needn't be afraid of telling me everything. I don't care what Mr. Bloomingdale or any one thinks; I shall be proud of them for it; I shall be glad!" Mrs. Meredith saw with terror that the girl's fancy had kindled with some romantic conjecture. "Who *was* my grandfather?"

"I know very little about him, Rhoda," said Mrs. Meredith, seeking to rest in this neutral truth. "Your father never told me much, except that he was a Creole, and—and rich; and—and—respected, as those things went there, among his people—"

"Was he some old slaver, like those in Mr. Cable's books? I shouldn't care for that! But that would have been his fault, and it wouldn't have been any great disgrace; and you said— And my grandmother—who was *she?*"

"She was—not his wife."

"Oh!" said the girl, with a quick breath, as if she had been struck over the heart. "*That* was how the dishonor—" She stopped, with an absent stare fixed upon her aunt, who waited in silence for her to realize this evil which was still so far short of the worst. Where she sat she could not see the blush of shame that gradually stained the girl's face to her throat and forehead. "*Who* was she?"

Mrs. Meredith tried to think how the words would sound as she said them, and simultaneously she said them, "She was his slave."

The girl was silent and motionless. With her head defined against the open window, her face showed quite black toward her aunt, as if the fact of her mother's race had remanded her to its primordial hue in touching her consciousness. Mrs. Meredith had risen, and sat with one hand grasping the wrap that still covered her feet, as if ready to cast it loose and fly her victim's presence, if it became intolerable. But she found herself too weak to stand up, and she waited, throbbing and quaking, for Rhoda to speak. The girl gave a little, low, faltering laugh, an inarticulate note of such pathetic fear and pitiful entreaty that it went through the woman's heart. "Aunt Caroline, are you crazy?"

"Crazy?" The word gave her an instant of strange respite. Was she really mad, and had she long dreamed this thing in the cloudy deliriums of a sick brain? The fact of her hopeless sanity repossessed her from this tricksy conjecture. "If I were *only* crazy!"

"And you mean to say—to tell me—that—that—I am—*black?*"

"Oh, no, poor child! You are as white as I am—as any one. No one would ever think—"

"But I have that blood in me? It is the same thing!" An awful silence followed again, and then the girl said: "And you let me grow up thinking I was white, like other girls, when you knew— You let me pass myself off on myself and every one else, for what I wasn't! Oh, Aunt Caroline, what are you telling me this ghastly thing for? It *isn't* true! You couldn't have let me live on all these years thinking I was a white person, when— You would have told me from the very beginning, as soon as I could begin to understand anything. You wouldn't have told me all those things about my mother's family, and their being great people, and disowning her, and all that! If this is true you wouldn't have let me believe that, you and Uncle Meredith?"

"We let you believe it, but you made it up yourself; we never told you anything."

"But you couldn't have thought that was being honest, and so you couldn't have done it—*you* couldn't. And so it isn't any of it true that you've just told me. But why did you tell me such a thing? I don't believe you *have* told me it. Why, I must be dreaming. It's as if—as if—you were to come to a perfectly well person, and tell them that they were going to die in half an hour. Don't you see? How can you tell me such a thing? Don't you understand that it tears my whole life up, and flings it out on the ground? But you *know* it isn't true. Oh, my, I think my head will burst! Why don't you speak to me, and tell me why you said such a thing? Is it because you don't want me to marry Mr. Bloomingdale? Well, I won't marry him. *Now* will you say it?"

"Rhoda!" her aunt began, "whether you married Mr. Bloomingdale or not, the time had come—"

"No! The time had gone. It had come as soon as I could speak or understand the first word. Then would have been the time for you to tell me such a thing if it were true, so that I might have grown up knowing it, and trying to bear it. But it isn't true, and you're just saying it for some other reason. What has happened to you, Aunt Caroline? I am going to send for Dr. Olney; you're not well. It's something in that medicine of his, I know it is. Let me look at you!" She ran suddenly toward Mrs. Meredith, who recoiled, crouching back into the corner of her sofa. The girl broke into a hysterical laugh. "Do you think I will hurt you? Oh, Aunt Caroline, take it back, take it back! See, I'll get on my knees to you!" She threw herself down before the sofa where Mrs. Meredith crouched. "Oh, you *couldn't* have been so wicked as to live such a lie as that!"

"It was a lie, the basest, the vilest," said Mrs. Meredith, with a sort of hopeless gasp. "But I never saw the time when I *must* tell you the truth—and so I couldn't."

"Oh, no, no! Don't take yourself from me!" The girl dropped her head on the woman's knees, and broke into a wild sobbing. "I don't know what you're doing this for. It can't be true—it can't be real. Shall I *never* wake from it, and have you back? You were all I had in the world, and now, if you were not what I thought you, so true and good, I haven't even you any more. Oh, oh, oh!"

"Oh, it was all wrong," said Mrs. Meredith, in a tearless misery, a dry pang of the heart for which her words were no relief. "There hasn't been a day or an hour when I haven't felt it; and I have always prayed for light to see my duty, and strength to do it. God knows that if I could bear this for you, how gladly I would do it. I have borne it all these years, and the guilt of the concealment besides; that is something, though it is nothing to what you are suffering. I know that—I know that!"

The girl sobbed on and on, and the woman repeated the same things over and over, a babble of words in which there was no comfort, no help, but which sufficed to tide them both over from the past which had dropped into chaos behind them to a new present in which they must try to gain a footing once more.

The girl suddenly ceased to bemoan herself, and lifted her head, to look into her aunt's face. "And my mother," she said, ignoring the piteous sympathy she saw, "was she my *father's* slave, too?"

"She was your father's wife. Slavery was past then, and he was too good a man for anything else, though he knew his marriage would ruin him, as it did."

"At least there is *some* one I can honor, then; I can honor *him*," said the girl, with an unpitying hardness in her tone. She rose to her feet, and turned away toward the door of her own room.

"Is there—is there anything else that I can tell—that you wish to know?" her aunt entreated. "Oh, child! If you could only understand—"

"I do understand," said the girl.

Mrs. Meredith, in her millionfold prefigurations of this moment, had often suffered from the necessity of insinuating to the ignorance of girlhood all the sad details of the social tragedy of which she was the victim. But she perceived that this at least was to be spared her, that the girl had somehow instantly realized the whole affair in these aspects. In middle life we often forget, amidst the accumulations of experience, how early the main bases of it were laid in our consciousness. We suppose, when we are experienced, that knowledge comes solely from experience; but knowledge, or if not knowledge, then truth, comes largely from perception, from instinct, from divination, from the intelligence of our mere potentialities. A man can be anything along the vast range from angel to devil; without living either the good thing or the bad thing in which his fancy dramatizes him, he can perceive it. His intelligence may want accuracy, though after-experience often startlingly verifies it; but it does not want truth. The materials of knowledge accumulate from innumerable un-remembered sources. All at once, some vital interest precipitates the latent electricity of the cloudy mass in a flash that illumines the world with a shadowless brilliancy and shows everything in its very form and meaning. Then the witness perceives that some-how from the beginning of conscious being he had understood all this before, and every influence and circumstance had tended to the significance revealed.

The proud, pure girl who had been told that her mother was slave-born and sin-born had lived as carefully sheltered from the guilt and shame that are in the world as tender love and pitying fear could keep her; but so much of the sad fact of evil had somehow reached her that she stood in a sudden glare of the reality. She understood, and she felt all scathed within by the intelligence, by whatever the cruelest foe could have told her with the most unsparing fulness, whatever the fondest friend could have wished her not to know. The swiftness of these mental processes no words can suggest; we can portray life, not living.

"I am going to my room, now," she said to her aunt, "and whatever happens, don't follow me, don't call me. If you are dying, don't speak to me. I have a right to be alone."

She crossed to the door of her chamber opening from the little parlor, and closed it behind her, and her aunt fell back again on her sofa. She was too weak to follow her if she had wished, and she was too wise to wish it. She lay there revolving the whole misery in her mind, turning it over and over ten thousand times. She said to herself that it was worse, far worse, than she had ever pictured it; but in fact it was better, for her. She pretended otherwise, but for her there was the relief in the situation of a lie owned, a truth spoken, and with whatever heart-wrung drops she told the throes of the anguish beyond that door, for herself she was glad. It was monstrous to be glad, she knew that; but she knew that she was glad.

After a while she began to be afraid of the absolute silence that continued in Rhoda's room, and then she did what men would say a man would not have done; she crept to the door and peeped and listened. She could not hear anything, but she saw Rhoda sitting by the table writing. She went back to her sofa, and lay there more patiently now; but as the time passed she began to be hungry; with shame that did not suffer her to ring and ask for anything to eat, she began to feel the weak and self-pitiful craving of an invalid for food.

The time passed till the travelling-clock on the mantel showed her that it was half past seven. Then Rhoda's door was flung open, and the girl stood before her with her hat on, and dressed to go out. She had a letter in her hand, and she said, with a mechanical hardness, "I have written to him, and I am going out with the letter. When I come back—"

"You can send your letter out," pleaded her aunt; she knew what the girl had written too well to ask. "It's almost dark; it's too late for you to be out on the streets alone."

"Oh, what could happen to *me?*" demanded Rhoda, scornfully. "Or if some one insulted a colored girl, what of it? When I come back I will pack for you, and in the morning we will start for New Orleans, and try to find out my mother's family."

Her aunt said nothing to this, but she set herself earnestly to plead with the girl not to go out. "It will be dark, Rhoda, and you don't know the streets. Indeed you mustn't go out. You haven't had any dinner— For my sake—"

"For *your* sake!" said Rhoda. She went on, as if that were answer enough, "I have written to him that all is over between us—it was, even before *this:* I could never have married him—and that when he arrives we shall be gone, and he must never try to see me again. I've told you all that you could ask, Aunt Caroline, and now there is one thing I want you to answer me. Is there any one else who knows this?"

"No, indeed, child!" answered Mrs. Meredith instantly, and she thought for the instant that she was telling the truth. "Not another living soul. No one ever knew but your uncle—"

"Be careful, Aunt Caroline," said the girl, coming up to her sofa, and looking gloomily down upon her. "You had better always tell me the truth, now. Have you told *no* one else?"

"No one."

"Not Dr. Olney?"

It was too late, now that Mrs. Meredith perceived her error. She could not draw back from it, and say that she had forgotten; Rhoda would never believe that. She could only say, "No, not Dr. Olney."

"Tell me the truth, if you expect ever to see me again, in this world or the next. Is it the truth? Swear it!"

"It is the truth," said the poor woman, feeling this new and astonishing lie triply riveted upon her soul; and she sank down upon the pillow from which she had partly lifted herself, and lay there as if crushed under the burden suddenly rolled back upon her.

"Then I forgive you," said the girl, stooping down to kiss her.

The woman pushed her feebly away. "Oh, I don't want your forgiveness, now," she whimpered, and she began to cry.

Rhoda made no answer, but turned and went out of the room.

Mrs. Meredith lay exhausted. She was no longer hungry, but she was weak for want of food. After a while she slid from the sofa, and then on her hands and knees she crept to the table where the bottle that held Dr. Olney's sleeping medicine stood. She drank it all off. She felt the need of escaping from herself; she did not believe it would kill her; but she must escape at any risk. So men die who mean to take their lives; but it is not certain that death even is an escape from ourselves.

VIII

IN THE STREET where Rhoda found herself the gas was already palely burning in the shops, and the moony glare of an electric globe was invading the flush of the sunset whose after-glow still filled the summer air in the western perspective. She did not know where she was going, but she went that way, down the slope of the slightly curving thoroughfare. She had the letter which she meant to post in her hand, but she passed the boxes on the lamp-posts without putting it in. She no longer knew what she meant to do, in any sort, or what she desired; but out of the turmoil of horror, which she whirled round and round in, some purpose that seemed at first exterior to herself began to evolve. The street was one where she would hardly have met ladies of the sort she had always supposed herself of; gentility fled it long ago, and the houses that had once been middle-class houses had fallen in the social scale to the grade of mechanics' lodgings, and the shops, which had never been fashionable, were adapted strictly to the needs of a neighborhood of poor and humble people. They were largely provision stores, full of fruit, especially watermelons; there were some groceries, and some pharmacies of that professional neatness which pharmacies are of everywhere. The roadway was at this hour pretty well deserted by the express wagons and butcher carts that bang through it in the earlier day; and the horse-cars, coming and going on its incline and its final westward level, were in the un-restricted enjoyment of the company's monopoly of the best part of its space.

At the first corner Rhoda had to find her way through groups of intense-faced suburbans who were waiting for their respective cars, and who heaped themselves on board as these arrived, and hurried to find places, more from force of habit than from necessity, for the pressure of the evening travel was already over. When she had passed these groups she began to meet the proper life of the street—the women who had come out to cheapen the next day's provisions at the markets, the men, in the brief leisure that their day's work had left them before bed-time, lounging at the lattice doors of the drinking shops, or standing listlessly about on the curb-stones smoking. Numbers of young fellows, of the sort whose leisure is day-long, exchanged the comfort of a mutual support with the house walls, and stared at her as she hurried by; and then she began to encoun-ter in greater and greater number the colored people who de-scended to this popular promenade from the uphill streets open-ing upon it. They politely made way for her, and at the first meeting that new agony of interest in them possessed her.

This was intensified by the deference they paid her as a young white lady, and the instant sense that she had no right to it in that quality. She could have borne better to have them rude and even insolent; there was something in the way they turned their black eyes in their large disks of white upon her, like dogs, with a mute animal appeal in them, that seemed to claim her and own her one of them, and to creep nearer and nearer and possess her in that late-found solidarity of race. She never knew before how hideous they were, with their flat wide-nostriled noses, their out-rolled thick lips, their mobile, bulging eyes set near together, their retreating chins and foreheads, and their smooth, shining skin: they seemed burlesques of humanity, worse than apes, because they were more like. But the men were not half so bad as the women, from the shrill-piped young girls, with their grotesque attempts at fashion, to the old grandmoth-ers, wrinkled or obese, who came down the sloping sidewalks in their bare heads, out of the courts and alleys where they lived, to get the evening air. Impish black children swarmed on these uphill sidewalks, and played their games, with shrill cries racing back and forth, catching and escaping one another.

These colored folk were of all tints and types, from the com-edy of the pure black to the closest tragical approach to white. She saw one girl, walking with a cloud of sable companions, who was as white as herself, and she wondered if she were of the same dilution of negro blood; she was laughing and chatter-ing with the rest, and seemed to feel no difference, but to be pleased and flattered with the court paid her by the inky dandy who sauntered beside her.

"She has always known it; she has never felt it!" she thought, bitterly. "It is nothing; it is natural to her; I might have been like her."

She began to calculate how many generations would carry her back, or that girl back, in hue to the blackest of those loathsome old women. She knew what an octoroon was, and she thought, "I am like her, and my mother was darker, and my grandmother darker, and my great-grander like a mulatto, and then it was a horrible old negress, a savage stolen from Africa, where she had been a cannibal."

A vision of palm-tree roofs and grass huts, as she had seen them in pictures, with skulls grinning from the eaves, floated before her eyes; then a desert, with a long coffle of captives passing by, and one black naked woman, fallen out from weakness, kneeling, with manacled hands, and her head pulled back, and the Arab slaver's knife at her throat. She walked in a nightmare of these sights; all the horror of the wrong by which she came to be, poured itself round and over her.

She emerged from it at moments with a refusal to accept the loss of her former self: like that of the mutilated man who looks where his arm was, and cannot believe it gone. Like him, she had the full sense of what was lost, the unbroken consciousness of what was lopped away. At these moments, all her pride reasserted itself; she wished to punish her aunt for what she had made her suffer, to make her pay pang for pang. Then the tide of reality overwhelmed her again, and she grovelled in self-loathing and despair. From that she rose in a frenzy of longing to rid herself of this shame that was not hers; to tear out the stain; to spill it with the last drop of her blood upon the ground. By flamy impulses she thrilled towards the mastery of her misery through its open acknowledgment. She seemed to see herself and hear herself stopping some of these revolting creatures, the dreadfulest of them, and saying, "I am black, too. Take me home with you, and let me live with you, and be like you every way." She thought, "Perhaps I have relations among them. Yes, it must be. I will send to the hotel for my things, and I will live here in some dirty little back court, and try to find them out."

The emotions, densely pressing upon each other, the dramatizations that took place as simultaneously and unsuccessively as the events of a dream, gave her a new measure of time; she compassed the experience of years in the seconds these sensations outnumbered.

All the while she seemed to be walking swiftly, flying forward; but the ground was uneven: it rose before her, and then suddenly fell. She felt her heart beat in the middle of her throat. Her head felt light, like the blowball of a dandelion. She wished to laugh. There seemed two selves of her, one that had lived before that awful knowledge, and one that had lived as long since, and again a third that knew and pitied them both. She wondered at the same time if this were what people meant by saying one's brain was turned; and she recalled the longing with which her aunt said, "If I were *only* crazy!" But she knew that her own exaltation was not madness, and she did not wish for escape that way. "There must be some other," she said to herself; "if I can find the courage for it, I can find the way. It's like a ghost: if I keep going towards it, it won't hurt me; I mustn't be afraid of it. Now, let me see! What *ought* I to do? Yes, that is the key: *Duty.*" Then her thought flew passionately off. "If *she* had done her duty all this might have been helped. But it was her cowardice that made her murder me. Yes, she has killed me!"

The tears gushed into her eyes, and all the bitterness of her trial returned upon her, with a pressure of lead on her brain.

In the double consciousness of trouble she was as fully aware of everything about her as she was of the world of misery within her; and she knew that this had so far shown itself without that some of the passers were noticing her. She stopped, fearful of their notice, at the corner of the street she had come to, and turned about to confront an old colored woman, yellow like saffron, with the mild, sad face we often see in mulattoes of

that type, and something peculiarly pitiful in the straight under-
lip of her appealing mouth, and the cast of her gentle eyes. The
expression might have been merely physical, or it might have
been a hereditary look, and no part of her own personality,
but Rhoda felt safe in it.

"What street is this?" she asked, thinking, suddenly, "She
is the color of my grandmother; that is the way she looked,"
but though she thought this she did not realize it, and she kept
an imperious attitude towards the old woman.

"Charles Street, lady."

"Oh, yes; Charles. Where are all the people going?"

"The colored folks, lady?"

"Yes."

"Well, lady, they's a kyind of an evenin' meetin' at ouah
choach to-night. Some of 'em's goin' there, I reckon; some of
'em's just out fo' a walk."

"Will you let me go with you?" Rhoda asked.

"Why, certainly, lady," said the old woman. She glanced up
at Rhoda's face as the girl turned again to accompany her.
"But *I'm* a-goin' to choach."

"Yes, yes. That's what I mean. I want to go to your church
with you. Are you from the South—Louisiana? She would be
the color," she thought. "It might be my mother's own mother."

"No, lady: from Voginny. I was bawn a slave; and I lived
there till after the wa'. Then I come Nawth."

"Oh," said Rhoda, disappointedly, for she had nerved herself to find this old woman her grandmother.

They walked on in silence for a while; then the old woman
said, "I thought you wasn't very well, when I noticed you at the
cawnah."

"I am well," Rhoda answered, feeling the tears start to her
eyes again at the note of motherly kindness in the old woman's
voice. "But I am in trouble; I am in trouble."

"Then you're gwine to the right place, lady," said the old
woman, and she repeated solemnly these words of hope and
promise which so many fainting hearts have stayed themselves

upon: " 'Come unto me, all ye that labor and are heavy laden, and I will give you rest unto your souls.' Them's the words, lady; the Lawd's own words. Glory be to God; glory be to God!" she added in a whisper.

"Yes, yes," said Rhoda, impatiently. "They are good words. But they are not for me. He can't make *my* burden light; He can't give *me* rest. If it were sin, He could; but it isn't sin; it's something worse than sin; more hopeless. If I were only a sinner, the vilest, the wickedest, how glad I should be!" Her heart uttered itself to this simple nature as freely as a child's to its mother.

"Why, sholy, lady," said the old woman, with a little shrinking from her as if she had blasphemed, "sholy you's a sinnah?"

"No, I am not!" said the girl, with nervous sharpness. "If I were a sinner, my sin could be forgiven me, and I could go free of my burden. But nothing can ever lift it from me."

"The Lawd kin do anything, the Bible says. He kin make the dead come to life. He done it oncet, too."

The girl turned abruptly on her. "Can He change your skin? Can He make black white?"

The old woman seemed daunted; she faltered. "I don't know as He ever tried, lady; the Bible don't tell." She added, more hopefully, "But I reckon He could do it if He wanted to."

"Then why doesn't He do it?" demanded the girl. "What does He leave you black for, when He could make you white?"

"I reckon He don't think it's worth while, if He can make me *willing to be black* so easy. Somebody's got to be black, and it might as well be me," said the old woman with a meek sigh.

"No, no one need be black!" said Rhoda, with a vehemence that this submissive sigh awakened in her. "If He cared for us, no one would be!"

" 'Sh!" said the old woman, gently.

They had reached the church porch, and Rhoda found herself in the tide of black worshippers who were drifting in. The faces of some were supernaturally solemn, and these rolled their large-whited eyes rebukingly on the young girls showing all their teeth in the smiles that gashed them from ear to ear, and carrying on subdued flirtations with the polite young fellows escorting them. It was no doubt the best colored society, and it was bearing itself with propriety and self-respect in the court of the temple. If their natural gayety and lightness of heart moved their youth to the betrayal of their pleasure in each other in the presence of their Maker, He was perhaps propitiated by the gloom of their elders.

" 'Tain't a regular evenin' meetin'," Rhoda's companion explained to her. "It's a kind o' lecture." She exchanged some stately courtesies of greeting with the old men and women as they pushed into the church; they called her sister, and they looked with at least as little surprise and offence at the beautiful young white lady with her as white Christians would have shown a colored girl come to worship with them. "De preacher's one o' the Southern students; I 'ain't hud him speak; but I reckon the Lawd's sent him, anyway."

Rhoda had no motive in being where she was except to confront herself as fully and closely with the trouble in her soul as she could. She thought, so far as such willing may be called thinking, that she could strengthen herself for what she had henceforth to bear, if she could concentrate and intensify the fact to her outward perception; she wished densely to surround herself with the blackness from which she had sprung, and to reconcile herself to it, by realizing and owning it with every sense.

She did not know what the speaker was talking about at first, but phrases and words now and then caught in her consciousness. He was entirely black, and he was dressed in black from head to foot, so that he stood behind the pulpit light like a thick, soft shadow cast upon the wall by an electric. His absolute sable was relieved only by the white points of his shirt collar, and the glare of his spectacles, which, when the light struck them, heightened the goblin effect of his presence. He had no discernible features, and when he turned his profile in addressing those who sat at the sides, it was only a wavering blur against the wall.

His voice was rich and tender, with those caressing notes in it which are the peculiar gift of his race.

The lecture opened with prayer and singing, and the lecturer took part in the singing; then he began to speak, and Rhoda's mind to wander, with her eyes, to the congregation. The prevailing blackness gave back the light here and there in the glint of a bald head or from a patch of white wool, or the cast of a rolling eye. Inside of the bonnets of the elder women, and under the gay hats of the young girls, it was mostly lost in a characterless dark; but nearer by, Rhoda distinguished faces, sad repulsive visages of a frog-like ugliness added to the repulsive black in all its shades, from the unalloyed brilliancy of the pure negro type to the pallid yellow of the quadroon. These mixed bloods were more odious to her than the others, because she felt herself more akin to them; but they were all abhorrent. Some of the elder people made fervent responses to thoughts and sentiments in the lecture as if it had been a sermon. "That is so!" they said. "Bless the Lord, that's the truth!" and "Glory to God!" One old woman who sat in the same line of pews with Rhoda opened her mouth like a catfish to emit these pious ejaculations.

The night was warm, and as the church filled, the musky exhalations of their bodies thickened the air, and made the girl faint; it seemed to her that she began to taste the odor; and these poor people, whom their Creator has made so hideous by the standards of all his other creatures, roused a cruel loathing in her, which expressed itself in a frantic refusal of their claim upon her. In her heart she cast them off with vindictive hate. "Yes," she thought, "I should have whipped them, too. They are animals; they are only fit to be slaves." But when she shut her eyes, and heard their wild, soft voices, her other senses were holden, and she was rapt by the music from her frenzy of abhorrence. In one of these suspenses, while she sat listening to the sound of the lecturer's voice, which now and then struck a plangent note, like some rich, melancholy bell, a meaning began to steal out of it to her whirling thoughts.

"Yes, my friends," it went on saying, "you got to commence doing a person good if you expect to love them as Jesus loved us when he died for us. And oh, if our white brethren could only understand—and they're gettin' to understand it—that if they would help us a little more, they needn't hate us so much, what a great thing," the lecturer lamely concluded—"what a great thing it would be all round!"

"Amen! Love's the thing," said the voice of the old woman with the catfish mouth; and Rhoda, who did not see her, did not shudder. Her response inspired the lecturer to go on. "I believe it's the one way out of all the trouble in this world. You can't fight your way out, and you can't steal your way out, and you can't lie your way out. But you can *love* your way out. And how can you love your way out? By helpin' somebody else! Yes, that's it. Somebody that needs your help. And now if there's any one here that's in trouble, and wants to get out of trouble, all he's got to do is to help somebody else out. Remember that when the collection is taken up durin' the singin' of the hymn. Our college needs help, and every person that helps our college helps himself. Let us pray!"

The application was apt enough, and Rhoda did not feel anything grotesque in it. She put into the plate which the old woman passed to her from the collector all the money she had in her purse, notes and silver, and two or three gold pieces that had remained over to her from her European travel. Her companion saw them, and interrupted herself in her singing to say, "The Lawd 'll bless it to you; He'll help them that helps others that can't help themselves."

"Yes, that is the clew," the girl said to herself. "That is the way out; the only way. I can endure them if I can love them, and I shall love them if I try to help them. This money will help them."

But she did not venture to look round at the objects of her beneficence; she was afraid that the sight of their faces would harden her heart against them in spite of her giving, and she kept her eyes shut, listening to their pathetic voices. She stood

forgetful after the lecturer had pronounced the benediction—
he was a divinity student, and he could not forego it—and her
companion had to touch her arm. Then she started with a
shiver, as if from a hypnotic trance.

Once out on the street she was afraid, and begged the old
woman to go back to her hotel with her.

"Why, sholy, lady," she consented.

But Rhoda did not hear. Her mind had begun suddenly to
fasten itself upon a single thought, a sole purpose, and "Yes,"
she pondered, "that is the first thing of all: to forgive her; to tell
her that I forgive her, and that I understand and pity her. But
how—how shall I begin? I shall have to do her some good to
begin with, and how can I do that when I hate her so? I do
hate her; I do hate her! It is her fault!"

As she hurried along, almost running, and heedless of the
old woman at her side, trying to keep up with her, it seemed to
her that if her aunt had told her long ago, when a child, what
she was, she would somehow not have been it now.

It was not with love, not with pardon, but with frantic hate
and accusal in her heart, that she burst into the room, and
rushed to Mrs. Meredith's sofa, where she lay still.

"Aunt Caroline, wake up! Can you sleep when you see me
going perfectly crazy? It is no time for sleeping! Wake!"

The moony pallor of an electric light suspended over the
street shone in through the naked window, and fell upon Mrs.
Meredith's face. It was white, and as the girl started back her
foot struck the empty bottle from which the woman had drained
the sleeping medicine, and let lie where she had let it fall upon
the floor. Rhoda caught it up, and flew with it to the light.

IX

THE THING that had been lurking in a dark corner of Olney's
mind, intangible if not wholly invisible, came out sensible to
touch and sight when he parted with Mrs. Meredith. At first
it masqueraded a little longer as resentment of that hapless

creature's fate, a creature so pretty, so proud, and by all the rights
of her youth and sex heiress of a prosperous and unclouded
future, the best love and the tenderest care that any man could
give her. Then it began to declare itself a fear lest the man
whose avowal had given him the right to know everything concerning her, might prove superior to it, and nobly renounce
his privilege, and gladly take her for what she had always
seemed, for what, except in so remote degree, she really was.
Then Olney knew that he was himself in love with her, and
that he was judging a rival's possibilities by his own, and dread-
ing them. He had an impulse to go back to Mrs. Meredith and
say that he was ready to take all these risks and chances which
she had counted so great, and laugh them to scorn in the glad-
ness of his heart if he could only hope that Rhoda would ever
love him. A few years before he would have obeyed his impulse,
and even now he dramatized an obedience to it, and exacted
from Mrs. Meredith a promise that she would not speak to Miss
Aldgate until he had found time to put his fortune to the touch,
and if he won, would never speak to her. But at thirty he had
his hesitations, his misgivings, not indeed as to the wish, but as
to the way. For one thing, he was too late, if Mrs. Meredith's
conjectures were right; and for another, he felt it dishonorable
to do what he longed in his heart to do, and steal from this man,
whom he began to hate, the love upon which his courageous
wooing had given him the right to count. Such a thing would be
not theft only in the possible but not probable case she did not
care for his rival, and he had no means of knowing the fact as
to that. It might be defended if not justified on the ground that
he wished to keep her forever in ignorance of what it was Mrs.
Meredith's clear duty otherwise to tell her; Olney comforted
himself with the theory that a woman who had delayed in her
duty so long would doubtless put it off till the last moment,
and that until this Mr. Bloomingdale actually appeared, and
there was no loop-hole left her, she would not cease attempting
to escape from her duty.

He postponed any duty which he himself had in the matter

through the love he now owned; he made it contingent upon hers; but all the same, he determined to forego no right it gave him. Again he had a mind to go back to Mrs. Meredith, and ask her to do nothing until Bloomingdale came, and then, before she spoke, to authorize him to approach the man as her family physician and deal tentatively, hypothetically, with the matter, and interpret his probable decision from his actual behavior.

This course, which appeared the only course open to him, commended itself more and more to Olney as he thought of it; here was something practicable, here was something that was perhaps even obligatory upon him; he tried to believe it was obligatory. But it occurred to him only after long turmoil of thinking and feeling in other directions, and it was half past seven o'clock before he returned from a walk he took as a final means of clearing his mind, and went to Mrs. Meredith's room to propose it to her. He knocked several times without response, and then went to the office to see if she had gone out and left her key with the clerk; he was now in a hurry to speak to her.

The clerk felt in the pigeon-hole of Mrs. Meredith's number. "Her key isn't here, but that's no sign she hasn't gone out. Ladies seldom leave their keys when they go out; we're only too glad if they leave 'em when they go away for good. I thought she was sick."

"She would be able to drive out."

Olney mastered his impatience as well as he could, and went in to his dinner. After dinner he knocked again at Mrs. Meredith's door, and confirmed himself in the belief that she had gone out. After that it was not so easy to wait for her to come back. He wished to remain of the mind he had been about speaking to her of Rhoda, and to avow himself her lover at all risks, but more and more he began to feel that he was too late, that he was quixotic, that he was ridiculous. He felt himself wavering from his purpose, and he held to it all the more tenaciously for that reason. If he was willing to hazard all upon the chance of being in time, that gave him the right to ask that the girl might be spared; but when he thought she and Mrs.

Meredith were probably spending the evening together with the Bloomingdales, his courage failed. It was but too imaginable that Miss Aldgate had made up her mind to accept that man, and that her aunt would tell her all that he longed to save her from knowing before he could prevent it.

When at last he went a third time to her door, he ventured to turn the knob, and the door opened to his inward pressure. It let in with him a glare of gas from the lamp in the entry, and by this light he saw Rhoda standing beside her aunt's sofa with the empty bottle in her hand. She had her hat on, and at the face she turned him across her shoulder, a shiver of prescience passed over him. It was the tragic mask, the inherited woe, unlit by a gleam of the brightness which had sometimes seemed Heaven's direct gift to the girl on whom that burden of ancestral sin and sorrow had descended.

"What is the matter?" he murmured.

Rhoda gave him the empty bottle. "She's drunk it all. She's dead."

"Oh no," he almost laughed. "It would be too soon." He dropped on his knees beside the insensible body, and satisfied himself by pulse and breath that the life had not yet left it. But to keep it there was now the business, and Olney began his losing fight with a sort of pluriscience in which it seemed to him that he was multiplied into three selves: one applying all the antidotes and using all the professional skill with instant coolness; another guarding the probable suicide from the conjecture of the hotel servants and keeping the whole affair as silent as possible; another devotedly vigilant of the poor girl who was so deeply concerned in the small chances of success perceptible to Olney, and who, whether he succeeded or not, was destined to so sad an orphanage. When he thought of the chance that fate was invisibly offering her, he almost wished he might fail, but he fought his battle through with relentless scientific conscience. At the end it was his part to say, "It's over; she's dead."

"I knew she was," Rhoda answered, apathetically. "I expected it."

"Where were you?" he asked, with the sort of sad futility with which, when all is done, the spirit continues its endeavor. "Was she alone?"

"Yes. I had gone out," Rhoda said.

"What time was that?" Olney wondered that he had not asked this before; perhaps he had made some mistake through not having verified the moment.

"It was about half past seven," answered the girl.

"You went out at half past seven! And when did you return?"

"We had a quarrel. I didn't come back till nearly ten—when you came in."

The poignancy of Olney's interest remained, but it took another direction. "You were out all the evening *alone?* Excuse my asking," he made haste to add. "But I don't understand—"

"I wasn't alone," said Rhoda. "I met an old colored woman on the street, and she went with me to the colored church. She came home with me." The girl said this quietly, as if there were nothing at all strange in it.

Her calm left Olney in the question which he was always pressing home to himself: whether her aunt had told her that thing. It was on his tongue to ask her why she went to the colored church, and what her quarrel with her aunt was about. He asked her instead, "Did you think, when you left her, that Mrs. Meredith seemed different at all—that—?"

"I didn't notice," said Rhoda. "No. She seemed as she often did. But I know she thought she hadn't taken enough of the medicine. She wanted to sleep more."

Rhoda sat by the window of the little parlor where she had sat when the dead woman told her that dreadful thing, and she remembered how she had glanced out of it and seen Olney in the street. The gas was now at full blaze in the room, but she glanced through the window again, and saw that the day was beginning to come outside. She turned from the chill of its pale light, and looked at Olney. Through the irresistible association of ideas, she looked for his baldness with the lack-lustre eyes she lifted to his face.

"Is there anything you wish me—anything I can do?" he

asked, after a silence, in which he got back to the level of practical affairs, though still stupefied from what Rhoda had said.

"No."

"I mean, notify your friends—your family—telegraph—"

"I have no friends—no relatives. We were alone; all our family are dead."

"But Mr. Meredith's family—there is surely some one you can call upon at this time."

A strong compassion swelled in Olney's heart; he yearned to take her in his arms and be all the world to one who had no one in all the world.

She remained as if dazed, and then she said, with a perplexed look: "I was trying to think who there was. Mr. Meredith's people lived in St. Louis; I remember some of them when I was little. Perhaps my aunt would have their address."

She went into the adjoining chamber where the dead woman lay, in the atmosphere of useless drugs and effectless antidotes, and Olney thought, "It's the mechanical operation of custom; she's going to ask her," but Rhoda came back with an address-book in her hand, as if she had gone directly to Mrs. Meredith's writing-case for it with no such error of cerebration.

"Here it is," she said.

"Very well. I'll telegraph them at once. But in the mean time what will you do, Miss Aldgate? You can't stay here in the hotel—*she* can't. How can I be of use to you?" Olney felt all the disinterestedness in the world in asking, but in what he asked next he had a distinct consciousness of self-interest, or at least of selfish curiosity. "Shall I let your friends at the Vendome—"

"Oh, no, no, no!" she broke out. "Not on any account! I couldn't bear to see them. Don't think of such a thing! No, *indeed*, I can't let you!"

The self-seeker is never fully rewarded, and Olney was left with a doubt whether this reluctance meant abhorrence of the Bloomingdales, or unwillingness to receive kindness from them which might involve some loss of her perfect independence to the spirited girl; she would not choose or be chosen for any reason but one. He could not make out from her manner as yet whether her aunt had spoken what was on her mind to speak or not; it seemed such a cruel invasion of her rights even to con-jecture that he tried to put the question out of his thoughts.

He began again while he was sensible of an unequal struggle with the question, which intruded itself in the swift whirl of his anxieties, as to what could immediately be done for her.

"Is there anything else you would suggest?"

"No," said the girl, in the dreamy quiet she seemed helpless to emerge from. "I suppose it wouldn't do, even if we could find her. I was thinking of the old woman I saw to-night," she explained. "I would like to go and stay with her if I could."

"Is it some one you know?"

"No, I don't know her. I just met her on the street, and we went to the colored people's church together. I went out after dinner, and left my aunt alone. That was when she drank it."

She added the vague sentences together with a child's heed-lessness as to their reaching her listener's intelligence, and she did not persist in her whimsical suggestion.

Olney left it too. "You must let me get you another room," he said; "you can't stay here any longer," and he made her take her hat and come with him to the hotel parlor. He went to arrange the business with the clerk, and to tell him of Mrs. Meredith's death; then he had to go about other duties con-nected with the case, which he rather welcomed as a distraction: to notify the fact and cause of Mrs. Meredith's death to the authorities, and to give the funeral preparations in charge. But when this was all done, and he could no longer play off the aggregate of these minor cares against his great one, he began to be harassed again about Miss Aldgate.

X

It was so much easier to dispose of the friendless dead than the friendless living, Olney thought, with a sardonic perception of one of the bitterest truths in the world; and he was not consoled by the reflection that it is often the man readiest to do all for a woman who can do nothing for her. At the same time he hurried along imagining a scene in which Rhoda owned her love for him, and for his sake and her own consented to throw convention to the winds, and to unite her fate with his in a marriage truly solemnized by the presence of death. He was aroused from this preposterous melodrama by a voice that said, with liking and astonishment, "Why, Dr. Olney!" and he found himself confronted with Mrs. Atherton, whom he had known as Miss Clara Kingsbury. In another moment she had flooded him with inquiry and explanation, from which he emerged with the dim consciousness that he had told her how he happened not to be in Florence, and had heard how she happened to be in Boston. Her presence in the city at such an untimely season was to be accounted for by the eccentric spirit in which she carried on her visiting for the Associated Charities; she visited her families in the summer, while most people looked after their families only in the winter. She excused herself by saying that Beverly was so near, and sometimes it gave her a chance for a little bohemian lunch with Mr. Atherton.

Olney laid his trouble before her. He knew from of old that if he could not count upon her tact, he could count upon her imagination, and he was quite prepared for the sympathy with which she rushed to his succor, a sympathy that in spite of the circumstances could not be called less than jubilant.

"Why, the poor, forlorn little helpless creature!" she exulted. "I'll go to the hotel at once with you, doctor; and she must come down to Beverly with me, and stay till her friends come on for her."

The question whether he was not bound in honor to tell Mrs. Atherton just what Miss Aldgate was, crazily visited him, and became a kind of longing before he could rid himself of it; he dismissed it only upon the terms of a self-promise to entertain it some other time; and he availed himself of her good offices almost as joyfully as she proposed them. He had to submit to the romantic supposition which he was aware Mrs. Atherton was keeping out of her words and looks, and he joined her in the conspicuous pretence she made throughout the affair that he was acting from the most disinterested, the most scientific motives.

It was not so hard as he had fancied it might be to get Miss Aldgate's consent to Mrs. Atherton's hospitality. It was the only possible thing for her, and she acquiesced simply, like one accustomed to favors; she expressed a sense of the kindness done her, with a delicate self-respect which Olney hardly knew how to account for upon the theory that Mrs. Meredith had spoken to her. Apparently she appreciated all the necessities of the case, and she did not troublesomely interpose any of the reluctances of grief which he had expected. If he could have wished any difference in her it would have been for rather less composure; but then this might have been the apathy following the great shock she had received. He willingly accepted Mrs. Atherton's theory, hurriedly whispered at parting, that she did not realize what had happened yet; Mrs. Atherton seemed to prize her the more for it.

He came back from seeing them off on the train to the hotel, where he found a telegram from Mrs. Meredith's connections in St. Louis. They were very sorry; they were unable to come on; they would write. Olney felt a grateful lift of the heart in thinking of Miss Aldgate in Mrs. Atherton's affectionate keeping, as he crumpled the despatch in his hand and tossed it on his dismal white marble hearth. He believed that he read between its words a revelation of the fact that the dead woman's husband had not kept Rhoda's secret from his family, and that these unable friends, whatever they wrote, were not likely to urge any claim to comfort the girl.

It was Mrs. Bloomingdale who came to do this with several of her large and passive daughters, about as long after the evening papers came out as would take her to drive over from the Vendome. Olney had been able to persuade the reporters who got hold of the case that there was nothing to work up in it, and the paragraph that Mrs. Bloomingdale saw was discreet enough; it attributed Mrs. Meredith's death to an overdose of the soporific prescribed for her, and it connected Olney's name with the matter as the physician who happened to be stopping in the hotel with the unfortunate lady.

"I came the instant I read it," Mrs. Bloomingdale explained, "for I couldn't believe the evidence of my senses," and she added such a circumstantial statement of her mental struggle with the fact projected into her consciousness as could leave no doubt that the fact itself was far less important than the effect produced upon her.

As Olney listened he lost entirely a lurking discomfort he had felt at Miss Aldgate's refusal to let those people have anything to do with her or for her in her calamity. Whatever the son might be, the mother was a vulgarly selfish woman, posing before him as a generous benefactress, who was also a martyr. "I asked for you, doctor," she went on, at the end of her personal history in connection with the affair, "because I preferred not to intrude upon that poor young creature without learning just how I ought to approach her. As I said to my daughter Roberta, in coming along"—she put the tallest and serenest of the big, still blondes in evidence with a wave of her hand—"I would be ruled entirely by what you said of the newspaper report."

Olney said of it dryly that it was quite correct.

"Oh, I am *so* relieved, doctor!" said Mrs. Bloomingdale. "I didn't know, don't you know—I thought perhaps that there were facts—details which you preferred to keep from the public; that there were peculiar circumstances—aberration, don't you know; and that kind of thing. But I'm so glad there wasn't!"

Olney felt a malicious desire to disturb this crowing complacency which he believed was the cover of mean anxieties and suspicions. He asked, "Do you mean suicide?"

"Well, no; not that exactly. But—" She stopped, and he merely said:

"There was no evidence of suicidal intent."

"Oh!" said Mrs. Bloomingdale, but, as he intended, not so crowingly this time. "And then—you think I can ask for Miss Aldgate?"

"Miss Aldgate is not here—" Olney began.

"Not here!"

"She is with Mrs. Atherton, at Beverly. She couldn't remain here, you know."

"And may I ask—do I understand— Why didn't Miss Aldgate let *us* know?"

Olney rejoiced to be able to say, "I suggested that, but she preferred not to disturb you."

"And *why* did she prefer that?" said Mrs. Bloomingdale, with rising crest.

"I'm sorry, I don't know. It was by accident that I met Mrs. Atherton on the street; she is a well-known lady here, and she at once took Miss Aldgate home with her."

At the bottom of his heart Olney did not feel altogether easy at what he knew of Miss Aldgate's relations to the Blooming-dale family. He would have liked to blind himself to facts that proved her weak or at least light-mindedly fond of any present pleasure at the cost of any future complication, but he was not quite able to do so, much as he wished to inculpate the Bloom-ingdales. He was silent, and attempted no farther explanation or defence of Rhoda's refusal to see them.

"I presume, Dr. Olney," Mrs. Bloomingdale went on, "that you know nothing of the circumstances of our acquaintance with Miss Aldgate; and I can't expect you to sympathize with my—my—surprise that she should have turned from us at such a time. But I must say that I am very greatly surprised. Or not surprised, exactly. Pained."

"I am very sorry," Olney said again. "I have no right to intervene in any matter so far beyond my functions as Mrs. Meredith's physician, but I venture to suggest that the blow which has fallen on Miss Aldgate is enough to account for what seems strange to you in—"

"Of course. Certainly. I make allowance for that," said Mrs. Bloomingdale; and Olney was aware of receiving this proof of her amiability, her liberality, with regret; he would have so willingly had it otherwise, in justification of Miss Aldgate. "And

I know that the past year has been one of great anxiety both to Mrs. Meredith and Miss Aldgate. You know they had lost their money?"

"No," said Olney, with a joyful throb of the heart, "I didn't."

"I have understood so. Miss Aldgate will be left without anything—in a manner. But that would have made no difference to us. We should have been only too glad to prove to her that it made no difference. But if she prefers not to see us— We expect my son by Wednesday's steamer in New York." She added this suddenly and with apparent irrelevance, but Olney perceived that she wished to test his knowledge of the whole case, and she had instantly learned from his face that he knew much more than he would own. But he made no verbal concession to her curiosity. "I think you met my son in Florence?" she said.

"I saw him at Professor Garofalo's one night."

"He was there a great deal. It was there he met—Mrs. Meredith." Olney said nothing, and Mrs. Bloomingdale rose, and as with the same motion her large daughters rose. "May I ask, Dr. Olney, that you will give Miss Aldgate our love, and say to her that if there is anything we can do, we shall be so— I suppose you have had to communicate with Mrs. Meredith's— or Mr. Meredith's rather—family?"

"Yes."

"They will be at the funeral, of course; and if—"

"They are not coming," said Olney. "They have telegraphed that they are unable to come."

"Oh," said Mrs. Bloomingdale; and after a little pause she said, "Good-afternoon," and led her girls out.

Olney felt that he had parted with an enemy, and that though he had in one sort tried to keep a conscientious neutrality, he had discharged himself of an offensive office in a hostile manner, that he had made her his enemy if not Miss Aldgate's enemy. She suspected him, he knew that, of having somehow come between her and Miss Aldgate of his own will as well as Rhoda's. In view of this fact he had to ask himself to be very explicit as to his feelings, his hopes, his intentions; and after a season of close question, the response was very clear. He could not doubt what he wished to do; the only doubt he had was as to how and where and whether he could do it.

XI

THE DAY of the funeral Bloomingdale arrived. None of his family had come to the last rites, though Olney had made it a point both of conscience and of honor to let them know when and where the ceremony would take place. He felt that their absence was an expression of resentment, but that it was a provisional resentment merely. There was a terrible provisionality about the whole business, beginning with the provisional deposition of the dead in the receiving-vault at Mount Auburn, till it could be decided where the long-tormented clay was finally to rest. Every decision concerning the affair seemed postponed, but he did not know till when; death had apparently decided nothing; he did not see how life should.

Bloomingdale came to see him in the evening, after dinner. His steamer had been late in getting up to her dock, and he had missed the first train on to Boston. He explained the fact briefly to Olney, and he said he had come directly to see him. He recalled their former meeting in Florence, but said, with somehow an effect of disappointment, that he had taken an older man whom he had seen at Professor Garofalo's for Dr. Olney. On his part Olney could have owned to an equal disappointment. He remembered perfectly that Mr. Bloomingdale was a slight, dark man; but the composite Bloomingdale type, from the successive impressions of his mother's and sisters' style, was so deeply stamped in his consciousness that he was surprised to find the young minister himself neither large nor blond. His mind wandered from him to the father whom he had never seen, but who had left so distinct a record of himself in his son, and not in his daughters, as fathers are supposed usually to do. Then Olney's thoughts turned to that whole vexed question of heredity, and he lost himself deeply in conjecture of Rhoda's ancestry, while Bloomingdale was feeling his way forward to inquiry about her through explanation and interest concerning Mrs. Meredith, and a fit sympathy, a most intelligent and delicate appreciation of the situation in all its details. Before the fact formulated itself in his mind Olney was aware of feeling that this man was as different from his family in the most essential and characteristic qualities as he was different from them in temperament and complexion.

"And now about Miss Aldgate, Dr. Olney," he said, with a kind of authority, which Olney instinctively, however unwillingly, admitted. "I shall have to tell you why I am so very anxious to know how she is—how she bears this blow. I am afraid my mother betrayed to you the hurt which she felt that Miss Aldgate should not have turned to her in her trouble; but I can understand how impossible it was she should. Without reflecting upon my mother at all for her feeling—for I can see how she would feel as she does—I must say I don't share it. While Miss Aldgate was still uncertain about—about myself— it was simply impossible that she should receive any sort of favor or kindness from my family even in such an exigency as this. It would have been indelicate; it must have been infinitely easier for her to accept the good offices of a total stranger, as she has done. Dr. Olney, I have to ask *your* good offices—and I have first to make you a confidence, as my reason for asking them. I'm *sure* you will understand me!"

In the fervor of his feeling the young man's voice trembled, and Olney felt himself moved with a curious involuntary kindness for him—the sort of admiring pity which men have been said to feel toward a brave foeman they mean to fight to the death. "I had a very great hope—and I think I had grounds for my hope—that Miss Aldgate would have consented to be my wife when she met me, if this terrible visitation—if all had gone well." The words sent a cold thrill through Olney's heart, and the mere suggestion that Rhoda could be anybody's wife but his own steeled it against this pretender to her love. "I offered myself to her in Liverpool before she sailed, and she was to have

given me her answer here when we met. Now, I don't know
what to do. I don't know anything. The whole world seems
tumbled back into chaos. I can't urge anything upon her at
such a time. I'm not even sure that I can decently ask to see her.
And yet if I don't, what may not she think? Can't you help me
in this matter? You were Mrs. Meredith's physician, and you
stand in a sort of relation to Miss Aldgate that would authorize
you to let her know that I am here, and very anxious to know
what her wish—her will—is as to our meeting. It might not be
professional, exactly, but—I came to you with the hope that
it might be possible. Does it seem asking too much? I should be
very sorry—"

Olney saw that the man's sensitiveness was taking fire, and
in spite of his resentment of a request which set aside all his
own secret hopes and intentions as non-existent, he could not
forbear a concession to his unwitting rival's generous feeling.
"Not at all," he said; "but I doubt my authority to intervene
in any way. I have no right—"

"Only the right I've suggested," the young man urged. "I
wouldn't have you assume anything for my sake. But I know
that the circumstances are more than ordinarily distressing, and
that Mrs. Merdith's death came in a way that might make Miss
Aldgate afraid that—that—there might be some shadow of
change in me on account of them. At such times we have misgivings about everybody; but I wish it to be understood that
no circumstance could influence my feeling toward her."

"I don't know whether I understand you exactly," said Olney,
with a growing dread of the man's generosity.

"Why, I suppose, from what I have been able to learn, that
poor Mrs. Meredith committed suicide."

"Not at all," Olney promptly returned. "There is no evidence
of that. There's every indication that she simply took an overdose of the medicine I prescribed. It wouldn't have killed her
of itself, but her forces were otherwise weakened."

"I'm glad, for her sake, to hear it," said Bloomingdale, "but
it would have made no difference with me if it had been differ-

ent. If she had taken her life in a fit of insanity, as I inferred, it would only have made me more constant in the feeling. There is no conceivable disadvantage which would not have endeared Miss Aldgate more to me. I could almost wish for the direst misfortune, the deepest disgrace," he went on, while the tears sprang to his eyes, "to befall her, if only that I might show her that it counted nothing against her, that it counted everything for her!"

Olney's heart sank within him, and he felt guilty before this unselfish frankness, which, if a little boyish, was still so noble. He knew very well that if such a lover could be told everything, it would not matter the least to him; that the girl might be as black as ebony, and his passion would paint her divinely fairer than the lily. Olney knew this from his own thoughts as well as from the other's words; he was himself like the spirit he conceived;

"Du gleichst dem Geist den du begreifst."

But he was aware of an instant purpose not to let his rival be brought to the test; and he was aware at the same time of a duty he had to let him somehow have his chance. "After all," he reflected, "what reason have I to suppose that she ever cared a moment for me, or ever could care? Very likely she likes this fellow; he is lovable; he is a fine fellow, though I hate him so; and what right have I to stand between them? He must have his chance." When he came to this point he said aloud, coldly, "I don't understand what you expect me to do."

"Nothing! Only this: to let me go and see the lady with whom Miss Aldgate is staying, and learn from her whether and when Miss Aldgate will see me. That's all I can reasonably ask. I ought to ask as much if I meant to give her up—and it's all that I ask meaning never to give her up. Yes, that's all I can ask!" he repeated, desperately.

"That will be a very simple matter," said Olney. "Miss Aldgate is with Mrs. Atherton, at Beverly. I can give you her address, and my card to her."

"Yes, yes! Thank you—thank you ever so much. But—but if I present myself without explanation, what will this lady think?"

"She'll give your name to Miss Aldgate, and that will be explanation enough," said Olney, finding something a little superfine in this hesitation, and refusing to himself to be the bearer of any sort of confidences to Mrs. Atherton, who would be only too likely to take a romantic interest in the devoted young minister. Olney meant to give him an even chance, but nothing more.

"True!" said Bloomingdale, nervously gnawing his lip. "True!" He drew a long breath, and added, "Of course, I can't go now till morning."

Olney said nothing as to this. He was writing on his card Mrs. Atherton's address and the introduction for Bloomingdale which he combined with it. He had resolved to go down himself that night. Bloomingdale clung fervently to his hand in parting.

"I can never thank you enough!" he palpitated.

"You have very little to thank me for," said Olney.

XII

IF MRS. ATHERTON thought it strange of Dr. Olney to drive up to her sea-side door at half past nine, out of a white fog that her hospitable hall lamp could pierce only a few paces down the roadway, she dissembled her surprise so well that he felt he was doing the most natural thing, not to say the most conventional thing, in the world. She was notoriously a woman of no tact, but of so much heart that where it was a question at once of friendship and of romance, as the question of Dr. Olney and of Miss Aldgate was with her, she exercised a sort of inspiration in dealing with it. She put herself so wholly at the service of their imagined exigency that she now made Olney feel his welcome most keenly: a welcome which expressed that she would have been equally glad and equally ready to receive him in her sweet-matted, warm-rugged, hearth-fire-lit little drawing-

room, if he had as suddenly appeared at half past two in the
morning. The Japanese portière had not ceased tinkling behind
him when she appeared through it, with outstretched hand. She
promptly refused his excuses. "I really believe I was somehow
expecting you to-night; and I'm ashamed that Mr. Atherton
isn't up to bear witness to my presentiment. But he's had rather
a tiresome day, in town, and he's gone to bed early. I'm glad
to say that Miss Aldgate has gone to her room, too. She's feeling
the reaction from the tension she's been in, and I hope it will
be a complete letting down for her. Have you heard anything
more from those strange people? Very odd they shouldn't any
of them have come on!"

Mrs. Atherton meant the St. Louis connections of Mrs. Meredith, and Olney said, with an embarrassed frown, "No, they
haven't made any sign yet."

"The strange thing about a tragedy of this kind is," Mrs.
Atherton remarked, "that you never can realize that it's ended.
You always think there's going to be something more of it. I
suppose I was thinking that you had heard something disagree-
able from those people, though I don't know what they could
say or do to heighten the tragedy."

"I don't, either," Olney answered. "But something else has
happened, Mrs. Atherton. You were quite right in your fore-
boding that the end was not yet." He paused with a gloomier
air than he knew, for Bloomingdale's appearance was to him
by far the most tragical phase of the affair. Then he went on
thoughtfully: "I hardly know how to approach the matter without seeming to meddle in it more than I mean to do. I wish
absolutely to put myself outside of it. But there's a kind of necessity that I should tell you about it." As he said this the kind of
necessity that he had thought there was instantly vanished, and
left him feeling rather blank. There was no necessity at all that
he should tell Mrs. Atherton what relation Bloomingdale bore,
and wished to bear, toward Miss Aldgate. All that he had to do,
if he had to do anything, was to tell her that he had given him
his card to her, and that she might expect him in the morning,

and so leave her to her conjectures. If he went beyond this, he must go very far beyond it, and not make any confidence for Bloomingdale without making a much ampler confidence for himself. "The fact is, I wish to submit a little case of conscience to you."

Mrs. Atherton was delighted; and if she had been drowsy before, this would have aroused her to the most vigilant alertness. She knew that the case of conscience must somehow have something to do with Miss Aldgate; she believed that it was nothing but a love affair in disguise, and a love affair, with a strong infusion of moral question in it, promised a pleasure to Mrs. Atherton's sympathetic nature which nothing else could give. "Yes?" she said.

"Mrs. Atherton," Olney resumed, "how far do you think a man is justified in pursuing an advantage which another has put in his hands unknowingly—say that another, who did not know that I was his enemy, had put in *my* hands?"

"Not very far, Dr. Olney," she answered, promptly. "In fact, not at all. That is, you might justify such a man if the case were some one else's. But you couldn't justify him if the case were yours."

"I was afraid you would say so; I knew you would say so. Well, the case is mine," said Olney, "and it's this. I've run down here to-night to tell you that I've given my card to a gentleman who will call here in the morning."

Olney paused, and Mrs. Atherton said, "I'm sure I shall be glad to see any friend of yours, Dr. Olney."

"He isn't my friend," Olney returned, gloomily.

"Then, any enemy," Mrs. Atherton suggested.

Olney put the little pleasantry by. "The day before Mrs. Meredith died, she told me something that I need not speak of except as it relates to this Mr. Bloomingdale."

"It's Mr. Bloomingdale who's coming, then?"

"Yes. Do you know anything about him?"

"Oh no! Only it's a very floral kind of name."

"I wish I could be light about the kind of person he is. But

I can't. He's a very formidable kind of person: very sensible, very frank, very generous."

Mrs. Atherton shook her head with a subtle intelligence. "Those might be very disheartening traits—in another."

"They are. They complicate the business for me. This Mr. Bloomingdale has offered himself to Miss Aldgate." Mrs. Atherton's attentive gaze expressed no surprise; probably she had divined this from the beginning. "He was to have had his answer when he met her in Boston," Olney said, with an effect of finding the words a bad taste in his mouth. "That was the arrangement in Liverpool. But of course, now—"

He stopped, and Mrs. Atherton took the word, with a lofty courage:

"Of course now he has all the greater right to it."

"Yes," said Olney, though he did not see why.

"I shall be glad to see Mr. Bloomingdale when he comes," Mrs. Atherton went on; "and though it's an embarrassing moment, I must manage to prepare Miss Aldgate for his coming. She will certainly have her mind made up by this time."

There was something definitive in Mrs. Atherton's tone that made Olney feel as if he had transacted his business, and he rose. He had felt that he ought to tell Mrs. Atherton of his own hopes or purposes in regard to Miss Aldgate; but now that he had given Bloomingdale away, this did not seem necessary. In fact, by a sudden light that flashed upon it, he perceived that it would be allowing his rival a fairer chance if he let him have it without competition. Afterwards when he got out of the house he thought he was a fool to do this; but he could not go back and make his confesssion without appearing a greater fool; and he kept on to the station, and waited there till the last train for town came lagging along, and then he put himself beyond temptation, at least for the night.

He spent what was left of it in imaginary interviews, now with Mrs. Atherton, now with Bloomingdale, now with Rhoda, and now with all of them in various combinations, and constructed futures varying in character from the gayest happiness to the gloom of the darkest tragedy lit by the one high star of self-renunciation. Olney got almost as much satisfaction out of the renunciation as out of the fruition of his hopes. It is apt to be so in these hypothetical cases; perhaps it is often so in experience.

He waited heroically about all the next day to hear from Mrs. Atherton. Something in the pressure of her hand at parting had assured him that she understood everything, and that she was his friend; that they were people of honor, who were bound to do this thing at any cost to him, but that a just Providence would probably not let it cost him much, or at least not everything.

When her letter came at last, hurried forward by a special delivery stamp that spoke volumes in itself, it brought intelligence which at first made Olney feel that he must somehow have been guilty of an unfairness towards Bloomingdale, that he had tacitly if not explicitly prejudiced his case. There was a little magnanimous moment in which he could not rejoice that Miss Aldgate had absolutely refused to see Mr. Bloomingdale; that she had shown both surprise and indignation at his coming; and that no entreaty or argument of Mrs. Atherton's had prevailed with her to show him the slightest mercy, or to send him any message but that of abrupt refusal, which Mrs. Atherton softened to him as best she could. She wrote now that she was sure there must be some misunderstanding, but that in Miss Aldgate's state of nervous exaltation it was perfectly useless to urge anything in excuse of him, and she had to resign herself to the girl's decision. She coincided with Olney in his idea of Bloomingdale's character. She owned to a little fancy for him, and to a great deal of compassion. He had borne the severe treatment he received very manfully, and at the same time gently. He seemed to accept it as final, and he did not rebel against it by the slightest murmur. Olney perceived that Mrs. Atherton had been recognized as his rival's confidante far enough to be authorized to pour balm into his wounds, and that she probably had not spared the balm.

XIII

OLNEY EXPECTED, without being able to say why exactly, a second visit from the man who was now only his former rival. Perhaps it was because he believed he knew why Miss Aldgate had refused to see him that he rather thought the young man would come to ask him. But he did not come, and in the mean time Olney began to perceive that it would have been preposterous for him to have come. Till he learned by inquiry of the clerk at the Vendome that Bloomingdale had left there with his mother and sisters, he did not feel that the minister was out of the story, and that it remained for him alone to read it to the end. He took it for granted that Rhoda treated the man who had certainly a claim upon her kindness in that brusque, not to say brutal manner out of mere hysterical weakness. She had made up her mind to refuse him, and as she felt she might not have strength to endure the sight of the pain she must inflict, she had determined not to witness it. Whether she had loved him too well to afflict him with her secret, or not well enough to trust him with it, was what remained a question with Olney, and he turned from one point of it to the other with the wish to answer it in a sense different from both. What he wished to believe was that she did not love the poor young fellow at all, but this seemed to be too good to be true, and he could not believe it with the constancy of his desire. Nevertheless he had a fitful hold upon it, and it was this faith, wavering and elusive as it was, that encouraged him to think Miss Aldgate would not refuse to see him, and that he might at any rate go down at once to Mrs. Atherton's, and ask about her if not for her.

When he had reasoned to this conclusion, which he reached with electrical rapidity as soon as he knew that Bloomingdale was gone, he acted upon it. Mrs. Atherton received him with a cheerfulness that ignored, at least in Miss Aldgate's presence, the fact that lay hidden in their thoughts if not in hers. Olney was not obliged to ask about her or for her; she came down with Mrs. Atherton, as if it were entirely natural she should do so; and the pathetic confidingness of her reception of him as an old friend brightened almost into the gayety that was her first and principal charm for him. If it had appeared at once this gayety would have troubled him; he would have doubted it for that levity of nature, of race, for which Mrs. Meredith had seen it; but it came out slowly like sunshine through mist, and flattered him with the hope that he had evoked it upon her tragic mask. At the same time he was puzzled, if not shocked, that she seemed forgetful of the woman, so recently gone forever, who had been in all effects a mother to her, and who had sacrificed and borne more than most mothers for her sake. He was himself too inexperienced, as yet, to know that we grieve for the dead only by fits, by impulses; that the soul from time to time flings off with all its force the crushing burden, which then sinks slowly back and bows it in sorrow to the earth again; that if ever grief is constant, it is madness, it is death.

Mrs. Atherton could have told him of moments when the girl was prostrated by her bereavement, and realized to their whole meaning the desolation and despair which it had left her to. But she could not have told him of the stony weight of unforgiveness at the child's heart: of her unreasoning resentment of the dead woman's revelation, as if she had created the fact that she had felt so sorely bound to impart. The tragic circumstances of her death had not won her pardon for this: the girl felt through all that her aunt had somehow *made it so;* and for her, ignorant of it all her life till that avowal, she had indeed made it so. Whether a wiser and kinder conscience might not have found it possible to keep the secret, in which there was no guilt or responsibility for the girl, and trust the Judge of all the earth for the end, is a question which the casuist of Mrs. Meredith's school could not deal with. Duty with her could mean but one thing, and she had done her duty. Certainly she was not to be condemned for it; but neither was the affection which she had so sorely wounded to blame if it had conceived for her memory the bitter drop of hate which poisoned all Rhoda's thoughts of her. What the girl had constantly said to herself from the first was what she still said: that having kept this secret from her all her life, it was too late for her aunt to speak when she did speak at last. Another not involved in the consequences of her act might not have taken this view of it; but this was the view taken of it by the girl who felt herself its victim, and who helplessly resented it, in spite of all that had happened since.

Whether she was in any degree excusable, or whether she was wholly in the wrong in this feeling, must remain for each to decide, and to each must be left the question of how far the Puritan civilization has carried the cult of the personal conscience into mere dutiolatry. The daughter of an elder faith would have simplified the affair, and perhaps shirked the responsibility proper to her, by going first with her secret to her confessor, and then being ruled by him. Mrs. Meredith had indeed made a confessor of her physician, after the frequent manner of our shrill-nerved women, but even if Olney could have felt that he had the right to counsel her on the moral side, it is doubtful if she could have found the strength to submit to him.

Olney's interest in her was mainly confined to the episodes of the last few days, and vivid as these had been, it could not hold him long in censure of Miss Aldgate's behavior; he began to yield to the charm of her presence, and in a little while hazily to wonder what his reserves about her were. She was in the black that seems to grow upon women in the time of mourning, and it singularly became her. It is the color for the South, and for Southern beauty; like the inky shadow cast by the effulgence of tropical skies, it is the counterpart of the glister and flash of hair and eyes which no other hue could set off so well. The girl's splendor dazzled him from the sable cloud of her attire, and in Mrs. Atherton's blond presence, which also had its sumptuousness—she was large and handsome, and had as yet lost no grace of her girlhood—he felt the tameness of the Northern type. It was the elder world, the beauty of antiquity, which appealed to him in the lustre and sparkle of this girl; and the remote taint of her servile and savage origin gave her a kind of fascination which refuses to let itself be put in words: it was like the grace of a limp, the occult, indefinable lovableness of a deformity, but transcending these by its allurement in infinite degree, and going for the reason of its effect deep into the mysterious places of being where the spirit and the animal meet and part in us. When Olney followed some turn of her head, some movement of her person, a wave of the profoundest passion surged up in his heart, and he knew that he loved her with all his life, which he could make his death if it were a question of that. The mood was of his emotional nature alone; it sought and could have won no justification from his moral sense, which indeed it simply submerged and blotted out for the time.

There was no reason why he should not stay now as long as he liked, or why he should not come again as often as Mrs. Atherton could find pretexts for asking him. Between them they treated the matter very frankly. He took her advice upon the taste and upon the wisdom of urging his suit at so strange a time; and she decided that in the anomalous situation to which Miss Aldgate was left, her absolute friendlessness and helplessness, there were more reasons for his wooing than against it. They took Mrs. Atherton's husband into their confidence, and availed themselves of the daylight of a legal mind upon their problem. He greatly assisted to clear up the coarser difficulties by communicating as Miss Aldgate's lawyer with her aunt's connections in St. Louis. Mrs. Meredith had left to her niece the remnant of the property she had inherited from her husband; and his family willingly, almost eagerly, accepted the conditions of the will. They waived any right to question it in any sort, and they made no inquiries about Miss Aldgate, or her purposes or wishes.

Olney agreed with the Athertons that their behavior was very singular, but he kept his own conjectures as to the grounds of it. They were, in fact, hardly conjectures any more; they were convictions. He felt sure that they knew the secret which Mrs. Meredith believed her husband had kept from all the world;

but this did not concern him so deeply as the belief that had constantly grown upon him since their first meeting in Mrs. Atherton's presence, that Rhoda knew it too. He had no reasons for his belief; it was quite without palpable proofs; it was mere intuition; and yet he was more and more sure of the fact.

His assurance of it strengthened with his belief that the girl loved him, and had perhaps had her fancy for him from the moment they saw each other in Florence. The evidences that a woman gives of her love before it is asked are always easily re-solvable into something else; and in both these things Olney's beliefs were of the same quality, and they were of the same measure. But the one conviction began to taint and poison the other. The man's sweetest and fondest hope became a pang to him, because it involved the fear that the girl might have decided to accept his love and yet keep her secret. In any case he desired her love; as before himself he did not blame her for withholding her secret till she found what seemed to her the best time for imparting it; but for her own sake he could have wished that she would heroically choose the worst. This tacit demand upon her was made from his knowledge of how safe it would be for her to tell him everything, and it left out of the account the fact that till he asked her to be his wife he had no claim upon her, that he could have no terms from her till he owned himself won. Love is a war in which there can be no preliminaries for grace; the surrender must be unconditional, before these can even be mentioned.

There were times, of course, when Olney could not believe that the girl knew what at other times she seemed to withhold from him; but at all times the conjecture had to be kept to him-self. If she knew, she practised a perfect art in concealing her knowledge which made him fear for the future; and if she did not know, then she showed an indifference to her aunt's memory which seemed not less than unnatural. He conceived the truth concerning her when he said to himself that Rhoda must hold Mrs. Meredith responsible for the fact if she had imparted it; and that time alone could clear away her confusion of mind and enable her to be just to the means which she confounded with the cause of her suffering. But he could not have followed her into those fastnesses of the more intensely personalized feminine consciousness where the girl relentlessly punished her aunt in thought not for doing her duty, but for doing it too late, when she could remain through life only the unreconciled victim of her origin, instead of revealing it early enough to enable her to accept it and annul it by conforming herself to it.

As this was what Rhoda had never ceased to believe would have been possible, her heart remained sore with resentment in the midst of the love which she could not help letting Olney divine. Circumstance had drawn their lives into a sudden intimacy which neither would or could withdraw from; they drifted on toward the only possible conclusion together. For the most part the sense of their love preoccupied them. She turned from her desperate retrospect and blindly strove to keep herself in the present, and to shun the future as she tried to escape the past; he made sure of nothing to build on except the fact that at least she did not know that Mrs. Meredith had confided her secret to him. With this certain, he could take all chances. He could trust time to soften her heart toward the dead, and he could forgive the concealment toward himself which she used.

One thing that he could not understand was her apparent willingness to remain just where and as she was indefinitely; he did not realize that it was apparent only, and as a man he did not account for her patience—if it were patience—as an effect of the abeyance in which the whole training of women teaches them to keep themselves. The moral of their education from the moment they can be instructed in anything is passivity, and to take any positive course must be a negation almost of their being; it must cost an effort unimaginable to a man.

The summer weeks faded away into September, when one morning Olney came to see Rhoda, and found her sitting on a bench to the seaward of a group of birches. The trees had already dropped a few yellow leaves on the lawn, which looked like flowers strewn in the still vividly green grass. It was one of those pale mornings when a silvery mist blots the edge of the sea and lets the sails melt into it. She was looking wistfully out at them, across Mrs. Atherton's wall, which struggled so conscientiously to look wild and unkempt, with its nasturtiums clambering over it; but she did not affect to be startled when Olney's steps made themselves heard on the gravel-walk coming toward her.

She flushed with the same joy that thrilled in his heart, and waited for him to come near enough to take her hand before she asked, "Oh! didn't you see Mrs. Atherton?"

"She sent me word that you were here, as if that were what I wanted," he answered, smiling over the hand he held.

"Well, I can tell you myself, then," she said, sitting down again.

"Yes; or not, as you like," he returned.

"No, it isn't whether I like or not. I am going away."

"Yes," he said, quietly. "Where?"

"To—to New Orleans. To look up my mother's family." She lifted her eyes anxiously to his face, and then helplessly let her glance fall. "I have been talking it over with Mrs. Atherton, and she thinks too that I ought to try to find them."

Olney's heart gave a leap. He knew that she was hovering on the verge of a confession, which she longed to make for his sake, and that he ought not to suffer her till he had made his own confession. He had the joy of realizing her truth, and he rested nervelessly in that a moment, before he could say lightly, "I don't see why you should do that."

"Don't you think—think—that it's my duty?" she pleaded.

"Not in the least! From the experience I've had with the St. Louis branch of your family I don't think it's your duty to look *any* of them up. Why do you think it is your duty? Have they tried to find you?"

"They are very poor and humble people—the humblest," she faltered piteously. "They—"

Her breath went in silence, and he cried, "Rhoda! Don't go away! Stay! Stay with me. Or, if you must go somewhere, go back with me to Florence, where the happiness of my life began when I first knew you were in the world. I love you! I ask you to be my wife!"

She let her hand seem to sink deeper in his hold, which had somehow not released it yet; she almost pushed it in for an instant, and then she pulled it violently away. "Never!" She sprang to her feet and gasped hoarsely out, "I am a negress!"

Something in her tragedy affected Olney comically; perhaps the belief that she had often rehearsed these words as an answer to his demand. He smiled. "Well, not a very black one. Besides, what of it, if I love you?"

"What of it?" she echoed. "But don't you *know?* You *mustn't!*"

The simpleness of the words made him laugh outright; these she had not rehearsed. She had dramatized his instant renunciation of her when he knew the fatal truth.

"Why not? I love you, whether I must or not!"

As tragedy the whole affair had fallen to ruin. It could be reconstructed, if at all, only upon an octave much below the operatic pitch. It must be treated in no lurid twilight gloom, but in plain, simple, matter-of-fact noonday.

"I can't let you," she began, in a vain effort to catch up some fragments of her meditated melodrama about her. "You don't understand. My grandmother was a slave."

"The more shame to the man that called himself her master!" said Olney. "But I *do* understand—I understand everything—I know everything!" He had not meant to say this. He had always imagined keeping his knowledge from her till they were married, and then in some favored moment confessing that her aunt had told him, and making her forgive her for having told him. But now, in his eagerness to spare her the story which he saw she had it on her conscience to tell him in full, the truth had escaped him.

"You know it!" she exclaimed, with a fierce recoil. "*How* do you know it?"

"Your aunt told me," he answered, hardily. He must now make the best of the worst.

"Then she was false to me with her last breath! Oh, I will never forgive her!"

"Oh, yes you will, my dear," said Olney, with the quiet which he felt to be his only hope with her. "She had to tell me, to advise with me, before she told you. I wish she had never told you, but if she had not told me, she would have defrauded me of the sweetest thing in life."

"The privilege of stooping to such a creature as I?" she demanded, bitterly.

He took her hand and kissed it, and kept it in his. "No: the right of saying that you are all the dearer to me for being just what you are, and that I'm prouder of you for it. And now, don't say you will not forgive that poor soul, who suffered years for every hour that you have suffered from that cause. She felt herself sacredly bound to tell you."

"It was too late then," said the girl, with starting tears. "She killed me. I *can't* forgive her."

"Well, what can that matter to her? She can forgive you; and that's the great thing."

"What do you mean?" she asked, weakly trying to get her hand away.

"How came she to tell you that she hadn't told me?"

"I—I made her," faltered the girl. "I asked her if she had. I was frantic."

"Yes. You had no right to do that. Of course she had to deny it, and you made her take a new lie on her conscience when she had just escaped from one that she had carried for you all your life." Olney gave her back her hand. "Whatever you do with me, for your own sake put away all thoughts of hardness toward that poor woman."

There was a long silence. Then the girl broke into sudden tears. "I do! I will! I see it now! It was cruel, *cruel!* But I couldn't see it then; I couldn't see anything but myself; the world was filled with *me*—blotted out with *me*! Ah, *can* she ever forgive me? If I could only have one word with her, to say that there never was any *real* hardness in me toward her, and I didn't know what

I was doing! Do you think I made her kill herself? Tell me if you do! I can bear it—I deserve to bear it!"

"She never meant to kill herself," said Olney, sincerely. "I feel sure of that. But she's gone, and you are here; the question's of you, not of her; and I only asked you to be just to yourself. I didn't mean to tell you now that I knew your secret from her, but I'm not sorry I told you, if it's helped you to substitute a regret for a resentment."

"It's done that for all my life long."

"Ah, I didn't mean it to go so far as that!" said Olney, smiling.

"No matter! It's what I must bear. It's a just punishment." She rose suddenly, and put out her hand to him. "Good-by."

"What for?" he asked. "I'm not going."

"But *I* am. I'm going away to find my mother's people, if I can—to help them and acknowledge them. I tried to talk with Mrs. Atherton about it, the other day, but I couldn't rightly, for I couldn't let her understand fully. But it's true—and be serious about it, and don't laugh at me! Oughtn't I to go down there and help them; try to educate them, and elevate them; give my life to them? Isn't it base and cowardly to desert them, and live happily apart from them, when—"

"When you might live so miserably with them?" Olney asked. "Ah, that's the kind of question that I suspect your poor aunt used to torment herself with! But if you wish me to be really serious with you about it, I will say, Yes, you would have some such duty toward them, perhaps, if you had voluntarily chosen your part with them—if you had ever *consented* to be of their kind. Then it *would* be base and cowardly to desert them; it would be a treason of the vilest sort. But you never did that, or anything like it, and there is no more specific obligation upon you to give your life to their elevation than there is upon me. Besides, I doubt if that sort of specific devotion would do much good. The way to elevate them is to elevate *us*, to begin with. It will be an easy matter to deal with those simple-hearted folks after we've got into the right way ourselves. No, if you must give your life to the improvement of any particular race, give it to mine. Begin with *me*. You won't find me unreasonable. All that I shall ask of you are the fifteen-sixteenths or so of you that belong to my race by heredity; and I will cheerfully consent to your giving our colored connections their one-sixteenth."

Olney broke off, and laughed at his joke, and she joined him helplessly. "Oh! don't laugh at me!"

"Laugh at you? I feel a great deal more like crying. If you go down there to elevate the blacks, what is to become of me? I don't really object to your going, but I want to go with you."

"What do you mean?" she entreated, piteously.

"What I said just now. I love you, and I ask you to be my wife."

"I said I couldn't. You know why."

"But you didn't mean it, or you'd have given me some reason."

"Some reason?"

"Yes. What you said was only an excuse. I can't accept it. Rhoda," he added, seriously, "I'm afraid *you* don't understand! Can't you understand that what you told me—what I knew already—didn't make the slightest difference to me, and couldn't, to any man who was any sort of a man? Or yes, it does make a difference! But such a kind of difference that if I could have you other than you are by wishing it, I wouldn't—for my own selfish sake at least, I wouldn't wish it for the world. Can't you understand that?"

"No, I can't understand that. It seems to me that it must make you loathe me. Oh!" she shuddered. "You don't know how hideous they are—a whole churchful, as I saw them that night. And I'm like them!"

Olney's heart ached for her, but he could not help his laugh. "Well, you don't look it. Oh, you poor child! Why do you torment yourself?"

"I can't help it. It's burnt into me. It's branded me one of *them*. I *am* one. No, I can't escape. And the best way is to go and live among them and own it. Then perhaps I can learn to bear it, and not hate them so. But I *do* hate them. I do, I do! I can't help it, and I don't blame you for hating *me !*"

"I don't happen to hate even you," said Olney, going back to his lightness. "My trouble's another kind. Perhaps I should hate you, and hate them, if I'd come of a race of slave-holders, as you have. But my people never injured those poor creatures, and so I don't hate them, or their infinitesimal part in you."

He found himself, whenever it came to the worst with her in this crisis, taking a tone of levity which was so little of his own volition that it seemed rather to take him. He was physician enough already to flatter his patient for her good, and instinctively he treated Rhoda as if she were his patient. It did flatter her to have that side of her ancestry dwelt upon, and to be treated as the daughter of slave-holders; she who could not reconcile herself to her servile origin, listened with a kind of fascination to his tender mockery, in which she felt herself swayed by the deep undercurrent of his faithful love.

"Come, come!" he went on, and at his touch she dropped weakly back into her seat again, and let him take her hand and hold it. "I know how this fact has seized upon you and blotted everything else out of the world. But life's made up of a great deal else; and you are but one little part injured to many parts injurer. You belong incomparably more to the oppressors than to the oppressed, and what I'm afraid of is that you'll keep me in hopeless slavery as long as I live. Who would ever imagine that you were as black as you say? Who would think—"

"Ah, you've confessed it! You would be ashamed of me, if people knew! That is it!"

"If you'll answer me as I wish, I'll go up with you to the house and tell Mrs. Atherton. I've rather a fancy for seeing how she would take it. But I can't, unless you'll let me share in the disgrace with you. Will you?"

"Never! It shall never be known! For *your* sake! *I* can bear it; but *you* shall not. Promise me that you'll never tell a living soul!" She caught him nervously by the arm, and clung to him. It was her sign of surrender.

He accepted it, and said: "Very well, I promise it. But only on one condition: that you believe I'm not afraid to tell it. Otherwise my self-respect will oblige me to go round shouting it to everybody. Do you promise?"

"Yes, I promise;" and now she yielded to the gayety of his mood, and a succession of flashing smiles lit up her face, in which her doom was transmuted to the happiest fortune. She kept smiling, with her hands linked through his arm and her form drawn close to him; while their talk flowed fantastically away from all her awful questions. Their love performed the effect of common-sense for them, and in its purple light they saw the every-day duties of life plain before them. They spoke frankly of the incidents of the past few days, and he told her now of his interview with the Bloomingdale family, and how he felt that he had hardened Mrs. Bloomingdale's heart against her by his unsympathetic behavior in denying them an interview with Rhoda herself.

This made her laugh, but she said, with a shudder: "I couldn't have borne to look at them. From the first moment after my aunt *told* me, I felt that I must prevent their ever seeing me again. I wrote to him, and I carried the letter out with me to post it, and make sure it went; and then somehow I forgot to post it."

"Ah," said Olney, "I suppose that's the reason why he came to see me, and to ask where he could find you."

"Yes," answered Rhoda, placidly.

"There is only one thing in the whole affair that really troubles me," said Olney, "and that's the very short shrift you gave that poor fellow."

"Why, when I had written to him I would not see him again, I supposed he was persisting, and it was only the other day that I found the letter, which I'd forgotten to post. It was in the pocket of the dress I wore that night to the church."

"And you don't think his persisting—his caring so much for you—gave him the right to see you?"

"Not the least."

"Ah, a man never understands a woman's position on that question."

"Why, of course, if I had cared for *him*—"

"I don't know but I've a little case of conscience here myself. I had awful qualms when that poor fellow was talking with me. I perceived that he was as magnanimous as I was on the subject of heredity, and that, I thought, ought to count in his favor. Will you let it?"

"No."

"Why not?"

"Because I don't care for him."

"How simple it is! Well, he's off my conscience, at any rate."

She began to grieve a little. "But if you are sorry—"

"Sorry?"

"If you think you will ever regret—if you're not sure that you'll never be troubled by—by—*that*, then we had better—"

"My dear child," said Olney, "I'm going to leave all the trouble of that to you. I assure you that from this on I shall never think of it. I am going to provide for your future, and let you look after your past."

She dropped her head with a sob upon his shoulder, and as he gathered her in his arms he felt as if he had literally rescued her from her own thoughts of herself.

He was young and strong, and he believed that he would always be able to make her trust him against them, because now in the fulness of their happiness he prevailed.

There are few men who, when the struggle of life is mainly over, do not wonder at the risks they took in the days of their youth and strength; and it could not be pretended that Olney found more than the common share of happiness in the lot he chose; but then it could be said honestly enough that he did not consider either life or love valuable for the happiness they could yield. They were enough in themselves. He was not a seeker after happiness, and when he saw that even his love failed at times to make life happy for his wife, he pitied her, and he did not blame her. He knew that in her hours of despondency there was that war between her temperament and her character which is the fruitful cause of misery in the world, where all strains are now so crossed and intertangled that there is no definite and unbroken direction any more in any of us. In her, the confusion was only a little greater than in most others, and if Olney ever had any regret it was that the sunny-natured antetypes of her mother's race had not endowed her with more of the heaven-born cheerfulness with which it meets contumely and injustice. His struggle was with that hypochondria of the soul into which the Puritanism of her father's race had sickened in her, and which so often seems to satisfy its crazy claim upon conscience by enforcing some aimless act of self-sacrifice. The silence in which they lived concerning her origin weighed upon her sometimes with the sense of a guilty deceit, and it was her remorse for this that he had to reason her out of. The question whether it ought not to be told to each of their acquaintance who became a friend had always to be solved anew, especially if the acquaintance was an American; but as yet their secret remains their own. They are settled at Rome, after a brief experiment of a narrower field of practice at Florence; and the most fanciful of Olney's compatriot patients does not dream that his wife ought to suffer shame from her. She is thought to look so very Italian that you would really take her for an Italian, and he represents to her that it would not be the ancestral color, which is much the same in other races, but the ancestral condition which their American friends would despise if they knew of it; that this is a quality of the despite in which hard work is held all the world over, and has always followed the children of the man who earns his bread with his hands, especially if he earns other people's bread too.

THE END

Notes to the Text

62.1–2   " 'Come unto me . . .' ": a telescoping of two verses in
Matthew, XI, 28–29.

81.17   From Goethe's *Faust*, Part I, scene 1, l. 512.

TEXTUAL APPARATUS

Textual Commentary

No manuscript or proof stage of *An Imperative Duty* is known to exist. The text was first printed in *Harper's Monthly* in four installments between July and October 1891. The first book edition (BAL 9659) was published by Harper and Brothers in New York in a first impression of 1,500 copies, with a title-page date of 1892, although the book was deposited for copyright on 14 November 1891.[1] The 1892 text exists in three hard-cover bindings; but collation of several copies in the different bindings offers no evidence for identifying distinct impressions. The one re-impression of this edition in 1893 has been noted both in boards and in the paperbound Harper's Franklin Square Library series. Finally, the British Edition, prepared by David Douglas of Edinburgh for his "American Authors" series, was printed in a first impression of 5,000 copies on 27 November 1891 and carries a title-page date of 1891.[2] Another impression was printed in 1903. No other printings or editions of the book were called for during Howells' lifetime.[3]

---

1. Information on the size of the first impression comes from Harper Memorandum Books, 1887–1891, p. 107. The records are in the "Treasure Chest" at Harper & Row, Publishers; for a discussion of these materials, see Edwin and Virginia Price Barber, "A Description of Old Harper and Brothers Publishing Records Recently Come to Light," *Bulletin of Bibliography*, XXV (1967), 1–6, 29–34, 39–40.

2. These figures are drawn from the records of T. & A. Constable, London, and are cited with the permission of P. J. W. Kilpatrick.

3. The following printed items, including at least first and last known impressions, were collated in the preparation of the present text: copies of *Harper's Monthly* in the Indiana University and University of California at Santa Barbara libraries; copies of the Harper edition of 1892, BAL 9659, in the Illinois (813.H83i), Lilly (PS2025.I5, PS2025.I5, copy 2), Indiana University (PS2025.I32) and University

In accordance with his working procedure at that time, Howells probably submitted his manuscript (or some typed version of it) to *Harper's Monthly*, and then sent proof of the magazine text to David Douglas in Edinburgh, where type was to be set and the plates made which Howells would supply to Harper and Brothers under his contract with them. A letter from Douglas of 7 May 1891 acknowledges Howells' letter of 25 April "with its enclosure consisting of the first part of 'An Imperative Duty.' "[4] But Douglas wonders whether he will be able to set type and get plates to the U.S. before 1 July, when, he speculates, the new international copyright law—denying American copyright to any book not set in type first in the United States—would probably go into effect.[5] Apparently it was decided soon after that Douglas would not be able to meet the July deadline, for on 2 October he again wrote to Howells, to thank him for a full set of proofs—presumably of the Harper book edition—of *An Imperative Duty* and to inform him that because of the new copyright law he had cancelled the 32 pages of text which had already been set in "fscp 8°," since "It was mainly to afford you a set of stereotypes at a less cost than you could get them in New York that I adopted the larger size."[6]

Given this information and the evidence provided by collation of the three available texts, the stages of Howells' work on the book as it was finally published seem to be as follows. He sent proof of the magazine version, possibly with some corrections, to Douglas for

of California at Santa Barbara (PS2025.I46) libraries, and of the 1893 re-impression in the University of Chicago (PS2025.I35 1893), Temple (PS2025.I6) and University of Texas (Z813.H839i) libraries; and of the Douglas edition in the Library of Congress (PZ3.H84 Im), Islington Public Libraries, and the Ohio Wesleyan (813.4 H85i, copy 2), British Museum (12704.aa.20) and Harvard College (*AC-85.H83951im) libraries.

4. MS in the Harvard College Library. Permission to quote has been granted by William White Howells for the heirs of the Howells Estate and by the Harvard College Library.

5. Formerly, Douglas' preparation of book plates helped Howells in two ways: Douglas could secure British copyright for him by setting and depositing some form of his edition in Great Britain before American publication, and he could provide plates at a better price to Howells than he could get in the United States. In return, Douglas could print a small edition from these plates himself first, with the sales of this edition financing the preparation of the plates for his own smaller-format "American Authors" edition.

6. MS at Harvard. The same page of the Constable Records which enumerates the cost for printing the first Douglas edition of the book notes also the cost of setting 44 pages (rather than 32) of this same book "which were cancelled."

preparation of plates and Douglas sent proof of his work to Howells as the text was being set; but Douglas stopped work on these plates and destroyed them, thus also destroying whatever evidence could be provided about revisions Howells might have made at this stage of the text (the edition Douglas finally published shows no signs of independent revision which might have had a source in revision on the magazine proof sent to Douglas). Then Howells sent proof or tear sheets of the *Harper's Monthly* text to the printing firm of S. J. Parkhill of Boston, where the plates eventually to be used by Harper and Brothers were prepared. It is possible that before sending magazine proof to Parkhill and again after receiving first book proof, Howells made some minor corrections (for example, the changes from the magazine in the sentence at 89.3–4, which are reproduced in both the Harper and British editions), and then returned one set of this book proof to Parkhill and forwarded a duplicate to David Douglas, so that Douglas could set his regular "American Authors" text from it. After this stage, however, Howells made much more extensive revisions in proof of the text being prepared by Parkhill—revisions not communicated to Douglas, so that the Harper text represents a later stage of revision than the version published by Douglas; the emendation at 4.12–13, for example, appears only in the Harper edition, while the Douglas text reproduces the original serial reading.

Clearly, then, the *Harper's Monthly* version should be copy-text for the present edition; it is the extant text closest to Howells' hand and thus most likely to reflect his intentions in spelling, punctuation, and other aspects of form. It is this text, reproduced in all essential details (except for visual styling, type format, spacing of paragraph indentation and styling of chapter headings) which is the basis for the present text. Into it have been introduced those changes in substantives made in the Harper edition which appear to have Howells' authority.[7] We have not introduced into this text generally accidentals in the Harper text which are at variance with the magazine, even in those few cases where the Harper edition differs from a reading common to the magazine and the Douglas edition; the number and kind of the accidentals unique to the Harper book text are not conclusive

---

7. This text therefore accords with both the intention and the practices outlined in the Center for Editions of American Authors, *Statement of Editorial Principles: A Working Manual for Editing Nineteenth Century American Texts*, July 1967.

evidence of Howells' revision of these accidentals in the later stage of proof of the Harper text. We have, however, emended certain accidentals, but because they constitute necessary corrections and not because they appear to have Howells' authority.

All emendations in substantives and accidentals accepted into the *Harper's Monthly* copy-text are recorded on the Emendations list. Rejected Substantives records all substantive variants from the serial in the book texts which do not appear to have Howells' authority. These variants are of three general classes: non-authorial alterations made in the preparation of the Harper edition and repeated in the Douglas text; readings in the Douglas text which duplicate the serial and fail to correspond to Howells' later Harper revisions; and independent substantive variants in the Douglas edition (except for necessary corrections made therein; see 24.26 and 81.17 in Emendations), which appear to have been made without Howells' authority.

D. J. N.

Textual Notes

19.2   The agreement of serial and British edition at this point is a good indication that the change from "poetical" to "poetic" is an authorial emendation made at some later stage of proof of the Harper text.

24.26   The British edition provides the correct spelling of the name of a character in George Eliot's *Romola*.

81.17   The British edition corrects the misquotation of Goethe's *Faust* made in the serial and repeated in the Harper edition.

Emendations

The following list records all substantive and accidental changes introduced into the copy-text. The reading of the present edition appears to the left of the bracket; the authority for that reading, followed by a semicolon, copy-text reading, and copy-text symbol appear to the right of the bracket. The curved dash ~ represents the same word that appears before the bracket and is used in recording punctuation variants. Occasionally changes in accidentals have been made on the authority of the Howells Edition, with the first book edition which records them cited as their source, though these editions of course have no general authority for accidentals; that is, an edition is cited because it is the first to incorporate a change and not because the change is thought to have resulted from Howells' intervention. *Om.* means that the reading to the left of the bracket does not appear in the text cited to the right of the semicolon. An asterisk indicates that the reading is discussed in the Textual Notes. The reading of any text which falls between the copy-text and the authority cited for the present edition may be assumed to agree substantively with the copy-text reading if not listed; accidental variants in these uncited texts have not been recorded here.

The following texts are referred to:

S   *Harper's Monthly,* LXXXIII (July–October 1891)
A   Harper and Brothers, 1892: First Edition
B   David Douglas, 1891: British Edition

4.12–13   sturdy, old-world peasants,] A; ugly old peasant women, often with the simian cast of features which affords the caricaturist such an unmistakable Irish physiognomy; S
4.13   girls] A; women S
4.15   from their . . . conditions,] A; *om.* S
4.16–17   They . . . shops; they] A; They S
4.21   survived] A; survive S

4.24	painful] A; painful, and it was not pretty in manner any more than in matter S
4.26	he found] A; *om.* S
4.27	bearing] A; bearing was S
4.27	aggressive,] A; aggressive, and sometimes rude, S
5.29	hotel] A; hotel instead of those Irishmen S
15.23	three] A; five S
*19.2	poetic] A; poetical S
19.9	"We] A; "I'm sure the Irish are twice as stupid as the colored people, and not half as sweet! We S
19.10	white] A; Irish S
20.35–36	fancy." ¶ Mrs.] A; fancy. But I've known of two marriages here between white women and colored men, and in both cases the wives were Irish Catholics." ¶ "Really?" asked Miss Aldgate. Mrs. S
21.1	eyes.] A; eyes. "I shouldn't have thought that Irish—" S
21.19–20	memory." ¶ She stood] A; memory. I was thinking at dinner yesterday, how much more delicate the colored waiters used to be in their insinuations." ¶ "Were they? Yes, I'm sure they were!" she said, S
23.13	bore] A; ignored S
23.14	had] A; has S
23.16	the] A; *om.* S
*24.26	Melema] B; Malema S
27.2	drama] A; human drama S
27.21	fancy] A; fancy is S
29.17	Ohio,] A; Sandusky, Ohio—I think it's Sandusky— S
30.19	tendency] A; celebrity S
46.14	young] A; *om.* S
53.14	chaos] A; chaos ruin S
53.32	moment,] A; ~ S
59.6	calculate] A; speculate S
60.8	sensations] A; emotions S
62.6	*my*] A; my S
62.7	*me*] A; me S
69.25	using] A; seeking S
69.25	skill] A; help S
73.3	imagining] A; dramatizing S
*81.17	den] B; dem S

89.3	Another] A; Whether another S
89.4	might not have taken] A; could take S
89.4	it] A; it is doubtful S
93.15	away.] A; ∼ ? S
99.4	promise?] A; ∼ ! S

Rejected Substantives

The following list records all substantive variants in editions published after copy-text and rejected as non-authorial in the present text. The reading of the present edition appears to the left of the bracket; the authority for that reading, followed by a semicolon, the variant reading and its source appear to the right of the bracket. The curved dash ~ represents the same word that appears before the bracket and is used in recording punctuation and paragraphing variants. *Om.* means that the reading to the left of the bracket does not appear in the text cited to the right of the semicolon. The reading of any unlisted text, other than copy-text, may be presumed to agree with the reading to the left of the bracket, unless recorded in Emendations. If the authority cited for the reading of the present text is other than copy-text, the reading of the copy-text and any text which falls between it and the authority for the present reading are recorded in Emendations.

The following texts are referred to:

S   *Harper's Monthly*, LXXXIII (July–October 1891)
A   Harper and Brothers, 1892: First Edition
B   David Douglas, 1891: British Edition

4.12–13	sturdy, old-world peasants,] A; ugly old peasant women, often with the simian cast of features which affords the caricaturist such an unmistakable Irish physiognomy; B
4.13	girls] A; women B
4.15	from their . . . conditions,] A; *om.* B
4.16–17	They . . . shops; they] A; They B
4.24	painful] A; painful, and it was not pretty in manner any more than in matter B
4.26	he found] A; *om.* B
4.27	bearing] A; bearing was B
4.27	aggressive,] A; aggressive, and sometimes rude, B
5.29	hotel,] A; hotel, instead of those Irishmen, B
11.2	first passed its] S; passed its first B
15.23	three] A; five B

17.8–9   said, ¶ "If] S; ~, "~ A–B
18.13   man] S; wan B
18.35–36   and ¶ "We] S; ~ "~ B
19.2   poetic] A; poetical B
19.10   white] A; Irish B
20.35–36   fancy." ¶ Mrs.] A; fancy. But I've known of two mar-
            riages here between white women and coloured men, and
            in both cases the wives were Irish Catholics." ¶ "Real-
            ly?" asked Miss Aldgate. Mrs. B
21.1   eyes.] A; eyes. "I shouldn't have thought that Irish—" B
21.19–20   memory." ¶ She stood] A; memory. I was thinking at
            dinner yesterday how much more delicate the coloured
            waiters used to be in their insinuations." ¶ "Were they?
            Yes, I'm sure they were!" she said, B
23.13   bore] A; ignored B
23.16   the] A; *om.* B
24.9   amongst] S; against B
25.9   might] S; may B
25.13   those] S; these A
26.30   They are] S; They're A–B
27.2   drama] A; human drama B
27.8–9   Olney?" Yet] S; ~?" ¶ ~ B
27.21   fancy] A; fancy is B
30.19   tendency] A; celebrity B
31.12   anxieties] S; anxiety A–B
31.23   was] S; was an A–B
33.19   Then] S; And then A–B
33.31   social] S; the social A–B
34.22   might] S; might at B
34.24   nor] S; or A
37.9   It is] S; It's A–B
38.29   I've] S; I have A–B
39.17   other-race] S; other race B
40.17   that] S; *om.* A–B
40.24   his] S; this A–B
42.1   wasn't] S; was not A–B
42.31   laughed. "I'll] S; ~. ¶ "~ B
44.16   that] S; *om.* A–B
45.3   be] S; he A

49.17	paltered] S; faltered A–B
50.9	in] S; *om.* A–B
50.25	books] S; book A–B
52.33	knees] S; knee A–B
53.25	away] S; *om.* A–B
55.9	a while] S; awhile A
56.14	late,] S; ~ ; B
56.14–15	error. She] S; error, she B
57.10	what] S; what else A–B
58.17	and own her] S; *om.* A–B
60.6	unsuccessively] S; insuccessively A–B
60.14	had] S; *om.* A–B
60.20	exaltation] S; exultation B
61.4	a] S; an A–B
61.19	again] S; *om.* A–B
62.10	child's] S; child A–B
62.15	sin] S; sins A–B
62.17	kin do] S; can do A–B
64.13	quadroon. These] S; quadroon, and these A–B
65.27	others] S; them A–B
65.33	round] S; around A–B
67.12	these] S; those A–B
70.29	woman] S; woman had A–B
71.7	one] S; one that A–B
77.2	know] S; knew A–B
79.2	inquiry] S; inquire A–B
83.1	as] S; *om.* A–B
86.26	exaltation] S; exultation B
91.24	won. Love] S; ~ . ¶ ~ B
93.15	it] S; it is A
94.5	violently away] S; away violently A–B
94.8	an] S; *om.* A–B
94.25	*do* understand] S; *do* know A–B
95.13	say] S; say that A–B
98.11	already] S; *om.* A–B
98.14	could] S; would A–B
98.31	you'll] S; you B
101.7	antetypes] S; antitypes B
101.32	THE END] S; *om.* A–B

Word-Division

List A records compounds or possible compounds hyphenated at the end of the line in copy-text and resolved as hyphenated or one word as listed below. If Howells' manuscripts of this period fairly consistently followed one practice respecting the particular compound or possible compound, the resolution was made on that basis. Otherwise his *Harper's* or other periodical texts of this period were used as guides. List B is a guide to transcription of compounds or possible compounds hyphenated at the end of the line in the present text: compounds recorded here should be transcribed as given; words divided at the end of the line and not listed should be transcribed as one word.

	LIST A		
6.24	side-hill	80.15	non-existent
7.26	overhead	82.6	superfine
10.17–18	close-shuttered	82.34	hearth-fire-
13.28	clergyman	98.14	slave-holders
32.19	granddaughter		
32.24–25	death-bed		LIST B
34.20	grandfather's	5.31	simple-heartedness
42.1	formal-minded	11.9	fellow-countryman
50.20	grandfather	19.20	fellow-feeling
50.28	grandmother	32.24	death-bed
53.31	prefigurations	39.26	easy-chair
54.20	sin-born	42.18	middle-aged
57.20	watermelons	46.12	young-ladyishness
58.4	day-long	48.11	light-hearted
58.8	uphill	54.9	after-experience
58.24	shrill-piped	55.5	heart-wrung
58.25–26	grandmothers	58.19	wide-nostriled
59.10	great-grander	59.28	self-loathing
59.18–19	nightmare	71.19	address-book
62.36	large-whited	82.34	drawing-room
71.21	writing-case	101.8	heaven-born

114